Earth, Air, Fire and Custard

By Tom Holt

EXPECTING SOMEONE TALLER
WHO'S AFRAID OF BEOWULF?
FLYING DUTCH
YE GODS!
OVERTIME
HERE COMES THE SUN
GRAILBLAZERS
FAUST AMONG EQUALS
ODDS AND GODS
DJINN RUMMY
MY HERO
PAINT YOUR DRAGON
OPEN SESAME
WISH YOU WERE HERE
ONLY HUMAN
SNOW WHITE AND THE SEVEN SAMURAI
VALHALLA
NOTHING BUT BLUE SKIES
FALLING SIDEWAYS
LITTLE PEOPLE
THE PORTABLE DOOR
IN YOUR DREAMS
EARTH, AIR, FIRE AND CUSTARD

DEAD FUNNY: OMNIBUS 1
MIGHTIER THAN THE SWORD: OMNIBUS 2
THE DIVINE COMEDIES: OMNIBUS 3
FOR TWO NIGHTS ONLY: OMNIBUS 4
TALL STORIES: OMNIBUS 5
SAINTS AND SINNERS: OMNIBUS 6
FISHY WISHES: OMNIBUS 7

THE WALLED ORCHARD
ALEXANDER AT THE WORLD'S END
OLYMPIAD
A SONG FOR NERO

I, MARGARET

LUCIA TRIUMPHANT
LUCIA IN WARTIME

TOM HOLT

Earth, Air, Fire and Custard

orbit

www.orbitbooks.co.uk

An *Orbit* Book

First published in Great Britain by Orbit 2005

Copyright © The One Reluctant Lemming Co. Ltd 2005

The moral right of the author has been asserted.

A CIP catalogue record for this book
is available from the British Library.

ISBN 1 84149 281 7

Typeset in Plantin by M Rules
Printed and bound in Great Britain
by Clays Ltd, St Ives plc

Orbit
An imprint of
Time Warner Book Group UK
Brettenham House
Lancaster Place
London WC2E 7EN

For Cassandra Claire

(back atcha)

&

TH, the artist,

with thanks

CHAPTER ONE

The soft, blurred light of dawn. A small, lonely island at the mouth of a sheer-sided fjord. A sparkle pierces the muffling sea fret; the flat clang of steel on steel troubles the eerie silence.

A small boat bobs at the water's edge. Two sets of footprints in the sand lead up the beach towards the thin grass. Two men stand facing each other, catching their breath by unspoken mutual consent. Both are exhausted, their hair spiked with sweat. One, gripping a sword, peers nervously over the rim of a hacked and splintered shield; the other leans heavily on the shaft of an axe.

Simultaneously they take a step forward, their bodies immediately tense as drawn bowstrings. The swordsman takes a low guard, while his opponent hefts the long Danish-pattern axe and waits, analysing the swordsman's defence. Presumably he sees something, because he plunges forward and swings the axe round his head and down, pulling the swing a little to one side at the last moment. The bright cannel-ground edge strikes the shield's rim but skids off, and the axe bites deep into the turf; spotting an unexpected advantage, the swordsman pushes forward with his shield and pivots his right shoulder for a devastating diagonal cut—

'Hold it,' grunts the axeman. 'Offside.'

The swordsman checks the stroke painfully in mid-air. 'It was not!' he protests.

'Offside,' the axeman repeats firmly. 'Look at where you've got your feet.'

The swordsman glances down, tries to draw his left foot back. 'I saw that,' the axeman says.

'All right,' the swordsman sighs. 'I suppose, technically—'

'Technically be buggered,' the axeman interrupts, 'offside is offside. Free hit to me.'

'Yes, all right,' grunts the swordsman. 'Though if we're going to be all picky about it—'

With a tremendous effort, the axeman heaves the axe-head out of the turf and swirls it round his head in a flashing arc, while his enemy stands perfectly still behind his ruined shield. The axe impacts on the rim, shearing through the steel band and deep into the timber, only just stopping short of the swordsman's left hand. In reply the swordsman jerks the shield and the trapped axe-head sideways, nearly disarming his opponent—

'You're doing it again,' the axeman points out.

'What?' Another quick glance. 'Oh, snot. It's ever since they changed the LBS rule,' the swordsman complains bitterly. 'I'd only just figured out what the old rule was, too.'

'There's nothing to figure out,' the axeman says coldly. 'Left foot no more than five inches in front of the shield-boss, or it's a foul shot. Perfectly simple. A child of four could understand it.'

'Yes, well.' The swordsman isn't happy, but he lets his left arm drop enough for the axeman to dislodge his blade. 'I can't see what was so bad about the old rule. If they'd only leave well alone and stop fiddling with it—'

'Another free hit to me,' the axeman points out, with a smirk. 'You aren't doing terribly well so far, are you?'

The swordsman grins back at him. 'Given that you've had six free hits and I'm still standing,' he said, 'looks like I'm not the only one. If you ask me, you're trying to hit too hard. Relax, loosen up, let the axe do the work instead of trying to force it.'

The axeman pulls a face and tries again. This time, perhaps because he's tired and irritated, he manages to miss completely. The swordsman sniggers.

'While we're on the subject of rules,' the axeman replies, tugging his blade out of the turf once more and stepping back into a defensive back-guard, 'what about rule 46, section 3, no unnecessary talking?'

'That's a bit rich coming from you,' says the swordsman huffily. 'Talk about your pot and kettle—'

Before he can finish his sentence the axeman swings again, bending his knees and drawing the stroke very low as he aims for the swordsman's ankles. But the swordsman reads the cut perfectly and jumps high in the air from a standstill, so that the blade passes harmlessly under his feet. As he lands, one foot jams the axe-shaft down, ripping it out of the other man's hands. Almost before the swordsman gets his balance he swings; the axeman rears away, arching his back, and just manages to avoid the sword-blade, but the sudden violent effort unbalances him. He seems to hang in the air for a moment, both hands waving helplessly, before crashing down on his back. As soon as he's down the swordsman cuts again; the axeman wriggles sideways, almost but not quite far enough, as the very tip of the blade engraves a line across his forehead, about an inch above eye-level.

'And on a double-wound score, too,' the swordsman gloats. 'Now then—'

'Just a minute,' sighs the axeman. 'You haven't got a clue, have you?'

The swordsman scowls horribly, but stays put. 'Now what?'

'Rule 27,' replies the axeman smugly, 'section 14. Gotcha!' he adds.

The swordsman's eyebrows bunch together like huddling sheep. 'Remind me,' he growls.

'With pleasure. The back-foot rule.'

'Oh.'

'Exactly. When making an offensive stroke at a fallen or unbalanced opponent, the back foot must be in contact with the ground at all times. The ground, please note; not the other bloke's axe-handle.' He smiles unpleasantly. '*Another* free hit to me.'

The swordsman clicks his tongue. 'Get on with it, then,' he

mutters. 'And this time, don't bunch your shoulders together like that. You want to be careful you don't chop your own foot off.'

With a scowl that'd curdle mercury the axeman starts to get to his feet.

'Hang on,' the swordsman objects. 'Just what do you think you're doing?'

'What does it look like?'

The swordsman beams like the sunrise. 'Rule 17,' he says, 'section 8. All free hits to be taken from the position the striker is in when the foul shot occurred.' He licks his lips. 'Free hit to *me*,' he adds cheerfully.

'It doesn't say that.'

'Yes, it does.'

'Doesn't'

'It *does*.' The swordsman's face is a study in baffled rage. 'Are you calling me a liar or something?'

The axeman nods. 'Yes,' he says.

'You take that back or I'll smash your face in . . . Oh, nuts,' the swordsman adds. The axeman chuckles, and slowly gets to his feet.

'Supervening fresh challenge,' the axeman says cheerfully. 'Rule 92. The current bout is declared null and void, start all over again.'

The swordsman makes a growling noise. 'You did that on purpose,' he mutters. 'Tricked me into a fresh challenge.'

'Yes,' the axeman agrees. 'Perfectly legal,' he adds. 'You can check if you like.'

'When you're ready,' grunts the swordsman, icily polite.

His opponent retrieves his axe, spits on his hands. 'In your own time,' he replies.

For a moment the swordsman hesitates; then he darts sideways, feinting a lunge to the other man's left knee, converting it effortlessly into a rising backhand slash. The axeman parries just in time with the axe-handle, but the swordsman's blade slices it neatly in two, leaving his enemy gripping eighteen inches of headless shaft. Before the axeman can move or cite rule 38 the swordsman rocks back on his heels and lunges again—

—And thrusts his sword deep into a thick patch of swirling grey mist, which instantly dissolves. 'Oh, for crying out loud,' the swordsman yells. 'That's cheating.'

The last few wisps of mist wriggle like maggots in the air and glow briefly with yellow-gold fire, spelling out the words *So report me* in twelve-inch runes. The swordsman throws his sword on the ground and jumps on it. Then he frowns, stoops down and picks up a handful of fine-grained dirt, which he tosses into the air where the letters had appeared. The dirt flares vividly into sparkling light, revealing the outline of a door or gateway, complete with lintel, hinges and big round doorknob.

'Right,' the swordsman grunts; sheathing his sword, he reaches out, grabs the outline of the doorknob and twists it sharply a quarter-turn—

—And vanishes, never to be seen in this timeline again.

Paul Carpenter was dragged out of a singularly nasty dream – in which he was being chased through a thick, bramble-draped forest by the teddy bear he'd owned when he was six – by a knock at the door. He sat up, opened his eyes and realised that he'd fallen asleep in his chair in front of the TV. That in itself was hardly surprising, since there's never anything good on in the summer. Who, on the other hand, would want to pay him a visit at this time of night?

Paul scrabbled for the remote, hit the standby button, and stood up. There it was again: knuckles on the woodwork. He'd had the television's sound turned right down, so it couldn't be upstairs complaining about the noise; and door-to-door salesmen rarely wasted their energy trudging up the four flights of badly lit stairs. As he opened the door with his right hand, he pinched sleep out of his eyes with his left.

'Hello,' said a familiar voice.

'Uncle Ken.'

'I know that. Can I come in?'

The yawn got past Paul's defences and escaped before he could do anything about it, but Uncle Ken wasn't the sort to be offended by yawns, or indeed anything that didn't actually draw blood. He ducked under Paul's arm (no great feat for a man of his minimal stature) and scuttled like a startled lizard into the living-room. By the time Paul caught up with him, he'd poured himself a large glass of the fine malt whisky that Paul had been given for his birthday two years ago, and was sitting in the only comfortable chair. Paul slumped a little and perched on the other one. 'Didn't know you were in town, Uncle Ken,' he said.

'I guessed as much,' Uncle Ken replied, 'otherwise you'd have locked up your booze and put the chain on the door. Got any corned beef?'

Corned beef. Paul thought about that for a moment and shook his head.

'Oh. Not to worry, anything'll do, cheese or ham or tongue. Not too much butter on the bread. Oh, and a bit of fruit'd go down nicely.'

Paul smiled grimly, went into the kitchen and made two rounds of industrial-chicken sandwiches. On the side of the plate he perched the apple he'd been saving for tomorrow; then, to save himself another trip, he opened the fridge (*Sod it*, he said to himself, *the little light's on the blink again*) and took out the very last can of beer.

'Cheers,' Uncle Ken said, pulling the ring with his usual surprising grace. Five feet nothing in his cowboy boots, sausage-fingered and practically circular, Uncle Ken nevertheless managed to do even the simplest thing with the elegant poise of a geisha pouring tea. 'You not having anything?'

Paul shook his head. 'So,' he said, trying to sound cheerful. 'Have you got a gig in these parts or something?'

'No such luck, son,' Uncle Ken replied with his mouth full. Paul had known what the answer to his question was likely to be before he asked it. For the last twenty years, Uncle Ken had been pecking out a sparse living doing stand-up comedy in obscure, short-lived clubs and bars up and down the country, with occasional enforced sabbaticals in the construction, catering and retail-petrol industries. Ironic, really; Paul's mum had chosen him to be her only son's godfather because at that time he'd been an ineffably respectable actuary, and because he was the most boring man she'd ever met. Whether it was the strain of turning up at Paul's christening and forking out for a small imitation pewter tankard that'd pushed Uncle Ken over the edge into the nomadic life he now pursued, Paul had no idea. He hadn't lost much sleep over it.

Watching someone else eat the food you'd hoped would tide you over till pay day isn't the most fun you can have with the lights on, and Paul couldn't help feeling slightly annoyed. But being small-minded about it wouldn't bring his bread and sliced chicken back, so he dredged up a smile from somewhere and asked politely after his godfather's health and general well-being.

'Not so hot,' Uncle Ken replied. 'Did three nights in Peterborough in January, went over very nicely, not a huge crowd, probably the venue getting flooded out by a burst sewer the week before didn't help. Joined up with with an experimental performance-arts collective for a bit – interesting bunch, there was a bloke who welded bits of angle-iron while his girlfriend sang medieval plainsong and played the zither, and another girl who juggled with razor blades stuck into apples – she left the group at Redcar – and a couple of those living-statue blokes, only they were so good the audience never figured out they weren't real, and a lad who did barefoot tightrope-walking on an electric fence, and me, of course. We were planning to take the show over to Canada for the Saskatchewan Arts Festival but we couldn't afford the fare. How about you?'

Paul grinned. 'Oh, nothing exciting,' he said.

'Last I heard, you were just about to start a new job.'

Paul nodded. 'That's right. Been there nine months now.'

'Liking it?'

'Not a lot.'

Uncle Ken shrugged. 'Pack it in, then. You're young, no ties, find something you really want to do and do it. Like I did.'

Paul shook his head slowly. 'Nice idea,' he said, 'but I can't.'

'Can't find anything you like doing?'

'Can't quit. Long story,' he added, stifling another yawn. 'But the bottom line is, I'm stuck there for the foreseeable future. Bummer, but there it is.'

Uncle Ken frowned. 'That's no kind of an attitude,' he said. 'I was the same when I was your age; I'd just finished college, got my qualifications, people had expectations I had to live up to, all that crap. Just meant I wasted the best years of my life, doing a stupid rotten job I hated. You want to get out there, have adventures, strange new worlds and all.'

Paul laughed, like a dry stick breaking. 'Oh, there's plenty of that kind of thing where I'm working now,' he said. 'It's the adventures and the strange new worlds that're the problem, not the mindless tedium and stuff. I can handle mindless tedium, it's—' He stopped, then shook his head. 'You don't want to hear about that,' he said. 'So, tell me, this girl who juggled the apples—'

'You can tell me about it if you want to.'

'Yes, but I don't. Did she wear gloves, or did she just have particularly hard skin on her hands, or what?'

'Yes, you do.'

'No, I don't.'

Uncle Ken was giving Paul a stern look from behind his enormously thick spectacle lenses. Seen from the wrong angle, they made his eyes look like huge hard-boiled eggs. 'I've known you since before you were born,' he said, 'and there's something you want to tell someone about, but you're hesitating because you think it'll sound stupid, or I won't believe it, or something. I'm right, aren't I?'

'Yes,' Paul confessed. 'But you don't want to hear about it. Really. Trust me.'

'Bollocks.' Uncle Ken poured himself another glass of whisky and rolled an extremely thin cigarette. 'I'm a very good listener, me.'

'Yes, but you don't want—'

'Yes, I do.'

'No, you—' Paul stopped and thought for a moment. 'All right,' he said. 'Stop me when you're prepared to admit I was right, which won't take long. And if you're going to smoke in here—'

'Get on with it.'

So Paul told him all about it: how he'd got a job as a junior clerk with a firm called J. W. Wells & Co in the City, without knowing what it was they actually did; how it'd come as rather a shock to him when he found out that they were one of the top six firms of family and commercial magicians in the UK, specialising in the entertainment and media, mining and mineral resources, construction, dispute resolution, applied sorcery and pest-control sectors; how he'd almost immediately tried to resign, and how he'd found out a little while later that the reason why they wouldn't let him was that his parents had financed their early retirement to Florida by selling him to the partners of JWW, who wanted him because the knack of doing magic ran in his family to such an extent that it was inevitable that he'd have it too; how he'd briefly found true love with Sophie, the other junior clerk, shortly before she was abducted by Contessa Judy di Castel Bianco, the firm's entertainments and PR partner and hereditary Queen of the Fey, who permanently erased Sophie's feelings for Paul from her mind; how he'd learned scrying for mineral deposits from Mr Tanner, who was half-goblin on his mother's side, and heroism and dragonslaying from Ricky Wurmtoter, the pest-control partner, and a bit of applied sorcery from the younger Mr Wells (before the elder Mr Wells turned him into a photocopier); and how he'd just started learning spatio-temporal displacement theory with Theodorus Van Spee, former professor of classical witchcraft at the University of Leiden and inventor of the portable folding parking-space; oh, and how he'd died, twice (only the second time was an accident) and been put on deposit for a while in the firm's account at the Bank of the Dead—

'Told you,' Paul said. 'But you wouldn't listen.'

Uncle Ken's eyebrows had risen so high that they'd popped up above the rims of his glasses, like hairy slugs surfing a really high wave. 'All right,' he said, 'I'm surprised, I'll give you that.'

'Surprised,' Paul repeated.

Uncle Ken nodded. 'And a bit disappointed,' he said. 'I thought I'd talked your dad out of that idea when you were born. Not fair on the lad, I told him; just because he can do all that stuff, doesn't necessarily follow that he'll want to. But to be honest with you, I never did trust him much.'

Over the last nine months, Paul thought he'd more or less lost the knack of being shocked. 'You knew?'

''Course I *knew*, it's not exactly a secret in your family.' He scowled. 'Only, I suppose your dad kept quiet about it, if he was planning to sell you all along; what you don't know, you can't get bolshy about. But I could've told him you wouldn't like it. All down to temperament, see. I mean, obviously you'd have the talent, with your Uncle Ernie being— You know about your Uncle Ernie?'

Paul nodded. 'Oh yes,' he said. 'I know all about him.'

'Well, there you are, then. He was all right, actually, until just before the end. He'd have been proud to think you were carrying on the tradition.'

Paul shook his head. 'No, he's not. He doesn't like me very much. Mind you, it's my fault he's stranded for ever in the vaults of the Bank of the Dead, so I suppose he's got grounds for being all snotty about it. But for crying out loud, Uncle Ken. You might have told me.'

Uncle Ken shrugged. 'Not my place to interfere,' he said. 'Your mum would never've forgiven me. Anyhow, would you have believed me if I had told you?'

'Yes, but—' Paul sighed, and slumped back in his chair; a bad idea, since there wasn't much holding it together apart from force of habit. 'It just really pisses me off,' he said, 'everybody in the whole world turning out to know all about this magic thing apart from me. And nobody telling me,' he added bitterly. 'The first I knew about it was when I stayed late in the office one night and nearly got eaten alive by goblins.'

'No chance of that,' Uncle Ken said, shaking his head gravely. 'Contrary to what you hear, they're mostly not dangerous unless you provoke them. And—'

'Yes,' Paul snapped, 'I know, apparently I'm part goblin myself, and they hardly ever eat family. It'd have been nice if someone had prepared me for *that* particular revelation, just a bit. Not that I've got anything against them particularly – well, that's not true, they scare the shit out of me, but so do most things in life. But even so—'

'Never mind about that,' Uncle Ken said quickly. 'Tell me more about this bird of yours. Sophie, was it?'

Bird, thought Paul; *hail to thee, blithe spirit, bird thou never wert.* 'She isn't, any longer,' he said sharply. 'I told you, Countess Judy scrubbed all that out of her mind, and now it won't come back. So that's that,' he said, trying to sound brave. 'It's a real bitch, because we still have to work together, and she can't quit either; another judicious purchase by the partners, you see.'

Uncle Ken nodded slowly. 'Always was your trouble,' he said, 'falling in love with anything that stays still long enough. 'Course,' he went on, 'it's not real. It's because you know nothing's ever going to come of it, you know that as soon as you start getting obvious, they always burst out laughing or tell you to get lost, so it's safe – oh, right,' he added, with a grin. 'You're going to tell me it wasn't like that this time.'

Paul had gone a deep beetroot colour. 'Actually,' he said, 'it was going just fine till Countess Judy ruined everything. I mean, we'd moved in together, we were making plans for the future . . .'

'Bloody hell,' Uncle Ken interrupted. 'No wonder you were scared.'

'I was not scared.' Well, of course he'd been scared; more so, in fact, than when Ricky Wurmtoter had pointed the crossbow at his heart and pressed the trigger and killed him. 'It was wonderful. We really loved each other. And then—'

'And then, at the very last minute, you escaped.' Uncle Ken raised a hand, before Paul could interrupt or find something to use as a weapon. 'Didn't seem like that at the time, I know. It hurt like buggery, I'm sure. Probably you felt just like shit quiche on a bed of wild rice. But really, deep down, you knew you'd got out just in time, before the roof caved in. You can't kid me, son, I've known you too long.'

'It wasn't like that.' Why did it matter so much that Uncle Ken wouldn't believe him? 'It wasn't like that at all. I didn't want it to end. I'd have done anything—'

There must've been something in his voice, like a tiny drop of blood in shark-infested water. Uncle Ken smiled faintly. 'But you didn't, did you?'

'I couldn't, it wouldn't have been— How do you know about it, anyway?'

'I don't. But you're just about to tell me.'

Paul gave in. 'It was after we'd rescued her,' he said, 'and she realised what that evil bitch had done to her. JWW make this thing called a love philtre, you drink it and fall in love with the first person you see. Cast-iron guaranteed, they've been selling it for two hundred years and it's never failed. She offered to drink it, so things'd be back to how they were. But I said no.'

'You said no. I see.'

'Because it wouldn't have been real,' Paul protested. 'It'd have been as though I'd snuck up when she wasn't looking and spiked her coffee with it or something.'

'You'd have done anything,' Uncle Ken said slowly. 'Only you didn't. You were a chicken standing on the conveyor belt, looking straight at the plucking machine, and suddenly the power goes off. You weren't about to go jumping up, saying you'd got fifty pee for the meter. Admit it, Paul. That's exactly how it was.'

Paul shook his head. 'You're right,' he said, 'about how I used to be. But it was different with Sophie, and now—'

Uncle Ken laughed out loud. 'And now you've got a bloody wonderful excuse, you've got a note from God saying you're let off PE for ever. Believe me, it doesn't work like that. Next bird you see that doesn't look like a garden gnome with warts, it'll be the same old story all over again. Come on, Paul, be honest with yourself. Remember Mandy Bolsover?'

Paul winced. 'Uncle Ken, I was fourteen. You can't blame someone for—'

'Mandy Bolsover,' Uncle Ken repeated. 'Big girl, captain of the shot-put team. You spent a whole term drooping around like a poisoned goldfish, then you wrote a suicide note and took four paracetamol. And you'd never said a single word to her.'

Paul gave him a look that'd have stripped the Teflon off a space shuttle. 'Anyway,' he said. 'It's not going to happen ever again, I've already seen to that. I mean it,' he added. 'Really.'

'Oddly enough, that's exactly what I say every time I pack in smoking,' Uncle Ken said sadly. 'I did really well the year before last,' he added, 'I lasted thirty-six hours, twelve minutes and fourteen seconds. The fourteen seconds were because my lighter wouldn't work and I had to run to the kitchen for matches, but the thirty-six hours were sheer will-power.'

'No,' Paul said. 'Because, finally, I've found a bit of the magic stuff that's actually useful for something other than making money for the partners. Here,' he added, opening a drawer and taking out a folded, dog-eared sheet of paper. 'Go on, take a look.'

Uncle Ken shrugged, took the paper and squinted at it over his glasses. 'What's this supposed to be, then?'

'Recipe,' Paul replied. 'Or probably they'd call it a formula, but as far as I can see it's just cooking. I photocopied it from one of Professor Van Spee's books. It's the opposite of the love philtre thing. If you drink it every six months, you're guaranteed not to fall in love.'

For once, Uncle Ken seemed impressed. 'You're kidding.'

'Absolutely not. And it's dead easy to make, all nice simple ingredients, apart from the crème fraiche, whatever that is—'

'You can get that in Sainsbury's,' Uncle Ken interrupted. 'Delia Smith bungs it in everything. Probably runs her car on it. What's this, though? Two milligrams Van Spee's crystals.'

'Oh, that.' Paul looked away. 'Yes, well, that's a bit unusual. But Professor Van Spee's got a big jar of it in his desk drawer. I think he invented it or something. Anyhow, I sneaked in one time when I knew he wouldn't be there and nicked some.'

'Really. Weren't you afraid he'd notice?'

Actually, the thought hadn't occurred to Paul before. 'Nah,' he said. 'It was a big jar, and I only took an aspirin-bottleful. And it's been a week and he hasn't said anything.'

'Oh well, that's all right, then.' Uncle Ken pulled a face. 'And you're actually going to swallow this stuff?'

'You bet. I've mixed up a batch, all except the crème thing, and apparently you add that last, once the mixture's stood for at least a week. It's still got a day to go, so if I can get the crème whatever in the supermarket—'

'You aren't worried it'll turn you into a frog or something?'

Paul shook his head. 'No chance of that,' he said. 'Completely different sort of magic, turning people into things. And no, I don't know if the medicine's safe to drink because, obviously, I've never made it before. But as far as I'm concerned, it's well worth the risk. You were absolutely right about how I used to be. But I've had enough of all that crap, and this'll be an end of it.'

Uncle Ken stood up. 'Where's the biscuit jar?' he said.

'What?'

'The biscuit jar. Oh, don't bother, I'll find it.' Uncle Ken went into the kitchen and came back munching. 'Fact is,' he said, 'I've been neglecting my duty as a godfather. Looking after your moral and spiritual welfare, and all that stuff. You need taking in hand, you do, before you make a right cow of your life.'

Paul looked him over, from his worn-out line-dancing boots to his masking-tape-bound spectacles, pausing midway at the bulge in his pocket where he'd helped himself generously to Paul's chocolate digestives. 'A right cow,' he said. 'Thanks, Uncle Ken, I'm sure that'll be a real help. Maybe if I get my act together and make a real effort, I could get to be just like you.'

Uncle Ken shook his head. 'You wish,' he said. 'But there's no harm in trying. You couldn't lend us a fiver, could you? Just till the end of the week.'

Paul paid up without a word, and Uncle Ken thanked him. 'See,' he added, 'I've only been on the job five minutes and already I've made you a better human being. Talking of which, you wouldn't happen to have any spare socks you don't need for anything? Only—'

'Top drawer of the chest of drawers, help yourself,' Paul said wearily. 'Uncle Ken, I'm not sure I really want to be a better person after all. Can't I just stay a mess and—?'

After Uncle Ken had gone, Paul made himself some cheese on toast and did a quick stocktake in the kitchen cupboard. His first faltering steps along the road to self-improvement had cost him two packets of biscuits, a jar of instant coffee, the bag of sugar he'd just opened that morning and a big tin of custard powder. Extending the inventory to the bedroom, he found he was morally and spiritually better off by the absence of three pairs of socks, two shirts, three pairs of pants and his nail scissors. On the other hand, he'd somehow managed to acquire a Canadian ten-cent piece, which he found in the empty desert where once several pairs of socks had safely grazed, like the buffalo before Bill Cody came along. He looked at it for a moment, frowned, and dropped it back in the drawer.

Crème fraiche, he thought; *Sainsbury's. I'll stop off there on my way home from work tomorrow, and then that'll be that done, and one less thing to worry about. Wonder if they also sell lockable biscuit jars?*

The cheese on toast tasted of plastic and cardboard, and then Paul went to bed. On his bedside table was a book. It had been there for several days, and each night, before groping for the light switch, he'd done his best to read a couple of pages, because Professor Van Spee had told him that it was essential reading if he was to get the hang of the work they'd be doing over the next three months. Unfortunately, the book itself appeared to be an exceptionally powerful magical object, with the power to put to sleep anybody who so much as opened its covers. Time was getting on, and all he'd managed to do so far was read the first page and a half six times. It still didn't make any sense—

Let this visible world, he read for the seventh time, *be a biscuit. Above, the immeasurable span of time; below, the limitless possibility of space. Sandwiched between them, the custard filling of elsewhere and elsewhen.*

The world is in haste, and rushes to its end. The world is narrow, and tapers headlong through entropy towards the sharp point where the angels dance. Only in the eye of the storm, through which a camel cannot pass into the Kingdom of Heaven, is there room to manoeuvre, time to reflect, a remote possibility of doubt. Only in philosophy is there a keyhole in the door of the future, through which one can spy on yesterday.

It is our business, therefore, to find room for a fingernail between the upper and the lower inevitabilities, so that they can be prised apart, if only for a little while. To this end, let us consider that all things are formed out of five elements: earth, air, fire, water—

Paul yawned. *Sheer unmitigated doggy-poo,* he reflected, and fell asleep.

– Not so much fell; glided, like a leaf drifting down from a tree on a still day, and when Paul reached the ground he was standing beside a single-track road on a bleak moor. On the other side of the road, the ground sloped sharply away to jagged bleak rocks and an angry steel-grey sea. Off in the distance he could hear the scream of many powerful engines, revving high and changing gear. A seagull wheeled overhead, and changed course when it saw him.

He wasn't alone. A small round man with a bald head and glasses was standing next to him, but either he hadn't seen him or was pretending. Paul was sure that he knew who it was; but it was as though the man had control over that part of Paul's brain that dealt with recognition, and he wasn't allowing him to fit a name to the face. Fair enough: Paul could take a hint. He looked away for a moment, the way you do, and when he turned back the man had vanished.

Then he saw someone walking towards him, and it was just as well he knew that this was only a dream, brought on by stale cheese untimely eaten, because otherwise he'd have been distinctly nervous about the stranger. He was tall and huge with fiery red hair that stuck out from his head in all directions, like a dandelion clock; he was wrapped in a damp cloak or blanket, and in his right hand he held a sword.

Paul groaned. He'd gone off swords, ever since the time when he'd had to share his somewhat cramped living quarters with a huge sword in a stone, an unexplained and unsolicited gift from Old Mr Wells. It had turned out to be a magical key and he'd managed to get rid of it eventually, but not before he'd cut himself several times and pulled a muscle in his back trying to get the thing out through the door on his own. After that, as far as Paul was concerned, swords meant trouble: horrible JWW-based intrusions of weirdness into his free time, which he could well do without. But the man walked straight up to him, just as it began to rain.

'Here,' he said, in a strong foreign accent. 'You're getting wet. Take this.'

Whereupon he swung the sword high above his head, flipped a catch or pressed a button or something, and opened the sword out into a perfectly normal golf umbrella. Paul thanked him but the man walked away without looking back, and then the mist closed around him and he was gone.

Never mind, it was better than getting wet. The engines sounded very close now, and Paul peered down the road to see. There was someone beside him, looking over his shoulder; she had long brown hair, slightly frizzy, with golden streaks in it so light that they were almost silver. 'I'll give you five to one on the Kawasaki,' she said, and for some reason he shook his head and replied that it had to be the Norton, and it'd be outright theft to take her money. Then nine motorcycles roared past them, each rider waving as they went by (to the girl, not to Paul). He saw their hair floating in the slipstream as they passed, and the girl next to him pointed out that he owed her five pounds.

'Sorry,' he said, 'but I gave my last fiver to Uncle Ken.'

'Oh.' That seemed to be an acceptable reason for not paying. 'Well, anyway,' she said, 'we'd best be getting back, before anybody notices we've gone.' Paul hadn't looked round at any point, so he hadn't seen her face. It was rather important that he didn't, in fact, and he felt vaguely proud of himself for resisting the temptation to peek. Her voice was cold and hard, which more than made up for the fact (he had no idea how he knew this) that she was very beautiful and had freckled shoulders to die for. *Great*, he told himself, *the medicine works, wait till I tell Sophie—*

And there she was, right in front of him, her hair plastered to her head by the rain, looking small and thin and very, very wet. 'For crying out loud, Paul,' she said, very deliberately not noticing the redhead standing next to him. 'Do you realise, we're *twenty minutes late?* Now come on.'

He followed her, up a steep hillside towards a ruined tower overlooking a misty grey creek where two small wooden ships lay at anchor. 'This is the last time I come looking for you,' she went on, as they dragged up a winding narrow stone staircase – the steps were worn and slippery, and the only light was a grey blur round the edges of arrow slits – 'and I'm really, really tired of covering up for you, just because you're too bloody idle to do your reading assignments.'

'I'm sorry,' Paul mumbled. 'But every time I open the stupid book, it sends me straight to sleep.'

She sighed. 'You clown,' she said. 'It's *supposed* to. Now pay attention—'

Then it all burst around him like a flood: so many things he suddenly knew how to do, so many answers and explanations, everything that had been puzzling and bewildering him and driving him to distraction and despair since he'd first joined JWW, all those things that everybody else seemed to know except him, and he really hated that— It was like standing directly under a huge volcano as it burst into furious life, belching out fire and enlightenment and useful practical information, formulae, specifications, procedures, detailed recipes, easy-to-follow step-by-step instructions and a huge cloud of yellow ash that blotted out the sun, as though God had perched a bag of custard powder on top of the door of Infinity as a practical joke, and it had landed *kersplat* on top of his head. Meanwhile Sophie was yelling, 'The crème fraiche, don't forget the crème fraiche,' and then Paul woke up.

CHAPTER TWO

Nine o'clock sharp – sharper, indeed, than the proverbial serpent's tooth – and Paul was standing outside the front door of 70 St Mary Axe, waiting for the bolts to be shot back and the wards of the massive, church-door-type lock to be graunched round, so that he could slouch in and start another day. It was less than nine months since he'd stood on this very step, and a single round red eye had glared out at him through the letter box; he hadn't known about goblins then. It seemed like another life.

The door opened, and behind the front desk sat a bewilderingly lovely girl, skin the colour of coffee and eyes like deep, dark pools. He'd never seen her before, of course.

'Morning, Paul,' she called out. 'You haven't forgotten, have you?'

'No, of course not.' He stopped, then shrugged. 'All right, yes, I have. Forgotten what?'

'Bastard. Rehearsal, six o'clock tonight. You promised you'd remember.'

Mr Tanner's mother – *call me Rosie*, she'd told him, but Paul knew it wasn't her real name – was a thoroughbred goblin of impeccable ancestry, with her species's unnerving ability to change shape at will, and an even more disturbing habit of developing serious crushes on human males, in particular tall, thin, weedy-looking, feckless specimens like himself. Subtle as an explosion in a fireworks factory, she'd been after him more or less since the day he'd joined the firm. Every day there was a completely different beautiful girl on reception, but they all had the same hungry grin. That aside, Paul minded Mr Tanner's mum least of all the inhabitants of the office; and when he'd found out a few months ago that he was part goblin himself, she'd asked him, rather touchingly, to be the godfather to her latest offspring, who'd been born a fortnight ago. Now, apparently, she was dead set on holding him to his rash promise. He wasn't looking forward to the experience, mostly because she'd been dropping all sorts of dark hints about what a goblin godfather had to do at the ceremony. All he'd been able to prise out of her so far was that it wasn't as dangerous as it sounded.

'Oh, and our Dennis wants to see you,' she added, flashing him a smile which, under any other circumstances, would've turned his knees to jelly. 'In his office, five minutes. Don't ask me what it's about.'

Paul nodded glumly and trudged down the long, gloomy corridors to his dog-kennel office. He didn't know why Dennis Tanner, the firm's mining and mineral rights specialist, should want to see him first thing on a Monday morning, but he was sure it wouldn't be about anything nice. At best, it'd mean a huge great batch of aerial photographs of seemingly identical patches of featureless desert, which he'd have to scry for bauxite deposits. It sounded impressive, but all it meant was running his fingertip across the surface of the picture until he felt a mild electric shock, and then ringing the precise spot with black marker pen. It was one of the few magical talents he'd so far manifested, and as far as unwanted gifts went it was up there in his all-time top ten, along with socks and the latest Martin Amis in hardback.

Having sloughed his coat, he checked his desk for memos, yellow stickies, post and other hazards; just one today, a handwritten note from Professor Van Spee—

From: TCVS
To: PAC

You have finally read the first chapter of the book I asked you to read three weeks ago; accordingly, you are now in a position to help me with the Macziejewski account.

Dennis Tanner will want to see you at 9.05; you will be free again at 9.35. Kindly call at 16 Jowett Street (just off the Charing Cross Road) and collect a parcel for me. You will be back at the office at 11.15; please come and see me.

Paul read the note twice, then shrugged. Ever since he'd first encountered Professor Van Spee, he'd made a conscious effort not to let this omniscience thing bother him. So far, he'd just about managed, but the strain was getting worse all the time. He was about to drop the note into the home-brew coal seam he called his filing tray when he noticed a postscript he'd missed earlier—

PS: Leave now, *or else you will be late for your appointment with Mr Tanner.*

According to Mr Tanner's mum and various other goblins whose word he was prepared to take on the subject, Dennis Tanner was related to him, something like his fifth cousin thrice removed. The revelation had brought him no comfort whatsoever. Every time he saw Mr Tanner, his first instinct was to run and hide. This wasn't anything to do with Mr Tanner being half-goblin; he looked mostly human, a bit like a freeze-dried child, with curly brown hair going slightly grey, big brown eyes and his mother's horrible grin. It was rather more to do with Mr Tanner being an unmitigated bastard—

'Come in,' he heard through the chunky panelled door. Mr Tanner was in his usual place behind the desk, wreathed in blue cigar smoke like a tiny, malevolent volcano. On the other side of the desk was someone Paul hadn't seen before.

Paul was on the tall, thin side himself; but he was an obese dwarf compared to the stranger, who was wearing a perfectly ordinary blue suit, shirt and tie but looked as though he'd been poked down the shirt collar like a pipe-cleaner and somehow got stuck. He had a long neck, like a turkey, and his head was absurdly too small for the rest of him. He had tiny round glasses and very short grey hair, like the bristles on a nail brush.

'You're here, then,' Mr Tanner said. 'Right, I'd like you to meet Frank Laertides. I'm delighted to be able to tell you, Frank's agreed to join us as our new PR and media partner.'

Paul immediately froze, and stared at the newcomer with undisguised trepidation. PR and media had been Judy di Castel Bianco's department, and three months ago Paul had, after a desperate struggle, succeded in thwarting her attempt to subjugate the human race to her own people, the dream-inhabiting Fey. When last heard of, Countess Judy had been trapped on the Isle of Avalon, whence (Paul devoutly hoped) she could never return. The reason he was panicking now was that (according to Countess Judy) only the Fey had the innate abilities needed to perform the kinds of magic needed for PR and media work; in which case—

'Relax.' It was the newcomer speaking, but it was hard to believe that such a friendly, pleasant voice could've come from the strange creature sitting at Mr Tanner's desk. 'I know what happened a while back, and you needn't worry, I'm not one of Judy's mob.' Mr Laertides smiled, and his whole appearance seemed to change. Instead of being a cartoon Frankenstein's monster drawn by L. S. Lowry, he became just a nice man who happened to be rather tall. 'So you're Paul Carpenter,' he went on, steepling his impossibly long fingers. 'The chap who took on the Fey and won. Got to admit, I've been looking forward to meeting you.'

The fear started to ebb away, but suspicion remained. At the time, Paul had been left in precious little doubt by the partners that the defeat of Countess Judy, though quite probably the salvation of the human race and civilised life as we know it, had been a nasty blow for the firm, and so far from being pleased with him, they'd only just managed to forgive him for depriving them of the staggering sums of money she'd brought in every year. This Mr Laertides, on the other hand, appeared to think he'd done something clever, and was pleased to meet him—

(*Well, quite*, Paul told himself. *If I hadn't got rid of Countess Judy, Stick-Insect Guy wouldn't have landed her old job. That's got to be the reason*—)

Paul smiled awkwardly, unable to think of anything appropriate to say. Mr Laertides nodded, then glanced back at Mr Tanner, who cleared his throat and looked down at his desk. If Paul hadn't known better, he'd have thought he was embarrassed.

'The other thing,' Mr Tanner went on, in a rather strained voice, not like his usual cheerfully abrasive self, 'is, we, my partners and I, we've been giving some thought to your, um, position in the firm. I take it,' he added, in a strangled sort of voice, 'you're happy here at JWW?'

It'd have been rude to laugh; and obviously Mr Tanner didn't want to hear the truth, or he wouldn't have asked the question. 'Yes, rather,' Paul heard himself say. 'Absolutely.'

'Excellent,' muttered Mr Tanner. 'Because we, my partners and I, we're very pleased with the work you've been doing for us, we think you've settled in very nicely, and –' here he paused, and maybe he closed his eyes just for a fraction of a second '– and so we'd like to, um, promote you, from junior clerk to assistant sorcerer, if you're happy with that.' Mr Tanner's dribble of words finally dried up completely, like the last trickle from a Saharan explorer's water bottle, and he buried his face in his hands for a moment. To his credit, he managed to pull himself together again in a matter of seconds. 'It'll mean more money, of course,' he said grimly. 'Plus extra holiday allowance—' He paused. 'How much holiday do you get at the moment?'

'Um.' Paul thought about it. 'None.'

'Ah, right. Well, from now on you can have seven days off a year. Just be sure to clear the dates with me first.' It was as though some huge, invisible bird of prey was ripping the words out of Mr Tanner's chest with its talons. 'Also you get a company car, a proper one this time, and there's other stuff too, but I won't bore you with it now.'

Oh, Paul thought. *Oh well, never mind.*

'In return –' Mr Tanner seemed to have cheered up just a bit '– we'll be looking for that extra bit of effort and commitment on your part; I mean, it's not going to be just a job any more, you're joining the JWW family, if you want to look at it that way, and the way we look at things is, we all pull our weight and do our best and—' Mr Tanner seemed to go all boneless, as though he simply couldn't go on any further, no matter what anybody did to him. 'That sort of thing,' he concluded. 'Look, do you want it or not?'

If Paul had really had a genuine choice in the matter, it'd have been different. But he didn't. He knew perfectly well that his parents had sold him to the firm just over a year ago. He even knew how much they'd got for him. Watching Mr Tanner suffer, on the other hand, was the most fun he'd had in ages. 'Yes, please,' he said quickly. 'And thanks. This means a lot to me, it really does.'

'Mm.' Mr Tanner nodded. 'I bet. Well, there you are, then, and I hope you'll be really happy. Now, you'd better get out of here and go and pick up that parcel for Theo Van Spee, before he starts giving me attitude for keeping you.' He shuddered, from his toes upwards, and looked away. The tall, thin bloke (Mr Laertides, Paul remembered) smiled pleasantly and nodded. 'Glad to meet you, Paul,' he said. 'I'll drop in your office later and we can have a chat.'

'Um, right,' Paul mumbled, and fled while he still had the use of his legs.

He had to go and do Professor Van Spee's shopping next; but instead, he went straight to the front office, where the lovely girl was lolling in her chair, sharpening her fingernails with a farrier's rasp.

'It was you, wasn't it?' Paul said.

She looked up, frowned a little. 'Probably,' she said. 'What the hell are you talking about?'

'This promotion thing. You made Mr Ta— your son, you made him do it. The pay rise, the holiday—' He stopped and looked at her. 'It wasn't you, then.'

She shook her head. 'Sorry,' she replied. 'Nothing to do with me.'

For some reason, Paul felt distinctly uneasy. 'You sure?'

'Absolutely. I mean,' she went on, 'if our Dennis has given you a raise, I'm really thrilled and of course you deserve it and all that crap. But it's the first I've heard of it.'

'So it wasn't just you trying to—' Paul stopped dead and turned beetroot. Mr Tanner's mum giggled.

'Look,' she said. 'Yes, if I thought it'd do any good, and if I could've made our Dennis do it, that's just the sort of thing I'd be capable of. But it doesn't work like that. For one thing, Dennis can't make decisions like that on his own, he'd have to clear it with the rest of the gang first. And if I asked him to do this one small favour for his dear old mum, he'd tell me to piss off and die in a ditch. If you've just got a promotion – well,' she added, with a grin, 'maybe it's because they really like you and they think you're an asset to the firm. Or there could be some other reason,' she added blithely. 'But it's none of my doing. Hope you're not too disappointed,' she added, and her tone of voice had him out of the front office and halfway up the stairs before he realised he was going the wrong way.

Annoying. 70 St Mary Axe had no back or side door; to get out onto the street, you had no choice but to go past the front desk, and Paul didn't want to have to run the gauntlet of Mr Tanner's mum's industrial-grade heavy leering again. Trying to explain all that to Professor Van Spee was, of course, completely out of the question, as was failing to obey a direct order from the Great Man. He hesitated, like a rubber ball on top of a fountain, kept in place by the two opposing forces of fear and embarrassment—

'They make the world go round, you know,' said a voice behind him. He spun round so fast that he nearly lost his balance and toppled backwards through the banister rail, like an inept sniper in a Western. Mr Laertides, Stick-Insect Guy, had materialised on the step below, and so offensively excessive was his height that he still towered over Paul like the London Eye. Where he'd come from or how he'd got there, Paul didn't even bother to wonder.

'According to the songwriters,' Mr Laertides went on, 'it's Love, but that's just silly. Science would have you believe that it's the gravitational pull of the sun, but bless them, they've got research grants to justify, so we'll forgive them a little white lie or two. Seven large vodka martinis on an empty stomach will make the world go round for a while, but then you fall over and pass out, so it's a temporary expedient at best.'

Paul stared at him as though he'd just sprouted an extra head; although, after nine months at JWW, he might well have been able to take that in his stride. 'I'm sorry,' he said, 'I don't quite follow.'

'Embarrassment and fear,' said Mr Laertides. 'You were just thinking about them.' He smiled, and Paul's bewilderment melted like grilled ice-cream. So what if he didn't have a clue what Mr Laertides was talking about? It just confirmed that he was a whole lot smarter than Paul, and Paul knew that already. 'The mainsprings of human motivation. You're afraid of getting looked at sternly if you turn up for your appointment with Theo without the parcel, but the thought of facing Rosie Tanner turns your spine to jelly. What you need, therefore, is a third option. Right?'

Paul felt his head bob up and down, though he couldn't recall asking it to.

'No problem.' Mr Laertides inserted a splayed-octopus hand into the inside pocket of his jacket, and pulled out a big, thick book that couldn't possibly ever have fitted inside it. 'Go on, take it,' he said. 'It won't bite. You can have it, by the way. Plenty more where they came from.'

Frowning, Paul opened the front cover. It was a book of carpet samples; maybe two dozen of them, with fibre backings and little sticky labels on the undersides telling you what they were.

'But not the whole truth,' Mr Laertides said. 'Bit more to it than that. Three guesses? All right, they're carpet samples, yes, but carpet samples with a difference. A bloke in Muscat makes them for me. You just use them once and throw them away.'

'Muscat,' Paul repeated. 'That's in France, isn't it?'

Mr Laertides smiled. 'Oman,' he said, 'on what used to be called the Persian Gulf. Still haven't figured it out? Fine. They're *flying* carpet samples. You just unclip these two rings up the middle, see, and take out one of the carpet squares, and tap it very gently with the side of your left index finger—'

Abruptly, the carpet sample lifted into the air, levelled off, straightened out its creases, and hung motionless in front of him, about four feet off the ground. 'That's a flying carpet?' Paul asked breathlessly.

'Well, it's carpet,' Mr Laertides replied, 'and there it is, flying.

Just for once, a great leap of faith isn't absolutely essential. And before you ask, it's dead easy. You just stand in the middle of it and say where you want to go; and next thing, there you are. A nice little added bonus is, the carpet zips along so fast, it can't be seen by the naked eye. Pretty neat bit of kit, though I do say so myself. You've just got to be a bit careful about low doorways and unusually tall coffee tables, that's all.'

'That's amazing,' Paul said doubtfully. 'But I still don't see—'

'Oh.' Mr Laertides's left eyebrow shot up. 'You surprise me. I'd have thought the guy who outsmarted Countess Judy'd have figured it out for himself a while back. Hop aboard, and it'll whiz you past Rosie's desk without being seen. It won't take you all the way to Jowett Street, unfortunately; even the best of them – that's the beige deep-pile Wilton knock-off with the faint herringbone pattern – its maximum range is only about four hundred yards. That one you've got there, the light blue imitation Axminster, ought to get you out the door and fifty yards down the street. Well, don't just stand there gawping like that, give it a go.'

'But—' Paul was going to ask some pertinent question or other. Unfortunately, his subconscious had been trying to work out how far down St Mary Axe from the front door fifty yards was, and a mental image of the bus stop flitted across his mind.

Immediately, he felt something jerk viciously at his right wrist, and a shield-wall of air hit him hard in the face as he shot upwards and forward. *Fuck, I'm flying*, he thought, *just like bloody Superman*— Then something very hard and chunky slammed into his shoulder, and he dropped to the ground. When he came round after a brief holiday from consciousness, he realised that he was sitting on the pavement next to the lamp-post from which the bus-stop sign hung, and he was holding a small square of light blue carpet in his right hand.

'That,' continued Mr Laertides, who was leaning on the lamp-post like an absurdly elongated George Formby (and he looked as though he'd been there all along, waiting for Paul to show up), 'is why it's better to start off kneeling or sitting on the carpet, like I told you, only you had to know best. Maybe next time you'll try it my way. Also, don't forget the light tap with the left forefinger, it helps slow the bugger down so you don't get your neck sprained by the slipstream.'

Paul looked up to reply, but Mr Laertides wasn't there any more. Several passers-by looked at him, and one woman made a point of crossing the street to avoid him. He couldn't blame her in the least.

As he stood up (Mr Laertides had forgotten to include unexpected high-velocity flight followed by a sharp blow in his list of things that made the world go round; odd, since it was a doozy), Paul felt something heavy in his offside jacket pocket, and instinctively reached in and drew it out. It was the carpet-sample book, still far too big to fit in any jacket pocket ever made; but when he tried to put it back, it dropped in quite happily as though it was no larger than a matchbox.

Gift-horses' teeth, Paul told himself. Of course, he knew that it couldn't possibly be real, but on the other hand it didn't take much imagination to realise that if it did actually work, under certain circumstances it could be amazingly useful. He shrugged. Mr Laertides was, after all, a specialist in what Countess Judy had called effective magic; the point about which was that if you believed something was true, quite often it would be, assuming you'd first made out a sufficiently large cheque in favour of J. W. Wells & Co. He'd sort of got the impression from Countess Judy that he was one of the very few non-Fey who had the innate knack of doing effective magic, which perhaps explained why the carpet had responded so readily to him. The pain in his arm reminded him that sometimes a very strong but completely untrained latent ability could be more of a liability than an asset.

What the hell; in any event, he'd got past Mr Tanner's mum without rupturing any blood vessels through excessive blushing, so that was all right. Paul found a rubbish bin and dumped the used-up carpet square (if only she could have seen him, his mother would've been so proud). Now all he had to do was find Jowett Street and pick up the professor's parcel.

When he'd read the memo that morning and seen the words *just off the Charing Cross Road* and *collect a parcel for me*, he'd known immediately what to expect. Charing Cross Road was where all the funny little second-hand bookshops were; it was the sort of neighbourhood where eccentricity was the rule rather than the exception, and even a specialist in magical texts and spell books would count as boringly normal. Obviously, therefore, the professor was sending him to collect a book. 16 Jowett Street, however, wasn't a bookshop at all; in fact, it was a small Italian café. Sensibly he'd brought the memo with him, and he took it out and checked it again, just to be sure. But there it was, unambiguous as a kick in the face: 16, Jowett Street. A little bell tinged as he walked in, and a short, stocky man with a perfectly spherical head, thick glasses and a grin that looked as though it was larger than his face asked him what he wanted.

'Um,' he said.

The short man laughed. 'What you want to eat?' he repeated.

'Nothing,' Paul replied; then, quickly, he added: 'Look, I've probably come to the wrong place, but have you got anything for a Professor Van Spee?'

The short man's grin widened so alarmingly that Paul had visions of his face coming unzipped and falling off. 'Theo,' he said. *Uno momento, per favore.*' He vanished, then popped up again at the other end of the counter holding a white cardboard box, the sort cakes are packed in. '*Ecco,*' he said. 'Zabaglione alla Romana.' He thrust the box at Paul like a fly-half passing the ball. 'For my good friend *il professore. Buon' appetito.*'

Zabaglione? That was some sort of Italian bandit, wasn't it? No, it wasn't, it was a cake, or trifle or something. 'Um, thanks,' Paul said. 'How much do I—?'

The man roared with laughter, as if the idea of paying for something was the funniest thing he'd come across in years. 'Is on the 'ouse,' he chuckled. 'And something for you,' he added. 'Any friend of Theo's is friend of mine.' He lunged at Paul with some species of choux pastry, chocolate-swathed and gushing cream at every splitting seam. 'You sit, eat, have a cup of coffee. Plenty of time,' he said; and Paul, catching sight of the clock on the wall, realised it was only just gone ten, and he wasn't due to meet the professor till 11.15. Also, he hadn't had any breakfast, and there are no grey areas or complex moral issues where chocolate-covered cream cakes are concerned. If one presents itself, you eat it. Simple as that.

So he sat down with his cake, and the short man brought him a large frothy coffee with cocoa powder on the top, and while he was busy guzzling the choux thing a slice of exquisite-looking cheesecake somehow found its way onto the table just by his elbow, so he ate that too, and time passed swiftly and agreeably, the way it usually doesn't during the course of the average working day. A small part of him was trying to brew up a degree of indignation at being sent out like some kind of serf to fetch yummy puddings (and him a fully fledged assistant magician), but it was fighting a losing battle, and it knew it. So far, working for Theo Van Spee had been a tense business. Mostly he'd been summoned to the presence, given books to read and been politely dismissed; and each time the process was repeated, the professor would look at him thoughtfully for ten seconds or so and tell him that he wasn't ready yet. That was fine, in a way; no filing or photocopying or prodding 8 x 4s of assorted bits of Outback or filling in bewildering forms, nothing scary or disgusting or even particularly bizarre. Theo Van Spee was odd, of course, because everyone at JWW was odd; he was tall and thin and elderly and grave, so you hardly dared breathe in his presence, and his room was as dark as a bag (he had a great many ancient manuscripts, he'd explained, which would suffer horribly if exposed to the harsh glare of electric light; so the blinds were drawn, and the only illumination was a single oil lamp and a handful of chubby white candles), and of course he did have that unnerving habit of telling you things about yourself and other people that he couldn't possibly have known, not to mention his even creepier knack of seeming to know exactly what you'd been doing and what you were about to do, and always getting it absolutely right . . . But when Paul had been assigned to Mr Wells junior, he'd tried to maroon him for ever in a small room with no doors or windows; and Countess Judy had tried to kill him in his sleep; and Benny Shumway had made him fight a dragon (albeit a very small one, and he'd killed it quite accidentally, by tripping over it and sitting on it) and had sent him into the kingdom of the dead to do the daily banking; and Ricky

Wurmtoter had used him as live bait in his feud with Countess Judy, and shot him at point-blank range with a crossbow, killing him stone dead . . . Fetching cakes, by comparison, wasn't so bad after all, and neither, if he was going to be perfectly honest, was being sent to his office to read books, even if he couldn't make head nor tail of them.

'*Scusi.*' The short man's voice snapped Paul out of his contemplative daze. 'Is ten forty-five. Thank you so much. Goodbye.'

No point even being faintly surprised that the short, round-headed man knew when Paul had to be back at the office. He got up, said thank you politely for the nice cakes, and left, taking care not to squash the white box with the professor's zabaglione in it. Mr Tanner's mum was still on reception when he got back – for some reason she'd turned into a willowy Swedish blonde; but she changed shapes the way a daytime soap star changes outfits, so he wasn't at all fazed thereby – but she let him past with nothing more intrusive than a further reminder about the rehearsal tomorrow evening. He started to climb the stairs, and on the second-floor landing he collided with Sophie, who was coming out of the room where the big laser printer lurked. She was holding a huge wodge of papers, and of course he knocked them out of her hands all over the floor.

'It's all right,' she snarled, as she knelt down to pick them up (small, dark, painfully thin; enormous eyes, like one of those fish that live right down at the bottom of the sea). 'I can manage. What are you doing with a cake box?'

'Something I had to fetch for the professor,' Paul mumbled. He tried to gather a stray sheet of paper, but she blocked him with her shoulder and grabbed it. 'My fault,' he said, 'wasn't looking where I was—'

'No,' she said. 'And I just spent half an hour getting them in order, but don't let it bother you, I'm sure you had really important stuff on your mind at the time.'

He wasn't sure he followed that. 'What?'

'Now you've been *promoted*.' The word came out like the first hiss of steam from a volcano on the point of eruption, and Paul took a step back, felt the edge of the stair under his heel, and grabbed the banister to keep himself from toppling over. 'So please don't let me hold you up,' she went on. 'I'm sure you've got an important executive meeting to go to, or clients to see, or you're expecting a really important call from Minneapolis or Dar-es-bloody-Salaam.' She grabbed his ankle, lifted it like a farrier shoeing a horse, and retrieved a stray page from under his foot. 'I just hope I haven't held you up too terribly much, that's all.'

It simply hadn't occurred to Paul that Sophie hadn't been promoted too, and his mind emptied of helpful things to say as though someone had just phoned in a bomb threat. 'Look,' he muttered, 'it wasn't my idea, and you know what they're like, it's probably some horrible devious plan—'

'Yes, right,' Sophie snapped. 'They've doubled your wages and given you holidays and everything because they're toying with you, trying to lull you into a true sense of security. The bastards,' she added, with a ferocious scowl.

That was just a millitad more than Paul could stand. 'Oh come on, Sophe,' he wailed. 'Be reasonable. What do you think I ought to've done?'

'Refused,' she snapped. 'Of course. Otherwise, it's – it's *collaborating*. But I don't expect *you* to see that.'

The same tiny cell of his mind that had got all stroppy about fetching cakes now speculated about whether she'd have turned down a pay rise if she'd been offered it, but Paul knew better than to pay any heed to subconscious troublemakers. 'I'm sorry,' he said. 'But I just assumed they'd promoted you as well, because—'

'Balls,' she interrupted crisply. 'You knew perfectly well. It's because you're a man, so obviously you get the promotion and the extra money and the BMW and the key to the executive toilet, and I'm stuck in the photocopier room copying bloody leases all morning. Honestly, Paul, I really thought you weren't like that, I really thought you had a shred of decency— Do you mind,' she added, 'you're standing on my hand.'

Which was true, unfortunately. He hopped like a sparrow, and she made rather a show of rubbing her knuckles and biting her lip stoically. 'Sophe—'

'Please don't call me that,' she said, in a voice you could've smashed into chunks and put in gin and tonic. 'Now, if you'll excuse me, I'd better go and sort this lot into order. Again.'

Paul opened his mouth for a bit more abject pleading, but it occurred to him that anything he said would only make things worse, and by now he must be late for Theo Van Spee. 'Sorry,' he mumbled, and charged up the stairs as fast as he could go, tripping over his feet once or twice because the light on the stairs had blown, until he was standing outside the professor's room. Just before knocking, he glanced down at his watch. 11.15 precisely. Then, just as his knuckles were about to impact on the door, it swung open, with the result that he tapped Professor Van Spee lightly on the chest, as though examining his tie for signs of dry rot.

(*Didn't predict that, though, you bastard*, he said to himself by way of consolation; *otherwise you'd have stood a step to the right.*)

'Please sit down,' the professor said. 'You have collected my parcel. Please put it carefully on the sheet of newspaper I have laid out on the desk.'

He did so, observing without being even slightly interested that it was the Court Circular page of the *Montreal Herald*. 'You wanted to see me,' he said.

The professor nodded very slightly, and sat down on his side of the desk. He was backlit by one of the chubby candles, which cast a pale honey-coloured halo round his shoulders while effectively silhouetting his profile. *Poseur*, Paul decided. 'Since you have at last tackled the first section of the book I asked you to read, you are now ready to help me with my current project. I have to recalibrate a number of rather delicate thaumaturgical instruments, and I need you to work out for me the mean differences and standard variations. You have not brought a calculator with you; I keep one in the second drawer down on your left.'

'Excuse me,' Paul interrupted, 'but there wasn't anything in the book about what you just said. It was all about the world being a biscuit and stuff.'

The professor sighed. 'You opened the book and started to read. You glanced at a couple of paragraphs, and then fell asleep.

You had a strange dream, which you cannot now remember. Correct?'

Paul nodded.

'Excellent. We will begin with the differential field-polarity gauges.' Van Spee reached across the desk, picked up a flat rosewood box slightly larger than a paperback book, and flipped the dainty little catches to open it. Inside, snuggled in frayed green baize, lay a pair of tiny little brass gadgets, with jaws and thumbwheels and bits that slid in and out, and scales of numbers lightly engraved in teeny-tiny lettering, so faint and elegant and fine he couldn't actually read them. The professor picked one up, wound the jaws open and blew on it very lightly; then he picked a pin out of the lapel of his coat, whistled the opening bars of the 'Blue Danube', and held the sharp end of the pin between the jaws.

'Eight hundred and thirty-six,' he said. 'Do you concur?'

Paul was about to object that he hadn't got the faintest idea what the professor was talking about when his eyes blurred over, the way they do when you've just been crying or peeling onions. But it wasn't anything like that, he realised; they were just out of focus, like binoculars someone else has adjusted. Parallax; they'd done it at school but he'd been daydreaming, as usual. He lifted his head a little and tried to concentrate on something a bit further away. When he reached the professor's brass gadget, he found it was perfectly clear, amazingly so – in fact, the minute little numbers on the thing's sides were as deep and broad as ditches, and the figures themselves were almost too big to recognise. He blinked, then noticed the point of the pin; it was crawling with tiny moving things, small and busy as ants but darting about in a markedly orderly fashion, and in time to the professor's rather tuneless whistling.

'The ants,' he said. 'Are they dancing?'

'Not ants,' the professor replied, and Paul realised that they had little lacy wings, like mayflies. The professor gave up the waltz and started humming 'Blue Suede Shoes'; whereupon the mayflies stopped dead in their tracks for a split second, and then began whirling around even faster.

'Jitterbugs?' Paul asked.

'No,' the professor told him. 'Look carefully.'

Not insects of any kind; they had minuscule legs and arms, they were even wearing clothes – long white smocks like old-fashioned nightshirts. Beyond question they were dancing, though—

'Eight hundred and thirty-six,' the professor repeated. 'Is that what you make it?'

Paul wasn't aware of making a decision to count them; there was a moment when he quite simply knew that there were eight hundred and seventeen of them. Presumably in his excitement he said the total out loud. The professor sighed. 'Nineteen,' he said. 'Too large a margin of error.' He moved a thumbwheel on a couple of clicks and said, 'Try again.'

He'd been right. Not ants or mayflies, and even though the professor had stopped humming, they kept on dipping and whirling, waving their tiny arms about in time with the gap in nature where the tune had been.

'Angels,' Paul said.

'Correct.' The professor was peering down at the little brass gadget. 'Eight hundred and twenty-one,' he said. 'Do you agree?'

'Eight hundred and nineteen,' Paul heard himself say. 'Only two out this time.'

'That'll do,' the professor said, and he put the gadget he'd been playing with back in its box and took out its twin. 'Now I make it eight hundred and twenty-three.'

'Twenty-one,' Paul insisted.

'Excellent,' replied the professor. 'Down to a standard deviation of two – that's very helpful.' He shook the pin, like a nurse with a thermometer, and went through the same procedure, holding it between the jaws of the gadget and fiddling with the little wheels. 'Eight hundred and fifty-two.'

'Yes,' Paul said, 'I make it that, too. Professor, how come I can see them when they're that small?'

Either Professor Van Spee hadn't heard him, or he was deliberately taking no notice. He shook the pin again, and Paul realised he was clearing the angels off, then waiting for a new batch to settle on it so he could count them with the little brass doodad. This time round, Paul's total (he had no idea how he was doing the counting) was three less than the professor's, but that didn't seem to worry Van Spee as he put the brass callipers back in the box and closed the lid.

'Most satisfactory.' The professor finished making notes in a small red book and glanced at the grandfather clock leaning against the opposite wall. 'Now you must excuse me for a moment, while I use the dimensional abacus. Once I have finished the job, I shall know whether it needs retuning.'

The dimensional abacus looked like a doll's-house harp, only round and with very small dots or blobs strung out on the wires. There were eight of them, all different combinations of colours, like marbles; there was a silvery one, and a red one, and a blue-green one, and further back a big brown one with a single dot, and one that appeared to have a thin, sharp-edged disc round it—

'Professor—' Paul started to say, but Van Spee was engrossed in what he was doing, teasing the balls along the wires with the tip of a biro. A tiny spark jumped across the frame, grazed the edge of the big yellow blob in the centre, and vanished in a bright blue flare.

'Lefkowitz's Comet,' the professor explained. 'Due to collide with Mars in five hundred and seventy-six years' time. The result would have been substantial damage to the planet, resulting in a cloud of asteroids which would have bombarded Earth. A similar collision many millions of years ago led to the ice age which wiped out the dinosaurs.'

Paul nodded slowly; he was feeling numb from the shoulders up. 'But it's not going to happen now,' he mumbled. 'Is it?'

The professor dipped his head. 'A tiny alteration in the solar orbit of Neptune will cause the gravitational field of Jupiter to draw the comet half a million miles or so off its original course. This divergence will increase as the comet continues its journey; it will miss Mars by a comfortable margin, fall into the sun and burn up harmlessly. There will be some perceptible effects here on Earth – increased rainfall in the southern hemisphere for a year or two, and there will be bumper harvests of cocoa and soya beans in 2579 – but beyond that, nothing of any consequence.'

Paul breathed out slowly through his nose. 'And you did that,' he said, 'nudging the blob things round with a pen.'

'In a sense,' the professor replied mildly. 'This instrument,' he went on, 'is somewhat akin to a computer mouse; by moving it, one can initiate parallel movements in the world outside. One can, for example, make minor adjustments to a planet's orbit. It's a modern adaptation of a very old system of procedures commonly known as sympathetic magic – the same system that makes it possible to harm someone by sticking needles into a wax doll. Simple as it seems, it is in fact a tremendously complex and involved process, requiring many millions of complicated mathematical calculations.'

'Right,' Paul said, fascinated in spite of himself. 'Which is what you need the abacus for.'

'Excellent.' The professor's shadowy top lip moved a touch, just possibly a smile. 'No doubt you've heard one or other of the popularised versions of chaos theory – the most commonly cited example is the butterfly that flaps its wings in the Amazonian jungle, thereby giving rise to storms and tempests over Northern Europe. That is, of course, a gross oversimplification. However, the abacus may be considered as the equivalent of the butterfly in that scenario. The difference is that the movement of the ball-bearing along the wire is deliberate and calculated with the utmost care and attention to all possible operating factors.'

'I see,' Paul said, bending the truth like a bowstring. His head was hurting, a real Force Eight little-men-with-pickaxes job, but he ignored it. 'So I was right, and it was you that made Neptune get out of the way.'

'Of course not. I merely moved a ball-bearing along a wire.' The professor sighed audibly. 'Think it over, Mr Carpenter, and it will come to you, I'm sure. Meanwhile, we must retune the abacus. I suspect it may be as much as 0.00000000000000000001 picohertz out of true, which for fine work would render it not merely useless but dangerous as well.'

Paul knew that he should know better; but he couldn't let it pass so lightly. 'Professor,' he said, 'you just saved the world. And the human race and things. Isn't that—?'

'Business.' A mild click of the tongue, a patient man tolerating the fact that his good nature is being taken advantage of. 'You wish me to explain my motivations, Mr Carpenter, when we should be recalibrating this instrument. However.' He tutted, more in sorrow than in irritation, and shifted just a tad in his chair. 'I suppose we should clear up this issue now, before it causes problems. Mr Carpenter, the procedure you have just witnessed, one small movement of a metal bead along a short length of ordinary fuse wire, was the culmination of over three hundred hours of intensive calculation and research, and my time is neither infinite nor entirely without value. Why would I want to do a thing like that?'

'To save the planet, of course,' Paul said, relieved that for once someone at JWW had asked him a question he could answer. 'Otherwise there'd have been an ice age, and we'd all—'

'No.' The professor was trying to be kind, but he wasn't finding it easy. 'For money, Mr Carpenter. To make money for the firm's clients, and for my partners and myself. There is no other reason. One must earn a living, after all.'

'Sure,' Paul said, 'the same way doctors get paid for curing sick people. But really—'

'Not at all.' There were tiny flecks of annoyance in the professor's bland voice. 'We are retained by a major food-processing and retailing multinational. They are aware that sunspot activity results in climate change, which in turn affects the growth of crops. A glut of any given commodity allows them to reduce the price they pay to their suppliers, which means increased margins and greater profits. Since even VogMart cannot afford the cost of launching nuclear missiles at the sun, they hired us to cause sunspots. This I have done; the adjustment in Neptune's orbit will have an immediate effect, and next year there will be the required glut of coffee and bananas. The English summer will also be the wettest in thirty years, resulting in a rash of late foreign-holiday bookings, which will justify the trust placed in us by our clients in the travel and aviation sectors. And that,' he added, absently scratching his chin with his forefinger, 'is all there is to it.'

'But—' Paul struggled to find the words he needed. 'You really mean to say that saving the world was, like, a coincidence?' The professor's laugh was not entirely kind. 'Hardly,' he said. 'Economy of effort is the key to productivity and profitability. By choosing very carefully the timing and nature of my intervention, I was able – what is the proverb, now? – to kill multiple birds with one projectile. I told you just now that there would be bumper harvests of cocoa and soya beans in 2579. I shall still be very much alive when that happens, and my stockbrokers will still be in business. An investment of twenty-five pence now, suitably managed over the intervening period, will provide the funds necessary to buy a controlling interest in the commodities markets in good time for me to take maximum advantage of those exceptional harvests. In 2580, I shall be the third richest man on the planet.'

Whatever it was Paul had intended to say to that, it came out as a muted whimper. The professor clicked his tongue again, and went on: 'Finally, there is the regulatory aspect to be considered. Our industry is governed by a voluntary ethical-standards agreement. Basically, if we fulfil our quota of good works, we are left alone by government. The agreement has to be self-regulating, since only we can understand it; we work on the honesty principle, like people who leave trays of tomato plants outside their houses and trust you to put money in a coffee tin when you take some. We fill our quota, because we must, but it's entirely up to us to choose which good works we do. And today, I have saved the human race from extinction five centuries hence. I will send a detailed report to the relevant department of the Home Office, and they will pass on my data to their scientists, who will eventually confirm, once they have progressed far enough in their understanding of astronomy, that Neptune did indeed shift in its orbit for no readily apparent reason, and that Lefkowitz's Comet is currently on a collision course with Mars, and that the adjustment in Neptune's orbit has obviated that threat. There, you see: three birds for my stone, all of which taken together exactly justify the expense of time and resources I have devoted to this project. In taking the time to explain these simple facts to you, I have regrettably reduced the profit element of the project by 0.413 per cent, so I trust you will agree that we should now get on with the recalibrations without further delay.'

That was Paul told; and for the rest of the day he helped the professor recalibrate the dimensional abacus, the mode reintegrator, the ⅜″ serendipity wrench, the Wogelsang Keys and the self-centring entropy clamps. He didn't ask what any of the things did, and the professor didn't tell him. At twenty-five past five precisely, he tightened up the locking screws on the last clamp.

'Thank you,' the professor said (it was the first thing he'd said for over an hour). 'You will be here at nine-seventeen tomorrow morning, and we will field-strip the Emmotson projector. Your front-door key has slipped through a hole in the pocket of your overcoat, but you will find it trapped in the lining just above the bottom hem.'

As soon as Paul got back to his office, where his coat hung on the back of the door, he checked to see if the professor had been right. As he fished the key out through the hole in the pocket, he wondered if any of the things that Van Spee had told him earlier offered a hint of an explanation of how the hell he did that stuff. Someone who could shift the orbit of a planet – And then he frowned, because it had been rather hot in the professor's room and there had been a useful-looking electric fan on his desk; but when Paul had asked if he could turn it on, the professor had shrugged and said it didn't work . . . A man who could heave planets about, but who couldn't replace a blown fuse. And if Van Spee was really all-seeing and all-knowing, wouldn't he have realised that the fuse was about to blow? Or maybe he simply didn't feel the heat.

He glanced at his watch, and swore. Five twenty-nine; he really didn't want to find himself locked in, even though he wasn't afraid of the goblins any more. Grabbing his coat, he jogged down the corridors and made it to the front office just as Mr Tanner was reaching for the top bolt.

'Cutting it fine,' Mr Tanner growled. 'Try and keep an eye on the time, will you?'

Paul apologised, and scuttled through the door as quickly as he could. Outside it was bright and sunny, or maybe it just seemed that way after a day cooped up in the Professor's office, with the blinds drawn. On such a fine evening as this, Paul didn't feel like going home straight away to his sparse and miserable flat. There was already quite a crowd of people sitting outside the pub just down the road, and his throat was dry enough to justify a quick drink. A virtual coin spun in his mind and came up heads; it was a double-sided coin, but that's often the way.

It took him a while to fight his way to the bar, and almost as long to thread his way back through the dense forest of drinkers without spilling his lemonade shandy. Worn out by his adventure, he propped himself up against the wall, just clear of the doorway, and took a couple of deep breaths. The warmth of the sun and the fiery strength of the shandy made him feel almost absurdly relaxed. No hurry to go home, or go anywhere in particular. Being out of the office, in blissfully normal, magic-free surroundings, was solace enough. He might even stay a while, have the other half—

Someone dug him in the ribs, and he convulsed, slopping shandy all over his cuff.

'Careful,' said a voice he'd never heard before but recognised immediately. 'You're a bit jumpy this evening. Nervous about tomorrow?'

Mr Tanner's bloody mother. Of course it was her, even though she'd disguised herself as a slim, flame-haired enchantress in a red sundress. 'No,' Paul replied. 'I've just got this thing about getting stabbed with sharp fingernails. Did you have to do that?'

'You looked so sweet standing there,' Mr Tanner's mum replied cheerfully, 'I couldn't resist. Haven't you got a home to go to, then?'

'Yes, but it's horrible,' Paul said. 'It smells of cabbage and the plumbing makes disgusting noises. What's wrong with having a quick drink before I go home?'

She tutted. 'Touchy,' she said. 'Girl trouble.'

'No, it isn't.' The reply a tad too vehement, perhaps? Like he cared. 'Nothing of the kind,' he said stiffly. 'And anyhow, won't be long now before I'm through with all that stuff for ever. Can't wait,' he added, trying to look nonchalant as he sipped the foam on the top of his shandy.

'You're joining a monastery.'

'Better than that,' Paul said, 'because I don't like getting up early in the morning and I'm allergic to bee-stings. No, it's much better than that, thanks for asking.'

The gorgeous redhead frowned. 'Why bee-stings?'

'Monks,' Paul said. 'They all keep bees, don't they? Anyhow, screw bee-stings, that's not the point. Pretty soon, my falling-in-love-again, heart-of-glass days will soon be over. Just you wait and see.'

Mr Tanner's mum shrugged. 'Oh, you mean that recipe you found in Theo's book,' she said. 'That old thing. Pure snake oil. Doesn't work.'

Paul's stomach lurched slightly. 'What do you mean, it doesn't work? How do you know about it, anyway?'

'Ah, well.' Mr Tanner's mum grinned. 'I know a lot of stuff, I do. And I happen to know, for a fact, you can't brew that muck without the special secret ingredient, Van Spee's crystals. And of course, you can't buy them anywhere, because only Theo knows how to make them, and he controls the supply.'

'That's what you think,' Paul said, smirking insufferably. 'Because I've got some Van Spee's crystals. Loads of them.'

'Really.' Her tone of voice cut through the smug fug in his brain like a razor. 'Where did you get them from, then?'

There was hardly any delay before Paul replied, 'Oh, I asked the professor for some and he gave them to me. From a big jar in his desk. Very pleasant he was about it, but he did say not to tell anybody about it, or they'd all want some. So if you wouldn't mind keeping it to yourself—'

'Sure.' She nodded thoughtfully. 'Well, that's lucky,' she said. 'Only, he must like you an awful lot. You know how much that stuff is worth?'

'You just said you can't buy it.'

Scorn, intense enough to strip varnish. 'You can buy anything,' Mr Tanner's mum said, 'so long as you've got enough money. How much did he give you, then?'

'Oh, about an ounce, I suppose. An aspirin-bottleful.'

'Bloody hell.' Not often Paul saw Mr Tanner's mum lose her cool. 'You may be interested to know, your mate Theo gave you enough stuff to buy a four-bedroom detached house in Surrey. Pretty remarkable, don't you think? He must fancy you, or something.'

Paul ignored that; he had other things to worry about. True, the professor hadn't said anything about missing crystals, so he'd assumed that the old fool hadn't noticed. Other explanations now came to mind, most of them involving diabolical forms of retribution that took a week or so to set up. 'Oh well,' he mumbled. 'Like you said, very generous of him.'

'Very. And everybody says what a mean, miserly old git he is. Well, see you tomorrow, then. Take care,' she added, as she swayed off down the street, all heels and hips, and two dozen young stockbrokers forgot what they'd been about to say and stared until she was out of sight.

Take care, she'd said; was that just a conventional form of words meaning goodbye, or was it a warning? Maybe if he managed to get the crystals back into the professor's desk before he noticed – and how much was a four-bedroom detached house in Surrey worth these days? Half a million? Three-quarters—?

'Psst.' Someone was standing on Paul's foot. Someone very small, because the whisper came from round about elbow height; but someone also very heavy, because his foot hurt quite a lot, and he couldn't move it for the weight. He looked down, and saw a very short, very stocky little man in a raincoat four sizes too big for him. He was also wearing very dark shades, which he lifted just for a split second, revealing a pair of bright blood-red eyes.

'You're a goblin,' Paul said.

The little man nodded. 'That's right,' he said. 'And speak up, I think there's a bloke on the other side of the street who didn't hear you.'

'What? Oh, right, sorry. But you are, aren't you? A gob—'

'All right, yes. Actually, I'm your third cousin, eight times removed. Call me Colin.'

'If you like,' Paul said. 'But what're you doing out here? You aren't supposed to wander about like this. You should be inside, with the others.'

Colin laughed. 'Screw that,' he said, 'I don't belong to the colony. Actually, I'm a naturalised human. Like you,' he added, with a revolting grin.

Paul knew better than to rise to that one. 'Pleased to meet you,' he said. 'Look, was there something, only I really ought to be getting home—'

'Bollocks,' Colin said. 'I was listening to you and our Rosie just now.'

'Oh. Were you?'

Colin nodded his oversized, noticeably pointed head. 'Heard some very interesting stuff about Van Spee's crystals. About an aspirin-bottleful.'

Paul winced. 'Look,' he said, 'I just decided, I'm going to put it back where I got it from, just don't—'

'Are you? Oh.' Colin looked profoundly underconvinced. 'That'd be a real pity, really, because I just happen to know a bloke who knows a bloke who'd pay top dollar for a few grams of Van Spee's crystals. Provided that's what they really are, of course,' he added, with a slight scowl.

'I'm pretty sure they are,' Paul said. 'Only, that's what it said on the label, and it was in Van Spee's desk drawer—' Maybe, just possibly, he shouldn't have said that. Too late now, though.

But Colin only grinned a bit wider. 'Easy enough to tell,' he hissed. 'I mean, I could tell you right now, if you happened to have them on you.'

As it happened, the bottle was in Paul's overcoat pocket, the one without the hole (and if Van Spee knew about the hole, surely it stood to reason – A mental image of the professor, pale and shrunken, hopping around on all fours muttering '*What has it got in its pocketses?*' slipped into his mind, and took quite a bit of getting rid of). 'All right,' Paul whispered back, 'but not here. People'll think we're dealing drugs or something.'

For some reason, Colin seemed to think that was funny, but he nodded his head sideways. 'Round the back,' he said. 'Alleyway, couple of lock-up garages. I got a key. Count to twenty and follow me.'

Paul couldn't remember having seen an alleyway near the pub, in fact he could've sworn it was an architectural impossibility, given the age and nature of the buildings. But apparently he was wrong; there was an alley, small and dark, like an American's visualisation of Dickens, and halfway down it stood two small garages, so shabby as to be picturesque. The sliding door of one of them was open, and Colin beckoned to him as he approached.

'Anybody follow you?' he muttered.

'Don't think so,' Paul replied (the thought hadn't even crossed his mind). 'Look, I'm not sure about this. Even if I'm going to keep the stuff, I don't think selling it'd be a terribly—'

'Quiet.' Colin peered up and down the alley a couple of times, then heaved the garage door down and flipped on a light. The garage was completely empty, apart from a few swatches of dusty cobweb swathed across the walls like tinsel on a Christmas tree. If someone had hired Lawrence Llewelyn-Bowen to decorate a garage in Furtive Noir, it couldn't have been more perfect. 'All right,' he said, 'let's see the stuff.'

'Look—'

'Please?' Now the goblin was doing that sad, beseeching look, like a red-eyed puppy dog. 'Come on, it can't hurt, letting me just look at it. And I can tell you if it's the real thing, or just coffee sugar.'

There was that, of course. Paul was proposing to use the stuff in the recipe; if it turned out to be something else, like strychnine, that the professor had put in the jar as a merry prank, it might be as well to find out about it now rather than later. 'Oh, all right then,' he said and fished out the bottle.

The effect on Colin was rather remarkable: a cross between someone finding a thick roll of banknotes in the street and Sir Lancelot kneeling before the Grail. 'If that's the real deal,' he said in a small, wobbly voice, 'then that's a hell of a lot of crystals. Mind if I—?'

Paul shrugged. 'Whatever.'

Very carefully, Colin unscrewed the cap; he paused as though saying grace, then grew a long, thin claw from the little finger of his left hand. He dipped the end of the claw into the bottle and licked it, and his face lit up with a sort of religious glow. 'That's the stuff,' he whispered. 'Definitely the stuff. All right,' he went on, pulling himself together with an almost audible snap. 'Tell you what I'll do, seeing you're family and I like you and everything. A million US dollars, cash. What do you reckon?'

It was the look on Colin's face that made Paul's mind up for him: that frantic, almost haunted look of unbearable longing and greed. 'Sorry,' Paul said, 'but it's going back. I just hope the professor hasn't noticed it's gone.'

Colin winced as though someone had just stubbed out a cigarette in his ear. 'Sorry,' he said. 'Sorry, sorry, sorry, serves me right for trying to rip off my own third cousin. What I meant to say was, two million. Pounds. For what's left,' he added quickly, 'after you've had what you need for your medicine.'

Two million pounds. Two million useless, worthless pounds, because of course he could never spend it; not Paul Carpenter, who'd been sold to JWW and could never quit. Mr Tanner's mum had said you can buy anything, but she'd been wrong. Paul couldn't buy anything, because he no longer owned himself—

'With three million quid,' Colin was saying, quietly and insidiously, 'you could do a deal. With them. Our Dennis's lot. With three and a *half* million,' he went on – he was sweating slightly, Paul noticed – 'you could buy *yourself.*'

Paul hadn't thought of that. How much was he worth to the partnership, exactly? He knew how much they'd paid for him, four hundred and twenty-five thousand, enough to buy Paul's parents their Florida home and their Winnebago. Would three and a half million strike them as a good deal, or not? How could he possibly be worth more than that to anybody? Even on a good day, he wasn't worth twenty quid and a book of stamps to himself—

'When I said three and a half,' Colin said, 'I was just kidding. Four and a quarter, I should've said.'

– But even a real idiot, a worthless clown like Paul Carpenter, knew better than to offer to buy anything from the partnership with their own money; and all he had to do was look into Colin's eyes to know that the stuff in the bottle wasn't going to do him any good. Rather the reverse, in fact.

'Sorry,' he said. 'I don't think so.'

For a moment, Paul was sure that the goblin was going to attack; and that'd be that, he thought, goblins being ferocious natural killers, armed with claws like razors and teeth like needles. Instead, however, Colin handed him the bottle and shrugged. A few tiny specks of greyish-white powder were scattered round the neck of the bottle; Paul quickly wiped them away with his cuff.

'Can't blame a bloke for trying,' Colin said. 'If you change your mind, Rosie'll tell you where to find me. Look after yourself, right?'

Then he snapped his fingers. The garage seemed to burst like a balloon, and Paul found himself standing outside the pub. The crowd had gone, he was holding an empty glass, in which someone had dropped a cigarette end, and it had started to rain.

CHAPTER THREE

G etting the crystals in the first place had been easy, sheer serendipity. Putting them back proved to be another matter entirely.

For one thing, Professor Van Spee never left his office. It was one of those things that everybody else in the building (the secretaries, the partners, Mr Tanner's mum, the cleaners, even the strange mad woman who came in once a month to talk nicely to the computers) knew and he didn't. Because he'd bumped into Van Spee once in the photocopier room, and then, some time later, been left alone in the professor's office while the great man went to see old Mr Wells, Paul had assumed he was vaguely nomadic, like everybody else in the building. At the very least, he'd reasoned, he must toddle off a couple of times a day to take a leak. Apparently not so. At one point in the fraught day that followed Paul's encounter with Colin, he almost made up his mind to confess, but he didn't. A right fool he'd feel, he decided, if he nerved himself to throw himself on the professor's mercy, only to find out in mid-air, so to speak, that he hadn't got one.

The day was long as well as nerve-racking. First, as promised, they dismantled the Emmotson projector, an astoundingly bizarre object that looked like a cross between a bird-scarer and a washing machine, apparently used to isolate moments in the past that marked crucial turning points in courses of events.

How it did that, Paul couldn't begin to guess and the professor wasn't inclined to explain. Instead, Paul had to crawl about on the floor on his back with a spanner and a set of Allen keys, undoing nuts and bolts, pulling off casings and covers, dodging tiny little springs that came hurtling out like rocketing pheasants every time he undid something, then squirting cans of various cleaners and lubricants into ferocious-looking batteries of cams and cogs and wiping gunk and slime out of slots and keyways with a bit of wodged-up paper towel. It was another hot day, even in the professor's office, which was always noticeably cooler than everywhere else, and Paul had to stop every few minutes to wipe sweat off his face with his sleeve. What with the sweat and the stale lemonade shandy from yesterday, it didn't smell very nice and tasted worse; furthermore, he soon developed a thirst that would've disabled a hardened desert explorer, but the professor didn't seem to have heard of coffee breaks or anything of that sort. By the time he'd fitted back the last panel and tightened up the last locking nut and grub screw, his watch told him it was ten past eleven, but he could've sworn he'd been playing about with the horrible thing for at least five hours. All that time, of course, the professor hadn't moved from his chair; he'd just sat there and told Paul what to do, in his flat, slightly bleating voice, with special reference to procedures that Paul had either forgotten or wasn't to be trusted not to forget. Opportunities to sneak the crystals back into the jar in the desk: none.

At least the next job on the list of things to do was sitting-down work; that, however, was the best that could be said for it—

'Here is a copy of an agreement,' the professor said. 'I have another copy of the same document. You will kindly read it out to me, so that I can check my copy for spelling mistakes and other errors. This is a very important contract, and it is essential that it should be word-perfect.'

So Paul started to read (he hated reading aloud); and mostly to begin with it was just incomprehensible legal drivel, all *whereas the parties hereto* and *hereinafter where the context so permits defined as* and other great big galumphing phrases with huge hairy eyebrows and too many syllables. Slowly, though, Paul started to get an idea of what it was about. It was an agreement for the sale and purchase of a soul.

'Correct,' the professor confirmed, when at last they'd reached the end, and Paul's curiosity drove him to ask if his guess was accurate. 'Ordinarily, spiritual conveyancing is not a major part of the workload of this department. Till recently, the younger Mr Wells dealt with it. However, since his departure –' here the professor paused for a moment and looked at him, because of course it was Paul's doing that Mr Wells junior had lost the power struggle with his uncle and been turned into a photocopier '– I have looked after such matters. It is tedious work, and I must confess that I have little sympathy for our clients. We generally act,' he added, deadpan, 'for the purchasers in these transactions. However, it needs to be done and it must be done carefully.' He was silent for a minute or so, as he examined the thick wodge of paper in his hand; then he passed it to Paul across the desk. 'Perhaps you would be so kind as to take this down to the typing pool and ask them to make the necessary corrections by one o'clock. It can then be checked again and bound up, in time for Mr Shumway to deliver it by hand when he goes to the Bank.'

Paul knew all about Benny Shumway's daily excursion to the Bank of the Dead, since he'd had to do the run himself on several memorable occasions. 'Right,' he said, as he stood up, delighted to be able to stretch his legs after sitting still for so long. 'Um, where is the typing pool, exactly? I don't think I've ever—'

The professor gave him directions, which Paul was sure he wouldn't be able to follow; to a substantial extent, he believed they were physically and topographically impossible, because there'd be walls and things in the way. But he was wrong as usual. Doorways he'd somehow failed to notice in walls in corridors that he'd walked up and down ten times a day for nine months turned out to be exactly where the professor had said they'd be. Stairwells sprang up at his feet like Jack's beanstalk at the end of passages that had been cul-de-sacs only days before. There was even a small, square open-air courtyard to cross, a sort of cloister arrangement with a fountain and lemon trees in the middle, in what his sense of direction told him should have been the middle of the building next door. On the other hand, all Paul's relatives had told him many times that he was capable of getting lost in a matchbox, even if all the matches were still in it, so he guessed he was imagining it.

Eventually he came to a door marked *Typing* and knocked. No answer; presumably you didn't knock, you just barged in, so he pushed it open and stepped through; and found himself standing on the tiled edge of a huge indoor swimming-bath.

The walls were blue, the roof was glass, and the whole place looked like something out of one of those underwater nature documentaries. The light danced on the ripples of the water, sending white dots and dashes careening up and down the walls. Instead of the usual chlorine smell, the air was thick with a strange blend of sea-salt, coconut and banana. For a moment, Paul thought the bath was deserted; then, as he was about to turn and leave, something broke up through the still blue meniscus like a whale coming up to breathe.

Fuck a ferret sideways, Paul thought. *A mermaid.*

She bobbed up and down in the water a couple of times, sweeping her mane of wet brown hair out of her eyes; then she became aware of Paul's presence, turned and waved. One of the tips of her tail broke the surface of the water, like the fin of a small shark. Mermaids don't wear swimming costumes, or tops of any kind. Paul spun round and faced the door he'd just come through, his face burning.

'Hello,' said the mermaid. 'I'm Vicky. Who're you?'

At that particular moment, that was a very good question, because for the life of him Paul couldn't remember. Somehow he pulled himself together, but it took some doing. 'Paul Carpenter,' he said. 'Sorry.'

'That's all right, I don't suppose you can help it.' A faint giggle. 'What are you sorry about?'

'I didn't know – I mean, I wasn't staring or anything, you just sort of popped up, before I could . . .'

'Before you could what?'

Paul cleared his throat. 'Excuse me,' he said. 'I was looking for the typing pool.'

As he said the words, the penny came crashing down like a thunderbolt. Typing *pool*. The mermaid giggled again.

'You found it. Have you got something for us to do?'

Paul nodded. 'From Professor Van Spee. He says, can you please have it ready for one o'clock?'

The mermaid groaned. 'Not that horrible long contract,' she complained. 'I've done it five times already. Now what's wrong with the bloody thing?'

'Oh, just a few minor bits and pieces,' Paul said, and for some reason his voice was all wobbly. 'Won't take five minutes on the computer—'

'We don't use computers, silly,' Vicky the mermaid interrupted. 'We live underwater. Water's not very good for electrical appliances.'

'Oh.'

'Yes, oh.' He heard her sigh. 'Big old-fashioned sit-up-and-beg typewriters are what we use, only they're all stainless steel, so they won't rust. Which means I'll have to do the whole rotten thing all over again from scratch. Never mind,' she added, her tone of voice changing slightly, 'can't be helped, and I don't suppose it's your fault.'

'Thanks,' Paul said. 'And, um, sorry.'

'I forgive you.' Pause. 'Well?'

'Sorry?'

'Would you mind awfully bringing it over here, so I can get on with it? I can't come over there and fetch it, you see, on account of not having any legs.'

Paul cringed. A part of him told him he was being a bit bloody silly, since obviously the mermaid didn't mind a bit, and what he'd seen in the split second before he shut his eyes had been very nice. But he was still very much Paul Carpenter; so he made a valiant effort to judge the distance and, eyes still glued to the door, started to walk backwards.

It took a whole ten seconds for the inevitable to happen; then he was falling through the air for perhaps a quarter of a second, and then the water hit him on the back of his head and wrapped itself all round him.

To be fair to him, Paul knew how to swim. He even had a

piece of paper somewhere to prove it. But that was proper deliberate swimming-on-purpose, where you take your clothes off and fold them neatly and put on bathing trunks and climb in backwards down a little ladder. Swimming where you're suddenly submerged in freezing cold water that fills your mouth and ears, and you're wearing lace-up shoes and a jacket and tie hadn't been covered in the syllabus when he earned his little piece of paper, and he realised he didn't know how to do it. Drowning, on the other hand, was apparently something that just comes naturally.

'Keep *still*,' said a voice in his ear, or maybe inside his head. Then something hit him on the point of the jaw, and all the lights went out.

He was a ship, drifting alone on a yellow sea. He was a hawk wheeling alone through yellow clouds, until he saw a gap and through it, far below, a flat green landscape and a grey stone tower. He swooped, and as he got closer to the ground the tower grew, reaching up to meet him like a stone arm pushing up out of the earth. He landed on a weathered battlement and folded his wings.

Below him lay the main courtyard, where the tower's garrison were busy with their chores: grooming horses, burnishing armour with handfuls of sand and straw, practising archery at the butts, carting hay, raking muck out of the stables, drying newly washed linen. Unnoticed by these busy people, he fluttered down and perched on the edge of an open door, next to a large grindstone on which someone was sharpening a wide-bladed axe. He recognised the axe, had a feeling that at some stage he might even have known its name. A few yards to his right, a pig had nosed and shouldered its way out of its pen, and was having a wonderful time being chased round the yard by half a dozen tired, angry men. They were shouting at it in a strange dialect of French; most of the vocabulary was unfamiliar to him, but that didn't stop him getting the general idea.

The main stable door swung open, and two men led out a fine black horse, tall and broad enough to pull a brewer's dray but fine-boned and immaculately turned out. Over a rich red saddle-cloth lay a saddle of tooled green leather, highlighted in gold leaf, with gilded stirrups swinging from the straps. The grooms led the horse to a mounting block standing against the court-yard's north wall, where a tall man in extravagantly ostentatious clothes was waiting, accompanied by half a dozen servants. The well-dressed man, clearly a great lord, swung himself easily into the saddle, picked up the reins in his left hand and held out his right arm, hand gauntleted and clenched. It was a gesture of invitation and summons; so he spread his wings and fluttered head-high across the yard, turned and dropped neatly onto the lord's wrist, a suitably perfect landing. Today, the great man told him in a soft, firm voice, they were going out after doves, pheasant and woodcock on the edge of the large stand of pine on the southern boundary of the park; and he must make a special effort and hunt diligently, because tomorrow the king himself would be a guest at the castle, as he broke his journey east from Toronto to the capital—

'You're all wet,' said the mermaid.

This was true. Paul was very wet indeed. There was enough water in his socks alone to wash out all fourteen days of Wimbledon. When he opened his eyes they stung, and he rubbed them.

'You fell in,' the mermaid told him. 'It was your own silly fault, you were walking backwards, so you couldn't see where you were going. Can't you swim?'

'Yes,' Paul said. 'Well, a bit. I was doing fine, actually, till somebody hit me.'

'Sure you were,' the mermaid said. Her face was only inches away from his, and her thick, wavy brown hair seemed perfectly dry. It had golden highlights, so pale they were almost white. They reminded Paul of something, but he couldn't for the life of him think what.

'Professor Van Spee's contract,' he croaked. 'Did I mention, it's really urgent.'

'Done,' the mermaid replied. 'While you were out cold. It's all ready, top copy and two carbons. You need to get out of those wet things before you catch your death.'

'No, really, I'm fine,' Paul said, all together in a rush. 'There's a radiator in my office, I'll dry off. I'd better be getting back or the professor'll wonder why I'm taking so long.'

She only smiled, and started peeling off his jacket. Her eyes were exactly the colour of the water, blue and deep enough to drown in, if you happened not to be a strong swimmer. 'How's your jaw?' she was saying. 'I didn't mean to hit you quite so hard, but you were thrashing about like a gaffed shark.'

'It's fine,' Paul said, as the sleeves of his jacket slithered past his hands; then her fingers were at his throat, prising apart the knot of his tie.

'Don't you ever stop wriggling about?' she asked him. 'The way you're carrying on, anybody'd think you were the fish out of water.'

Good point. He was, he realised, on the tiled edge of the pool, and she was kneeling over him, something that ought not to be possible without something to kneel with. He made a point of not looking down, and mumbled, 'Shouldn't you be—?'

She laughed. 'Hans Christian Andersen to you,' she said. 'And it's all right, you're safe, you can look.'

He ventured a quick, furtive glance, and saw that she was wearing a white blouse and a plain navy blue skirt. He relaxed a bit, but she was still very close, and her fingernails were brushing the skin of his neck.

'I go walking three times a week,' she said proudly. 'Last Tuesday I walked seventeen lengths. And I borrowed Christine's catalogue and sent off for a pair of shoes. The pointy ones with the big nail things sticking out of the back end.' She frowned. 'You probably know this,' she went on, 'but what's the nail thing for, exactly? I'm guessing it's like a sort of claw, for holding your prey still while you finish it off.'

Paul smiled feebly. 'Something like that,' he said.

'Thought so. And what about the net things you wear round your legs? What're they for? Christine says you're supposed to pull them right up over your thighs, but I can't see what makes them stay up. And do men wear them, or only women?'

She'd overcome his tie and started on his shirt buttons. *First thing when I get home this evening*, he promised himself, *I'm*

going to make that medicine, and bugger giving back the crystals.
'Look,' he said, swiping her hand away as though swatting a
huge fly, 'it's really kind of you, but I'll, um, change when I get
home. Bit of water never hurt anybody.' Then he sneezed.
'Anyway, thanks very much for saving me from drowning, but
I really ought to get on. You wouldn't happen to know the
time, would you?'

She frowned thoughtfully. 'Time,' she repeated. 'No, can't
say as I do. What does it look like?'

That'll do me, Paul thought, *I'm out of here.* 'Thanks again,' he
spluttered, jumped to his feet, slithered and bounded toward the
door. Then he realised that he'd forgotten Van Spee's stupid
contract. The mermaid was standing behind him, smiling
sweetly, holding it out for him. He took it from her – it weighed
a ton, and he felt the tendons in his wrist twang like guitar
strings – and fled, letting the door slam behind him.

In the corridor he stopped, caught his breath and tucked the
contract carefully under his arm.

Water dripped from Paul's trousers and puddled embarrassingly
on the carpet. A fat drop trickled down his forehead and into his
right eye. He looked at his watch, but of course it had stopped.
Wearily, he squelched back the way he'd come, happily not
meeting anybody on the way. They still hadn't got around to
replacing the blown light bulb on the third floor stairs. The
world, Paul decided, was a wretched, miserable place.

'You are wet,' Theo Van Spee told him, as he shuffled through
the door. 'There is a towel on your chair, and dry clothes in the
Marks & Spencer bag on the floor to your right, next to the
waste-paper basket. You will wish to get changed in the lavatory
at the end of the corridor. Nobody else will want to use it today,
and you may therefore hang up your wet clothes to dry. You will
just be in time to catch Mr Shumway before he leaves for the
Bank. I shall not need you any more today.'

Benny seemed preoccupied, and didn't hang around to chat;
Paul knew that even now he dreaded the daily banking run, and
with good reason; so he dumped the contract on the desk and
left, heading back to his office. When he got there, he found the

new partner, Mr Laertides, sitting on the edge of his desk, eating an apple.

'Your hair's all wet,' Mr Laertides said. 'Raining out, is it?'

For all I know, Paul decided, *it could very well be*. 'Yes,' he said. 'Is there anything I can do for you?'

Mr Laertides took another bite of his apple; he sank his teeth into it, then pulled his hand away, so that a chunk of apple-flesh was torn off. Then he dumped the core in Paul's bin. 'So tell me,' he said, 'what was it really like, fighting it out with Countess Judy? Scary, I bet.'

Paul nodded. 'Would it be all right if I didn't talk about it?' he said.

'Please yourself,' Mr Laertides said with his mouth full. 'Point is, you never actually finished your stint in Media and PR. I know you're working with Theo Van Spee right now, and after that you're booked for two months with Cas Suslowicz, castles in the air and so forth. Just thought, though, you might like to sandwich in a few weeks with me. Only, I'm building a rather juicy deal right now that'll be starting to get interesting about the time you're due to finish with Theo, and I thought you might like to be in on it. I saw in your personnel file, Judy reckoned you've got the knack. And say what you like about her, she was bloody good at the job. What do you say?'

Difficult, Paul thought. The truth was, of course, that he'd rather scrub sewers with a toothbrush than have anything to do with magic of any sort; but, since he didn't have that option, one form of unspeakableness was pretty much the same as any other. On the other hand, Mr Suslowicz had struck him as the least offensive of the JWW gang; on Paul's first day in the job he'd sent him down a map of the building so that he could find his way about through the nightmare tangle of corridors and staircases. True, Mr Suslowicz's map had turned out to be no more than forty per cent accurate, and where it was wrong it was usually disastrously wrong – the first floor small interview room had proved to be a store for eight-foot-tall man-shaped wicker cages, and Mr Suslowicz had marked the blue door opposite the window on the second floor landing as a stationery cupboard, when in fact it was a ladies' toilet. In spite of that, Paul had been sort-of-looking-forward to two months in Civil Engineering, whereas Mr Laertides was very much an unknown quantity. Fortunately, inspiration struck; 'I'll ask Mr Tanner what he thinks,' Paul said. 'He's sort of in charge of that kind of arrangement, so—'

'Fair enough.' Mr Laertides stood up. He moved jerkily, like bad animation. 'Well, see you at Rosie's later, for the rehearsal.' On his way to the door, he paused. 'One last thing,' he added, rather in the style of Lieutenant Columbo. 'Have you had a chance to brew up the medicine yet?'

As far as Paul was concerned, his life over the last nine months had turned into the sort of experience you'd expect if Dante had designed the rides at Alton Towers. Mostly he seemed to be trapped in the one where you're swept along down a pitch-dark underground river in an open boat, and the branches of overhanging trees keep smacking you in the face. 'Medicine,' he repeated.

'You know,' said Mr Laertides, with a hint of impatience, 'the jollop. The stuff that'll stop you falling in love every two minutes. Theo told me you went ferreting about in his old books one time when you thought he wasn't looking. Then you nicked a load of his special patent wonder-crystals from the jar in his desk drawer, so Theo guessed you were planning on making the stuff. Bloody good idea, he thought, it'll help you keep your mind on your work, instead of drooping round the place like a weasel with malaria. Well? Only if you haven't done it yet, maybe you'd like a hand. It's not exactly rocket science, chucking a few ingredients in a saucepan, but it's not exactly defrosting an Asda cannelloni, either.' Mr Laertides frowned; his whole face seemed to clench inwards, as if an invisible hand was squeezing it. 'You want my help or don't you? Up to you, of course, but I do happen to have a master's degree in supernatural chemistry, whereas you can just about boil an egg without blowing up most of north-west London.'

The last part was true enough. 'Excuse me,' Paul said cautiously, 'but why would you, a partner and all, want to spend valuable fee-earning time helping me do something that's nothing to do with work?'

Mr Laertides's face went blank for a moment; then he laughed. 'Suspicious soul, aren't you? No bad thing, either, in this trade, and after the Countess Judy business and all I don't blame you. Always wise to have a gander at a gift horse's teeth, just in case they're about to meet in your neck.' He reached out a hand – it was almost as though he had a telescopic arm that extended from the elbow – and dealt Paul a staggering blow on the shoulder. 'But it's okay,' he said, 'you don't need to worry about me. Fact is, we're going to be working together from now on, and I don't hold with all that stuffy them-and-us crap, it's completely counter-productive in my experience. If we're going to be on the same team, I'd like us to be mates, and mates help each other, right? Or would you rather stick with the unappeasable-hatred school of industrial relations?'

'Well, no,' Paul said, when the silence got too much for him. 'No, obviously. I just didn't want to, um, trespass on your good nature or anything.'

'Bollocks,' said Mr Laertides, and his face dissolved and reformed into a jovial scowl. 'You're thinking, this bloke's up to something, and he's a partner, so he's got to be a right bastard. Which is fine,' he added, 'but it's not getting your medicine brewed, and you don't even know where to buy crème fraiche. Whereas I just happen to have a spare half-hour and a pot of the stuff upstairs in the staffroom fridge. So, you up for it or not?'

You can lead a horse to water, and even though you can't necessarily make it drink, you can stick a hosepipe up its nose and turn on the tap. 'Yes,' Paul said. 'I mean, thanks, that'd be really great. So long as you're sure it's no bother.'

'No trouble at all.' Mr Laertides immediately became a smile on legs. 'You scratch my back, I scratch yours, that's what makes the world go round.' From the top pocket of his suit jacket, he pulled a piece of paper, a photocopy of a page from a book. 'Now then, apart from the crystals and the crème fraiche, we need anchovies, floor wax, trichloroethylene, fresh cucumber, turpentine, paracetamol, mutton fat, charcoal, chalk dust, black lead, extra-virgin olive oil, salt, sulphur, cornflour, starch, Epsom salts, butter, eggs, flour, monosodium glutamate and permitted colourants and flavourings.' He was ticking items off the list with a stub of pencil that had materialised behind his ear as soon as he reached up for it. 'No problems there, we've got all of that in the stores. Equipment; let's see, we'll want a Groeninger crucible – well, that's easy enough, just cut the neck off a plastic milk bottle – an ethane burner rated to 3,000,000 BTU, triple-action refractory chamber, yes, got that, all just standard lab kit really, and a tin-opener, of course. No,' he concluded, folding the paper up and vanishing it into the palm of his hand, 'no difficulties there. You've got the crystals, we'll stop off at the staffroom and then press on to the lab on the fourth floor. Piece of cake, really.'

As Paul followed Mr Laertides up the stairs it occurred to him, when he could spare a moment or two from trying to catch his breath, that 70 St Mary Axe didn't have a fourth floor. He kept quiet, however, and that proved to be just as well, because he'd only have shown his ignorance. Mr Laertides led the way past Professor Van Spee's office, down a corridor that Paul had never explored to a small door painted an improbable shade of primrose yellow. It opened onto a narrow circular staircase, the sort of thing you'd expect to find in a church steeple or a castle tower; at the top was another yellow door, on which someone had painted

DEFENSE D'ENTRER

in huge green letters. It opened a split second before Mr Laertides gave it a shove, and beyond it lay a long, bright, sparse room, lined with melamine-topped workbenches cluttered with retorts, Bunsen burners, fume cupboards, old-fashioned brass microscopes and all manner of scientific junk the likes of which Paul hadn't seen since his last school chemistry lesson. On hooks on the butter-coloured wall hung a row of several dozen brown lab coats. Mr Laertides grabbed two as he swept past, tossed one over his shoulder to Paul and wriggled into the other without breaking stride.

'Lots to do,' he called out without looking round; he was pulling open a huge store cupboard at the back of the room, hauling out jars and packets and bottles without needing to look at the labels. 'Light up a Bunsen, would you, and fill a couple of those five-litre beakers with clean water.'

After a long and frustrating search, Paul found a matchbox containing precisely one match, and lit the gas. By now, the pile of ingredients was so tall that he could only just see the top of Mr Laertides's head. He drew the water from the tap in the middle of the centre bench. The room, he noticed, had a frosted-glass roof but no windows, and no electric light. No electric points, either, or electrical equipment of any kind; odd, surely, for a modern laboratory. Mr Laertides was humming as he worked, but he was a lousy hummer, and the tune sounded like nothing on Earth.

Filling the beakers turned out to be the last chore assigned to him. Mr Laertides did everything else himself, shuffling and scuttling up and down the workbenches like a huge long-legged crab. Pretty soon he had no less than half a dozen Bunsens roaring away, each one warming a big glass vessel on a tripod stand. Fiddly arrangements of rubber and glass tube linked each vessel to its neighbours; there were filters, like yuppie coffee-makers, and things gripped in steel claws on clamps, and vents where waste gas was burned off. It all looked like a cross between a black-and-white Frankenstein's workshop and the old Mousetrap game that Paul had played with as a kid. Presumably there was a point to it all.

'Coming along, coming along,' Mr Laertides chirruped. 'Fuck, where did I just put the litmus paper? Tell me if the stuff in that end flask goes purple, if it does we'll have seven seconds to get out before the whole lot blows and they start flying in emergency cartographers from the Continent to redraw all the maps. Oh, that's good, that's excellent.' Here, Mr Laertides paused to admire the bubbles rising from a pool of clear liquid in the bottom of a beaker. 'Told you there was nothing to it really.'

Paul cleared his throat. 'Mr Laertides.'

'Frank. Just call me Frank.'

'Sorry to bother you,' Paul said. 'But I don't remember any of this from when I copied the recipe out of the book.'

Mr Laertides grinned. 'Just as well I stepped in, then, isn't it? See, that formula was written for the trade, it's assumed you know how to use it, all the different basic techniques. Like it says, *clarify two ounces of mutton fat dissolved in turpentine.* Sounds like you don't know how to clarify. Well, do you? Thought not. I didn't spend twenty years learning all this stuff just for something to do, you know.'

Paul could take a hint, especially one which landed with the terminal velocity of a large meteorite. He stood back, stayed out of the way while Mr Laertides worked and tried to keep himself amused by reading the labels of the bottles in the store cupboard. There was aqua regia and aqua fortis, sweet spirits of nitre and salt of wormwood, lunar caustic and oil of Mars and peach ash and pearl ash and calomel, butter and bloom and glance of antimony, bitter salts and blue vitriol, killed spirits, tincture of steel, liver of sulphur and corrosive sublimate, and not a single newt's eye or frog's toe to be found anywhere. At the very back of the cupboard, among the wreaths of cobweb and moraines of dust, he found a tiny bottle whose label read *Van Spee's crystals*, but it was empty.

'All done,' sang out Mr Laertides. 'Complete, finito, come and get it while it's hot.' He was holding out a clear plastic pot, marginally bigger than an upturned thimble. 'I'd knock it back in one if I were you,' he went on. 'Probably doesn't taste too wonderful, I don't know. I haven't actually tried it, for obvious reasons.'

Paul looked at it with a certain degree of horror, then did as he was told. It was only slightly warm, and had no perceptible taste whatever.

'Is that it?' he said.

'Yes,' Mr Laertides confirmed. He was red in the face and sweating a little. He'd taken off his jacket at some point and rolled up his sleeves, revealing long, thin white forearms, completely hairless. 'My guess is, it'll be about half an hour before it takes effect, and you may feel a bit drowsy, so don't drive or operate heavy machinery. Aside from that, though, that should be you seen to for at least six months before you need topping up.' He was putting things away, wiping the desktop, stoppering bottles and jars, dismantling glass and rubber tubing. 'And the good part is, we'll be testing it straight away, because there's bound to be one or two cute chicks at the rehearsal this evening. But now you'll be able to look 'em in the eye and walk straight past, and that's one less set of hideous complications in your life.'

Paul thought about that. 'Thanks,' he said. 'Thanks very much Mr La— Sorry, Frank. You've got no idea how much this'll mean to me. And you're sure it'll work?' he couldn't help adding.

'You bet.' Mr Laertides nodded his head four times in rapid succession. 'Fact is, though I've never made this one before, it's quite like all your basic love-philtre recipes – stands to reason if you think about it – and I've been making them for thirty years.' He'd just put something in his pocket, absent-mindedly and without thinking. Now he paused, frowned, took it out again. 'Silly me,' he said and opened his hand, revealing the aspirin bottle still nearly full of yellow crystals. 'I expect you'll want to hang on to these,' he continued. 'I sort of got the impression that Theo wasn't expecting to get them back, and you never know when they might come in handy.'

Paul didn't make any attempt to take them. 'Aren't they, well, sort of valuable?' he asked.

'What? Oh, I see what you mean. Yes, a bit. I suppose this lot'd be worth a bob or two on the black market. But if you sell them, what'll you do in six months time, when you've got to make the next batch? Up to you, of course, but—'

'That's all right,' Paul said firmly, taking the bottle. 'I'll make sure I keep them very safe. You, um, you think the professor didn't mind me helping myself like that?'

Mr Laertides grinned. 'The fact that you're standing there would tend to suggest that,' he said. 'If Theo was upset with you, by now you'd be nothing but a memory and a faint smell of burning. Don't worry, though, he makes the stuff, so there's plenty more where that came from, far as he's concerned. What's the time, by the way? It's just struck me, I'd better go and get changed if I'm going to this rehearsal thing. Can't show up at Rosie's shindig looking like this, can I?'

Mr Laertides was wearing a plain blue suit. So was Paul. 'Can't you? I mean, ought I to change as well? She didn't say anything—'

'Don't worry about it,' Mr Laertides said. 'What you're

wearing will be the least of your problems.' He held the door open so Paul could go through. 'You carry on,' he said. 'I'll just make sure everything's shipshape, then lock up.'

Half an hour, he'd said. Paul went slowly down the stairs and made for his office. The brewing process had taken a bit longer than Mr Laertides had predicted, an hour rather than thirty minutes. That left half an hour till going-home time; just long enough for the medicine to work. He sat down at his desk, which was noteless and memo-free, and rested his elbows on top.

If it works, he thought. If it worked, if only, then it'd be good-bye to a whacking great chunk of the pain of being Paul Carpenter, and wouldn't that be good? No more falling in love, no more wild, hopeless crushes, no more drifting around bumping into things and absent-mindedly walking through shop windows. No more drooping, sighing, yearning, making an utter and unmitigated prat of himself. He'd be able to walk down the street without needing to look down or away every time a girl came into view. He grinned, as a picture formed in his mind of his arch-persecutor Cupid, who'd hounded him all these years like a chubby pink Captain Ahab, howling at him in baffled fury from his white fluffy cloud. Safe, for the first time since he was eleven. Assuming it worked, of course.

But if it worked, what a wonderful world this would be. They could do what they liked; girls of every shape, size, height and weight, they could hunt him in packs for all he cared but it wouldn't do them any good. Just imagine, a world without fear. Only an hour or two ago, he'd been ambushed by Vicky the mermaid, been lucky to get out of that one with nothing worse than a plunge into deep water. Before that there'd been the fake Demelza Horrocks, a hateful trap set for him by Countess Judy into which he'd blundered like a honey-starved heffalump; and before that – before that, there'd been Sophie, and look where that had led. *Thank you*, he thought; *thank you, nice Mr Laertides, even if you are as weird as nine pink ferrets in a blender. If I can be spared another sleigh-ride down the plumbing like that, I can't ever thank you enough.* If it worked, it'd almost be enough to reconcile him to all this magic stuff for ever.

Almost.

The door swung open and Paul looked up. For once, Mr Tanner's mum hadn't bothered to disguise herself; she stood in the doorway in her goblin face and skin, all long, curved teeth, round red eyes and short bristles. He knew she wasn't really supposed to walk around like that before the office closed for the evening, and somehow he knew that it was meant as a friendly gesture, like a white flag denoting a brief ceasefire, a short interval during which they could share cups of tea in no man's land and sing 'Silent Night' together until the howitzers started up again. Of course, it was only because he was doing her a favour, coming to her stupid rehearsal.

'Thought I'd make sure you didn't forget and slip away early,' she said, parking herself on the edge of his desk. 'You tend to do things like that. Tea-bag memory, as my Uncle Howard would say.'

Paul grinned feebly. 'How are we getting there?' he said. 'I don't even know where we're going.'

'Don't worry about it,' she replied. 'I'll make sure you get there. Besides, we aren't going far. Walking distance.'

He followed her; down the corridor past the closed file-store, up the back stairs to the photocopier room, along the passage leading to Mr Suslowicz's office (though last week it had been on the first floor, and now it was on the second), through the staffroom fire escape, which actually led down a tunnel, a marble-faced tube eight feet in diameter going straight ahead and slightly uphill, which if he stopped to think about it was absolutely impossible . . . Down the tunnel for what felt like half a mile, through a massive steel door—

'It's not much,' said Mr Tanner's mum, 'but it's home.'

It was a huge open space; sand-floored, like an arena, circular, the bottom of another vast tube, so tall that the other end, a dazzling blue circle, looked no bigger than a sequin. Paul realised that he was facing the stands of an amphitheatre; row upon row of stone benches raked steeply uphill, almost but not entirely surrounding him. Three hundred degrees of seats, and every single one appeared to have a goblin in it.

'Meet the folks,' Mr Tanner's mum whispered in his ear. 'Just think, every single one of them's your long-lost cousin.'

Her claws were gripping his shoulder like a G-clamp, so running for it wasn't on the cards, unless he fancied leaving his arm behind. 'Now what?' he hissed back. 'You never did tell me what I'm supposed to do.'

'No,' she replied. 'I didn't.'

Then he felt her hand in the small of his back, and he shot forward, scrambling furiously to keep from treading on his own feet. A devastating wall of sound hit him; it was the goblins, all cheering at the same time. Paul had always wondered what it'd be like to be really popular, but in his daydreams it hadn't been like this.

'You know I told you this was a rehearsal?' Mr Tanner's mum whispered in his ear.

'Yes?'

'I lied. This is the real thing. Not something you can rehearse, if you get my meaning.'

The rampart of faces staring at him were blurring, melding into one vast composite goblin grin. 'It'd lose that fresh impromptu edge, you mean?' he said.

'That too. But think about it. What things are there you can only ever do once in a lifetime?'

Before Paul could say anything, he sensed that she'd gone, and he stood there, alone in front of maybe twenty thousand goblins, reflecting on the last thing she'd said. Offhand, his mental agility somewhat impaired by the context, he could think of three things that fitted her criteria. None of them were things he'd want to do in front of a crowd, and two of them he'd done already.

No, belay that. All three.

Even so. A polished bronze trapdoor, twelve feet square, appeared in the sand in front of him and gradually slid open, with much rumbling of chains and graunching of badly lubricated moving parts. No prizes for guessing which of the three Mr Tanner's mum had in mind. Something fell at his feet with a thud, just missing his toes; he glanced down and saw a long,wide-bladed sword, with a pink ribbon incongruously fastened around the handle. *In this life*, he could distinctly remember his dad saying when he was fourteen and asking for the money to go on a school trip to Bruges, *there are times when you just have to make sacrifices.* Among the goblin community, it seemed, christenings were just such an occasion.

Help, he thought, but without any great enthusiasm. No point, and it'd be too bad if the last emotion he ever experienced was disappointment. Meanwhile the trapdoor had slid wide open, and up through it on a slowly rising platform appeared—

A cake. A huge, enormous ziggurat of a cake, with battlements of piped white icing, candles like ships' masts, spun-sugar bobbles like cannon balls and a single glacé cherry on the top like the dome of the Kremlin. Its bottom tier was fenced around with a silver-foil wrapper as tall as the ramparts of Constantinople, and written on it in prussian-blue letters five yards high were the words *Happy Christening Paul Azog Tanner.*

Something you only do once in a lifetime: cut the first slice off a fucking great big cake. *Well,* Paul thought, *of course. Silly me not to have figured it out earlier.*

'Go on, then,' hissed a voice offstage; so he pottered across the sand towards it. It took him two minutes to get there, and he was trying not to dawdle. The crowd had gone deathly quiet; here and there flashguns popped, but otherwise there was no movement in the encircling goblin cliffs. When he reached the foot of the cake, he craned his neck up until it hurt, and still couldn't see the top.

Never mind; he was here now, he could do his job and then, presumably, that was his part in the proceedings over with. Deep breath; then he swung the sword up over his head and buried it up to the hilt in the cake wall before him.

It went in easily enough. Fist-sized shards of white sugar cracked off and rained down around him, like plaster from a ceiling, and around the wound he'd made great cracks and fissures started to appear. Paul dragged the sword free and stepped back; crushed flat by an avalanche of cake crumbs would be a really silly way to die. The cake was definitely starting to split open – he could hear the groans and creaks of stressed fabric, like a great tree torn apart with wedges. Suddenly, in a fraction of a second, the wall gave way; and out through the side of the cake burst a bevy (only word for it) of beautiful young women in spangly bikinis, with tinsel wreaths wound in their piled-up blonde hair. They rushed forward towards him, squealing.

Goblin taste, he thought; just what you'd expect from a people in whose mythology the sun was formed from the bronzed baby shoe of the sky-god. Utterly naff, but nevertheless harmless enough, in its way—

Then the party girls were all round him, and Paul suddenly (but too late) remembered the one thing about goblins he'd been sure he'd never ever forget, as the bimbo nearest to him changed seamlessly back into her true shape and swung at the side of his head with a double-headed battleaxe. Somehow he managed to get his sword up to block the slash; he could feel the shock of impact jarring the tendons of his arms right down into both elbows. The goblin hissed furiously through her curved yellow fangs and stepped back to start another swing; meanwhile the goblin next to her was lunging at his solar plexus with a triple-barbed lance. He avoided that too, mainly because his shoelace had come undone and he'd stood on it, and the ensuing stumble took him out of the way of the lance's needle-sharp point. Unfortunately, as he staggered and fell, a goblin to his right stepped forward and jabbed at him with a halberd, and there was absolutely nothing he could do about it. Paul heard an explosion of cheering as the blade slid into him, and as the light grew pale and the focus softened, his last conscious thought was that, just for once, he appeared to have lived up to someone's expectations. Well, not lived up, actually the exact opposite, but—

CHAPTER FOUR

He was sitting in a chair; a tubular chrome and vinyl one, next to a smoked-glass table, opposite another similar chair, in which sat a bronzed, well-groomed middle-aged man in a blue shirt with a bit of wire sticking out of it. Behind the man's head he could see a large camera, while overhead swayed a couple of microphones on long steel poles. The man was smiling and staring past him at something: a screen on the wall, where a mob of savage and hideous goblins were stabbing and hacking at some object lying in the dust.

'So, Paul,' said the man, and the camera started to edge forward on its hydraulic boom. 'How do you think it went?'

Paul could feel the corners of his mouth pull apart in a smile, and he heard himself say, 'Well, David, obviously we're a bit disappointed with the final result, but we know we gave it our best shot, the lads all done brilliant on the day, it's just a shame someone's got to come second, really.'

The man nodded gravely, as though he'd just got a straight answer out of Plato. 'I'd like to take you through a few of the key moments from the game, Paul, if I may. Let's kick off with the beginning, shall we? On reflection, maybe not the best start you could've got off to.'

On the screen, Paul saw a hospital ward, a nurse handing a bundle to a woman lying in bed; close-up of his mother's face (he recognised it from old photographs) then a smart cut across to the ugliest-looking baby Paul had ever seen, wriggling and grizzling and waving its little fists in the air. 'Well, David, the lads felt the conditions were dead against us, I mean obviously they weren't what we'd have chosen for ourselves, but that's the game, you got to play the cards you're given and just get out there and give it a hundred and ten per cent, which maybe we didn't quite manage to do on this occasion. But it's been a learning experience for all of us, and—'

Now the screen showed a sullen-looking kid in a navy-blue blazer, tie knotted under his chin, standing on his own in the corner of a crowded playground. Cut to the same small boy crouched sobbing in the corner of a large, sparse school bathroom, while a bunch of larger, more cheerful kids methodically flushed the contents of his school bag down a toilet. 'For me,' the man called Dave was saying, 'it was pretty much lost and won here, right in the opening stages, and afterwards you never really had a chance to climb back into the game. Is that a fair assessment, do you think?'

Paul's head nodded of its own accord. 'Absolutely, David,' he said. 'Their lads were absolutely magic, can't take anything away from them, and we're going to be going over the videos of this stage of the game very carefully over the summer.' As his mouth moved, a little voice was whispering inside his mind, in the dark corners where nobody ever needed to go: *goblin taste, goblin humour, goblin appearances; don't forget the one thing about goblins you really need to remember.* At this point, Paul noticed he was still holding the sword.

Meanwhile: 'How would you react,' the man called Dave was asking him, 'to the guys in the media who've been saying all along that your leadership style's been too laid back and sloppy and you didn't train nearly hard enough and that really, you've let down the fans back home who actually believed you could pull it off?'

Paul grinned. 'Like this,' he said, and with a single sweep of his arm, he sliced Dave's head off with the sword and watched it sail across the room, bounce off the opposite wall and land with absolute precision in a small metal dustbin. Quite a few of the cameramen cheered, and someone let off an air-horn.

Smiling, Paul stood up and walked away. Outside the glaring circle of the studio lights it was dark and cool, and he was feeling quite tired. *Goblins*, he thought; *bless them*. It stood to reason that at a goblin party you had to have beautiful girls jump up out of a cake and attack you with savage weapons, just as the goblin idea of your past life flashing in front of your eyes at the point of death was inevitably a *Grandstand* interview. He was also absolutely convinced, though he had no data on the subject, that goblinkind's favourite TV show was Benny Hill, but Forrest Gumped with cutting-edge computer-graphics technology to include scenes of gratuitous slaughter. *My relatives*, he told himself. Devious, vulgar and blessed with a degree of cunning that it was fatally easy to underestimate, but flawed nevertheless with the assumption that everyone was like them, deep down. Outside the immediate confines of the genome, however, they hadn't got a clue.

Of course, he reflected as he walked further into the darkness, he did have the fairly unique advantage of having died twice already. Arguably, if he didn't have that rather unusual insight, which quite possibly they weren't aware of, it was quite likely that he would believe he'd just been killed, and that this was the underworld, the afterlife, the kingdom of the dead. In any event, he felt he'd established beyond reasonable doubt that that was what they wanted him to think. Which led on to the thorny question, why? What good was it doing them, and how could it possibly be relevant to the christening of baby Paul Azog?

Paul wrestled with that one for a while, but try as he might he couldn't find a satisfactory answer, so he shelved the question and began to speculate about what might happen next. Not that it mattered. After all, none of this was real, so none of it mattered. He knew it wasn't real, because he knew precisely what the realm of the dead looked like: dark, flat, featureless, neither hot nor cold, dry nor wet, nothing so positive; and after a while, when you got bored with strolling across a blank canvas, you came to the entrance to the Bank of the Dead, where Mr Dao would be waiting to greet him—

'Paul?'

The voice was familiar. He looked round, trying to see where it was coming from, but realised that he was completely disorientated in this dark, flat, featureless landscape.

Pause. Rewind. Freeze.

Come to think of it, he muttered to himself, *it's also neither cold nor hot, wet nor dry.* And the voice he'd just heard was that of Benny Shumway. He opened his mouth to yell, but nothing came out.

'Shit, Paul, I didn't know,' Benny's voice went on. 'Nobody ever tells me anything around here. Bloody hell, mate, I'm so sorry.' Hesitation, rather than a pause for a reply. Benny had been here often enough (once a day, to pay in the cheques, draw the petty cash, check the automated credits) to know that the dead can't answer back or see you, they can only just hear your voice, faint and coming from no particular direction. 'Well,' Benny continued awkwardly, 'I just hope it was painless and quick, and tomorrow I'll see about bringing you something, a drop of goat's blood or a bit of raw liver. I really am sorry, chum. You got right up my nose sometimes and I can never forgive you for sending Judy away, but some of the time I actually did quite like you.'

Benny. Benny, wait for me, get me out of here, there's been a terrible mistake, don't go. Paul could just hear an echo of the words inside his own head, but no voice speaking them; really, nothing more than the shape and shadow of the thoughts, and that only because he was so recently arrived. Of course Benny couldn't hear him, because Benny was still alive.

Desperately, Paul tried to see something, any damn thing; or hear, or smell, or touch, or taste. No dice. Then, just as he'd found a crumb of reassurance in the fact that he hadn't seen the Bank or Mr Dao, another familiar voice spoke out of the darkness and spoiled all that for ever.

'Mr Carpenter,' Mr Dao said. 'Again. What on earth brings you here?'

And there he was, exactly the way Paul remembered him: grave, distinguished, almost sympathetic and kindly but not quite. Mr Dao, manager of the Bank, walked out of the absence of light and bowed formally to him.

'Mr Dao. Look, this is wrong. I shouldn't be here.'

A gentle glow of pity and understanding in his eyes, deep as an artesian well. 'Alas,' Mr Dao said. 'How often I've heard those very words, and always so true. Of course you shouldn't be here, Mr Carpenter. Nobody should be here. But—' He shrugged, thin shoulders lifting a little under the deep blue silk of his robes. 'We all have our cross to bear, Mr Carpenter, and in the end all we can do is make the best of it. You'll find it isn't as bad as all that here; we have a bridge club, if you play at all, and a very strong choral society; or you can sign up for an excellent choice of evening classes. Only the other day, for instance, we added flower arranging, conversational Turkish and beginners'-level lawnmower maintenance. I won't pretend that everything here isn't agonisingly boring and point-less, but we do make an effort.'

'This is wrong,' Paul repeated helplessly. *This is wrong, it's just Mr Tanner's mum and her loathsome relatives playing a stupid trick on me. You aren't the real Mr Dao, you're just—*

'His ghost.' Mr Dao smiled wanly. 'To coin a phrase, this is as real as I get.' He folded his arms and tucked his hands into his capacious sleeves. 'Mr Carpenter,' he said, then made a supreme effort. 'Paul, if I may. I'm sorry. There has been no mistake. Your name is there on the arrivals board, which is why I came out specially to meet you. There is an explanatory note; it says, "killed by goblins", if that's any help to you in understanding the sequence of events. Not that it matters. You must face this fact: as far as you are concerned, nothing matters, nothing will ever matter again. We used to have a banner, Paul, we rigged it out over the front entrance every time new guests arrived until the time-and-motion consultants pointed out that it was depressing and counter-productive and made us throw it away. But I dis-agree with them. It said: "*Abandon hope, all you who enter here*"; and I still maintain that it was the best and most constructive advice that can be given to someone in your present situation. You must accept this, Paul; down here, hope is not your friend. There is nothing to hope for here, just as there is nothing to be afraid of. Quite simply, there is nothing. Deal with it.'

Paul stared at Mr Dao for a moment; then it was as though

he'd just woken up out of a particularly vivid and disturbing dream to find himself in his bed, in his red and white striped pyjamas, suddenly and rather foolishly aware that he'd got himself into a dreadful state over nothing at all. Just as the dream fades and gets thin and evaporates as the light bleaches it away, so his memories of having been alive, all the stuff he'd tried to bring with him and now realised that he wouldn't be needing after all, began to melt and thaw away; because he'd woken up out of a strange and disturbing dream about being alive, but it was all right now, and he knew that it had all been just a—

'No,' he said. 'No,' he repeated. 'Sorry, but it can't be like that. I mean, they wouldn't have killed me, they had no reason to. I was being little Paul Azog's godfather.'

Mr Dao was frowning sympathetically, but frowning nonetheless. 'They're goblins, Paul,' he said. 'That's reason enough. Human sacrifice is part of their rich cultural heritage. But you mustn't worry about that any more. The important thing is that you're here, and this time you're here to stay. Now I'm prepared to bend the rules for you a bit until you've got yourself settled in, but there is a very definite limit to what I can do; and in a day or so, once you're acclimatised—'

'No.' It wasn't in Paul's nature to shout at people he didn't know well, but the circumstances seemed to warrant making an exception. 'I'm not going to get acclimatised, because I'm not staying. This isn't happening. I demand to see the manager.'

Mr Dao only shook his head. 'I am the manager,' he said.

'No, you aren't.' No, it occurred to Paul to consider, he wasn't the manager, at that. 'You're in charge of the bank, you're not the government around here. I want to see whoever's in charge. And that's not you.'

Mr Dao smiled wryly. 'Take me to your leader, in other words. I'm sorry, but we haven't got one. No need, you see. There's nobody in charge because there's nothing to be in charge of. Except the Bank, of course. Please, I must ask you to calm down and try and behave in a rather less unseemly fashion. Perhaps,' he added, with a friendly gesture, 'I can get you something to eat or drink. A cup of tea, perhaps, and a plate of mixed biscuits.'

And maybe it was Paul's imagination, or maybe as he said that, Mr Dao winked; a tiny flicker of the lid of his logically non-existent eye, a hint—

Of course. He was still holding the sword.

You can't take it with you, they say; but sometimes, Paul realised with a jolt, they lie. He was still holding the sword, with which he'd so lightly and easily decapitated the annoying TV anchorman. As he swung it up and looked at the blade (a deep, rich glowing brown, flecked here and there with swirls and squiggles of vivid silver), he imagined that he saw Mr Dao's chin dip just a tiny bit, almost as if he was nodding in approval, in confirmation. *How* could he still have the sword if he was really dead? Vaguely he remembered: Magnus Magnusson or someone like that, telling him through a plate-glass screen that dead Vikings always liked to be buried with their swords, to have something to defend themselves with in the next world. Magnus had made it sound pretty silly, but here he was in the next world, and here was this sword in his hand – a hand he shouldn't still have; but somehow the realness of the sword was soaking through into his skin. He thought of a film he'd seen once, a sci-fi thing about an invisible man; and they'd caught him by spraying paint about from aerosols. The skin of his hand was real where it touched the sword in the same way that the invisible man's face could be seen by the infinitesimally thin layer of paint covering it.

Cool, he thought; and then he took another look at the sword-blade.

'Excuse me,' Paul said to Mr Dao; then he lifted the blade to his mouth and carefully licked along the line of the cutting edge, feeling his tongue become real again as it touched the cold, smooth metal. There was only a very thin smear of blood there, but he knew from his two previous visits that a tiny, tiny drop of the red stuff was all it took.

It was as though he was a line drawing in a child's colouring book, and the child had just coloured him in, gaudily and mess-ily with a broad-nibbed felt-tip pen. He was suddenly so full of life that it was sloshing about inside him like water in a bucket, spilling out of him, dripping off him like wet paint. 'Sorry,' he heard himself say, 'can't stop. Thanks for everything.' Mr Dao lifted his hand in a very small wave as Paul spun on his heel – he had heels to spin on once again, wasn't that *amazing*? – and sprinted like hell in what he devoutly hoped was the direction of the little postern gate that opened into Benny Shumway's office.

As he ran, he worried. He'd been in this position before, of course. There was a door linking the cashier's room at JWW with the land of the dead; but as soon as Benny got back from his daily trip to the Bank, the door was bolted and locked and chained and barred, and wouldn't be opened again for twenty-three and a half hours; by which time, the tiny lease of life afforded him by the tiny smear of blood he'd licked off the sword would have expired, and that'd be that. But he'd met Benny not all that long ago, and Benny didn't run home from doing the banking, he tended to trudge wearily, like a man wading through waist-deep porridge. If he could get to the door before Benny did, he was saved. If not, forget it. Simple as that.

A bit like running for a train, Paul thought, *except that there won't be another one if I miss this one, not ever.* He was running into complete darkness, nothing to navigate by, nothing under-foot even, to confirm that he was moving rather than standing still. That wasn't a nice thought, but he made an effort and ran faster anyhow; and then there was a tiny point of light, no bigger than a star, which he knew was the glow from the sixty-watt bulb in the cashier's room, seen through the keyhole. Time for an extra-special effort; because if he could see the light, it was because the door was still unlocked and the keyhole cover hadn't been swung back. He also yelled, 'Benny, Benny,' at the top of his voice, but he couldn't hear his own words.

Then there was Benny; briefcase in one hand, big folder of papers wedged under the other arm. There he was, and there was the door, but he was right on the doorstep and Paul was still a hundred yards or a thousand yards or a million miles away, and he wasn't going to get there in time, because Benny was way too smart to look back over his shoulder when he was in the Kingdom of the Dead. Paul watched him reach for the door handle – his fingers were on the knob, about to turn it; but a couple of sheets of paper slipped out of the folder and drifted to the absence-of-ground, and Benny swore under his breath and stooped to pick them up. *'BENNY!'* Paul yelled, pounding forward like a racehorse, *'IT'S ME! BENNY, WAIT FOR—'*

No more than ten yards away now, three strides; but Benny had picked up his papers and turned the door handle and opened the door. At the last moment, Paul shut his eyes tight and leapt like a deer into the blinding rectangle of light—

And crashed into something profoundly solid, bounced off and landed on his back, stunned and breathless. He lay unable to move, as the sound of bolts and keys and chains and latches crashed and graunched at him through the woodwork. A fraction of a second later he was on his feet again, hammering with both fists against the rough oak panels, howling and yelling and screaming, but he knew he was wasting his time. Benny Shumway hadn't lasted this long without knowing that this was one door you never answered, no matter what you heard on the other side.

That was it, then. Screwed.

Paul slumped to the lack-of-ground, almost too weak to move. The desperate exertion of all that running, yelling and bashing had used up most of his little wispy smear of extra life, and in a few seconds it'd all be gone, and so would he. Suddenly he thought of the sword. Maybe there was an atom or so of blood left on the blade that he'd missed, or maybe the sword, being magical, could cut through two inches of oak like a cake slice through lemon meringue. But the sword wasn't there; either it had gone through the doorway before Benny shut the door, or Paul had dropped it at some point in his wild dash, out there in the total absence of light, where he'd never find it again even if he had all eternity to look, which he would.

Fuck, he thought.

He'd believed he was going to make it, right up to the point where his face slammed into the closed door; he'd been utterly, unshakeably convinced that this wasn't the end; he'd had the sword, and it wasn't fair anyhow, being suddenly murdered by goblins when he was the one doing them a favour. If it was the end, why bother giving him the sword and sacrificing the life of a TV presenter just so there'd be blood on it when blood was needed, and why have Benny Shumway there at precisely the critical moment – even the pantomime with the dropped papers – to buy him the essential fraction of a second? But apparently not. Abandon hope, all you who enter here.

Goblin humour, he thought; round about now, it'd be just his luck to see Jonathan Ross or Barry Norman floating eerily in the gloom – *because now's the time for a frank, trenchant review of my life, now that it's over, now that the fat lady's straining for the high notes.*

Conclusions, anyone? First, it was all a waste of time, because nothing worthwhile would end this way (massacred by pretty girls jumping out of a cake, leaping headlong into a shut door) *Second, if I had my time over again—*

There had been a very brief moment, a split second, when the road of Paul's life had forked, and he'd had a genuine choice. After Sophie had told him about how Countess Judy had leeched out all her feelings for him, as though they'd never existed, Sophie had made him a remarkable and genuine offer. She'd said that if he wanted her to, she would drink the justly celebrated JWW patent love philtre and make herself fall in love with him, unconditionally, for ever. He'd looked at her in amazement and horror, because it wasn't fair to confront him with a choice like that. As his world spun around him, upside down and out of control, he'd struggled to find some fixed point whereby to make his choice; and of course he'd hit upon *What's the right thing to do?* Once he'd made that call, the rest was easy. No, he couldn't let Sophie drink the philtre, because then her love for him would be a lie, synthetic, involuntary; like plastic flowers or British lager, not real, lifeless, worthless. So he'd done what he knew was the right thing, and both of them had lived wretchedly ever after. Until now, of course.

There had been a very brief moment, a split second; and Paul had chosen to do what he thought was right. Which was fine, in a way, because at least it was a criterion, albeit a totally random and arbitrary one, like choosing someone to be Prime Minister by the length of their toenails. At the time he'd had no way of knowing that it was also a wretched, stupid mistake, which he could now say with total accuracy he'd regretted for the rest of his life. Annoying, really, since it'd been (he now realised, with the benefit of hindsight, not to mention the added clarity which comes with being effectively dead) the only decision he'd ever faced which really mattered. He'd loved and won and lost and—

—And screwed up. *Regrets*, he thought, *I've had a few, but then again, too few to mention*; except for that one colossal and unforgivable exception, that howling, staring, screaming example of taking his eye off the ball when it had really mattered. Which was why it was basically a pretty bad break for him, dying like this with his one great act of stupidity unpurged and now incapable of absolution. *I let some trivial shit like right-and-wrong come between me and the girl I actually, genuinely, truly love. That was not good. I wish I hadn't done that. But now it's too late to set it right, and accordingly the world will be out of true for ever.* While there'd been life, there'd been hope. Now there was just anger, frustration, and the infuriating knowledge that he'd lived, and died, an idiot.

I would really, Paul thought, really *like to see the manager. I have a few things to say about the way this outfit is run.*

'You did your best,' said Mr Dao, somewhere behind him. 'I knew you wouldn't be able to accept, truly accept, until it was brought home to you in the most unequivocal terms.'

'You aren't the manager,' Paul growled back, not looking round. (Because you didn't: Benny had taught him that. Just like the living must never accept food or drink in the land of the dead.)

'True. There is no manager, therefore it follows that I am not him. At least now you should've got hope out of your system.'

'Go away,' Paul said; and he knew he was being rude, and he didn't care. 'I've still got a second or two left, I can feel it. Come back later, when you're entitled.'

'As you wish.' Mr Dao didn't sound offended, just rather sad. 'If you insist on it, you still have three minutes and twenty-seven seconds. I fear, however, that in the context of eternity—'

'Say that again,' Paul interrupted.

'Three minutes and twenty-seven seconds. Twenty-four seconds now, of course.'

'Mr Dao.' Paul stood up, faced his interlocutor and smiled broadly. 'Is the Bank still open? I want to make a withdrawal.'

One minute, six seconds to walk to the Bank. Fifteen seconds to fill in the necessary forms. One minute, thirty-two seconds to walk down the corridor and down the stairs to the safety-deposit vault. Five seconds to find the box with his name on it, rip it out of the rack and tear off the lid.

'Really, Mr Carpenter,' said Mr Dao. (*So I'm Mr Carpenter again, am I? Fine.*) 'Are you sure?'

One second to say 'Fuck you,' to Mr Dao, three seconds to unroll the thin sheet of plastic from its cardboard tube and press it against the vault wall. One second to open it and say, 'Home.'

Piece of cake, Paul thought, as he stumbled through and slammed the door behind him.

The door – the Acme Portable Door – slowly peeled off the back wall of his bedroom and landed in a heap on the floor. *Piece of cake*, Paul thought again, as his legs buckled under him and he collapsed on the bed, bounced twice and lay absolutely still, listening to the pounding of his real, functional heart. One whole second to spare. *And to think, for a moment there I was starting to fret.*

His hands felt sticky. Well, they would, after all that, and it was also a miracle he hadn't thrown up or wet himself. But it wasn't that kind of sticky. Blood? He scrunched his fingertips across his palms: squidgy, but not like blood. Thicker. Purely out of curiosity, he lifted one hand and looked at it. Some kind of yellow slime; yuck. He wiped his hands on the duvet, shut his eyes and – because he'd earned it, he deserved it and now he was going to enjoy it, so there – he screamed.

'Charming,' said a voice.

Never, not even in the ecstatic throes of terror or relief, a moment's bloody peace. Paul choked off his scream and sat bolt upright. 'You,' he squawked, because of all the things he'd seen in the last twenty-four hours, this was the hardest to believe in. 'What the *fuck*—?'

'I brought you a piece of cake,' said Mr Tanner's mum, and she held out a paper plate on which rested a rather meagre slice of squished-up fruit and some crumbled white plaster. 'Since you couldn't be there for the party afterwards.'

'Couldn't be there,' Paul repeated in a dazed voice, as though he was asking the voice from the burning bush, *Hold on a second, tell me again, what was that bit just after Thou shalt not?* 'You horrible bloody lunatic, you *killed* me.'

Mr Tanner's mum grinned at him; smile and long, sharp teeth in roughly equal parts. 'You're looking well on it, I must say. Anyhow, I think it went off pretty well, all things considered. You missed the speeches, of course, Uncle Jerry went on far too long, but—'

Desperately, Paul wanted to throw something at her or hit her with something, but there wasn't anything within easy reach except a pillow and his pyjamas. 'Did you hear what I just said? You fucking *murdered* me. I *died*. Did you know that? I actually *died*.'

She nodded. 'Well, of course,' she said. 'But I knew you'd be all right. That was the whole point, after all.'

Trying to be hysterically angry with Mr Tanner's mum was a bit like trying to put out an Australian bush fire by crying on it. 'You're mad,' he said. 'Completely out of your tree. How the hell could you know I'd be all right?'

A click of her scaly red tongue, mildly reproachful, a sort of motherly don't-do-that-dear unspoken rebuke. 'I knew you'd be all right,' she repeated, 'and you are. I knew what you'd do, and you did it. What's hard to grasp about that?'

'You—' There comes a point where you can be too bewildered to be angry. 'How could you possibly know what I was going to do? I didn't know until I only had three minutes left. I got out of there with one fucking second to spare.'

'Really? But it was so obvious. You told me yourself, when Countess Judy got put away in Avalon, you'd taken the Portable Door and stashed it away in the Bank so nobody could ever get their hands on it again and misuse it for their own evil ends. And you knew perfectly well that the Door will get you into or out of absolutely anywhere at all. So naturally, as soon as you realised you were dead, you went to the Bank, got it out of your safe-deposit box and came home through it. Not exactly rocket science.' She paused, then frowned at him. 'You're saying that wasn't the first thought that crossed your mind, right?'

Put like that, it did sound fairly reasonable. 'I was confused,' Paul said, just a smidgeon defensively. 'Also bewildered and scared absolutely shitless. And—'

'You panicked.'

'No. Yes. Yes, of course I panicked, I'd just been killed by goblins. Goblins,' Paul added bitterly, 'in spandex catsuits and little white bunny tails jumping out of a cake. Whatever else I may eventually forgive you for, I will never ever—'

'That wasn't my idea,' Mr Tanner's mum said quickly. 'That was our Dennis. Said he thought it'd appeal to your offbeat sense of humour, whatever that means. Anyhow, you got off lightly if you ask me. Cousin Howard and Uncle Tony had set their heart on a bevy of kissogram girls with obsidian daggers. I'm afraid he's a bit unregenerate, my Uncle Tony.'

'But—' There was a whirlwind of questions inside Paul's head, and for a long time he couldn't pick out which one he really needed an answer to. 'Why?' he eventually chose.

'Why what?'

'Why did you have me murdered, you evil bitch? Just to see if I could escape? What was it, a bet or something?'

'Don't be ridiculous. No, you had to go to the Bank to collect little Paul Azog's christening present. That is, somebody had to go, and you're the only person we could think of who'd be able to get back again.'

'Christening present—' Paul broke off and stared at her. 'What, I was supposed to pick up some rotten little pewter tankard or something? Well, you've had that, because I didn't.'

Patient little sigh. 'Yes, you have, silly. There it is, look, on the floor over there. Wouldn't have been any need,' she added reproachfully, 'if you hadn't gone and put it there in the first place. Your own silly fault, really.'

Paul turned his head to look, just in case he'd overlooked something. 'What are you talking about?'

'The door thing, stupid. The Acme Portable Door. Paul Azog's prezzie.'

All the rage and fury came back at once, like water gushing

from a broken pipe. 'But that's – he can't have that, it's mine.'

'Your own,' Mr Tanner's mum sighed, 'your precious. Sorry, but you're forgetting something, aren't you? Like, how you came by it in the first place.'

Paul opened his mouth, then shut it again. 'I found it,' he muttered. 'In my desk.'

'In the top left-hand drawer of your desk,' Mr Tanner's mum confirmed. 'Where I left it for you. A loan,' she added, 'not a gift. And now you've got to give it back. Sorry,' she added, 'but you should've guessed at the time. It's a really, really powerful magical object, stands to reason it must belong to someone. And who else around here likes you enough to lend you something like that, when you really needed it?'

'Yes, but—' But what? Paul couldn't think of anything to say.

'And then, when you'd finished with it, you went and stuck it in the Bank, where nobody but you could ever get at it again. So,' she went on, with a mild sigh, 'it's not like we had any choice in the matter. You put it there, you had to go and get it back. Thanks,' she added. 'Sorry for any inconvenience. Eat your cake, it's not nearly as revolting as it looks.'

Paul looked at the plate lying on the bed beside him. 'No, thanks,' he said stiffly, 'it's had goblins in it. All right, so it's your Door, but why the hell couldn't you have told me, instead of having me killed like that? Have you got any idea how close I came to—?'

'Well, I can't help it if you're not nearly as bright as I assumed you were. And besides,' she went on, 'if I'd come to you and said, actually, that was my Door, can I have it back, pretty please? Do you really expect me to believe you'd have just meekly handed it over?'

'Yes.'

'Really?' Mr Tanner's mum looked at him. 'I wouldn't, if I'd been you. Absolutely no way in hell I'd have given it back without a fight. But there we are, probably just as well we aren't all alike. Anyway, here's the Door and no harm done.'

'No harm.' *No harm*, Paul thought; and he remembered for the first time what Mr Dao had told him, when he'd entrusted the Door to him for safekeeping—

(*'I should warn you,' Mr Dao had said, 'that you will be able to retrieve it one time only; once it has been withdrawn from our keeping, the Bank's standard terms and conditions clearly state that should you wish to return it to store, a standard administration fee will be payable.'*

'Oh,' *Paul had said, thinking:* Aggravating, but that's banks for you. *'How much?'*

'A life.')

– Which raised the question he'd faced three months ago, when he'd decided to put the wretched thing safely out of harm's way: was the Door the kind of thing that ought to be left lying around, practically begging every nutcase and psycho and wannabe Dark Lord to get his claws on it? Was it really a suitable present for a two-week-old baby, or wouldn't a nice bear or a box of building bricks be more suitable? But Mr Tanner's mum had strolled round, picked it up and tucked it down inside her profoundly intimidating goblin cleavage. Threat to civilisation as we know it or no threat to civilisation as we know it, Paul was buggered if he was going to try and get it back from there.

Fine, he decided. *Not my problem any more.* 'So that's it, is it?' he said, suddenly feeling very tired. 'Because if you don't need me for anything else today, I think I'd like to pass out from shock and trauma for a bit.'

Mr Tanner's mum nodded. 'You go ahead,' she said. 'I'll see myself out.'

After she'd gone, Paul lay still and quiet on the bed for about ten minutes, then drifted into the kitchen to see if there was anything to eat. But the fridge was empty and so was the bread bin and the biscuit jar, and he didn't have the strength to trail down the stairs and yomp the fifty endless yards to the corner shop. Nothing else for it, therefore, but to drive a stake through his finer feelings and eat the slice of christening cake. It was sticky, bitter and tasted disconcertingly of sulphur, but it was marginally better than nothing at all. He pulled a face as he crunched up the last scraps of icing – rather like eating the chalk out of the little wooden tray under the blackboard back at school – and then it occurred to him to wonder what was likely to be on the menu at Mr Dao's place; nothing, followed by nothing with a null salad. The thought took away his appetite completely, and he lay on his back on top of the duvet (shoes still on; his mother would have had a fit) staring at the cracks in the ceiling plaster. Three times he'd been there now, not counting the banking trips with and without Benny Shumway. The first time he'd gone voluntarily, or at least intentionally, unable to see any other course of action, but driven by the absolute necessity of saving Sophie that overrode all other priorities. The second time had been a screw-up, a dumb misunderstanding by Ricky Wurmtoter, but even as the crossbow bolt had sheared through the tissue of Paul's heart, he'd known that there was a way back, a get-out-of-jail-free card nestling in his sleeve lining. This time he hadn't really believed he was dead until practically the last minute, and then there'd been a couple of lucky chances – the blood on the sword, the Portable Door in his safe-deposit box. For all he knew there'd be a fourth or a fifth time, and he'd find himself back in the land of the living by the skin of his teeth, thanks to some clever magic trick or prudently stockpiled artefact. But eventually, because of what he was and the terms and conditions governing his existence, a time would come when he'd be there and there'd be no way back; he'd be stuck there for ever; like hanging around an airport lounge for all eternity, parted from all his companions and possessions, nothing to eat or drink or read or do, waiting for a flight that had been delayed permanently. The time would come, and everything he did until then was pointless and stupid, building sandcastles in the face of the incoming tide.

Paul thought of Mr Dao's well-meant advice: please deposit all hope tidily in the receptacles provided, because you'll be better off without. Wasn't hope just another lethal addiction, starting as a jolt of something to help you through the day, developing into a habit, then a craving, then a slow poison? Hope binds the addict to his needle, nurturing the old lie that each beat of the heart, each lungful of air is a useful prevarication, keeping all options open. The truth was Mr Dao and the floor that was no floor and the sky that wasn't actually there, and sitting watching stalactites grow and the slow drip from the leak in the roof gouging the Grand Canyon out of solid rock. When Paul had been a boy, he'd lain awake worrying himself sick about what would happen when the sun burnt itself out and the sky went cold, only a billion or so years from now. But he'd fretted unnecessarily, he realised, because whatever happened to stars and planets and galaxies, whether they burned up or crashed into asteroids or broke up into dust and got caught up in the drag of a dead gas giant, swirling for ever like the skirts of a pirouetting dancer, it'd make no difference at all. Mr Dao would still be there when all the stars had gone out and the whole skyful of flying rocks had eventually come to rest. Even if, by diabolical cunning and supreme sublime genius Paul outlasted the last little drop of water and grain of sand, he'd still have a reservation in the kingdom of the dead, a place assigned and waiting for him, a home to go to when the adventures were all over.

Nice cheerful things to think about at three o'clock in the morning.

At one minute past nine the next morning, Paul rang JWW and, knowing the drill, asked to speak to Christine, Mr Tanner's secretary.

'It's Paul,' he said. 'Just to let you know I'm not feeling well, so I won't be coming in today.'

He could picture the stormy crease of her eyebrows. 'What's wrong with you?'

'I died.'

Pause. 'You don't sound very dead to me.'

'I sort of got better,' Paul admitted. 'But it's only temporary. Sooner or later I'll have a relapse and then that'll be it, kerboom, finito. So really, there's not a lot of point me coming in, is there?'

Christine wasn't the sharpest serpent's tooth in the kindergarten, but she could spot a rhetorical question when she heard one. 'Have you got a doctor's note?'

'What? No, I haven't. But you could ask Benny Shumway to check with Mr Dao at the Bank if you like. He'll tell you that I'm telling the truth, and you can't get more authoritative than that, can you?'

But Christine wasn't so easily fobbed off. 'It says in the book you're entitled to sick leave,' she said. 'Doesn't say anything about death leave. You hang on there a minute while I go and check with Mr Tanner.'

To Paul's great surprise, Mr Tanner was prepared to let him have a day off; not just one, in fact, but the traditional three. If, however, he hadn't risen again from the dead on the third day, he'd better be able to have a death certificate, a valid will and a little urn of ashes ready for inspection when he finally did condescend to show up, or the old cliché about a fate worse than death might suddenly take on new and startlingly vivid penumbras of meaning. At first, Paul was taken aback by this unexpected display of compassion; then it occurred to him that Mr Tanner might well be taking his orders in the matter from his mother.

Three whole days . . . True, Paul remained painfully conscious of the fact that he was still squatting in a cell on Nature's Death Row waiting for his rendezvous with the big chair, but even so, the thought of three days off – five, in fact, since tomorrow was Saturday, and even Mr Tanner couldn't expect him to be dead on his own time – was enough to bring a huge grin to his face. As soon as he'd hung up the phone, he grabbed a sheet of paper and did some calculations. His finances were in their usual dismal state, but if he scrimped and saved for the rest of the month and made do with mousetrap cheese on plastic toast washed down with tap water, he could just about afford a little impromptu holiday. He could—

He could go away. The prospect stunned him. It had been nine months, more than nine months, since he'd been out of London except on grim and horrible official business. It was, he remembered, summer; he could borrow a tent, get on a coach, head off into the green and pleasant stuff, to fresh air and lush green grass and soldier ants in the groundsheet. He hadn't been camping since he was a kid – actually, he'd loathed the one time they'd gone camping and had spent the whole holiday praying for the rain to wash the tent away so that they could go home. But camping was all he could afford, and what the hell was the point in being temporarily officially dead if you had to spend your limited ration of afterlife cooped up in a grotty bedsit watching daytime TV?

By an amazing coincidence, the unemployed guitarist who lived on the floor above had a tent, which he wouldn't be needing again until Glastonbury; Paul bumped into him on the stairs as he went to empty the bins, raised the subject hopefully and five minutes later returned to base with the black plastic sack containing the tent tucked safely under his arm. *Great*, he thought as he threw a few items of clothing into a Tescos bag, *I've got everything I need, including my portable shelter. Wonderful; I've scrambled so far up the evolutionary ladder that I'm almost on equal terms with a snail.*

It had to be the seaside; because the only happy memory from his childhood that Paul could still call back every time, without fail, with perfect focus and total recall, was a week he'd spent at Weston-super-Mare when he'd been eight. True, it had rained for five of the seven days, and while it was raining his parents had sulked and snapped, and he'd read his comic at least two dozen times, to the point where, even now, he could draw most of it with his eyes shut. But when it hadn't been raining they'd sat on the beach and he'd built sandcastles, and played beach football with Dad, and paddled in rock pools and persecuted small, strange-looking crustaceans among the seaweed. As he sat in the train, eyes shut, waiting for the slightly vertiginous judder that meant they were under way, he played back the scene one more time, just to make sure it was still there. Anybody looking at him would have assumed he was asleep and dreaming, but it was far, far better than any dream, because it had come true, once, and the past is perfect; it's closed off and sealed, watertight and timetight, so that nothing can leak into it and spoil it. He knew he was grinning all over his face, and the other passengers in the compartment probably thought he was drunk or stoned or peculiar, but he didn't care. He'd died often enough not to worry about what people on trains thought about him.

Then a flexing of the seat cushion under his bum told Paul that someone had sat down next to him. Instinctively he shifted to make room, and opened his eyes.

Shit, he thought.

'Thought it was you,' said Mr Laertides, frowning at him. 'What're you doing on a train? You're supposed to be ill in bed.'

As always, Mr Laertides had a disconcertingly unfinished look about him, the sort of mildly annoying failure to convince you'd associate with computer-generated animation in the movies. The light and shadows didn't seem quite right under his eyes and beside his nose, and there were gaps in the way he moved, as though a few frames were missing.

'Um,' Paul said.

'I was looking for you first thing,' Mr Laertides went on. 'You weren't in your room, so I asked Christine, and she said you were off sick. At death's door, she said.'

Paul sighed. There had been a time when something like this, being caught skiving by the boss, would've been his worst nightmare. He was still fundamentally the same person who used to think that way, and it was a habit that he needed to break. Oddly enough, dying the first two times hadn't cured him of his naughty-schoolboy complex; but this last time he'd come so close . . . So he grinned. 'Yup,' he said. 'Literally. Only some clown locked it just as I was about to go through, so I had to go the long way round.'

Mr Laertides froze for a moment; the look on his face put Paul in mind of a diplomat at the United Nations, waiting for the simultaneous translation. 'Presumably you mean the door in the cashier's office,' he said. 'I heard about that. But surely that was months ago, before I even joined the firm.'

That hadn't been what Paul was expecting; still, he wasn't being told off, either. 'This was yesterday,' he said. 'Actually,' he added, frowning, 'yesterday and the day before, because the christening was in the evening, right? After work. But when I tried to get through Benny's door, he was just coming back from the Bank. I must've been down there a whole *day*.'

Mr Laertides raised a faintly two-dimensional eyebrow. 'I haven't got the faintest idea what you're talking about,' he said. 'And talking of the christening, where did you get to? You were supposed to be the godfather, weren't you? But I didn't see you there.'

'You didn't?' A tiny flicker of doubt snagged Paul's attention, like a trout fly dragged through murky water. 'You didn't see the cake, with the girls jumping out?'

'Cake? Oh, right, yes, I saw that.'

'But you didn't see me? I was the one cutting it, and then—'

'Ah, got you.' Mr Laertides nodded. 'That would explain a lot. What you were doing on the wrong side of Mr Shumway's door, for one thing. But you got back, evidently.'

It was as though someone else was running Paul's mind. Not an invasion or a hostile takeover, more as though a kind friend had said to him, *You look really tired, you relax for ten minutes and I'll hold the fort for you.* Now this kind friend was telling him that it'd be good to confide in Mr Laertides, who seemed a nice enough bloke, even if he was a partner; and he'd be far less likely to get into trouble for skiving off work if he just fessed up and told the truth. Personally, Paul thought the kind friend was either drunk or exceptionally stupid, but it was out of his hands, unfortunately. 'I saw Mr Dao and got the Door,' he heard himself say. 'Oh, and I was able to get that far because there was still a bit of blood left on the sword.'

Mr Laertides was perfectly still, apart from a tiny flicker round the edges. 'Maybe you'd like to start at the beginning,' he said.

So Paul told him all about it, straight through to the point where Mr Tanner's mum had brought him the slice of cake and left him to eat it. When he'd finished, Mr Laertides steepled his fingers and pressed them to his lips, a study in profound thought by an undistinguished pupil of Rodin. 'But that doesn't make sense,' he said.

Paul had to grin at that. 'Which bit did you have in mind?' he said.

'The sword,' Mr Laertides said. 'Everything else is pretty straightforward – though, if you don't mind me saying so, I think you might be a bit more careful choosing your friends in future. It's fine for Rosie Tanner to say it was simple and obvious, what you had to do to escape, but she wasn't the one having to do it. But that's beside the point, and we can all be a tad thoughtless at times. No, what I can't figure out is this sword thing.'

Mr Laertides wasn't making any effort to keep his voice down, but the other passengers in the compartment (which was almost full) didn't seem to be taking any notice. 'Don't worry about it,' he said with a faint smile, as though he could read Paul's thoughts. 'They can't see us chatting. What they think they can see is you fast asleep, and me talking very loudly into my mobile phone about some really boring meeting I'm late for. So, they aren't listening to me. A simple first-level glamour, your basic Jedi mind trick. I can teach you how to do that in five minutes flat, if you're interested.'

'Can you? I mean, that'd be really kind of you, of course, only—'

Mr Laertides shrugged. 'The offer's still open – working in my department for a couple of months, once you're finished with Theo. Entirely up to you, and you don't have to decide yet, of course. But about the sword. You said you kept it with you, after you—'

'Died,' Paul said. 'That's right. The goblins killed me, and the next thing I knew I was sitting in this television studio; and I still had the sword in my hand.'

'Extraordinary,' Mr Laertides said, and the intensity in his voice was rather unsettling. 'That's not supposed to happen, really it isn't. You know the saying, you can't take it with you. Absolutely true, no exceptions. The very most you can do is have it sent on to await arrival, but that's a different procedure entirely.' He sat scowling thoughtfully for three seconds, then leaned forward a little. 'So what became of it?' he asked. 'The sword, I mean. Did you leave it down there, in the Underworld?'

Paul shrugged. 'I'm not sure,' he said. 'I think I must still have had it when I ran at the door, but after that I'm not sure. No, hang on; I remember wondering where it had got to after I tried to get through the door and it was shut. I suppose I must've dropped it down there somewhere; but I didn't get around to looking for it because that was when Mr Dao showed up again, and I suddenly thought of using the Portable Door, and of course that shoved the sword clean out of my mind.'

'Ah.' Mr Laertides didn't relax, but he turned down the volume of his body language a little. 'In which case, presumably, it's lost down there for ever. Which is a pity – I'd have liked to have seen this remarkable object. Where did you say you got it from?'

At the christening. It sort of fell at my feet out of nowhere. Or they chucked it down for me to use. There was a bit of pink ribbon wrapped round the hilt, if that's any help.'

'Pink?'

Paul nodded. 'Pink. That's one thing I'm positive about. Goblin taste, you see.'

But Mr Laertides shook his head. 'Clearly you don't know,' he said, 'but goblins – in their own proper shape, as opposed to masquerading as humans or other species – are violently allergic to the colour pink. It hurts them, literally, like burning. They can't touch anything pink, they can't even look at it for very long unless they're wearing special red-filter sunglasses.' He looked up, and his eyes were very deep, the follow-you-round-the-room eyes of a high-class painting. 'So it wasn't the goblins who gave you the sword. In fact, whoever put it there for you to find also boobytrapped it, so to speak, so that no goblin would touch it.'

'I see,' Paul said, and if the Brothers Grimm had been running the universe, his nose would've grown maybe a quarter of an inch. 'So—'

'So,' Mr Laertides said, 'it must've been put there by someone who wanted to help you. A friend. Someone,' he added, 'who also knew in advance what you were likely to be up against, presumably.'

'Really? Why's that?'

'Maybe there are still people in this world who go around carrying magic swords with them wherever they go as a matter of course. But the pink ribbon, the goblin-proofing if you like, strongly suggests forethought and preparation. So you've got an anonymous ally. A well-informed anonymous ally, which is even better. Lucky you. At some more appropriate time you can try and figure out who it could possibly have been. That still doesn't explain,' he went on, 'what you're doing out of the office during working hours when there isn't actually anything wrong with you.'

Oh, Paul thought. 'Really?' he said. 'Dying doesn't count as being ill, then.'

'But you aren't dead. And otherwise you're as fit as a fiddle.'

'Mr Tanner gave me the day off,' Paul suddenly remembered. 'Three days, actually. I phoned Christine this morning and she checked with him. He said it'd be all right.'

'Ah.' Mr Laertides nodded gravely. 'That's all right, then. And presumably you're headed for the coast in the hope that a bit of fresh sea air will put the roses back in your cheeks. Yes, that seems to be in order.' He smiled, and Paul felt himself relax. 'How far are you going?' he said.

'Brighton,' Paul replied.

'Really? There's a coincidence, that's where I'm headed. Party conference,' he explained, 'we have quite a few heavyweight political clients, as you'd expect. A simple glamour, like the one I told you about just now, and for a few minutes, just as long as it takes to make a speech, people will actually believe what they say. Very basic, level-one stuff, but we make them pay through the nose for it.' He paused, and gave Paul a look that he didn't like at all. 'Funny coincidence, really, because the reason I went looking for you this morning back at the office was, I was going to ask you if you felt like joining me, helping out with a few things.'

Heavy hint; and Paul was just grateful he hadn't been standing directly underneath as it crashed to Earth, or he'd have been flattened. 'Great,' he said, with all the sincerity of a government apology. 'That'd be—' He couldn't quite find words to describe what that would be, but Mr Laertides grinned like a furnace and said, 'Excellent,' as though he'd just invented a way of bottling sunshine. Paul gave his mind a savage kick, and it sputtered reluctantly into life.

'Just a moment, though,' he said. 'I haven't got any clothes with me, apart from a spare shirt and, um, things. No suit, I mean. And it wouldn't reflect well on the firm, your assistant turning up in scruffy old T-shirt and jeans—'

Mr Laertides laughed; he sounded like a studio audience. 'That's not a problem,' he said. 'Lean across, you can see your reflection in the window.'

Paul did as he was told. There was his face, he'd know it anywhere. But under his chin was a clean white collar and sober blue and grey tie, and across his shoulders a high-class charcoal-grey suit. His hair was neatly trimmed and combed. He looked like an actuary.

'Glamour,' Mr Laertides explained, as Paul glanced quickly down at himself and saw the clothes he'd put on that morning. 'Simple little trick but well worth mastering. For one thing, you can save a fortune. I mean, since when can you afford Armani on what JWW pays you?'

Paul thought about that. 'So anybody looking at me—'

'Will see you as you appear in the window, yes. Take me, for instance,' Mr Laertides went on, brushing a spot of lint off his immaculate navy chalk-stripe lapel. 'I'm wearing a pyjama jacket with coffee stains down the front, jogging trousers and a pair of old gardening shoes. And, of course, it doesn't only apply to clothes.' He smiled. 'No offence,' he said, 'but I'll bet there've been times in your life when you wished you looked like *that*.' He pointed at the window, and Paul peered over his arm. He saw Mr Laertides's reflection, and next to it a man he'd never seen before (he'd have remembered if he had): a tall, fair-haired, broad-shouldered, blue-eyed youth, good-looking, intelligent, endlessly likeable, the Greek god of being nice. Instinctively, Paul looked round, but there was nobody on the seat apart from Mr Laertides and himself. 'That's *me*?' he mumbled, and Mr Laertides grinned and shook his head.

'Of course it isn't,' he said. 'Actually, if you really want to know, that's my wife's cousin Larry. Nice enough bloke, got a job in a building society in Cobham, but he happens to be the most good-looking man I can think of offhand. Of course,' he went on, as the image faded and was replaced, heartbreakingly, with the long, skinny halfwit Paul had gradually reconciled himself to seeing in mirrors over the years, 'that look works wonders with middle-aged women in government offices, but it won't do you much good with the chicks. Too clean-cut. Sensible. Reliable. Boring. They'd be much more likely to go for something like – now then, let me see.'

Paul must have looked away for a split second, because the

reflection in the grubby window-glass was suddenly quite different: leaner, darker, sharper, more sardonic and above all, indescribably cool in a black leather jacket and faded denims with ripped knees. 'James Dean,' Mr Laertides was saying. 'John Travolta. The Fonze. Elvis. Totally retro, of course, but practically a classic, you'd be fighting them off with a baseball bat. Or maybe you'd prefer—'

'No,' Paul said, extremely quickly, 'that'd do fine, really. Except—' He hesitated. 'It's not me, though, is it? I'd look ridiculous in something like that.'

Mr Laertides shrugged. 'Millions of people all over the world look ridiculous,' he said, 'but they can't do anything about it, poor bastards. You, on the other hand—'

'Yes?' Paul said hopefully, rubbing his chin with his hand. The man in the window had enough designer stubble to provide habitat for four dozen partridges, but Paul's chin felt as smooth as glass and familiarly clammy. 'Me?'

'You can decide for yourself.' Paul craned his neck, but all he could see in the window now were trees, cows and countryside. 'All you have to do is learn a few words. It's perfectly safe, no nasty side effects, no selling your soul to the devil or ugly old paintings hidden up in the loft. From fridge magnet to babe magnet in one easy step. Or,' Mr Laertides added, as the train shot into a tunnel and the window went dark, 'maybe you've got scruples about cheating, or you simpy can't be bothered. I mean, only very shallow people judge by appearances, and you'd rather soldier on, waiting for Miss Right to love you for who you really are deep down. Or maybe you'd have deep ethical reservations about inducing someone to love you by supernatural means.' He smiled very faintly. 'Some people have issues about that sort of thing, though God only knows why.'

'No,' Paul heard himself shout. 'I mean, yes, that sounds like it might be, um, rather useful. And it'd get over the problem,' he added desperately, 'of me not having anything smart to wear for this job we're going to.'

'Indeed,' Mr Laertides said gravely. 'There's that as well. Anyhow, you take your time and think it over, and when you've reached a decision—'

'Yes please,' Paul snapped. 'Yes, I'd really like to learn how to do that, if it wouldn't be any bother.'

'Fine.' Mr Laertides held up his hand, palm facing outwards. 'You don't actually need the hand movements, but it's easier to learn doing it this way. All you've got to do,' he went on, 'is this.'

He turned his hand round, pressed it against his face and started pressing, squeezing, moving things about. First he pushed his eyebrows back a little; then he squidged the sides of his mouth together, pulled his nose to make it longer, used his thumb and forefinger to lift and smooth out his cheekbones, as though his face was a lump of wet clay and he was carefully moulding it into shape. It only took him a few moments, and when he took his hand away, his face had changed completely. Not, it turned out, for the better. He'd made himself look exactly like Paul.

'See?' he said. 'The first few times you try it, it helps to have a mirror. Otherwise you might find you come out looking like cheese on toast, or a Dali watch. Here,' he added, and once again he held his hand up. This time, his palm seemed to have turned to glass, and Paul could see himself reflected in it.

'I'm not sure about this,' he muttered doubtfully. 'I mean, surely there's more to it than that, or else—'

''Course there is,' said Mr Laertides. 'There's the small matter of natural ability, which is only granted to maybe one person in twenty million. But you've got it, just like your Uncle Ernie, rest his vicious soul, so that's all right. Go ahead,' he went on, 'try it. If you don't like the result, just shake your head a couple of times and it'll reset to zero.'

Well, Paul thought, *why the hell not?* Very cautiously, he touched his fingertips to his face and pressed, watching the skin move. *What first,* he asked himself, *where to begin?* There were so many things about his appearance that he hated that for a while he couldn't decide what to tackle first. But his upper lip; that had always annoyed him – he was convinced that it made him look like a chipmunk eating a biscuit. Tentatively he drew it down with the top of his forefinger, pressing it gently against his front teeth. As he let go he expected to see the skin move back to where it should be, but it didn't.

'It works,' he whispered.

'Of course it *works*, silly,' said Mr Laertides. 'I do this sort of thing for a living, remember. Go on, don't stop, you're doing fine.'

So Paul tried again. This time he pushed his nose back a little with the heel of his hand, smoothed out the irritating bump halfway along, squidged the ridge between finger and thumb to make it thinner and less pudgy. That didn't look quite right, though; in order to be any good, it needed the cheeks to be a bit flatter, the chin a tad more pointed, and he definitely had to do something about his ghastly wing-mirror ears—

'Too much, steady on,' Mr Laertides warned. 'Your problem is, you know what you don't like, you're not so sure about what you want instead. What you've done, you don't look handsome, you just look like someone's pressed you in a book like a daisy. What I usually suggest is, get an idea in your mind of what you're working towards. Easy way is to think of a face you know, a movie star or a TV personality, and try and make yourself look like that. In your case,' he mused, 'I'd go for either Leo DiCaprio or the young Hugh Grant. Oh, and don't forget the teeth,' he added. 'That's a mistake a lot of people make: they get the rest of their faces just right and then as soon as they open their mouths they look like a shark trying to swallow a keyboard.'

Paul had always been hopeless with plasticene and making clay models in Art at school, but he found that if he just con- centrated on the picture in his mind and stopped looking at his reflection, it was much easier. 'There,' he said, a few minutes later, 'how's that looking?'

'It's an improvement,' Mr Laertides said. 'Has to be admitted, though, that's not saying a whole lot. No reflection on you, no pun intended, but you've got the sort of looks that most things improve, second-degree burns included.'

It all seemed to take for ever; and then, quite suddenly, every- thing seemed to come right and fit together. 'That's it,' Mr Laertides called out, 'you've got it now. See? Told you it was dead simple. Actually,' he added, his eyebrows drawing together, 'that's not bad, not bad at all. Didn't I say I thought you had a flair for this sort of work?'

Paul looked away from the window for a moment or so to reset his perceptions, then looked back. The face he saw in the glass was— Years of thoroughly justifiable modesty were getting in the way, but there was no call for any of that, since the face wasn't *his*, after all. But it was strikingly handsome: straight nose, high cheekbones, square jaw, finely tapered chin, large well-spaced eyes, firm mouth not too narrow or too broad, a basically serious face but fully equipped to handle a wide spectrum of emotions . . . He ventured a smile, and was agreeably startled by the flash of warmth, like sunlight breaking through clouds and flooding a deep valley. He tried a laugh; when Paul Carpenter laughed he looked like a baboon, but you could practically see the great golden soul behind this face peeping out at you through the windows of the eyes. He ran through a basic repertoire of expressions – brave, stern, compassionate, caring, happy, sad, serious, playful – and stopped because it was unbearably frustrating; because this was the face he *should* have been born with, if only there had been any justice in the world. With a face like this, he could have been somebody, a contender . . . Not just because it was cute and hunky and guaranteed sure-fire girl catnip, though of course that'd have solved or more likely preempted a great many of the personality defects that the real Paul Carpenter had had to live with all these years. It was more than that, though. He could've been himself in a face like this, instead of having to tailor his hopes, aspirations, objectives, expectations to suit the jumble of skin, bone, muscle and cartilege he'd been issued with when he was born. All his life, he realised bitterly, he'd had to be the boy who looked like a bolted Brussels-sprout plant (the clown, the butt, always left over when teams were picked, always on his own in the playground during break); and how stupid, how arbitrary to allocate him to village-idiot duties simply on the basis of nose length and ear configuration. You might as well choose somebody to be the President of the USA on the grounds that he could spit further than anybody else.

'What's the matter?' Mr Laertides was saying. 'You look like someone's just filled your inside pocket with treacle. Don't you like it?'

'Oh, I like it a lot,' Paul mumbled. 'That's the problem.'

'Is it? Why?'

Paul turned sharply and looked away. 'Because it's not me, is why. Because I've got to give it back and carry on being Chimp Boy for the rest of my life. It's not . . .'

'Not fair?' Mr Laertides chuckled, and for some reason the floor under Paul's feet shook slightly. 'Come on, sunshine, how old are you? Nine? Is that hypocrisy, or what? You're getting all stressy because it's not fair that people judge by appearances, but what the hell else are you doing every time you fall in love at first sight? Think about it; *at first sight*. What kind of attitude is that, for crying out loud? You must be so shallow, it's a miracle you haven't evaporated yet.'

'Yeah, well.' Paul shrugged. 'Like it'd have made a whole lot of difference if I'd fallen in love with girls because they're warm, caring human beings who want to work with disabled childen and dream about world peace. They'd still have told me to drop dead, because I've got a face like a Disney character. Not that it matters, anyhow,' he added briskly, 'because I'm through with all that now. Thanks,' he added with a slight frown, 'to you and that medicine you made for me. I mean, because of that, isn't all this sort of thing a bit irrelevant?'

'There's other things in life,' said Mr Laertides, 'besides getting off with girls, or had you forgotten about that? No, really. There's being taken seriously, for a start; having people predisposed to like you, willing to hear you out, listen to what you've got to say. I know, none of that stuff's in the same league as being able to pick up women in bars, but it might just be worth making a tiny effort now and again, don't you think?'

Paul nodded. 'You're right,' he said. 'I'm sorry. But it still doesn't matter a toss, because sooner or later I've got to go back to being Coco the Clown. That's where I live,' he said harshly, 'and anything else'd just be a short holiday I couldn't afford to pay for.'

Mr Laertides's face was completely expressionless. 'Not necessarily,' he said.

'Not necessarily?' Paul was aware that his voice was raised and messy-sounding, but there wasn't anything he could do about it;

he was angry, and he needed to say his piece. 'Oh, sure. Like I can walk into the office on Monday morning looking like this. Nobody would believe it was me.'

'True,' said Mr Laertides quietly. 'They'd think you were a client, or a rep or something.'

'Exactly. I'd be kissing goodbye to my job, for one thing.'

Probably because of the angle of the sun slanting through the train window, Mr Laertides's face was in shadow. 'Right,' he said. 'And that'd be a bad thing, of course.'

The implied *yeah, right* stopped Paul short like a cow standing dead still on a railway line. 'Well, of course it would,' he said. 'Look, being me isn't a barrel of laughs, but that's who I am. I can't suddenly stop it and go and be someone else.'

Mr Laertides shrugged just a little. 'You think so,' he said.

'Oh, for— It doesn't matter what I think. It's not a matter of opinion. It's one of those things, that's all.'

'I see. So you're resigned to it, in other words. You're so sure, you wouldn't even try something else, even if you had the chance.'

Paul shook his head. For some reason, Mr Laertides seemed to be having trouble understanding him. 'Look,' he said, 'I'd love a chance of being someone else, like *him*.' He jerked his head sideways in the direcion of the window. 'But it's not possible, so what the hell. Right?'

'No.'

It was probably his tone of voice that did it. Paul looked up sharply. 'Sorry?'

'I said no,' Mr Laertides said. 'Meaning, if you want to be the bloke in the reflection there, that's no problem. Easy bloody peasy. All it'd take,' he added, 'would be for Paul Carpenter to die; and then, gradually and being tactful about it, you could take his place.'

'Yes, but—'

'And you've already done that,' Mr Laertides went on, 'so that's the hard part out of the way. The rest's easy, it's just telling a few lies over and over again until eventually they stop being lies and become true. Now, how much trouble could that be, compared with dying and coming back to life again?'

For a long time – long enough to make a sandwich or wrap a

small parcel – Paul said nothing. Then, in a little tiny voice, he asked: 'What did you have in mind?'

'Ah.' Mr Laertides's grin was back, gaping in his face like a volcanic fissure. 'Now we're getting somewhere. Here's what I had in mind. You come to Brighton with me and help me out with a few small jobs – nothing boring or yucky, not even doing any magic; just sitting in a corner during meetings making notes, running a few errands, stuff like that. In return, when I get back to the office on Monday, I'll tell them all you died. Yet again. Had a relapse of death, and this time you've copped it, you aren't coming back. And don't worry, they'll believe me, because when they go round to your flat they'll find a body, and it'll be you, and they'll have an inquest and then a funeral, and everything completely legal and above board. Or that's what they'll believe, at any rate. Just another basic glamour, really.'

Paul looked at him. 'You can do that?'

'In comparison,' Mr Laertides said confidently, 'you need two first-class honours degrees and a doctorate to fall off a log. Trust me,' he added with a grin, 'that's my job, it's what I do. So there you'll be, dead, no more boring, dumb-looking loser you. Then, after a decent interval, like maybe a week, I'll tell Dennis Tanner and the rest of them that I've found someone to take over your job. Enter the new you; and you carry on where you left off, but without the incredibly debilitating handicap of being you. What do you reckon? Sound good to you?'

'But—' Paul frowned. His mind was gridlocked with ideas, objections, worries, practicalities, trivia. 'Why have I got to go back to JWW?' he said. 'If you're so smart, can't you see I hate it there?'

'Only because you're a pathetic loser,' Mr Laertides pointed out. 'New improved Paul Carpenter will get on like a house on fire, probably realise what a really wonderful place it is and how incredibly lucky he is to work there. Besides,' he went on, 'the whole point of this gig from where I'm sitting is to get you to come and work for me. It's the price of the deal, take it or leave it. Up to you entirely.' Before Paul could stop him, he'd reached over, grabbed Paul's wrist and held his palm outwards in front of his nose. 'Your choice,' he added, as Paul gawped at the reflection suddenly showing there. 'You could be him, or you can stay being you. No rush to decide, the offer stays open for the next three seconds.'

Paul froze, counting in his head, *one-Mississippi, two-Mississippi.* One second left to make a choice like that, it was crazy. He couldn't be expected to make a decision like that in less than a fortnight. *Three-Missi—*

'Well?' asked Mr Laertides.

CHAPTER FIVE

It was bizarre, attending his own funeral. Being the kind of pathetic loser he'd always been, Paul had imagined what it might be like many times. Each time, he'd pictured a small (a pathetic loser, yes, but a realist) crowd of family and so-called friends, all torn apart with guilt and shame because they'd failed him, never understood him, been horrible to him and now it was too late to set things right. He'd pictured them over and over again, heads bowed as they stood in the rain beside his open grave – obviously it'd have to be raining – looking down at their shoes, miserable and wet, while his disembodied spirit floated above the treetops, sticking out its ectoplasmic tongue at them. It had always been a strangely comforting fantasy, which was why he'd kept coming back to it.

Instead—

'People keep staring at me,' he hissed at Mr Laertides, as they filed out of the crematorium into the painfully bright sunlight. 'They know it's me. I'm going to be in so much trouble—'

'Balls,' Mr Laertides replied, without any visible lip movement. 'None of them have ever seen you before, and they're all wondering who you are. Probably they think you're my boyfriend.'

'What? At my own funeral? That's so—'

'Keep your voice down,' Mr Laertides growled. 'Who's that

large woman with the luminous hair? Her over there, just ducked behind the laurel bushes for a smoke.'

'Who? Oh, that's my mother.' Paul frowned. His shoes were too tight for his new feet. 'It was nice of her to come, though, all the way from Florida. Pity Dad couldn't make it, but apparently he's in some posh golf tournament, and the quarter-finals are tomorrow. Bastard,' he added.

'You should go and talk to her,' Mr Laertides said. 'Offer her your sympathy at her sad loss. Who's that girl standing on her own at the back? Ex-girlfriend, by the look of her.'

Paul was about to point out that Sophie hadn't come when he realised who Mr Laertides had meant. 'That? Mr Tanner's mother. You know, from the office.'

'Are you sure? It doesn't look like her. No claws or fangs, for one thing.'

'She's in disguise. Well, not disguise, exactly. She likes to dress up as humans.'

Mr Laertides shrugged. 'Whatever. In any event, she's adding a bit of tone to the proceedings. Call no man's life wasted, I always say, when there's a mysterious beautiful girl in floods of tears at his funeral.'

Paul shook his head. 'That's not floods of tears,' he said. 'She's probably just picking her nose behind a handkerchief.'

'Floods of tears,' Mr Laertides repeated firmly. 'Though since it was her that had you killed, it may just be a show she's putting on for the lawyers, in case your family decides to sue.'

Paul shook his head, as his seven-year-old cousin Penny ran past, chasing a pigeon. 'No dice,' he said. 'They went to see a lawyer in Orlando, soon as they heard what happened. Apparently they lost all their rights to compensation when they sold me to JWW. You lot could sue, the firm, I mean, but I don't suppose Mr Tanner'd be too happy about suing his own mother.'

Mr Laertides grinned just a little. 'Dennis Tanner is incapable of happiness,' he replied. 'It just sort of soaks away into him like water in the desert. Are any of your friends here?'

'Dave and Chloe said they'd try and look in for the reception,' Paul replied. 'Howard sent my mum a nice card, with lilies on it.'

He looked away. 'Actually it was a birthday card, but he gummed a bit of white paper over the inscription.'

'Touching.' Mr Laertides yawned. 'I wonder what's taking so long,' he said. 'You didn't have any metal bits inside you, did you? You know, hip replacements, pacemakers, stuff like that?'

Paul thought for a moment. 'Tooth fillings,' he said, 'that's about it. Talking of which, who the hell decided on cremation? I've always thought it's a bit, you know, yucky.'

'Better than being eaten by worms, surely. I expect it was your mother, as next of kin.'

'Well, she might have asked me first – Look, they're coming out.' Paul pulled a face. 'I suppose that's me there, in that little box thing. I don't know the procedure at these things. What happens next?'

'Depends. Twelve, by the way.'

'Twelve what?'

'People here. Mourners. I counted. That's not including us, of course. Even so.'

'Fourteen,' Paul said defiantly. 'And there'd have been more if it wasn't for the football. England versus Kiribati.'

Mr Laertides dipped his head. 'I know,' he said. 'There was someone sitting behind us during the service, listening in on headphones. We were six-nil down at half-time, if you're interested.'

'You're right,' Paul said quietly, 'it's absolutely bloody ghastly. I shouldn't have come. It's so . . .' He shrugged. 'Twelve people,' he said. 'Not much to show for a life, is it?'

'Never mind,' Mr Laertides said, 'you'll just have to do better next time. Shouldn't be difficult,' he added. 'One dozen to beat. It'll give you something to work towards.'

Paul frowned. His mother was trying to get the lid off the little box; either she was going to scatter him in the Garden of Remembrance or use him as an ashtray. The lid popped off unexpectedly, fine wisps of grey powder went everywhere, and his mum sneezed.

'Figures,' Paul said. 'When I was alive she always said I got right up her nose sometimes. I'm pleased to see dying hasn't changed that.'

'It's good that you can make jokes about it,' Mr Laertides said indulgently. 'In case you were wondering, by the way, what's inside that little box is the ashes of two hunded copies of the *Financial Times*, glamourised to pass for your mortal remains. A suitably ephemeral note, I thought. So, have you seen enough already, or are you dead set on hanging on for the reception?'

Paul shrugged his shoulders. Thanks to the strong magic he'd learned over the last few days, he had something to shrug with, for a change. 'Let's go,' he said. 'I get the general idea.'

He turned his back on them and headed for the car park. So far, he had to admit, the great make-over of his existence hadn't gone precisely as he'd hoped. The biggest disappointment, of course, was that Sophie hadn't bothered to show up, but probably that was for the best too. Either she'd have been genuinely upset, which would've made him feel bad, or she wouldn't, which would've been worse. Maybe she couldn't get the time off work, he told himself. That would be JWW all over. Only twelve, though; that wasn't good. Even Uncle Ken was missing, he noticed; Uncle Ken had always remembered Paul's birthday, but apparently couldn't be bothered to make an effort for his death. It was enough to make him wish he'd made a will so he could have left nothing to any of them, except that there hadn't been anything to leave, apart from dirty laundry, inchoate washing-up and a few tins of baked beans.

'I'll miss the flat, though,' he said aloud. 'What's going to happen to all my stuff?'

'Sold,' Mr Laertides replied. 'The whole lot'll just about fetch enough to pay off the outstanding week's rent.' He grinned. 'Don't worry, I've seen to it. A friend of mine does house clearances, he bought the lot, you can owe it to me until you start work again and get your first pay cheque. While we're on the subject, I went and saw your landlord. Said my nephew was moving to London, and I heard there was a flat going. My friend's got all your stuff in cardboard boxes at his lock-up, and he'll put it back this afternoon. All right?'

'Oh,' Paul said. 'Thanks,' he added. 'I mean, it's only junk, but—' He didn't finish the sentence. He didn't want to have to say that everything his life had amounted to was there, so little of it, so worthless, just *things*, but it was all he'd got. 'Thanks,' he repeated. 'You've been to a lot of trouble.'

'It was my idea,' Mr Laertides replied. 'It's up to me to keep the inconvenience down to a minimum. Now, I don't know about you but I could do with some lunch.' He yawned. 'Ricky Wurmtoter didn't make it down, I noticed. I thought you and he got along all right. You saved his life or something.'

Paul shook his head. 'Not really,' he said. 'I helped him get shot of Countess Judy, but that didn't make us best buddies. Besides, he was probably off on business and couldn't get away.'

Mr Laertides got in the car. He had a huge open green Bentley, conspicuous as an exploding gas main. 'She wasn't there either,' he said. 'You're upset about that, I can see. Maybe she just couldn't face it.'

'Yeah, right.' Paul didn't want to talk about that. 'It doesn't matter,' he said. 'I couldn't care less, actually. I'd have missed my CD collection, but I can do without Sophie Pettingell. Or any of them,' he added, with a shrug. 'Which is just as well, really.'

'That's the spirit. What we need,' Mr Laertides said, starting the engine, 'is comfort food; which boils down to a simple choice, pizza or pie and chips. Your choice.'

'Pizza,' Paul replied. 'See?' he added. 'Decisive. I'm improving, aren't I?'

'Bloody, bold and resolute,' Mr Laertides replied gravely. 'I ought to point out that I detest pizza and it gives me wind, but this is your special day. My treat,' he added.

Paul looked round at him and thought, *Why's he doing this?* for the seventy-fifth time that day. He knew the answer in general terms, of course. Mr Laertides wanted something from him, something only he could do or get or be, in connection with some JWW-type scheme. There would be a great deal of money in it for him, none of which was likely to come Paul's way. It would almost certainly end in tears, and only a complete and utter idiot would've got involved in it in the first place. On the other hand – he happened to catch a glimpse of his new face in the wing mirror of Mr Laertides's beautiful car. *That's me*, he thought in wonder. And, since everything he'd ever done had always gone wrong anyway, and Man is born to sorrow as the toast falls buttered-side downwards, why the hell not?

'So that's you fixed up,' Mr Laertides was saying. 'You've got somewhere to live, a job to go to in the morning, and you look the way a Hollywood star thinks he looks when he checks himself out in the mirror.' He paused, stamping down on the accelerator to overtake a milk float. 'All you need now,' he said, 'is a name.'

'Philip Marlow,' Paul said, smiling. 'Mr Tanner should be expecting me. I'm the new assistant.'

The woman behind the desk scowled at him through her half-inch-thick glasses. 'I'll let him know you're here,' she said. 'Take a seat, he won't be long.'

No gorgeous blonde, sultry redhead, stunning brunette or lotus-eyed Oriental beauty on reception today; instead, a massive fifty-something with hair like steel wool stretched back in a bun, and a wart on her chin. It took Paul fifteen seconds to figure out that this was Mr Tanner's mum's equivalent of full mourning. He was touched, but obviously couldn't show it. He nodded politely, sat down and picked up a two-year-old colour supplement from the pile on the table.

Philip Marlow hadn't been his idea, not really. All through lunch he'd dithered, rejecting Mr Laertides's suggestions and making none of his own, until Mr Laertides had asked him, in an apparent change of subject, if he liked old black-and-white thrillers. He'd been unwise enough to say yes, he didn't mind them occasionally, and now here he was. At least it ought to be easy to remember—

'Mr Tanner's ready for you now,' said Mr Tanner's mum. He thanked her and set off towards the fire door that separated the front office from the rest of the building, only remembering as his hand made contact with the handle that he wasn't supposed to know the way. 'Can you tell me . . . ?' he began; Mr Tanner's mum nodded and reeled off a set of directions which would, he reckoned, leave him stranded in the third floor ladies' toilet. 'Got that?' she said.

Paul nodded. 'I'll find it,' he said, and set off up the stairs without looking back.

Things, he couldn't help thinking, were starting to look up already. For the first time since he'd joined the firm, he hadn't had the embarrassment of fighting off Mr Tanner's mum's extra-goblin brand of mild flirtation as he ran the gauntlet of the front office. He'd been a bit worried about that. She'd fancied him rotten when he was Paul The Mess Carpenter. Given her readily admitted weakness for cute humans, Paul had wondered how the hell Philip Marlow was going to get out of reception with a shred of clothing left on him. Apparently, though, she wasn't in the mood this morning; a blessing, Paul decided, as long as it lasted.

A minute or so later he was knocking on Mr Tanner's door. The first time he'd been in this room, he remembered as he picked his way across the file-strewn floor between the door and the desk, the general ambience of intimidating weirdness had struck him incoherent, and he'd gawped and gabbled like a clown with toothache. Now, being used to it all, he could move through the cigar-smoke fog and under the rows of neatly mounted razor-edged tomahawks that lined every wall without a second look. If he didn't know better, he'd have believed that Mr Tanner was impressed by such a display of insouciance; because instead of scowling at him and grunting, Mr Tanner stood up and held out his hand, like a real human being.

'Dennis Tanner,' he said, 'commodities and mineral rights. Can I offer you a cup of coffee?'

'Thanks,' Paul replied, and sat down. Of course, he now knew all about Mr Tanner's office chair, and lowered himself into it carefully and with precision. ('Don't let it sense you're afraid of it,' Benny Shumway had advised him once. 'Be afraid of it by all means, just don't let it know.') While he did this Mr Tanner buzzed for Christine and placed the coffee order.

'Well,' Mr Tanner went on, looking at him warily through his round, practically lidless eyes. 'Frank Laertides seems to think very highly of you.'

One of the many things that Philip Marlow could do and Paul Carpenter couldn't was fluent body language. A very slight dip of the head put across exactly the right blend of familiarity and respect. 'I've been lucky enough to work with him before, as you know,' Paul said. 'He reckons we make a good team.' A faint flicker of a deprecating smile. God, Paul couldn't help thinking, communication was really piss-easy when you didn't have to blunder about using stupid old *words*.

'If Frank wants you on board, that's good enough for us,' Mr Tanner was saying, in a tone of voice Paul had never heard before; practically ingratiating, almost as though Mr Tanner was glad he was here . . . A strange and sudden thought struck him. This was what it felt like, he realised, to get off on the right foot, make a good first impression. 'It was a stroke of luck you being available at precisely this moment,' Mr Tanner went on, 'since we've suddenly found ourselves short-staffed – I don't know if Frank's filled you in on the background, or—' Paul nodded, and Mr Tanner relaxed a little, clearly grateful not to have to go through a long and dreary story. 'I'm hoping you don't mind jumping right in at the deep end; it'd be a great help to all of us if you could see your way to starting right away, though if that's not convenient—'

'No problem,' Paul said. (Confident, decisive, short and to the point; everything Paul Carpenter had never been. Why, why the *fuck* did a slight rearrangement of his facial geography make such a vast difference?) 'I have the feeling that it won't take me very long at all to get settled in here. If I may say so, Mr Tanner, you run a tight ship.'

(What did that *mean*, exactly? A ship that never bought a round? A ship that kept getting wedged in the entrances to small harbours?) 'We do our best,' Mr Tanner replied, and Paul could actually see him swelling, froglike, just a tiny bit. 'We try and make it a happy ship too, of course. We've always found that just sort of comes along once you've got everything running as smoothly as you can. Anyhow,' he went on, 'according to Frank you know the work inside out; anything else you want any help with, just give me a shout and we'll get you fixed up in no time. Meanwhile, all I've got left to say is, welcome aboard.'

So much maritime imagery, Paul wouldn't have been surprised if Mr Tanner had hopped up onto his desk and started dancing a hornpipe. And the hypocrisy of it all; *run a tight ship,* indeed. Paul Carpenter could never have got away with any of that kind of twaddle in a million years. Was it really just because his nose was a bit straighter, his ears a tad less elephantine? Not that it mattered. He'd read somewhere that scientists had conclusively proved that the difference between drop-dead gorgeous and back-end-of-a-bus ugly was usually no more than twenty-five thousandths of an inch . . . He surfaced from his reflections in time to hear Mr Tanner buzzing someone else. 'I've asked Vicky to join us,' he was saying. 'She'll show you round, tell you where everything is. She'll be doing your general typing and filing. We've only just promoted her out of the typing pool, but she seems like a bright enough girl.'

Dear God, Paul thought, *they're giving me a* secretary. Somehow it struck him as bizarre, faintly barbaric, like an arranged marriage, or sacrificing a chicken to the gods. *But that'll mean giving orders, telling someone what to do; I can't do that. Correction: Paul Carpenter couldn't have done that. But Paul's not here any more, is he?*

'And if there's anything you need help with,' Mr Tanner was saying, 'there's always Sophie Pettingell, the junior clerk.' Mr Tanner paused, frowned. 'Her manner takes a bit of getting used to,' he went on, as though he was trying to sell Paul a semi-derelict second-hand car, 'but she's a good little worker when she sets her mind to it.'

Paul felt his right hand clench into a fist; but no, bashing Mr Tanner's face in wouldn't be a good idea, not even for popular, likeable Phil Marlow. *Besides,* he reminded himself, *this is Mr Tanner, you know he's an arsehole, so what do you expect?* A fundamental rule of life had just, he realised, become relevant to him for the first time ever: just because someone likes you, it's not obligatory to like them back.

'Sorry,' Paul said, 'what was that name again? Sophie—'

'Pettingell,' Mr Tanner repeated. 'I expect you'll run into her sooner or later. At the moment she's been drafted in to work with Theo van Spee.' Pause, and Mr Tanner looked at him; *you don't need me to explain why,* his expression was saying, gratefully.

Clearly the death of Paul Carpenter was something nobody wanted to talk about. *Fine by me*, Paul thought.

A knock at the door. Paul had his back to it, and so he heard the voice before he saw the face. By then, Mr Tanner was doing introductions: 'Vicky, this is Philip Marlow, who you're going to be working with.' She said how nice, or words to that effect; he knew her voice instantly, which was probably just as well. He wasn't sure he'd have recognised her without her tail.

'Hello,' she said, and smiled; and Paul thought, *Thank God for Mr Laertides and the medicine, without which—* Actually, he'd been completely wrong about one thing. He'd have recognised her straight away in any context, because of that hair; bright, soft auburn with gold streaks so light they could almost be silver. *Only just promoted her out of the typing pool*, Mr Tanner had said; that should've put him on notice, only he hadn't been paying attention. *Must stop that. Too slack, too Paul Carpenter*. Talking of which – he did a quick systems analysis, hoping he wasn't being too obvious about it, and was vastly relieved to find that, despite the hair and the voice and the smile, the medicine did appear to be working. 'Pleased to meet you,' he said brightly.

The next half-hour was awkward, to say the least. Vicky led him down the corridors and up the stairs, into offices and interview rooms and closed-file stores and kitchens; it was all completely familiar, of course, but also somehow strange, not because it had changed, but because *he* had – it was as though Robinson Crusoe had returned to his island incognito on a package tour and the guide had shown him his cave, his lookout, the beach where he'd seen the footprint. 'And this is the junior clerks' office,' she was saying, as she knocked on the door and Sophie's voice, typically petulant, called out 'Come in.'

She was sitting at the desk, and all Paul could see of her was the crown of her head, poking out over the top of a huge mound of Mortensen printouts. Then she disappeared completely for a moment, and emerged a second later round the side of the great pile. Her eyes had the dead look of the long-term paper-shuffler, and she looked at them both blankly without saying anything.

'This is Philip Marlow,' Vicky said, her cheerful tone faltering slightly in the face of Sophie's vacant stare. 'He's joined us as Mr

Laertides's assistant. Phil,' (at what point had he become Phil? Not that he minded, he just couldn't remember), 'this is Sophie Pettingell, the junior clerk.'

'Hi,' Sophie said.

Which was odd. Sophie didn't say 'Hi', in roughly the same way that she didn't run singing through meadows full of spring flowers while wearing floral-print dresses. Nor did she smile at people she'd never met before. For a split second he assumed that she was pleased to see Vicky, but apparently not; in fact, if she'd registered Vicky's existence at all it could only have been for an instant and then she'd dismissed it as irrelevant and unnecessary, possibly even unwelcome. No; she was smiling at him, and saying 'Hi' and—

Blushing?

Water doesn't flow uphill, the sun doesn't rise in the west, lead weights don't hover in mid-air when you drop them, and Sophie Pettingell never, ever blushed. It was just one of those things, a given, Scotty looking sad and moaning, '*I canna change the laws o' physics, cap'n.*' But her dark eyes were wide, and she was looking at him the way— He fumbled around in his memory and found what he was searching for. She was looking at him the way Paul Carpenter used to look at girls, at least until they noticed and asked him not to.

The same Paul Carpenter would've said 'Um' at this point, or something equally brilliant. But he was in his little box now, ashes to ashes. 'My God,' Paul said, 'you look busy. Is it always as bad as this around here?'

Sophie laughed, or rather simpered (and E announced that it had had enough of equalling mc^2, and was planning to start a new life in Patagonia with the square on the hypotenuse). 'Not usually,' she said. 'But it's been really, like, hectic since Paul – he was the other junior clerk, but he—' She stopped dead and shook herself like a wet dog. 'It's just me now, and so I've got to do all his work as well.'

'That's awful,' Paul said, and she nodded three times very quickly. 'It's not so bad,' she said bravely. 'So, you're working with Mr Laertides, then.'

'That's right.'

'I haven't actually met him yet, myself,' Sophie said. 'But I'm really, really interested in that side of the business.' She hesitated, and in one of those rare, brief flashes of insight that you get sometimes when you least expect them, Paul realised that she didn't actually know what Mr Laertides did. 'So maybe—'

'It's a fascinating area, media and public relations,' Paul said rapidly. 'And Frank's quite possibly the best there is, so if you do get a chance to sit in with us, you couldn't hope for a better start.' He smiled encouragingly, just in case there was the slightest possible ambiguity, and a sort of stuffed expression covered Sophie's face, one which was immediately familiar to Paul from a long succession of mirrors. 'So,' he said, 'who are you with right now?'

'Oh, nobody,' she said very quickly; then she blinked twice (he could almost hear the sucking sound of the mental foot being extracted) and said, 'I mean, I'm doing three months with Professor Van Spee, he's applied sorcery and stuff. But I've only got a few more weeks to go.'

A tongue ferociously clicked a few feet to Paul's left and made him break eye contact. Vicky was still smiling in a non-specific manner, like a water-cannon blasting an unruly mob, but there was a hard edge to her expression that you could've sharpened knives on. 'Actually,' she was saying, 'we've still got a lot to see, so maybe—' She tailed off, suddenly aware that she didn't have the sympathy of her audience. 'We ought to be getting on,' she added firmly. 'Really.'

'Oh, right,' Paul said. 'Well, it was nice meeting you, and I expect we'll be seeing more of each other quite soon.' Sophie nodded enthusiastically, like a seal watching the piece of fish in its trainer's hand. 'Best of luck with the Mortensens,' he added. 'I don't envy you that job.'

'Oh, someone's got to do it,' Sophie replied cheerfully. 'See you soon, I mean, bye.'

He could feel her eyes watching him all the way out of the door.

There was a slight edge to Vicky's manner as they finished off the tour, but Paul was too preoccupied to worry about it, or even to reflect in general terms about what Vicky was doing, on two legs, out of the typing pool. He felt like someone who's just been told something in a foreign language that he only knows a few words of, and it's either that he's won a million dollars on the lottery, or else he's under arrest for espionage and due to be shot at dawn, or possibly both. He'd shared his own sad company for enough years to recognise the symptoms, the lemming-like rush over the cliffs of At First Sight. The difference was that hitherto he'd always been the lemming, not the cliff. But there was no other way to account for Sophie's extraordinary behaviour; and if he was right, then that was absolutely wonderful.

Or, looked at from a slightly different perspective, a total and utter disaster.

'This is Mr Wurmtoter's office,' Vicky was saying, and either she was still royally ticked off about something, or she didn't like Ricky Wurmtoter very much. 'But apparently he's not in. Never mind, I expect you'll run into him sooner or later. Mr Wurmtoter kills things for a living,' she added, 'dragons and stuff. Now, just down here on the left—'

Yes, I know, you silly cow, that's the stationery cupboard where Julie hoards the pads of yellow stickies; shut up while I'm introspecting, for crying out loud. A total and utter fucking disaster, because it looks horribly as though Sophie's just fallen head over heels with someone, and it's not me. Or at least it is me, but—

'And that's about it,' Vicky was babbling, 'apart from Mr Laertides's room, of course, and your office, which is right next to it. Just down the passage here on your right, and—'

Paul stopped and looked at her. She looked back, and deep in her soft brown eyes he saw something he couldn't quite place but which made him take a step back, as though he'd just blundered in on a fight to the death between two strangers. 'Thanks for the tour,' he said. (That old Phil Marlow charm still running on autopilot, when what he really wanted to say was, 'Who *are* you?' or maybe just 'Eeek!') 'I think I'd better go and let Frank know I'm here. It's been—' Even suave, unflappable Phil couldn't quite put into words what it had been, except that in spite of the strange new experiences – Mr Tanner being polite, Sophie practically drooling down his shirt-front, Mr Tanner's mum *not* drooling down his shirt-front, and other wonders too bizarre to be comfortably contained in his mind – in spite of all that, it was still very much business as usual at 70 St Mary Axe, and that was both reassuring and infinitely depressing. Looking in the mirror and seeing drop-dead gorgeous (or in his case, having-dropped-dead gorgeous, which amounted to much the same thing) was all very well, but it was still an unsolicited free gift from a partner in the firm: beautifully gift-wrapped and, if he held it to his ear, audibly ticking. *What on Earth possessed me to do it?* he asked himself, not for the first time; and he knocked on Mr Laertides's door and went in quickly before his subconscious could provide him with an uncomfortable answer.

'There you are,' said Mr Laertides. He was sitting in front of the window, back to the door, looking out over the street. 'Well? How'd it go?'

'Odd,' Paul replied. 'Mr Tanner was, well, civil.'

'It's amazing what people can do when they really try. How about Ricky?'

'Out.'

Mr Laertides shrugged. 'I honestly don't think there's any danger of him recognising you. Or any of the others, come to that. Did you go and see Theo?'

Paul shook his head, then realised that Mr Laertides was facing the other way. Apparently, though, that didn't matter, because he said, 'Probably wise. Who else? Cas Suslowicz? Benny Shumway?'

What the hell, Paul thought, and nodded. 'And, um, Sophie. She was—'

'Rude. Brusque. Gauche.' Mr Laertides laughed. 'She's a caution, that Sophie, but she doesn't—'

'Actually,' Paul said. (And why the hell should he tell Mr Laertides, or why should he care, but anyhow.) 'Actually, she was quite friendly.'

'Oh.' Mr Laertides turned round slowly and looked at him. 'That's – interesting. So what happened? You knocked and went in, and—'

Paul nodded. 'And Vicky said, this is Philip Marlow, he's the new . . .'

'Hang on.' Mr Laertides's eyes had suddenly grown very small and bright. 'Who's Vicky?'

'Vicky the mermaid. Well, she's got legs now,' (*yes, indeed*) 'and they've made her my secretary. Tall girl, brown hair with shiny bits. Used to be in the typing pool.'

Mr Laertides frowned; parts of his face gathered together like a herd of migratory animals round a waterhole. 'Vicky,' he repeated, 'I don't think I've come across her. Anyway, not to worry.' His face opened again, and he looked almost mischievous, like a small boy watching the door he's just balanced a bag of flour on. 'What was it like? Different?'

'You could say that,' Paul mumbled. 'It may take some getting used to. People liking me,' he added, 'for no reason.'

Mr Laertides laughed; a barrel-chested, curly-bearded pirate-king laugh that it shouldn't have been possible to dredge out of his stick-insect body. 'There you are, you see,' he said. 'For no reason, that's your basic problem. You go through life believing you don't deserve to be liked, and that's what's caused a lifetime of misery, for you and a lot of other people.'

The last part left a barb in Paul's attention. 'Other people?'

'Of course. Your parents. Your family. You don't suppose that on the day you were born, the whole lot of them crowded round you, sniffed and made a decision that you were no good? Of course not. It was mostly you – gradually, over the years. If your parents made the decision to sell you to JWW, it wasn't just because they're unspeakable bastards. Partly it's that, of course; but you must've helped.'

'Thank you,' said Paul. 'Thank you so much.'

Mr Laertides shrugged; he was a great shrugger. 'Not that it matters any more,' he said. 'They're in Florida, you need never have anything to do with them any more. And everybody thinks you're dead. Now you've got a chance to be whatever you want. The key to not screwing it up this time round is knowing what you want. Simple as that.'

'Fine,' Paul said. 'And I suppose you know what that is?'

'Of course I do, it's not like you're a particularly complicated character. You just want true love. I could point out to you how shallow and incredibly self-limiting this is; it's as though I'm asking a six-year-old kid what she wants most of all in the whole world for her birthday and she tells me she wants to be seven. I could suggest a long list of better things to want, and I could probably make you realise how much more useful and beneficial they'd be. I could take you to meet a great many very unhappy people who've found true love but not, for example, money, or health, or freedom. But—' He made a wide gesture with his hands. 'That's none of my business. If you really want two pairs of socks for Christmas, that's what you'll get. Anyhow, I've fulfilled my side of the bargain.'

Click, Paul thought; *the sound of the pieces falling into place.* 'Bargain,' he repeated.

'Bargain, yes. I'm a businessman, not a charity.'

'But you said, if I helped you with what you were doing at the party convention—'

Mr Laertides shook his head. 'You don't believe that. You know the score, you were perfectly aware of what I was offering and what the price would be. The straight traditional barter, a body for a soul. Where I do business, innovation is frowned on.'

Paul looked at him for a while; he didn't move, not a flicker. 'My soul,' he said.

'Correct.'

'What does that mean, exactly?'

'Ah, well.' Mr Laertides smiled pleasantly. 'That's a matter of personal belief, isn't it? Though in your case, you have an advantage over most people – you know where we go when we die.'

'Those aren't souls,' Paul said straight away, without needing to think. 'They're just – well, leftovers. Scraps. You don't want anything like that.'

'Right again. What I want is something completely different. And the good part is, I'm guaranteed delivery.' Mr Laertides shrugged again. 'It's your choice,' he said. 'But so long as you wear that face, you're carrying out your side of the deal, that's all I'm saying. Now,' he went on, 'I think it's time we got some work done, don't you?'

'No, I don't,' Paul blurted out. 'I want you to tell me exactly what the hell you mean by all that stuff.'

'No.' Mr Laertides's face had set, still as a photograph. 'I can't do that, sorry. You're just going to have to take my word for this, but if I tell you what you want to know, it buggers up the whole thing. Don't interrupt,' he added, and Paul found that he couldn't, even if he'd wanted to; he had no words and no voice to say them with. 'I need your help,' Mr Laertides went on. 'You, and nobody else but you. The job I have to do is very important to me, and it's also my business and no one else's. Meanwhile, you've been very generously paid for your involvement: an unbreakable heart and the sublime gift of beauty. Cheer up, for crying out loud, you've got the fifth and sixth ace in Life's poker game – what else could you possibly want? Or need, come to that?'

'Cheer up,' Paul said. 'Why would I want to do that?'

Mr Laertides stood up slowly and walked towards him, making no noise, hardly disturbing the air. 'I could make you be cheerful,' he said. 'I could make you be happy. I could make it so that every day of your life is filled with sunshine and joy, whether you like it or not. All I have to do is decide, I don't even need to say the magic words or snap my fingers. But, out of the infinite kindness of my heart and because – for some bizarre reason I can't fathom – I like you, I'm not going to do that to you, not if you stop mucking me about and do as you're told. Do you understand me?'

No, Paul thought, *because you're talking drivel*. But before he could do or say anything, a memory flashed through his mind. He remembered Sophie, offering to drink the love philtre. Even now, there were times when he cursed himself for being so stupid as to refuse, but he knew that if she'd done it, even being in the same room with her would've been unbearable, because of the magnitude, the sheer horror of the lie. And suppose Mr Laertides could make good on his threat: perfect happiness and contentment for ever, no matter what. Wouldn't that be infinitely worse?

For a moment, Paul felt like he was going to be sick. He shut his eyes; and when he opened them again, there was Mr Laertides, offering him a glass of water.

'Sorry,' he said. 'I didn't want to have to upset you like that. But you're going to have to trust me, that's all.'

Paul sipped the water and pulled himself together. 'If you say so,' he said.

'I do say so. And now.' Mr Laertides sat down in his chair, stuck out his feet, put his hands behind his head. 'Let's clear the air and take our minds off all this unpleasantness by doing a little bit of actual paid work for a change. Someone's got to bring in the pennies, you know.'

There's nothing I can do, Paul thought. *I've walked into something nasty, I can't get out, I don't even know what it is. And – the one constant in an infinitely changing universe – there's bugger all I can do about it.*

Mr Laertides looked up. 'Well?'

'Sure,' Paul said. 'What do you want me to do?'

Working for Mr Laertides was rather different from what Paul had become used to over the last nine months.

Hitherto, to be sure, most of the time he hadn't understood what he was doing, or known what it was for or how the partners translated it into money; but at least it had felt reassuringly like work. Work isn't hard to recognise: it's boring, difficult, the antithesis of fun. (Because if it wasn't, it wouldn't be work at all. The universe is built up of polarities; it deals in such opposites as day and night, light and dark, good and evil, dead and alive, false and real, work and fun. Everything that isn't one is the other; the categories are separate and exclusive. If it's fun it can't be work, and vice versa.) But the tasks he had to perform for Mr Laertides, though hardly fun, didn't have that gritty, dry work texture about them. They were neither one thing nor the other; a third category, a hitherto undiscovered element, a pocket dimension.

Paul's first job had been to think of a flower. He had to sit still, eyes shut, hands on the arms of the chair, and think of a flower. It could be any shape or colour he liked, didn't have to be a real flower, it could be completely imaginary, just so long as it was a flower. *Screw this*, Paul thought, and sat still and quiet for a moment before saying, 'Right, done that.' But Mr Laertides said, 'No you haven't,' in a grim voice; so Paul admitted defeat and thought of a geranium. At least, he thought it was a geranium, but it could just as easily have been a dahlia or a chrysanthemum. Paul knew very little about flowers, and cared less.

'Excellent,' he heard Mr Laertides say, 'although if we're going to be annoyingly pedantic about things, that's actually a foxglove. Doesn't matter, though, and you're doing just fine. Now – you can open your eyes, by the way – I'd like you to describe for me the taste of an onion.'

Paul sat up. 'You what?'

'You heard me. Imagine I've never eaten an onion. What do they taste like?'

Paul frowned. 'No offence,' he said, 'but how exactly is this paying work? I thought you, well, sort of wrote speeches for people and worked out what their colours are and stuff.'

'That's right,' said Mr Laertides, 'up to a point. And that's why I need you to tell me what an onion tastes like.'

Fine, Paul thought, *just checking*. 'Well,' he said, 'it's sort of sharp and sour and a bit yuck, really, but it's also crunchy and a bit refreshing. That's when it's raw, of course. Cooked—'

'No, that's fine.' Mr Laertides stopped him with a wave of his hand. 'That's exactly what I needed, thank you. Now, would you mind telling me about the sexiest pair of wrists you ever saw?'

Paul just looked at him for a moment. 'Wrists,' he said.

'Wrists,' repeated Mr Laertides, with a hint of impatience. 'You know, the bit that joins the hands to the arms. Come on, you've spent your entire adult life gawping at girls. What constitutes a really cute wrist?'

After a long, long silence, Paul said, 'Absence of thick, curly hair is all that springs to mind. I'm sorry.'

'No, that's fine. You're doing really well, I promise you. Now, I suggest you have lunch early, because this afternoon I need you to nip down to Swindon and look at a tree.'

So Paul nipped. The tree was exactly where Mr Laertides said it would be, on the corner of Dunkeswell Street and Arundel Drive. It was slightly shorter than the other eleven trees in the row, and local government had splurged on a stake for it to lean on but not the little strap to tie it thereto. 'Look at it,' Mr Laertides had said, and beyond that he'd refused to be drawn, so

Paul looked at it, carefully, for five minutes. *It's a tree,* he eventually decided. *So fucking what?* Then he went home.

'It was about eight feet tall,' he started to say, first thing next morning. 'Sort of greenish leaves, I don't—'

But Mr Laertides held up his hand, as though conducting traffic. 'I said look at it,' he said, 'I don't need a description. Well done, though, we're making good progress so far. Which reminds me, here's a fiver, just pop down to Aldgate and buy me a toothbrush.'

It was five minutes past nine; way, way too early in the morning for that sort of thing. 'Aldgate,' Paul said. 'But that's half an hour's walk, and there's a Boots just round the—'

'Aldgate,' Mr Laertides insisted. 'It's got to be Aldgate, all right? Blue if there's a choice, if not whatever they've got. Take a cab, the firm's paying.'

So Paul took a taxi to Aldgate and spent half an hour traipsing up and down, looking in vain for a shop that sold toothbrushes. Anything else, apparently, he could've had his pick of, from microchips to elephants. If he wanted a toothbrush, however, the consensus was that he should nip round the corner, a hundred yards or so, to the chemist in the Arcade, where they'd be overjoyed to sell him the toothbrush of his dreams. He thanked them all, said he'd do that, and carried on down the street to the next remote possibility. He was just about to pack it in and go back when he saw a little tiny shop shoehorned in between an airline and a bookstore—

Demetrius Palaeologus (est: 1954)
Antiques – Rare Books – Prints – Maps – Vintage Scientific
Instruments – Toothbrushes

Mr Palaeologus, or his duly appointed representative, was a short, cheerful-looking man with a completely spherical bald head, round glasses and chins like a concertina; the face and the shape were more than a little familiar, something to do with coffee and cake, but Paul couldn't quite place it. Mr Palaeologus had a toothbrush for sale; he even had a blue toothbrush, though he admitted that he couldn't personally endorse that particular model, whereas the green one with the textured handle— No? The blue one, then. Fine.

'And you'd like that gift-wrapped,' the man said; a statement, not a question.

'Well, not really,' Paul said, but the man wasn't there any more; he'd darted into the back room, taking the toothbrush, and Mr Laertides's fiver, with him.

Paul settled down to wait. There wasn't a great deal in the shop to interest him; apart from the toothbrushes, distinctly separate in a perspex display of their very own on the far wall, it was just a few bits of tatty old furniture, some framed maps and a shelf of big, fat leather-bound books. After ten minutes of standing around, Paul pulled out one of the books and glanced at it, but the title page was in Latin and the rest of it was just a load of old-fashioned maps of (apparently) Nova Scotia, with a few line drawings of fallen-down old castles and the like. Eventually, the man came out holding a parcel the size of a shoebox, covered in bright red paper and festooned with curly ribbon. Biting back the truth, Paul thanked him, said it was very nice and left quickly. There were no taxis to be had, so he went back to the office on the bus. People stared at him all the way.

'This is *stupid*,' he complained, dumping the loathsome parcel down on Mr Laertides's desk. 'All right, the flower stuff was harmless and it wasn't bad getting out of the office to look at that tree, but—'

'Get a grip,' Mr Laertides said. 'Just imagine, it could've been pink.'

'It's not far off pink,' Paul maintained bitterly. 'Well, aren't you going to open the bloody thing, after I've been to all that trouble?'

Mr Laertides shook his head. 'That's all right,' he said, 'I trust you to know a blue toothbrush when you see one. Now—'

'Aren't you going to explain? Please?' Paul said hopefully. 'Just a hint'd do.'

'Sorry, not possible. Now, I want you to look through that big cardboard box over in the corner there, and choose the eight CDs you'd least like to be stranded on a desert island with.'

And so it went on, day after day. Carefully examine these seven identical steel washers and say which you think is the shiniest. If you could only eat one thing for the rest of your life, which would you choose, rice pudding or Rich Tea biscuits? Who do you think looks better in a hat, Robin Cook or Severiano Ballesteros? Imagine a goldfish, a claw hammer, a mountain, a pile of tins of grapefruit, a shoe, dawn over the Nile delta in February. If toothache had a colour, would it be red, black or yellow? Go to a suburban road in Dunstable and count the number of blue cars parked on the south-facing kerb.

Still, it was better than work; and Paul was getting out of the office quite regularly, and nobody seemed to notice or mind if he dawdled on his way back. The extra money was nice, too, as were the friendly smiles of the partners as he passed them in the corridors, and the general sense of not being a quarry species at a predators' convention. Mr Tanner's mum was back to her normal flamboyant self at the front desk, but so far she was leaving him well alone; he missed being able to talk to her, but he had other people to chat with now, and besides, he was busy, no time for idle banter . . . Actually, he realised, the being busy all the time was maybe the greatest improvement of all in his quality of life. Paul Carpenter had been able to shut out the weirdness, and even turn a blind eye to much of the sheer horror and fear, but the one thing he'd never figured out how to cope with was the boredom of hours sitting in his office with nothing to do. Popular Phil Marlow, on the other hand, might spend his working day carrying out one set of unfathomably bizarre orders after another, but at least he was kept occupied. And if the work he was doing seemed pointless, ridiculous and a total waste of time and effort, how was that different from the working lives of millions of his fellow citizens? The tasks that Mr Laertides set him were no more fatuous than the job descriptions of any number of civil servants, local government officers, Revenue officials and duly accredited inspectors of this and that; and unlike them, he wasn't doing anybody any harm, so what was there to complain about?

'Good work,' Mr Laertides said enthusiastically, as Paul reported back after a morning spent playing *Death Throes 2005* on the office computer. 'Thanks for that, I do believe we're beginning to make some progress at last. Now—'

Paul shut his eyes, but only for a moment.

'I want you,' Mr Laertides went on, 'to nip down to Trafalgar Square and feed the pigeons.'

Paul looked at him. 'Sorry?'

'Trafalgar Square,' Mr Laertides repeated, slowly and clearly. 'Pigeons.'

'There aren't any.'

Mr Laertides frowned. 'How do you mean?'

'There aren't any pigeons in Trafalgar Square these days,' Paul said. 'The government had them all gassed or something. It was on the news at the time.'

'Oh.' Mr Laertides shrugged. 'In that case, I want you to go to St James's Park and feed the ducks.' He paused. 'There are still ducks in St James's Park?'

'I think so.'

'They haven't all been lined up against the wall with little duck-sized blindfolds on or anything?'

'I don't think so.'

'Fine. In that case, here's a kilo and a half of birdseed,' he added, pointing to a fat paper bag on the desk. 'You'll need to take someone with you, give you a hand.'

'Just a moment,' Paul objected. Freedom of speech wasn't an issue with Mr Laertides, he could say pretty much what he liked, raise objections, ask questions, whatever. Of course, his questions weren't answered and his objections were ignored, but it was the principle of the thing. 'How could feeding the birds, tuppence a bag, possibly need two people?'

'You could take that secretary of yours,' Mr Laertides continued, with a grin, 'give the poor kid something to do for a change. She must be bored silly, waiting around for you to give her some typing or filing to do. What did you say her name was, again?'

Paul shook his head. 'I'd rather not, thanks,' he said. 'Look, is it extremely heavy birdseed or something? Or does one of us chuck it around while the other one takes notes?'

'Or,' Mr Laertides said, his face suddenly blank, 'you could ask her to help you.'

Sophie's name hadn't been mentioned in Mr Laertides's room before, but even so there was no need to ask who *her* was. Paul opened his mouth to refuse, then shut it again.

'And it'll take you a while,' Mr Laertides went on, 'and there's no point you both trudging back to the office at one o'clock and then back again at five past two, so you might as well have lunch out somewhere. Together,' he added.

Whenever Mr Laertides dropped hints, it made Paul think of some US Air Force bunker a mile under the roots of the Rocky Mountains, and frantic missile technicians trying to shoot the hint down with tactical nukes before it collided with Earth and started a new ice age. Nevertheless. He hadn't actually seen Sophie to talk to since Phil Marlow's first day; and a shared cappuccino and sandwich couldn't do any lasting harm, surely. 'All right,' he said. 'Should I—?'

Mr Laertides shook his head. 'I'll send Theo a memo asking if we can borrow her,' he replied; and just then there was a knock at the door, and Sophie came in.

Paul's first instinct was to look away, but he batted it aside like an over-persistent moth. She paused just inside the room, smiled at him, then handed Mr Laertides an envelope. He opened it, read the single sheet of paper inside it, smiled and handed it to Paul.

From: Theodorus Van Spee
To: Frank Laertides

You will wish to borrow Ms Pettingell to help with your current project. I can spare her until 3.45. She will wish to order a banana milk shake, but should be dissuaded from doing so as bananas bring her out in unsightly facial blemishes, a fact which her liking for bananas has led her to ignore.
  Cordially
  TVS

Paul straitjacketed his facial muscles, nodded and handed it back. 'That seems to be in order,' he said, and Mr Laertides inclined his head gravely. A few minutes later, Paul and Sophie were out in the open air, armed with birdseed and heading for St James's Park in a taxi.

'So,' Paul said after a long silence, during which Sophie had smiled at him at least three times. 'How's it going?'

'Don't ask.' She made a pantomime of rolling her eyes. 'Honestly, Van Spee can be absolutely bloody insufferable sometimes.' Pause, frown. 'Have you come across him yet?' she asked. 'Tall, thin bloke, white beard, cross between Mycroft Holmes and the Wizard of Oz.'

Paul shook his head. 'Haven't had that pleasure,' he replied. 'You're in his department, right?'

'Worse luck. Actually,' she added, 'it's not so bad; I mean, there's no goblins or demons or dragons or anything, you know, yetch. And he doesn't throw tantrums or shout or try and look down the front of my blouse or anything. It's just—'

'Weird,' Paul supplied.

'Weird,' she repeated. 'Absolutely and completely weird. Like, yesterday he had me colouring in a kid's colouring book all afternoon. And we spent three hours this morning playing chess.'

'Really? Who won?'

'I did,' Sophie replied, with a slight frown. 'Which is odd, because I'm rubbish and you'd have thought a bloke like that'd be brilliant at chess. But no, I beat him six times and drew twice.'

'Go you,' Paul said approvingly. 'But that's not the point, is it?'

She nodded briskly. 'Not the point at all. It's weird, and it's starting to freak me out. I mean, the filing and the photocopying and looking things up in books and traipsing up and down stairs carrying messages, it was boring and miserable but at least—' She shook her head. 'If it carries on like this, I'm going to go to Tanner and ask to be transferred. Talking of which,' she added, and maybe she'd got something in her eye, 'do you need any help in your department? Only it's always interested me a lot, public relations and media and, um, whatever.'

Paul grinned. 'Actually,' he said, 'I'm not sure you'd want to. For instance,' he went on before she could object, 'did anyone tell you what we're going to be doing?'

'Well, no,' Sophie replied. 'Van Spee just looked up at me suddenly from the papers he was reading, handed me that envelope – it was there on his desk all morning, ready – and told me to go and see you. Well, you plural,' she added in a hurry. 'So, what exactly are we doing?'

'Feeding the ducks in St James's Park,' Paul said. 'As witness, one paper bag full of birdseed.'

'Feeding the ducks? Why?'

Paul shrugged. 'Because he likes birds, or—' He couldn't think of a reason. 'Truth is, most of the stuff we do in PR and Media is like that. Bizarre and incomprehensible.'

Sophie paused and looked at him curiously. 'Bizarre and incomprehensible to the outside observer,' she said, 'but of course you know exactly what it's all in aid of, because it's your speciality. Yes?'

'Yes. Well,' Paul admitted, 'actually, no. Actually, I haven't got a clue. I just do as I'm told, and at the end of the month I get paid money. Presumably there's a point to it all, but—' He checked himself. He was sounding a little bit too much like Paul Carpenter back from the dead, and if anyone around JWW was likely to notice, it'd be Sophie. 'It's like when they were building the pyramids, or the great cathedrals,' he said, smiling cheerfully. 'Frank Laertides is the architect, I just haul on a rope and assume that he knows what he's doing. It's a very complicated branch of the trade,' he added grandly, 'takes a lifetime to learn, and even then you've got to have the gift or you'll never get anywhere.'

'I see,' Sophie replied, and there was a tiny hint of suspicion in her voice. 'You don't mind that? Not having a clue, I mean.'

Paul did a rather fine doesn't-bother-me gesture with his hands; completely spontaneous and unrehearsed, too. 'I go with the flow,' he said. 'Obviously, I pick up bits of theory and stuff as I go along; and once the job's finished, naturally you look at it and think, of course, that's what all that was for, how dumb of me not to figure it out.'

'Ah,' Sophie said. 'Traditional British apprenticeship, in other words. Left-handed screwdrivers and stuff.'

'In a sense,' Paul replied, a trifle huffily. 'I think of it more as being Dr Watson, and you only find out the solution to the case at the end, when Holmes explains it all. I rather like it that way,' he added defiantly. 'At least it keeps it from getting boring.'

'I guess,' Sophie said; and then the suspicion and scepticism seemed to drain out of her, like oil from the crankcase of a British motorbike, and Paul could have sworn that she almost sort of batted her eyelashes. Now it was his turn to be suspicious: the Sophie he'd known would rather have been staked out over an anthill in the desert than knowingly have batted an eyelash. Mr Tanner's mum, now: in her day, she'd left no eyelash unbatted, and had moistened her lips with the tip of her tongue so often it was a wonder she hadn't had permanent cold sores. But they'd walked past her at reception on their way out of the office, so it couldn't be her; and none of the other female goblins in the building had ever shown that sort of interest in him. Besides . . . a moment later, presumably without realising she was doing it, Sophie started cleaning out her ear with the tip of her index finger, and that was so definitively Sophie that it had to be her. In which case – *Don't go there*, Paul warned himself, and for once he had the good sense to listen to his own advice.

A wise man once said that in central London there are only two sorts of pedestrian, the quick and the dead. Having got out of the taxi on the south side of Birdcage Walk, they managed to sprint through a gap in the lava flow of traffic into the wrapper-strewn peace of the park and soon found themselves at the edge of the water, surrounded on all sides by a seething carpet of ducks. 'Well,' Paul said, 'here goes. Good luck.' He held out the birdseed bag, and Sophie gravely scooped up a handful.

'The ancient Romans reckoned they could predict the future by watching birds,' Sophie said, after a few distributions of largesse. 'Maybe that's what this is all about.'

'Interesting theory,' Paul replied, in his best Hugh Grant voice. 'You mean, if they climb on each others' backs and try to peck each others' eyes out, it means that there's going to be a general election.'

A strange moment: at first, Sophie started to frown, as she generally did just before she treated a feeble joke with the contempt she felt it deserved. But then she sort of froze for a heartbeat; and then she giggled. Sophie didn't often giggle, in the same way that deep pools of water are rarely set on fire by stray sparks. 'Something like that,' she said. 'Or if they all waddle about frantically with their bottoms in the air, it means—'

Paul, who'd been watching a fat brown duck with a limp, waited for her to finish the sentence, but she didn't. He looked round, but she wasn't there any more. He swivelled his head round like a tank turret; she couldn't have gone far, and they were at the edge of the pond, but he still couldn't see her. Then he turned back, and nearly fell over.

Where Sophie had been standing was a goblin; in broad daylight, all fangs and claws and round red eyes. And in its outstretched paw were a few grains of millet.

CHAPTER SIX

'What the fuck,' said the goblin, 'am I doing here?'

It had taken Paul a long time and a great deal of concentration to learn to tell goblins apart. It should've been easy, because some of them were rat-headed, some of them had faces like pigs or dogs, some of them could almost have passed for human but for the six-inch curved tusks and the third nostril. This one was basically dog with a hint of cat around the cheekbones, and it only took Paul about a second and a half to remember where he'd seen it before. He even remembered that he knew its name, except he'd forgotten it for the moment. 'You,' he said; and then, 'Where's she gone? What've you done with her?'

But the goblin only stared; first at Paul, then at the bits of grain in its paw. 'For crying out loud,' it hissed in a loud stage whisper, 'I can't be seen out like this – *do* something.'

A duck waddled up, stopped dead eighteen inches from the goblin's feet, opened its wings and flew away terribly fast. 'What? I mean, like what?'

The goblin had started quivering, like a guitar string. 'I don't bloody know, do I? Quick, take your coat off and give it here. *Quickly.* Your lot may be as perceptive as a box of small rocks, but any minute now someone's going to start screaming, and then we'll be up to our arses in the Filth.'

Valid point. Paul slipped off his jacket and draped it awkwardly round the goblin's shoulders. 'I know who you are,' he said. 'Colin. Colin the goblin. You overheard me talking about Van Spee's crystals and wanted to buy some off me.'

The goblin flinched as if it had misjudged climbing over a very powerful electric fence. 'Fuck you,' it said. 'Who are you, cops or something? That wasn't me, I wasn't even—'

'We went to your lock-up,' Paul went on. 'You offered me, what was it, four million?'

'How the hell do—?' The goblin peered closely at Paul's face, then took a step back. 'Look,' he said, 'I don't know who you are or what in buggery's going on; but the bloke I offered to buy the crystals off didn't look anything like you and anyway, I know for a fact he's dead, so you can't be him. And I didn't buy them anyhow, he wouldn't sell, and *failing utterly* to traffic in prohibited substances isn't a crime in anybody's book, not even if the judges were Dave Blunkett and Attila the Hun. So if you'll kindly stop frigging me about and send me back—'

'Send you back,' Paul repeated. 'I didn't bring you here. Talking of which—'

'What?' Colin the goblin opened his round little eyes wide, till they were the size of blood-red tennis balls. 'Well, I didn't get here by fucking taxi, sunshine. Last thing I knew, I was sitting in my office doing this month's VAT; and then, suddenly—'

'What do you mean, "then suddenly"?' A wave of panic broke over Paul like a surfer's dream. 'If you didn't – look, have you seen a girl? Human, about five two, straight dark brown hair—'

''Course not,' snarled Colin. 'I follow the rules, me; no going Topside until the doors're locked, keep out of the way of humans at all times. At least,' he added ferociously, 'I *try* to follow the rules, except of course when I'm suddenly whisked away by titanic supernatural forces and dumped in a wide open space full of humans and *birds*.'

'But—' Paul began to argue; and maybe he shifted his feet and accidentally trod on a questing duck, because one of them suddenly exploded off the ground in a flurry of wings, zooming straight up past his nose. Instinctively he jumped back and shut his eyes; and when he opened them again, there was Sophie, just as she'd been, with a stunned expression on her face and grains of birdseed dribbling out through her fingers.

'Did—?'

'Sophie,' Paul said quietly.

'Did I just – *go* somewhere?' She turned her head and looked at him, her face completely empty. 'Only I could've sworn—'

'Let me guess,' Paul interrupted quickly. 'You were sitting at a desk, and there were these forms—'

'VAT returns,' Sophie said, nodding. 'I know about them, I've got an accountant who's an uncle, I mean the other way round, and in the holidays I used to—' She shook herself like a wet dog. 'Screw that,' she said, 'I don't want to talk about that. How the *hell* do you know? About the desk, and the—'

'Because,' Paul said, trying to keep still and calm, 'you vanished; and where you're standing now there was this goblin, and he told me . . .'

'Goblin? Oh God, I think I'm going to throw up. I turned into a *goblin*.'

Paul shook his head. 'I don't think so,' he said. 'I think you just changed places for a second or two. Look, why don't we go somewhere, instead of discussing this in the middle of St James's bloody Park?'

'But the ducks—'

'Oh for—' Paul held out the hand with the birdseed bag in it and turned it over. Birdseed swamped his left foot, and immediately he could feel duck beaks drumming on his toe, like a host of elven chiropodists. 'There,' he said, 'all done. Now, shall we go somewhere a bit less bloody public?'

'All right.' Sophie staggered slightly as she followed him, across the park, over the road (suddenly no traffic) and into a pasta bar, which happened to be the nearest public building. Paul practically had to shove her into a seat.

'Well,' she said, smiling suddenly and without apparent provocation, 'while we're here, we might as well have lunch.'

'What?' It took Paul a moment to remember the meaning of the word 'lunch'; it was rather like hearing English unexpectedly when you've been living with a remote tribe in the heart of the rain forest for the last five years. 'Oh, right, lunch,' he said. 'Why not?'

'Great,' Sophie replied, 'I'm starving,' and she grabbed the tall, plastic-coated menu. 'Right, I think I'll go for the straight spag bol, but with—'

'Sophie.' He caught himself a touch too late; he'd said it the way Paul Carpenter used to say it, back when they were living together and she'd said or done something so outstandingly unreasonable that even he felt compelled to protest. 'Ms Pettingell,' he corrected, but that didn't sound right either. 'Look,' he compromised. 'Before we start getting all wrapped up in spaghetti,' he said, and his scowl was so fierce that the giggle evaporated on her lips, 'I want to get to the bottom of this vanishing business—'

'You said you wanted lunch.'

Oink? 'No, I didn't.'

'You said, let's nip across the road and find somewhere – All right, you didn't actually *say* lunch, but it sounded like—'

'Bloody hell.' Apparently Phil Marlow had a shorter temper than Paul Carpenter. 'All right, let me clarify the position. This is a serious enquiry into something really bizarre and scary. It's not a – a *date*. All right?'

Sophie looked at him, and it was like peering into a long, dark tunnel. 'Whatever,' she said. 'But I'm still starving. I can't handle a whole portion of garlic bread, so let's go halves.'

'Garlic bread,' Paul repeated. 'All right, yes, why the hell not? And then can we talk about you disappearing, and turning into a goblin called Colin?'

She opened both her eyes very wide. 'Colin?'

'I don't know, I think it's a goblin thing. They know we can't pronounce their real names, something like that. Doesn't matter. The point is, I recognised him. I met him before.'

Sophie frowned, as if groping for the point. 'Small world?' she suggested hopefully.

'And he,' Paul ground on – why was it he felt like he was reading out a scientific paper to an audience of small children and clowns? – 'he seemed just as surprised as you did, so my guess is it wasn't him who made it happen. I don't know,' he admitted, 'I was so scared you'd been – well, *vanished*, like the other time . . .' He stopped short. Did he even know about the other time? 'It was you, wasn't it?' he rallied bravely. 'Who got kidnapped by the elf woman, whatsername . . .'

'Countess Judy,' Sophie replied, with a faint shudder. 'And she wasn't an elf, they're pointed ears and lace wings and ballet costume. Countess Judy was the Queen of the Fey. Which is a totally different kettle of barracudas,' she added with feeling.

'That's right, I remember now. Anyhow, that was what I thought, and—' A waiter was standing over them. Sophie asked for something technical, bits of Italian, including one word which Paul had always thought meant 'typewriter'. He grunted 'Same for me,' and the waiter went away.

'That's really sweet,' Sophie was saying. 'That you were worried, I mean.'

Sweet? *Sweet?* It suddenly occurred to him that maybe the real Sophie was still missing, and that goblins can be anybody they choose; because Sophie didn't use the S-word, not ever. But goblins always gave themselves away, if you knew what to look for; there was a grin, a certain gleam in the eye, and he wasn't looking at it. Even so; *sweet*, for crying out loud. 'Well,' he said awkwardly, 'if there's even the remotest chance that Countess Judy's come back—'

'Oh.' Her face closed down again. 'That's what you were worried about, I see. Well, I don't think it was anything like that. I mean, I can remember exactly what it was like when the Fey got me, and you wouldn't mistake it for anything else. Trust me.'

The waiter came back, dumped two plates of spaghetti down in front of them and went away. Sophie grabbed her fork and started to twirl. That was perhaps the most reassuring piece of evidence so far. Paul had watched Sophie eat spaghetti many times, always with fascinated horror. The ruthless way she twirled the stuff onto her fork put him in mind of the propeller of a vast tanker getting tangled in fishermen's nets, and the culmination of the procedure, when she poked the entanglement into her face and went *slurp* was like that bit with the giant squid in *20,000 Leagues Under The Sea*.

'Let's not talk about it any more, okay?' she said, as the tines spun relentlessly in the tangled mess. 'Right, so it was like really weird, but a lot of weird things happen around JWW, and I'm still alive and in one piece, so it can't have been that big a deal.' She reached out a hand and grabbed the pepper mill. Another important clue, because Sophie couldn't eat a plate of mince in tomato effluent without first poisoning it beyond redemption with a thick lava-crust of ground black pepper.

'Good idea,' Paul said. 'In that case, maybe you could answer a question for me. It's not something I've felt able to ask anyone else in the office, but—'

Sophie looked at him over her fork. 'Fire away.'

'This bloke who was here before me,' he said, and paused, making a play of trying to remember a once-heard name. 'Carpenter?'

She nodded vigorously. 'Paul Carpenter. He joined the same time as I did.'

'Ah, right. So what exactly happened to him?'

'Oh, he died.' Paul froze; he could feel the ends of his fingers and the tips of his ears getting cold – because she hadn't said, '*He died*' in a low, strangled, choking-back-sobs way. It was that initial *Oh* that screwed everything up. 'Apparently he was at this really wild party with a load of goblins and everybody was pretty well pissed as rats, and there was an accident.'

Paul didn't say anything for a moment. He was waiting for some appropriate comment about what a tragedy it was, a promising young life cut short, we shall not see his like again. But Sophie just carried on twirling her fork, pitching the mess into her face, and sucking in the ends like a supercharged Dyson. That was it, then. He died, but it was his own silly fault.

Even so. 'That must've been quite a shock,' he said, 'if you'd been working with the bloke.'

'Well.' Slurp; another dozen thread-ends vanished between Sophie's thin lips. 'Yes, it was completely unexpected, of course, you're always a bit stunned when someone you know gets killed or something like that. But it's not like we were close or anything.'

You lying bitch. You pasta-sucking heartless cow. 'Ah, right,' Paul said. 'So, did he have any family?'

She shook her head. 'Parents emigrated, I think, and I never heard he had any other close relatives. Sad, really, being all on your own like that. He was all right, I suppose. A bit dozy most of the time, rather immature, but harmless enough. And of course I got stuck with all his work as well as my own. We were both helping Professor Van Spee – have you run into him at all? Very polite, but a bit creepy, and God only knows what this project he's working on is actually about. And of course he never explains anything, it's really annoying.'

Hardly a seamless change of subject. As far as Sophie was concerned, Paul Carpenter could be dismissed in a few rather disapproving sentences, because that was all he merited. 'Thanks,' Paul said, winching the Marlow smile across his face. 'Only, people around the office keep mentioning him but whenever I've asked, they just go all quiet and then start talking about something else. I was wondering if it was some deadly secret or something.'

Sophie shook her head, and the upturned ends of her straight, dark brown hair trailed lightly in her bolognese sauce, like a lover's fingertips traced delicately across your cheek. 'You'd expect there to be some desperate goings-on behind it all, what with all the weird shit that happens at JWW. But apparently it really was just a stupid accident. It was something really silly, like a giant cake collapsing and smothering him. It's not actually all that funny, of course, but if you'd ever met Paul you'd realise how – well, appropriate, really.' She smiled faintly, then went on: 'I think it was Rosie's party – that's Mr Tanner's mother, she works on reception. I have an idea that Paul had a crush on her, which sound a bit yuck, her being a goblin, but of course she can change her shape at will, and she's got this thing about turning herself into these really obvious tarty women. I'm afraid poor old Paul was a complete sucker for all that stuff.'

Possible explanation: *she knows who I really am, and she's punishing me deliberately for pretending to be someone else and not telling her I'm actually still alive. Possible, but rather unlikely.* 'He sounds like a real loser,' Paul snarled. 'No wonder you were glad to see the back of him.'

'Oh, he wasn't as bad as all that,' Sophie said; and she was smiling, with that faint glow he'd seen a few times in a girl's eyes, though never when they were pointed at him. Usually that glow was his cue to make an excuse and leave before things got nauseatingly embarrassing. How often he'd dreamed about the day when he'd be on the receiving end of a glow like that – and now, here it was, and all he really wanted to do was pick up his plate of spaghetti in tomato sauce and grind it into her face. *Not as bad as all that*; she'd loved him once, he knew it, even he couldn't have imagined it all, but she'd never glowed at him like that. It had been a fierce, reluctant love, almost as though she'd resented the completeness of her devotion to him. Indeed; now he thought about it, it struck him that she'd never enjoyed being in love with him. All the time it had been an intrusion, a weakness, almost a failing. Now, though, he could see a deep pleasure behind that glow; and if someone – Mr Laertides, maybe – were to sidle up to her and offer her an antidote guaranteed to cure her, purge every trace of it out of her system, she'd be all horrified and refuse. *The bitch*, he thought. *A cute nose, a pretty face, and they aren't even* real; *and suddenly she's floating-on-air, singin'-in-the-rain happy; how shallow can you get?* It was worse than if she'd taken the love philtre, because—

Paul broke off from his train of thought and opened his eyes wide. Oblivious in her joy, Sophie had wound two turns of her hair onto her fork, along with the spaghetti, and was just about to stuff it into her mouth. 'Um,' he said, but it was too late. She closed her mouth, removed the fork, did the big slurp and realised that, at a rather fundamental level, things weren't quite as they should be. 'Uck,' she spluttered. 'Oh, *hit!*'

Insensitive and immature he might have been, but Paul reckoned he knew Sophie quite well, well enough to predict what her reaction would be if he burst out laughing at this juncture. On the other hand, what with one thing and another, it'd been some time since he'd had a good laugh, and if anything in the whole world was genuinely, delightfully funny, it was the expression on her face—

Screw it, Paul thought; and then the laughter took over.

He was still laughing when Sophie jumped up, knocking over her chair, and fled; through the door and out into the street, with the end of her hair still in her mouth, entwined with spaghetti like ivy and Russian vine. Then he tried to pull himself together, but only because people were staring. More joy in heaven, he thought as he dragged money out of his wallet and dropped it on the table; he didn't dare try and finish his meal, for fear of choking to death. He found his way out into the street, leaned against a wall and laughed until he felt his stomach muscles twanging like guitar strings.

'So you fed them,' said Mr Laertides, leaning back in his chair with his hands clasped behind his head. 'Then what?'

Paul hesitated. By rights, of course, he ought to tell his boss the whole story. For all he knew, the business with Sophie vanishing and being replaced by Colin the goblin was the entire point of the experiment. The fact was, however, that there were elements of the story he didn't feel like explaining; how he'd first come across Colin, for example. Also, in spite of or perhaps precisely because of how helpful and nice Mr Laertides had been to him, he still didn't trust him as far as he could sneeze him through a blocked nostril. 'Nothing much,' he therefore replied. 'It was lunchtime, so we had lunch—'

'Where?'

'Some pasta place just across the road. Can't remember what it was called, sorry.'

'Pasta,' Mr Laertides replied. 'Never got on with the stuff myself, I have to admit. Irrational, I know, but I never could drum up any enthusiasm for eating string. Give me a nice bacon sandwich any day. So then what?'

'Then we came back here,' Paul said.

'That's all?'

'Yes.'

'Oh.' Mr Laertides shrugged. 'Well, we can't expect miracles. All right, here's what I want you to do this afternoon.' He leaned forward, grabbed a copy of the *Evening Standard* off his desk, and opened it. 'Odeon, Tottenham Court Road. Programme starts 2.30 – but that means there's twenty minutes of trailers and mobile-phone adverts, so really it means ten to three, which ought to give you plenty of time. Julia Roberts and Russell Crowe. Do a pink form when you get back for the tickets and popcorn.'

Tickets, plural, Paul noticed. 'Hang on,' he said. 'You want me to go to the pictures?'

Mr Laertides nodded. 'It's extremely important,' he replied, 'especially in light of this morning. Yes, I think it's got to be done. You'll need to take someone with you, of course.'

Paul stared at him. 'Will I?'

'Well, of course. Otherwise, there wouldn't be any point, the whole thing'd be a waste of time. Tell you what,' he went on, 'you might as well get that Pettingell female to go with you. Theo can manage on his own for one afternoon.'

Paul breathed out slowly through his nose before answering. 'Actually,' he said, 'that might not be a good idea. We, um, I think I might have offended her, when we were doing the ducks thing.'

'Really? What did you do? Make a pass at her?'

He wasn't sure why that made him so angry. Possibly the casual way Mr Laertides said it, as though Paul was the sort of person who went around making passes at girls, rather than just wanting to but not having the courage. 'No, of course I bloody didn't,' he said.

Mr Laertides shrugged. 'All right,' he said, 'keep your hair on. So what did you do?'

'I laughed.'

'Laughed?'

Paul nodded. 'She got a bit of her hair wound round her fork, along with the spaghetti. She didn't think it was very funny.'

'Silly cow.' Mr Laertides grinned. 'Really, she did that? What happened?'

'Anyway,' Paul said firmly, 'I don't think she'd want to go to the pictures with me after that. Not even if it's work.'

'She'll bloody well go if I tell her to,' Mr Laertides said. 'First rule of business, don't let your personal feelings and antipathies get in the way of the job.'

'Yes, right,' Paul said appeasingly. 'That's so true, yes. But if it's all the same to you – I mean, if she's sitting there feeling all sullen and resentful, then she won't be concentrating properly on, well, whatever it is we're there for. Will she?'

'I suppose not,' Mr Laertides replied. 'All right, find someone else.'

'Right,' Paul said; then, 'Who, though?' He paused. 'I suppose I could ask Mr Shumway.'

'No,' Mr Laertides said quickly. 'No, that'd be no good, he has to go and do the banking at four. Look, it doesn't necessarily have to be someone from the office, even. Don't you know any girls who'd—?' He hesitated. 'No, of course not, I keep forgetting you're dead, so you don't know anybody much.'

Paul frowned. 'I suppose there's always Mr Tanner's mother,' he said.

'No, absolutely not. I mean, she's needed on reception. Look, are you quite sure about the Pettingell girl? I'm sure if you apologise nicely—'

'No, really. I'll think of someone, I'm sure,' Paul added hopefully. 'Half-past two, did you say? In that case, I'd better be going.'

Mr Laertides nodded. 'No need to come back here when the film's finished,' he said. 'See you in the morning, all right?'

Paul was halfway to the street when the obvious answer struck him. He turned left and walked down the corridor to his office.

He hadn't been in there since he'd died and resurrected himself as Phil Marlow, so he wasn't prepared for what he found, which was nothing at all. The room had been stripped bare of contents; they'd even taken up the carpet and removed the light bulb. The only thing left was the phone, resting on the floor with its flex curled up round it like a cat's tail. He knelt down and dialled Vicky's extension.

'Hello,' he said. 'I, um, need someone to help with something. Are you free?'

'Well, I'm hardly rushed off my feet,' Vicky's voice replied. 'You haven't actually given me any work to do since you arrived. What have I got to do?'

A surge of embarrassment powerful enough to swamp a tropical atoll swept through Paul, and he replied, 'It's a bit complicated. Come down to my office, I'll tell you when you get here.'

Slight pause. 'Your office. You mean Mr Laer—'

'No, my office. Paul Carpenter's old room. I suppose it's my office – nobody else seems to want it for anything.'

Less than a minute later, Vicky knocked at the door and came in. Today she had her hair pinned and combed on one side, swept over her shoulder on the other. She smiled at him and said, 'Well?'

'First.' Paul took a step away from her, felt the wall against his back. 'First, I've got to tell you, this isn't my idea. In fact, it's a direct order from Mr Laertides, it's like vitally important for the job he's doing. Honest,' he added. 'You can ask him if you don't—'

'Hold it,' she interrupted. 'What is this thing you want me to do? You said you'd explain.'

'Yes, right.' Paul stopped, tried to appear calm, cool, at peace with the world. 'Look, Mr Laertides says I've got to go to Tottenham Court Road—'

'Right, got you. I'll have to just nip back upstairs and fetch my coat.'

'And watch a film,' Paul went on. 'Julia Roberts and Russell Crowe. And—' No way to cushion the shock, better just to blurt it out and have done. 'And I've got to take someone with me. And the person I first thought of wouldn't want to go, so I thought I'd ask you. Of course, if you're busy—'

'Not likely.' She grinned. 'Stay there, I'll be right back.'

The medicine, Paul muttered to himself as the door closed behind him; *thank God for the medicine, or we'd be in real trouble here.* It wasn't just that Vicky had somehow managed to grow even lovelier since he'd seen her last – he was used to that sort of thing thanks to Mr Tanner's mum, and he was practically immune; it was the sheer enthusiasm she'd displayed at the thought of going out with him. (*Hold it there,* he commanded himself; *just because we're going somewhere and it's out of the office, that doesn't make it going out.*) It had never been like that with Sophie, that unalloyed *cheerfulness.* With Sophie, it had always been a case of the two of them facing up to the unavoidable fact that they loved each other; along the lines of *we're both in this mess, so we'd better pull together, bit between the teeth, shoulders to the wheel, and make the best of it.* Happiness hadn't really been a factor, apart from a very solemn sort of happiness that an uninformed outsider could well have mistaken for stoical resignation. But Vicky had practically bounced out of the room, like Zebedee in *The Magic Roundabout*. Of course, a career victim might be led astray by that into thinking that she actually liked him, which would in turn inevitably lead to infatuation, rejection, heart-break—

Would it, though? What if she did actually like him?

The thought hit Paul like a kick from a mule. Now that he'd ditched Paul Carpenter and replaced him with handsome, confident, relaxed Phil Marlow, it was no longer utterly unthinkable that a girl might just possibly like him a bit, or even a bit plus; in which case there might be something rather more desirable than rejection and heartbreak waiting for him at the bottom of Life's cereal packet. Except, of course, that Paul Carpenter had taken the medicine, which meant Phil Marlow was incapable of falling in love—

Sod it, Paul thought, and looked round for something expendable to hit, but of course the room was empty.

'I'm ready.' Vicky was standing in the doorway, smiling at him, and for a moment he thought that maybe the medicine was starting to wear off; but he looked at her again and realised that what he'd thought might be the first flash of love's refining fire was probably only very mild indigestion. As he muttered, 'We'd better be going, then,' and shooed her out of the room, a little voice in the back of his mind asked him if his reaction would have been different if it had been Sophie standing in the doorway smiling. Luckily, he knew where listening to voices in one's head could lead to, and ignored it.

It wasn't a bad film, but Paul hadn't enjoyed it much. The producers had done their best, filling the screen with hurtling cars, chattering machine-guns and great big explosions with cauliflowers of orange and red fire (it was, after all, a romantic comedy), but they failed to engage his interest; he was far more concerned with the presence in the seat next to him. Even when the gunfire and detonations were at their loudest, he was sure that he could hear the sound of her breathing, maybe even the slow beat of her heart. His general well-being wasn't helped by agonising cramp caused by sitting absolutely still, to avoid any possibility of accidental bodily contact.

It was a long film, but not nearly long enough. As far as Paul was concerned, it raced along like the last day of the holidays, every passing second bringing closer the awful moment when the lights came up, and one or other of them would inevitably suggest rounding things off by going for a pizza. Even as poor Mr Crowe was locked in hand-to-hand combat with the villain twenty thousand feet in the air on the wing of a speeding 747, Paul had his eyes shut, to help him concentrate as he struggled to come up with an excuse that wouldn't sound too excruciatingly fatuous. Appointment with doctor, ditto dentist, optician, physiotherapist; birthday party for parent, sibling, friend; got to go back to the office and work was a non-starter, Vicky knew he didn't have anything to do because she was nominally his personal assistant. He was considering the merits of folding up like a dead spider and dropping to the ground, clutching his stomach and groaning – all right, so they might rush him into hospital and whip out his appendix, but that had to be preferable – when the lights came up and the screen was suddenly full of the names of assistant cameramen and location-unit accountants. He shot up out of his seat like toast from a toaster, and said, 'Sorry, but I've got to get back home, they're delivering a new fridge-freezer,' before he realised she hadn't said a word.

'Oh,' Vicky said. 'Right. Well, see you at the office tomorrow, then.' A few minutes later, Paul was standing in the Tottenham Court Road, alone apart from a quarter-million or so irrelevant and harmless strangers embarking on the evening homeward lemming-run. Against all the odds, he'd made it. Carpenter 1, Cupid 0.

That, he felt, called for a celebratory drink. He chose a pub doorway at random, oozed his way through the crush to the bar and eventually managed to get his hands on a full pint (moderation was for wimps) of ginger-beer shandy, which he carried off to an empty, smoke-shrouded corner. It was only once he'd finished his drink that he realised just how thirsty he was; but it had been dry work, sitting absolutely still in a confined place trying not to breathe too loudly. Paul fought his way back to the bar for a repeat prescription. The second pint made him feel much more lively. That suggested that it must be doing him some good, in which case it was practically his duty to have a couple more, so he did; at which point, boozer's relativity caught up with him, and he realised that what he needed most in the world was fresh air and a wall that kept still while he was leaning on it.

There must have been something wrong with the fresh air, because as soon as Paul left the pub, something else seemed to have gone wrong with his legs; furthermore, the wall he chose for support turned out to be one of those pesky slithering-about types. As a result, through no fault of his own, he staggered, tripped and cannoned into a small, bald, round-headed man who happened to be passing by.

'Steady on,' the man said, in an American accent; fortunately, he didn't seem to mind being trodden on, because he grinned pleasantly. Maybe he'd had trouble with slithery walls himself.

'Sorry,' Paul said; and then it occurred to him that the man's face was familiar. 'Hold on,' he said, 'I know you from somewhere.'

'Do you?'

'Sure I do. Seen you somewhere just recently.' He frowned. 'That's it, you're whatsit with the funny name. Shop. Toothbrushes and antique furniture.'

The man frowned. 'We met in a shop selling toothbrushes?'

'No, no.' Paul shook his head, which must've provoked the wall somehow, because it shifted most inconveniently. Also, the pavement started playing up, probably in sympathy with the wall. 'Your shop. You got a shop selling toothbrushes and old pictures and stuff.'

'I don't think so,' the man said. 'And I'm sure I'd be aware of it if I did.'

Carefully, Paul detached himself from the wall, took a cautious step forward and examined the man closely. 'No disrespect,' he said, 'but you're wrong there. It's you, definitely.'

The man raised his eyebrows. 'Well, I can agree with you on that score, because I am definitely me. It's the shop bit I'm having trouble with. Still, there you are. That's the thing I like about this country, there's scope for a wide range of different opinions.'

It occurred to Paul that it wasn't the end of the world, even if

146 • Tom Holt

the man wasn't prepared to admit to being the shopkeeper. Maybe he was self-conscious about it or something. 'Doesn't matter,' he said magnanimously. 'Not to worry. Sorry about your foot.'

The man shrugged. 'It's okay,' he said, 'I've got two.'

'That's all right, then. Cheers.'

The man smiled and walked away, and Paul shifted along a bit, in search of stabler walls and less stroppy pavements. It was odd, he thought; not that it figured tremendously in the vast overarching scheme of things, but the man he'd bumped into was quite definitely the man from the toothbrush shop, Mr, Mr Thing, Mr—

Palaeologus. For some reason he couldn't quite pronounce it, even speaking wordlessly to his inner ear, but he could sort of see the word in his head. Funny sort of a name; but that was Americans for you. Paul had been an earnest student of international affairs all his life, and nothing the Yanks got up to surprised him any more.

The pavements were against him all the way to the bus stop – a bit uncalled-for, he felt, since all he'd done was brush up against a wall who happened to be a friend of theirs. He fell asleep on the bus and woke up just in time to scramble out at his stop. While he'd been dozing the pavements had apparently found it in their stony hearts to forgive him, because they stayed more or less level as far as his front door. On the other hand, he'd got a bit of a headache, doubtless because he'd had his head at a funny angle or something of the sort. He trudged up the stairs and let himself in, but the lights weren't working. Fuse blown, he diagnosed instantly. *Bugger.*

But that was all right. Paul knew where the fuse box was, and all you had to do was look at a row of switches till you found the one that'd flipped itself down. There was just enough light seeping in from the street-lamps to see by, and he hopped up on a kitchen chair to investigate. Remarkably, he found that all the fuses must've blown simultaneously, because all the switches were pointing the same way. *Freak power surge*, he decided, probably a powerful electric storm. He flipped them all over, climbed down and tried the lights, which still didn't work. Funny.

'Silly,' said a voice. 'It's the bulb that's gone, not the fuse. And now you've turned them all off, so nothing works.'

'Ah, right,' Paul replied, feeling a trifle foolish. 'I'll just put them back, then.' He clambered back onto the chair, did the switches and then thought, *Just a second: voice?*

'Hello?' he said cautiously. 'Who's that?'

'Me,' the voice replied. 'Over here.'

'I can't see you.'

'That's because the bulb's gone, you pinhead.'

'Yes, but—' Maybe it was the befuddling effects of his nap on the bus, or dizziness from hopping on and off chairs, or just possibly it was a side effect of the ginger-beer shandies; but Paul couldn't quite marshal the words he needed to get across what he wanted to say; namely, who the hell are you and what are you doing in my flat? *Screw verbal communication anyway*, he decided. Why ask when he could see for himself, which he could do perfectly easily just as soon as he'd changed that annoying bulb? Which he couldn't do in the dark, because he couldn't find a spare—

But (and this was where he had an ace in the hole in this battle against the universe) he did know exactly where to lay his hand on a candle and a box of matches; right here on the kitchen shelf, next to the pasta jar.

Paul located the jar rather cleverly by touch (and the crash it made as it hit the tiles confirmed its identity); and there next to it, just as he'd thought, were the candle and the matchbox. He struck a match, tried to light his middle finger, decided that was a bad idea and lit the wick of the candle instead. Now he had light; armed with which, he was the equal of anything the world could throw at him. He picked up the candle and directed its glowing yellow circle around the room. Nobody there.

'Stop mucking about,' he ordered, because an Englishman's home is his castle, even though most Englishmen tend to end up in the dungeons. 'Where are you?'

'Here,' the voice said, sounding bored. 'Where I usually am.'

That didn't make a whole lot of sense; because if Paul had been sharing his flat with whoever the voice belonged to, he reckoned he'd have noticed it by now. 'Fine,' he said. 'Humour me. Where's that?'

'Right in front of you, of course. Between the sink and the washing machine.'

Paul frowned, and lifted the candle higher. There was the sink, right, yes; there was the washing machine. Between them, there was just the fridge, no gap large enough for anybody to hide in. 'No you aren't,' Paul pointed out.

'Yes, I am.'

'No, you bloody well aren't. Look,' he added, marching across the floor and standing next to the fridge door. 'No gap, see? Sink, fridge, washing machine. Nobody there.'

The voice sighed. 'You've been drinking,' it said. 'That'd account for it. Even you aren't generally this stupid.'

Paul froze. He had a nasty feeling that the voice was coming from inside the fridge. Nerving himself against what he might find, he grabbed the handle and pulled the door open. Nothing. The light didn't even come on and his candle flame showed him nothing except a sad-looking lump of antique cheese and a milk carton.

This was really stupid, but: 'Are you in there?'

This time the voice laughed. 'In a manner of speaking,' it said; at which point Paul realised that for the last few minutes he'd been having a conversation with his fridge.

He slammed the door shut and jumped back. 'You?'

'Finally.' A long sigh, and a faint gurgle of plumbing. 'For someone in your line of work, you're a bit bloody slow off the mark.'

'You're the fridge.'

'Yes, I'm the fridge. Of course, I knew that already.'

'But—' Pity about the four pints of intoxicant; this was a situation he'd have preferred to face without having to think his way through all that beer. 'You can't be, I've been keeping *food* in you for the last nine months. I mean, how long—?'

'I've always been here,' the fridge replied, and repeated the gurgling noise, which put Paul in mind of something or other he couldn't quite place. 'Looking after you, like I promised I would. But now I need you to do something for me.'

'Oh. What?'

'Switch me back on. He's been here. He turned me off at the mains. If I go cold, I'll die. It's all right, I've still got half an hour left, at least. But if you wouldn't mind—'

'Like you promised?' Paul said. 'Promised who?'

'The switch. Please.'

'Oh, sorry, yes.' Hot wax from the candle ran down over the back of his hand; he nearly dropped it. 'I'll just turn on the lamp here, so I can see—'

'Don't bother, it won't work. I told you, he was here. He's killed all the bulbs.'

Down on his hands and knees, Paul followed the line of the skirting board to find the electric point. 'There,' he said, as he flicked the switch. 'Is that better?'

The fridge gave a great sigh. 'Yes,' it said. 'Yes, that's fine.'

'Right.' Paul stood up, bumping his head against the worktop. 'Now, who did you promise you'd look after me to?'

'Ah.' The fridge gurgled again. 'Actually, I made two promises. The other one was not to tell you.'

The headache was much worse now. 'Look,' Paul said, 'that's silly. Just a moment,' he added, as something else the fridge had said battled its way through the shandy entanglement into his mind. 'Did you say someone's been here?'

'Yes. He tried to kill me, and he killed all the light bulbs.'

'And I suppose you aren't allowed to tell me—'

'Of course I am, stupid. I told you, it's my duty to protect you. It was Utgarth-Loke.'

Paul paused for a moment. 'Sorry,' he said. 'What did you just say?'

'It was Utgarth-Loke,' the fridge repeated. 'He came in here—'

'Who the hell is Utgarth-Loke?'

Stunned silence; then the fridge said, 'What do you mean?'

Orange juice from now on. 'I mean,' Paul said slowly, 'who's Utgarth-Loke?'

'He is.' Pause. 'Don't you understand?'

'No.'

'Oh, for—' Silence; Paul could almost hear the sound of the

fridge concentrating. 'Utgarth-Loke is *him*. That's who he is. That's his *name*. Look, what's so difficult about that?'

'You aren't making any sense,' Paul shouted. 'Listen, I've never heard of anybody called whatever it is you just said. It doesn't mean anything to me.'

'You've never heard—' The fridge started to whirr ominously. 'Of course you have, you must have. That's like saying you've never heard of Wiod. Or Dunor.'

'Who?'

There was a bang and the fridge door flew open, narrowly missing Paul's knee. 'Now look what you've made me do,' the fridge said bitterly. 'Bloody hell, don't you know *anything*?'

'Apparently not,' Paul replied. 'Can't you just start at the beginning? And was it one of those people you just said who made you promise—?'

'Just shut my door, will you? And while you're at it, get that disgusting piece of cheese out of me, there's *stuff* growing all over it. Thank you, right, yes.' The fridge appeared to have calmed down a little. 'That's better. It was horrible, like having toothache.'

'Please,' Paul said, 'can you explain what all this is about? Like, from the beginning. And who are all those people with the funny names?'

'Oh God.' The fridge sounded despondent. 'I'd have thought he'd have told you *something*, but apparently not. All right, it's like this. In the beginning, there was nothing but mist and fire and empty space. Then the fountain Hvergelmir surged up out of the darkness, and from it sprang twelve rivers—'

'Excuse me,' Paul interrupted, 'but what are you talking about?'

'You said begin at the beginning, so I am. As the waters of the twelve rivers cooled down and began to freeze—'

'Not *that* beginning,' Paul protested. 'Look, all I want to know is, who's this Utgarth person you keep talking about?'

'Began to freeze,' the fridge repeated icily, 'and when they congealed, they took the shape of the first living creature, the giant Ymir. Meanwhile Audumla, the Great Cow of Heaven—'

'All right,' Paul whined, 'all right, forget it. Sorry I asked.'

'But it's important,' the fridge said angrily.

'No, it's not.'

'How dare you!' the fridge roared, so loud that Paul nearly jumped out of his skin. 'What kind of attitude is that, for pity's sake? Here I've been all this time, doing everything I possibly could to keep you safe, and you can't even be bothered to listen. It's not right. You've passed two of the three great tests – more by luck than judgement, needless to say, but even so, technically you've passed, and now we've got to get you ready for the third one. Which is why you ought to know these things.'

'*Why?*' Paul yelled. 'Why's it important? What the hell does it matter to me, any of it? I'm just this small, inoffensive bloke who wants to have a quiet life and be left alone, and what do I get? Talking fridges and the Great Cow of Heaven. It's not bloody *fair*, really.'

Long pause; then – 'Have you quite finished?'

'Yes.'

'Better now?'

Paul nodded.

'Right, then. Just as well, because I don't think we've got much time. Where were we?'

'The Great Cow —'

'Oh, yes. From the udders of Audumla the Great Cow of Heaven dripped the four elements: earth, air, fire, water. From these elements, Ymir the giant created all things, the sky, the sea, the land, or at least, that's how it was in the beginning *originally*. But then – quite some time later, obviously, but also next – then Utgarth-Loke stole the Great Cow from her stall, and in secret, unsuspected by the other gods—'

'What other gods?' Paul interrupted. 'You said there was just this giant and the cow. And you never said where the cow came from, either.'

'She was formed out of droplets of sea spray breaking on the cliffs of Surtheim, obviously. But the gods came much later. This is all before that, or at least it *was*. That's the whole problem. Anyway, you're making me get ahead of myself. Utgarth-Loke stole the Great Cow and, unsuspected by the other gods, he drew from her udders a fifth element, purely for his own use: stronger, more versatile, infinitely more dangerous, easy to make at home from sustainable resources. This element, which is all around us every day, pervading every corner of our lives and posing a horrific threat to the fabric of the universe, is in fact click—'

The fridge didn't actually say the *click* part; that was a sound effect, coming from somewhere up above Paul's head and to the right. Paul waited for a moment, just in case the fridge was doing it on purpose to heighten the suspense; then he tore open the fridge door.

No light.

'Bloody fuses,' Paul snarled aloud. He groped for his candle and knocked it over. It went out. He tried feeling for the matchbox, then remembered that he'd left it over on the worktop. He got up, found the chair, stood on it and reset the fuse. No problems whatsoever with any of that. It was as he tried to get down off the chair that he trod in something slippery, wobbled for a moment, lost his balance, skated the length of the kitchen floor and slammed very hard indeed into the door frame. Then he went to sleep.

When Paul woke up, he had a bad, bad headache.

He also had a crick in his neck that made him whimper when he tried to get up; also, he noticed, he wasn't in bed. For some reason he'd chosen to go to sleep in the kitchen doorway, like someone's faithful dog. With the benefit of hindsight (and the light streaming in through the windows was so obnoxiously bright that even hindsight hurt) he could see that this hadn't been a good idea, and he wondered why he'd done it; also, why he was still fully dressed in his work suit.

Then memory began to seep back, like oil through a chip wrapper. The pub. Alcohol abuse. That, of course, explained everything – the headache, the lack of judgement as regards sleeping arrangements, even the hazy recollection at the back of his mind of a long and earnest conversation with his fridge. Something about a cow—

Talking of fridges; Paul stood up, wobbled and sat down again. Since he'd more or less mastered the walking business by the time he was two, he wondered what was wrong, but a quick survey of the floor, followed by cursory examination of the soles of his shoes revealed rather a lot of gungy, slippery yellow stuff; something he'd trodden in at some point in his adventures, and it was probably just as well he couldn't remember anything about it. He crawled to his knees and stumped across the floor to the fridge, opened the door and gazed blearily inside. Once he'd got used to the blinding glare of the light, he found what he needed: a beautifully chilled Coke can, which he pressed carefully against his throbbing temples. Blessed numbness gradually spread, and he sighed. Thirty seconds of the treatment, and he felt ready for stage two, a long drink of cold orange juice.

The fridge was unusually well stocked. As well as two cartons of orange juice, there were eggs, bacon, sausages (he shuddered), cold drinks, milk, a Tesco moussaka, even some salady leaf things. Paul couldn't remember buying them, but there was so much that he couldn't remember about the previous evening that one small detail was neither here nor there. He stuck his thumb gracelessly through the cardboard of one of the juice cartons and swilled down half the contents. Better; still not good, but better.

Phases three and four involved aspirin and coffee. Phase five was a scheduled R & R break, five minutes sitting motionless at the kitchen table with his head in his hands. He hadn't worked out phase six in any detail, since he'd hardly expected to live that long, but in the event he winged it; a shower, a shave, clean shirt and underwear left him looking more or less human, and with luck nobody would get close enough to know any different. By eight-fifteen, he was sentient, self-propelled and late for his bus.

Dragging into the office at twenty past nine, Paul expected, at the very least, scornful looks and a mild rebuke. But, most unusually, there was nobody on reception, the front office was deserted, the corridors were empty. Nobody to be seen, anywhere. Arguably it was a definite improvement, but not the sort of thing to spring on someone with a delicate head first thing in the morning.

For some reason he felt the need to walk very quietly as he made his way up the stairs, as though the building was asleep and wouldn't be pleased at being woken up. He stopped outside the door of Mr Laertides's office, knocked as usual, and waited. No reply; but inside he was sure he could hear curious shuffling noises. Then a voice he didn't know squeaked, 'Come.'

There was someone sitting in Mr Laertides's chair, but it wasn't Mr Laertides; quite the opposite, in fact. Mr Laertides was long and linear, whereas this bloke was short and built up out of curves and radii. His head was almost perfectly circular, its profile unmarred by even the faintest trace of hair, and was poised snugly above a nest of chins, like a cat sitting on a pile of cushions. Paul was sure he knew him from somewhere.

'Hello,' said the stranger.

Paul stared at him for a whole four seconds. 'Hello,' he replied. 'Um, who are you? And where's Mr Laertides?'

The round man smiled agreeably. 'Frank can't make it in today,' he said. 'He asked me to hold the fort for him till he gets back. My name's Constantine Porphyrogenitus, by the way, and you must be Paul Carpenter. Pleased to meet you.' He stuck out a paw fringed with chipolata fingers, and when Paul hesitated to have anything to do with it, he laughed again. 'It's all right,' he said. 'Frank briefed me about the Paul Carpenter-Phil Marlow business. Why Philip Marlow, by the way? Where's the raincoat, the fedora, the forty-five?'

Paul blinked. 'The forty-five what?'

Mr Porphyrogenitus narrowed his eyes. 'Like that, is it? I understand. Of course, it's mostly just dehydration – that's what causes the headache and the sense of having been raised from the dead after two months in a limepit. Next time, drink three glasses of water before you go to bed. You'll be amazed what a difference it makes. So,' he went on, as Paul flopped into a chair, 'how'd it go yesterday?'

Yesterday. What the hell had happened yesterday? 'Excuse me?'

'The pictures. With that long-legged bit from the typing pool. Get lucky?'

Paul's eyes opened wide, but he lacked the necessary

coherence to word a suitable protest. 'No,' he replied. 'At least, we had a nice time and enjoyed the film, and then I went home.'

'You went home.'

'Yes.'

'Alone.'

'Yes.'

Mr Porphyrogenitus sighed, and pressed the bridge of his nose between thumb and forefinger. 'Right,' he said. 'And then you drank yourself into a stupor and went to bed.'

'Um, no,' Paul said. Difficult to explain that he'd gone out drinking to celebrate his escape from having to go out for a pizza with a friendly and attractive young woman. 'I stopped off on the way home, and—'

'Whatever. All right,' the round man went on, 'I'll just ask you to nip across to the cashier's room and fetch me the files marked "2004 reconciliations".' He frowned, probably in reaction to the blank stare that Paul was sure he was wearing. 'Think of the 101 Dalmatians, it'll help you remember. They should be right there on the desk.'

As Paul traipsed up and down stairs on the way to Benny Shumway's room, he was thinking, *I know that man, I've seen him somewhere just recently.* But the librarian of his mental archive was obviously away for the day, and nothing came.

Benny wasn't in when he knocked, but the files were there on the desk, just as the round-headed man had said they would be. Paul was just about to leave when something in the corner of the room caught his eye.

Something about three feet long, wrapped in newspaper. It could have been a loaf of French bread, or an oversized clarinet, or an offcut of plastic water-pipe, but somehow he didn't think so. It was right next to the little door, the one with all the bolts and chains and Chubb locks and Yale locks on it that led to the Land of the Dead; the one that had slammed in his face, the night of the christening party.

Nothing to do with me, Paul told himself, but in his own mind he sounded like a child telling his mummy he's got a headache and shouldn't have to go to school, on the day of the big maths test. *Nothing to do with me, it's in someone else's room, I can't possibly just wander over there and take the wrappings off and look at it, what if Benny were to come back and catch me?* But by then he'd already picked it up and peeled off the paper at the top, revealing the hilt of a sword.

It was a small point of pride with Paul that he knew roughly as much about weapons as a shoebox knows about medieval Russian music. This sword-hilt, however – he recognised it immediately. Last time he'd seen it, he'd used it to cut a cake and then decapitate a TV anchorman. He'd worried a bit about the latter act from time to time since the event; but he was moderately certain in his mind that his victim hadn't been real, just a hallucinatory image planted in his brain by the goblins; further, or in the alternative, even if he *had* hacked a real head off real shoulders, killing a television presenter under any circumstances wasn't homicide so much as pesticide. But; the fact remained that the blood left behind on the sword-blade must've been real blood, because it had been good enough to get him, if not out of the Land of the Dead, at least as far as the doorway. With extreme caution, since he had reason to believe the edges were sharp, he slipped off the rest of the wrappings and studied the blade for a moment or so. Just as he remembered it; the most striking feature being the whirling, looping fountains of silver patterning, not engraving or inlay but deep in the grain of the metal, standing out clearly from the smooth, faintly glowing brown steel. It reminded him of something so strongly that he could almost see it—

Something, or someone.

He heard a noise and jumped away from the wall like a rubber ball bouncing. It was the sound of a key in a lock – which, in Benny's office, could only mean one thing. He swung round and stared at the connecting door, the one that led to Death and the Bank.

The top bolt was slowly drawing back, grinding and graunching slightly against its retaining hoops.

Which wasn't good, because the bolt was on the inside.

CHAPTER SEVEN

Each of us has a subconscious voice, an inner mother who tells us what we know we ought to do at precisely the time when we know we aren't going to do it. At that moment, the voice in Paul's head was yelling, *Get out of there, run away*, but it was wasting its breath. He wanted to obey, of course, but his motor functions weren't responding, and the little voice was running out of arguments. *You'll be in real trouble if you don't* was simply stating the obvious, and *You'll go to bed with no pudding* just wasn't cutting it.

The top bolt was all the way back; now the chains were shaking slightly, as though a heavy lorry was thundering past in the road below, and the knob of the big Yale lock was slowly starting to turn. Not Benny, then, not unless he'd won stupendous telekinetic powers in the office Christmas raffle. Not Benny coming back from the Bank. Somebody or something else.

At the very least you could try calling for help, tutted his inner voice. But Paul could see the flaw in that one. The building was apparently deserted, apart from Mr Porphywhatsit. Yelling would only bring him to the attention of whatever was coming through the door. *Honestly*, sighed the inner voice, *just wait till your father hears about this*. He backed away, and as he did so the sword, dangling forgotten from his right hand, banged against the edge of the desk. It gave him an idea.

What on Earth that's supposed to achieve I really couldn't say, sniffed the voice. But Paul took no notice; instead, he dug the needle-sharp point of the sword into the carpet, then jammed the pommel under the bottom edge of the Yale-lock housing. As he let go of the handle and stepped aside, the remaining bolts flew back like crossbow quarrels, the last chain fell away, and the tumblers of the bottom Chubb clunked into battery. *Run*, screeched the voice, but he couldn't move at all – he could hardly breathe. The door shifted.

And stopped. Then there was a moment of great stillness, followed by a loud thump on the other side of the door; then another, and another. Pause, followed by a tremendous crash, and the sword bent like a bow, the door opened an inch and a half, and darkness speared through the crack between it and the frame, darkness that was much, much more than a mere deficiency of light. Paul opened his mouth to scream, but the sword straightened up like a spring, pushing the door shut. Paul stared at the point where the pommel was jammed against the lock body; there was nothing holding the lock on except four perfectly ordinary, mundane little screws, the sort that come in a separate little compartment in the plastic bubble-wrap when you buy the lock. Four silly little bits of metal, screwed into a piece of board, standing between him and whatever was on the other side.

They held. *Bless them*, Paul thought. Bless whoever made them, whoever specified and ordered them, packed them, fitted them, because they'd done a good job in a world far more dangerous than they could ever begin to imagine. And the least he could do was try and give them a little bit of support. Gingerly, as though touching a hot pan-handle, he reached out and slid the top bolt home again. It didn't burn, bite or struggle, so he slammed back the rest of the bolts; and when the next thump came, the door didn't flex at all. Next he hooked up the chains, and mercifully they stayed put. The next assault cracked the plaster round the edge of the door frame, but nothing budged; and unless Paul was kidding himself, it wasn't quite as ferocious as the previous one, or the one before that. Was it possible that the thing on the other side was getting tired, running out of steam? He watched as the bolts quivered a little but didn't move.

One more thump, but it was more a venting of frustrated anger. Then nothing.

At this point, Paul realised that he'd been neglecting his breathing, and caught up. A few deep breaths and he was thinking better; in particular, he was remembering something a little voice had said to him about getting out of there, and now he came to think of it that wasn't a bad idea. First, however, he tapped the sword-hilt sideways with the palm of his hand, till the weapon came free and toppled over onto the floor. Pushing it out of the way with the side of his foot, he grabbed the big, heavy filing cabinet that stood beside the door (there was a cake box, of all things, on top of it, but he chucked that on the floor) and hauled it down onto its side; then he shoved, heaved and manhandled it up tight against the door. It wasn't much, but it was something; and besides, it wasn't his fault or his choice that he was in the position of defending the land of the living against invaders from the other side, with no resources at his disposal apart from office furniture. He knelt down, grabbed the sword and ran out of the office, slamming the door behind him. In the corridor, he paused, swore out loud, went back in, snatched the files he'd been sent to collect off the desk, and withdrew once more. This time, he didn't stop running till he was back in the passage outside Mr Laertides's office. He knocked and went in.

'What kept you?'

'Well, there was this—' Paul stopped, and stared. The man sitting behind the desk wasn't the round-headed Mr Porphyrothingummy. Instead, Mr Laertides was lounging in his usual slightly exaggerated manner, hands behind his head. 'When did you get back?'

Mr Laertides frowned. 'What?'

'I said, when did you get back?'

'I've been here all morning, as well you know. Look, have you got those files or not, because I've got a lot to get done before—'

'No, you haven't,' Paul said grimly. 'I got in at twenty past nine and you weren't here. There was this other bloke, Mr Por—' Screw it, he couldn't remember the name. 'This other bloke. Short, tubby, round head like a football.'

Both of Mr Laertides's eyebrows shot up. 'Are you feeling all right?' he said. 'I was here at half-eight this morning, and I've been here ever since. You were your usual punctual self; three minutes past nine.'

'Balls,' Paul said. 'You weren't here. Roundhead Guy was sitting there, right where you are. He sent me to get these files.'

Mr Laertides stretched forward – it was as though his upper torso was plasticene – and peered at the files in Paul's arms. 'Those are the files, all right. You found them on Benny Shumway's desk, yes?'

'Yes, that's – how did you know that?'

'Because I asked you to get them for me. Twenty minutes ago, actually, but you're here now, so—'

He reached out for the files, but Paul stepped back. Instinctively, he raised the sword a little. Mr Laertides couldn't have noticed it before; when he saw it, he went suddenly very still and quiet. 'What are you waving that thing around for?' he said in a flat, soft voice.

'I got here late,' Paul said. 'I had a hangover – I missed my bus. When I got in there was nobody about; nobody on reception, the front office was empty, nobody in the corridors or anything. You weren't here, but this round bloke was. He said you were away today, he was minding the store for you. He sent me to get these files—'

There was a knock on the door. Mr Laertides scowled, called out, 'Yes, come in', and Mr Tanner walked in. 'You got the Amalgamated Mouldings file?' he asked.

Mr Laertides nodded. 'Just beside you, look, on top of the filing cabinet.'

'Thanks.' Mr Tanner moved to get the file and caught sight of the sword in Paul's hand; maybe he did a very slight double take, or maybe not. Then he left, closing the door behind him.

Mr Laertides smiled. 'I think you'd just got to the bit where the building was completely deserted,' he said.

'It was,' Paul said resolutely. 'All right, I didn't search the place from top to bottom, but—'

Another knock. This time it was Cas Suslowicz, wanting to borrow Mr Laertides's twelve-dimensional calculator.

'But,' Paul went on, 'I came all the way here from the front office, then from here up to Benny's, and there was nobody about, and it was dead quiet.'

Mr Laertides shrugged. 'Whatever,' he said. 'So you got the files. Why the cold steel, by the way? You got a really stroppy letter to open, or something?'

'I found—' Paul hesitated. He had no idea why, but he was sure that it wouldn't be a good idea to tell Mr Laertides about the connecting door trying to open itself. 'I found it in Benny's room, but actually it's mine. I, um, left it there a while back, so while I was passing I thought I'd bring it along.'

Mr Laertides's smile widened, like the gap in the ozone layer. 'And why not?' he said. 'Do it now, I always say: if you leave it till later you'll forget all about it. Anyway,' he went on, yawning hugely, 'you've got the files I need, and you've got your sword back, so we're all happy, aren't we? And now, if it's all the same to you, perhaps we can get on and do some paying work.'

I could refuse, Paul thought. *I could refuse to give him these files unless he tells me what the hell's going on. But*— He remembered, for some reason, a history lesson at junior school, horrible batty old Miss Hook telling them the story of King Canute and the sea. Precisely; he could stand there and *command* the waves to go back, he could shout and wave his arms about and threaten to resign and anything else that occurred to him on the spur of the moment, but he was still going to end up with wet shoes and soggy socks. 'Here you are,' he said quietly, handing over the files. 'Anything you want me to do?'

Mr Laertides frowned, then shrugged. 'Can't think of anything offhand – no, wait a second, there *is* one thing you could do for me. Just nip across the road to Waterpebbles, see if the book I ordered last week's arrived yet.' He scribbled a few words on the back of a petty-cash slip. 'It's all paid for, you just need to pick it up.'

Paul nodded and left without a word. In the corridor, just past the closed-file store, he nearly bumped into Sophie, who was coming out of the stationery cupboard with a large box of paper clips. She mumbled a greeting and scuttled past, her gaze fixed on the carpet. As if that wasn't enough adventure for one day, a few yards further on he came face to face with Theo Van Spee himself.

'Mr—' Van Spee narrowed his eyes. 'You are Mr Marlow,' he said, but without his usual ring of absolute conviction. 'You work with Mr Laertides, and you're just going to collect a book for him. They have it in stock, but Mr Laertides has in fact not yet paid for it. You will give them a cheque, and Mr Laertides will reimburse you in cash. His favourite colour is grey. You are fond of crème brûlée and zabaglione, but you have never been to Toronto. The key to the problem that has been disturbing you for some time was until recently under your bed; now, however—' He hesitated and frowned a little; his lips moved but no words came out. Then he asked, 'Excuse me, but haven't we met before?'

'I don't think so,' Paul replied.

'Really? For a moment I was sure—' The professor closed his eyes just for a second. When he opened them again, he seemed much more composed. 'Your father loves you very deeply, unlike your mother. You should in future avoid strong drink whenever possible, and the alarm clock on your bedside table is four minutes slow. Quite soon you will cause the death of one of your colleagues, but not two. Something you are relying on is actually worthless and false, but this is no bad thing. You are standing on my left foot.'

'Sorry,' Paul said, and shifted slightly.

'It is of no consequence,' the professor replied, lifting his foot and wincing slightly. 'One of them loves you—' He scowled and shook his head. 'No, that's not true. That is, one of them does indeed love you, but not the one I thought it was or in the way I had anticipated. The fridge is, to a certain extent, the key, but first you must understand properly why you couldn't fix it. You are far less than you used to be, but will be far more in due course. I suggest that you glance at the book before you give it to Mr Laertides, and your worst nightmare will show you the way. Do you happen to have the right time? I fancy my watch is running fast.'

'Um,' Paul said; then he looked at the clock on the wall just behind the professor's head, and told him it was a quarter past ten.

'Thank you,' the professor said. 'I am very sorry to have met you. Good day.'

It took Paul several minutes to recover from all that. Working at JWW, however, had given him the knack of burying his head so deep in the sand that he could practically smell magma, and by the time he passed the front desk – Mr Tanner's mum was back on form again, a slim, curly-haired redhead with freckled shoulders and misty green eyes, but she ignored him completely – he was mostly wondering whether he dared make the most of his trip out of the office and stop off somewhere for a coffee and a snack.

As he crossed the road it occurred to him that Mr Laertides hadn't specified which branch of Waterpebbles. He took out the note he'd been given, and saw that the address was written down there, along with the right department to ask at, and which floor it was on, and of course the title of the book: *The Garden of Chivalry*. Whatever.

'The garden of what?' asked the girl behind the counter.

'Chivalry,' Paul replied. 'Or I suppose it could be cavalry.'

'You sure you don't mean *Landscaping Your Window Box With Alan Titchmarsh*?'

Paul thought for a moment. 'Yes,' he replied. 'Absolutely sure.'

'Oh. Or *Alan Titchmarsh's Big Book of Compost*?'

'Still sure, thanks.'

'Or *An Introduction By Alan Titchmarsh With A Book By Somebody Or Other*?'

'Not even that,' Paul said. 'Sorry.'

The girl shrugged. 'I'll see what I can do,' she said, with the air of a doctor prescribing aspirin for a bad case of death. 'But it doesn't sound like the sort of thing we usually sell.'

Paul nodded. 'Not by Alan Titchmarsh, you mean?'

The girl seemed offended. 'We've got books by other people as well, you know. Baby Spice, Scary Spice—'

'Old Spice?'

She ignored that. 'Desmond Lynam,' she went on, 'Delia Smith, Trinny and Susannah, Jamie whatsisname with the hair, that bloke who does the weather on BBC2. We've got *loads* of books, actually.'

'Great,' Paul said. 'Do you think you could go and have a look for this one?'

She sighed. 'Fine,' she said. 'Wait there.'

Ten minutes later she came back, holding a book and wearing a slightly stunned expression. 'This what you were after?'

'Possibly,' Paul replied. 'Can I have a look at it?'

'What? Oh, I suppose so.' She put it down on the desk and wiped her hands on her jeans. '*The Garden of Chivalry: Illuminated Manuscripts from Fourteenth-Century Saskatchewan*, by Jean-Paul de Saussignac.' She shook her head. 'You sure you want that?'

Paul smiled. 'It's for a friend,' he said.

'Oh, right.' That, apparently, explained everything. 'That'll be thirty-nine ninety-nine, then.'

There followed a circular and rather dreary little discussion about whether or not the book had been paid for in advance; then Paul wrote out a cheque, was issued with the book and a receipt, and left the shop before the girl could change her mind. Out in the fresh air, he caught a hefty reprise of his hangover. *Coffee*, he thought, *and a snack*. Fortunately, there was a Starbucksy sort of place a few yards down the street. He bought a cup of coffee and a custard slice and, not because Professor Van Spee had told him to, oh dear no, but because he had nothing else to beguile his mind with, opened Mr Laertides's book and started to read.

Mostly it was just pictures; a book of pictures of pictures in books, which struck Paul as faintly incestuous. As pictures, they were all right if you liked that sort of thing: knights in armour and droopy-looking women in blue holding flowers, in the margins of columns of strange-looking writing; Latin, he guessed, or possibly Klingon. Attractive in a wishy-washy sort of a way, but rather monotonous after a while; also, whoever had drawn them had a rotten eye for perspective. Here, for instance, was a picture of two men bashing each other up with sharp weapons on a tiny island the size of a rubber dinghy surrounded by unconvincing-looking water. On the opposite page there was a castle; but the men standing outside it shooting arrows and throwing rocks were almost as tall as the walls, and the people inside the castle were just as big, which meant there was only room for four of them. On the next page, a man with a curly beard and two extremely ugly women with wings were hovering in mid-air over the heads of some kneeling people, all of them face-on and looking hopelessly constipated. Facing that was a sort of cartoon strip: the same people appeared in each of the dozen small pictures, and one of them looked like he was carrying a building balanced on his right hand, like a waiter carrying a tray. Not, Paul decided, his cup of tea, particularly when his head felt more than a touch fragile. Silly, most of it, and the rest was just plain dull. *Bet you don't get rubbish like that in an Alan Titchmarsh book.*

'You want another coffee?' asked a voice behind his head. Conscious that he'd been sitting there with an empty cup for some time, taking up floor space that could have been earning revenue, he nodded several times and said, 'Yes, please.'

'Coming right up. You like the cake?'

'Mmm. Yes, fantastic, thanks.'

'You want another slice?'

'No.'

'All right. Just the coffee.'

Paul caught sight of his watch. He'd been there half an hour. 'Actually.' He stood up and closed the book with a snap. 'I have to go now. Thanks all the same.'

'Oh. You don't want the coffee?'

'No.'

'Is poured now already. You take. On the house.'

'It's not that,' Paul said, turning round to face the speaker, 'it's just that I lost track of the time and I'm going to be late, so—'

His mouth might have carried on moving for a split second or so, like the proverbial headless chicken running round the yard, but no words came out. The man who'd spoken to him was half-hidden behind the counter, but Paul could plainly see his round, perfectly circular bald head, balanced on top of a similarly spherical body, like a snowman. At the same moment he remembered a name he'd been groping for at some point in the recent past. Mr Palaeologus, the toothbrush-and-antique-prints man.

'You take,' the round man repeated, his tone of voice making it clear that this was an order rather than a suggestion. 'No money. Present.' He tipped coffee from a mug into a styrofoam cup, and pressed on a lid. 'Also more cake,' he added. 'Custard slice, is very popular. Many women in love with bad men come here to eat, makes them fat but happy.' He fished a slice off the tray with a big pair of steel tongs, dumped it in an open-ended cardboard box, and slid the box into a paper bag. 'Enjoy. You are in love too, maybe. Take mind off.'

Well, Paul thought, *why not?* He didn't wait for a reply, probably because, if it was at all accurate, it'd take way too long. 'Thanks,' he said. 'Thank you very much.'

'Welcome.'

'Um.' There was no point asking, and he had more chance of getting a straight answer out of a Cabinet minister, but even so. 'Do I know you?'

'You do now. Before—' The man shrugged. 'Is possible. I been here many years, many years.'

'You don't sort of run a map-and-toothbrush shop, in your spare time?'

The man looked at Paul as if he was drooling down his lapels. That was presumably a No.

'You don't have a twin brother or anything?'

The man shook his head. 'I come here from the old country twenty-seven years ago. No brother, no sister, not even aunt or second cousin.'

'Ah, right.' One last try, and then he'd done his duty to Curiosity, and could leave. 'The old country,' Paul said. 'Where would that be, exactly?'

'Manitoba,' the man replied. 'In the old days, before the war, we are dukes and counts and princes; much land, much money, we live in great palace. Then the war come and *pfft!* Is very sad, but—' The man shrugged. 'Is very bad, but we come here, we make new life. Is not like old country. Is shit compared to old country, but what you do? Now you take coffee, you take cake, have nice day. Goodbye.'

Manitoba, Paul thought as the door swung shut behind him. *It's all Miss Hook's fault; because if she hadn't been so horrible and so boring, maybe I'd have learned some geography and history and stuff back when I was eleven, and then I'd know where the hell Manitoba is.* Counts and dukes and princes; that sounded sort of eastern European, and of course they were always having wars out that way.

As he started to walk down the street, the book slipped out of its carrier bag and fell on the pavement. He stooped to pick it up; there was a dusty mark on the jacket and one corner was bruised; also, he'd contrived to drop a splodge of custard on the flyleaf. *Wonderful.*

It was getting late, and Mr Laertides would be wondering where the hell he'd got to. In spite of that, Paul got a taxi to Aldgate. As he'd rather expected, Mr Palaeologus's shop wasn't there any more. Then he headed back to the office.

Mr Laertides didn't notice the damage to his book; he took it from Paul's hands, wrote out a pink slip so that he could get the money back, then went on with the paperwork he'd been doing when Paul arrived. No, there wasn't anything else for now. Come back after lunch.

Paul stood in the corridor for a couple of minutes, still holding his cake and his coffee (now stone-cold and dribbling slightly from the air-hole in the lid) trying to decide what he ought to do. It was difficult, mostly because he couldn't quite put his finger on where the problem lay. Last time it had been pretty straightforward: there had been an enemy, Countess Judy, and a clear and present danger. It had taken him quite some time to get involved (though not nearly as long as he'd have liked) but at least he'd known what the problem was. Now, though, he could tell something wasn't right, but this was JWW, where everything was different, weird, not right at all; trying to track down a problem here was like trying to find last year's rain in the ocean – and besides, it wasn't his problem, his fault, his responsibility. More to the point, it wasn't anybody's fault. No, that wasn't strictly true. There was one person who'd failed in their duty, and who had to be made to put that failure right. If he could do that, he'd at least have a vague idea of where to look for the problem. Progress, as the deer said to the caveman who invented the bow and arrow.

On the first floor landing, Paul nearly collided with Ricky Wurmtoter; Paul had stopped to fish a bit of dust out of his eye in front of the mirror that hung there, and Ricky came charging up the passageway like a prop forward. A last-moment sidestep avoided serious impact damage, but most of Paul's coffee went down the front of his jacket.

'Sorry,' Ricky said. 'Wasn't looking where I was going.'

'Doesn't matter,' Paul replied, 'it was cold anyhow.'

'That's all right, then,' Ricky said. 'You're Philip, aren't you? Frank Laertides's assistant. Don't think we've met before, I've been a bit tied up recently, out of the office a lot. Fifty-headed hydra'd somehow managed to wriggle its way into the vaults of the Credit Lyonnais in Basle, real bitch getting at it down there without blowing up half the city, and you know how pernickety the Swiss can be. Eventually managed to flush it out with ultra-sonic waves and nailed it the old-fashioned way – the old cold steel, as Lance Corporal Jones would say. How about you? Settling in?'

'Fine, thanks,' Paul replied. 'I like it here, it's fun.'

'Great.' Ricky smiled at him, then caught sight of the paper bag in his hand. The paper had gone translucent in a couple of places, and the tell-tale yellow of confectioner's custard was peeking through. 'What've you got there, then? Custard slice?'

Paul nodded.

'Mmm, I love them,' Ricky said, shifting his attention away from the bag with a slight but still perceptible effort. 'They've got really great patisseries in Basle, of course, as you'd expect, but even so, I always reckon you can't beat a traditional English custard slice. Probably my favourite, though it's a close call between that and a proper old-fashioned sticky bun.'

Slight pause, as though Ricky was waiting for something. 'Actually,' Paul said, 'you can have this one if you like.'

'No, no, I couldn't.'

'No, really. I've had one already, so it'd just be greedy. Please, be my guest.'

If Ricky fought dragons with the same ferocious energy he brought to battling with his conscience, no wonder the Credit Lyonnais had sent for him straight away. 'Oh, go on, then,' Ricky said, practically snatching the bag from Paul's hand. 'Thanks, that's very kind of you. My shout next time, I know this really great little Monagasque place that does a mean crème tartuffe aux cerises.' He hurried away down the stairs, as though he was afraid that Paul would change his mind.

Shaking his head, Paul went to his office. After a brief, futile attempt to sponge coffee off his jacket with a screwed-up sheet of paper before it stained, he picked up the phone.

'Directory enquiries?'

Rather to his surprise, they were able to give him the number he wanted. He dialled it; it rang through. Holding his breath, he waited.

'Hello?' The voice was thinner, reedier, a little cracked, but Paul's mouth still went dry with fear. He screwed his eyes shut. 'Miss Hook?'

'That's right. Who's this?'

Deep breath. *Here we go.* 'You won't remember me, Miss Hook,' he said, 'but my name's Paul Carpenter, I was in your class back in ninety-one. You—'

'Oh, I remember you,' snarled Miss Hook. 'I remember you very well. You were always fidgeting, playing with bits of paper. You and that Demelza Horrocks.'

'Ah, right,' Paul said. 'Fancy you remembering me after all this time. Anyway, there's something—'

'Never paid attention,' Miss Hook went on, as if he hadn't spoken. 'Weren't interested. I might as well have tried teaching a brick wall. Trying to get homework out of you was a waste of time. And if I told you once, tuck your shirt tails in, straighten your tie, sit up straight—'

'Miss Hook,' Paul interrupted, 'I know I wasn't a very good student . . .'

'That's putting it mildly.'

'And I know I sort of missed out on a lot of stuff we did in class . . .'

'In one ear, out the other. I don't know why I even bothered to try.'

'Well,' Paul said firmly, 'I realise now how stupid that was of me, and I'm sorry. Really I am.'

Pause. 'You called me up after all these years just to apologise?'

'Yes,' Paul said. 'Partly. Also, there were some things I know I missed, and I was just wondering if we could go over them now. Make up for lost time, as it were.'

Paul felt he could hear the expression on her face. 'Isn't it a bit late for that?'

'It's never too late, Miss Hook,' Paul said. 'So, would it be all right? There's just a few specific questions, it won't take long.'

'All right. Though I really don't see what can be so important, thirteen years later.'

'Oh, it's important all right. First—'

Some time later, Paul put the phone down. He was shaking slightly, and his breathing was forced and quick, but he had half a page of notes jotted down on the piece of paper in front of him. They'd cost him more than blood, more than breaking and entering his own worst childhood memories, but they were worth it. Now at least he actually knew something.

He now knew that Manitoba was in Canada, and so was Saskatchewan; that Canada was first colonised by Westerners in the sixteenth century, although there'd been an abortive attempt nearly six hundred years earlier, when a bunch of Vikings led by someone called Leif Eirikson had briefly established a settlement in Labrador. But they'd given up and gone home almost immediately, and for the next six centuries the only inhabitants of Canada had been the indigenous Native American tribes. Aside from a few skirmishes around 1814, the last war fought on Canadian soil had taken place back in the eighteenth century. There were a lot of French-speaking people in Canada, and they were proud of their cultural heritage, but Miss Hook hadn't been able to tell him if they had a distinctly French Canadian school of cuisine; and even if they had, she'd pointed out, it wouldn't have been on the syllabus for eleven-year-olds, though they might just possibly have touched on it in a project or something. She'd also told him a few things about himself at eleven years old that she thought might have slipped his mind, but he hadn't bothered taking notes about them.

Paul read the paper through four or five times, his eyes skating over the scribbled words like a file on hardened steel. Now at least he knew what was wrong, and he had a faint shadow of an idea *why* it was wrong; also why Sophie had vanished and been replaced by Colin the goblin, who Mr Palaeologus was, and why the office had appeared to be deserted when he'd got there that morning. All well and good; but he was no nearer the truth than, say, a twenty-ninth century archaeologist trying to extrapolate the whole of twenty-first-century society from a Coke bottle and a Barbie doll. What he couldn't figure out for the life of him was where Vicky the ex-mermaid or the sword he'd cut the cake with fitted in, or why Mr Laertides moved like second-rate computer animation, or why the TV anchorman's blood on the sword had saved him in the Land of the Dead. Without answers to those questions, he was no better off than he'd been before.

He glanced at his watch. If he was quick and didn't bump into some chatty bastard on the way out, he could be through the front door before they bolted it for the lunch hour. He was hungry, and he had an experiment he wanted to try. If only he was still on flirting terms with Mr Tanner's mum . . . But that would involve long, complex explanations, and probably a slap round the face with her leather-palmed, scale-backed hand. Besides, there was no guarantee that the experiment would work, and if it failed he'd be in no danger at all.

There's never a bakery around when you want one. It felt like he'd been walking for hours before Paul finally stumbled across what he was looking for: a small, crowded sandwich bar under some railway arches, with a queue of office workers backed up into the street. When eventually he got to the head of the line, he saw what he'd been expecting to see. He smiled politely. 'Hello,' he said. 'Your name wouldn't happen to be Palaeologus, would it?'

The short, bald, round-headed man raised both eyebrows at him. 'You what?'

'All right, then. You wouldn't happen to be one of a set of identical triplets?'

'Uh?'

Paul shrugged. 'Never mind,' he said. 'Thought I knew you

from somewhere. Could I have two custard tarts, a custard slice, a custard doughnut and a Danish pastry, please?'

'What flavour Danish?'

'Custard.'

The man handed them over in a paper bag. 'You like custard, don't you?'

'No,' Paul said. 'Well, I can take it or leave it. Thanks.'

Next he needed somewhere quiet and peaceful. Fortunately, he wandered into a small public garden in the middle of a square: some sad-looking flower beds surrounding a patch of threadbare grass, with a few benches and a statue of some old general on a horse. It was still a bit public, and of course there was no prospect at all of any help if something went wrong, but that was only to be expected. And anyway, nothing was going to go wrong, because the experiment wasn't going to work, was it?

Paul began with the Danish, and nothing happened. Next he ate one of the custard tarts. It fell to bits as soon as he'd coaxed it out of its little foil cup, and a cascade of pastry shrapnel tumbled down his shirt-front and into his lap. The custard slice was messier still, and the custard doughnut squidged alarmingly under the pressure of his teeth, shooting sweet-smelling yellow goo up his nose. So far, so futile; and he was just starting to think what a prat he must look, sitting on a park bench on his own gorging himself on cakes, when he looked up and noticed something.

It was the green and brown bronze general, on his anatomically impossible, guano-streaked horse. Two minutes ago, he'd been facing east. Now he was pointing due north.

That was it; nothing else. If Paul hadn't made a point of taking note of every little detail that might possibly be relevant, he'd never have noticed anything, because who the hell pays any attention to mouldy old Victorian statues, or gives a damn which way they're pointing? Nevertheless, he stood up, walked over to the statue and read the inscription on the plinth:

Erected by public subscription in honour of His Royal Highness Louis-Philippe XXII, Prince of Saskatchewan, Grand Duke of

New Brunswick, Elector Palatine, to commemorate the 50th anniversary of the battle of Waterloo.

Fine, Paul thought, *so I proved my point. Now, how the fuck am I supposed to get back out of here?*

Should've thought of that earlier, shouldn't you? chided his inner voice, which was pretty much the sort of remark he'd come to expect from it. He sat down heavily on the bench and tried to rally his thoughts, but he knew he was wasting his time. If this place was where he thought it was, he was beyond help. It wasn't like falling asleep on the bus and having to walk home from the terminus. This was a place he could never walk home from if he marched all day for a thousand years.

Paul was, he knew perfectly well, approaching the problem from the wrong direction. That was another thing he knew; he'd really taken to this knowledge business, making up for lost time. Unfortunately, it was rather like the feeling you have in those dreams where you're both the main player and a spectator, where you watch yourself doing something really stupid but you can't tell yourself not to –

– And maybe that was the whole point, except of course he couldn't see it, not from here. Over there . . . Over there but invisible, sitting on precisely the same few square inches of this very bench, but looking at a mouldy old Victorian statue that faced east instead of north, was his old friend and worst enemy Paul Carpenter; he could feel the smug bastard's eyes watching him, knew for a certainty that bloody Carpenter knew what ought to be done, could most likely do it himself, easy as sneezing, but either couldn't be bothered or was maliciously refusing to help –

No; paranoia. Paul Carpenter was in the same dream, the one where you watch yourself walking out into the unmarked minefield and you yell warnings till your throat's rasped raw but you can't seem to make yourself heard. It was infuriating, because Carpenter was only ninety or two hundred and seventy degrees away, but without the right gadgetry or guaranteed stone-cold reliable method of cheating (damn Mr Tanner's mum to goblin hell for taking the bloody thing from him, just when he really, really needed it) he had no hope whatsoever of establishing contact between himselves. Semaphore wasn't going to get the job done, nor smoke signals, beacon fires, messages in bottles, sky-writing, e-mail or standing on the bench shouting very loud. Possibly, just possibly, if he set off walking in the opposite direction and kept on going right the way round the planet until eventually he came back to this exact spot and faced himself, as in a mirror . . . But there wasn't time for all that. No, it was a mess, and stupid Carpenter had got him into it. All Carpenter's fault. No wonder nobody had liked him in school.

He still had what he knew. He'd won the knowledge the hard way, by living it, not the easy way, reading it in a book or being told by someone who'd been in on the secret all along. He'd dug down deep to get it, as though he'd been retrieving someone else's buried treasure, with only a badly drawn, faded sketch where X marked the spot. And, of course, he'd wormed his way in here without giving any thought to how he was supposed to get out again, because deep down he'd refused to believe that the experiment might work. After all, he'd been basing everything on a hypothesis figured out by a known idiot, someone only a fool would ever believe. But he still had what he knew, for what that was worth—

'Hello, Paul.'

He recognised the voice; no need to turn his head and look at her. 'You,' he said ungraciously. 'Should've expected you'd be here.'

'Really?' The voice was the same, but not the tone. Paul still thought of her primarily as Vicky the mermaid, assuming that that was what she really was. 'Well, clever old you. What led you to that conclusion?'

'Not exactly rocket science, was it?' he thought aloud. 'The whole mermaid thing, for a start. After all, what's the most salient feature of mermaids?'

'Ooh, tricky one. Let's see. Big, dreamy brown eyes.'

'No.'

'Nice smile. Long, wavy hair. Great pair of—'

'No.'

'Good heavens,' she said gravely, 'don't say you look beyond the crudely obvious. Next thing, you'll be thinking with your brain, instead of your other very small organ.'

'Mermaids,' Paul went on, 'transcend elements. They're half creatures of air and half creatures of water. That makes them special.'

'True,' Vicky said, 'though the same goes for dolphins. Also frogs. Are frogs special too?'

'Doesn't matter,' Paul said, 'because you aren't really a mermaid.'

She laughed, very slightly shrill. 'Excellent,' she said. 'Well done. How'd you know?'

He carried on looking straight ahead. He had faith in the medicine, of course, he knew he couldn't really come to harm, catch any nasty visually transmitted emotional disorders, but it wasn't worth taking the risk. 'Your hair,' he said. 'Dark brown, with light streaks. Very distinctive.'

'You like it?'

'I recognised it. I knew I'd seen it before; that pattern, or something really similar. But I couldn't remember. It's like the memory is a book, but where it ought to be on the bookshelf there's a gap. I know there's a memory, but I don't know what it is. And if it's not there any more, the likeliest explanation is that someone's taken it away.'

Vicky sighed. 'I hate that,' she said, 'when someone borrows bits of my mind and forgets to give them back. You know, you're talking a real load of poo here.'

'You think so?' Paul shrugged. 'Trying to reconstruct what that memory might've been, that was a real cow of a job. But then I saw that pattern again. At Mr Tanner's mum's christening party.'

'That's when you died, right?'

He nodded. 'That's when I died. But just before that, I had to cut the stupid cake. And guess what they gave me to cut it with? A bloody great big sword.'

'Oh. Was it a big cake?'

'Enormous. But that's not the point. The point was, they gave me this sword; and the blade was a sort of plum-brown colour, with these really cute silver whorls and tendrils and what have you – not inlays or etched on or anything like that, they were right deep down in the metal. I think it's called damascening. I may have seen it on a history documentary or something.'

'Fascinating. What's that got to do with anything?'

'And I was thinking,' Paul went on, 'there's other things that transcend elements, as well as mermaids. Swords, for instance. Not,' he added, 'that I'm an expert. I mean, I could write out everything I know about metalworking in big capital letters on the back of a postage stamp and still have room for my name and address. But if I remember right – from this history programme I'm guessing I must've seen at some point, or else how would I know any of this shit? – if I'm right, a sword starts off as iron ore deep in the ground – that's earth – and then it gets heated up till it's red-hot – that's fire; and you get fire hot by blowing it with a bellows, so that's air, too—'

'Technically,' said Vicky, 'though I think you're pushing it.'

'And then,' Paul said, 'you make it hard and tough by dunking it in water; and there's your complete set. Earth, air, fire, water. A sword is equally at home in all four.'

'Assuming you're counting air,' Vicky objected. 'I still think that one's a bit iffy, myself.'

'I don't agree. I think a sword transcends all the elements. Which is why, I think, when Viking warriors died, they always had their swords buried along with them, because something that transcends elements like that is something you *can* take with you. Don't you think?'

'Nah. I think it's because they hated their relatives, so they wanted to make sure they didn't leave them any nice stuff when they snuffed it. People can be so petty. I had an uncle—'

'No,' Paul said. 'I don't believe you ever had an uncle, or any relatives of any sort. I think that when the goblins stabbed me at that party and I died, I took the sword with me, because swords transcend the elements. That's why I still had it in my hand when I woke up in that TV studio; and it must've been real, because there was real blood on it, just enough to keep me from fading away.'

'TV studio? I never knew you'd been on telly.'

'I don't think I was,' Paul replied. 'I think it was the goblin afterlife; I went there because I got killed by goblins, I'm a little bitty part goblin myself, and a TV show where they play back the shittiest moments of your life and ask you to comment on them is exactly the sort of thing you'd expect to find in the goblin hereafter. Which is why,' he added, with a slight shudder, 'I'm reasonably sure I didn't actually kill somebody, even though I cut off that bloke's head. I don't think he was real; at the very most, he was some kind of goblin angel, and I'm guessing he wasn't killed in any meaningful sense—'

'You *killed* someone? Why would you do a thing like that?'

'But,' Paul went on, 'later on, when I licked the blood off the sword, it was real blood, real enough to get me out of there, and that must be because being in contact with the sword *made* it real, because swords transcend the elements. They must do, actually,' he added, 'or else how could I have had a hand to hold it with, when I'd just died? That's it, must be. Touching the sword kept me real, or at any rate real enough. Is that right? Is that how it works?'

'What're you asking *me* for?'

'Well,' Paul said, 'you ought to know better than anybody. It was you, wasn't it? You're it. Brown hair with curly bright streaks in it, just like the patterns in the blade. You're the sword they gave me to cut the cake with. Well, aren't you?'

Pause.

'No,' Vicky said.

Deep in the smelly recesses of Paul's mind, a nasty thought stirred: the thought that he'd been barking up entirely the wrong tree, and he'd just made the nuttiest speech of his entire life to one of his work colleagues, who'd lose no time in telling everybody else around the office that he was barking mad and very, very strange indeed—

'No,' Vicky repeated, 'but you're close.'

'Am I? Oh good.'

'Very close, actually. But you're wrong about that. I'm not a sword. I'm a girl.'

'Oh. Right. Sorry.'

'Perfectly all right. I'm a girl, but the sword is my other half.' She paused. 'Is none of this ringing any bells?'

'No,' Paul confessed. 'No, it isn't.'

'Really?' She clicked her tongue. 'That Ricky Wurmtoter. Next time I see him, I'm going to kick his arse from here to Dagenham.'

Paul considered what she'd just said. 'Splendid idea and it's high time somebody did, but why? What's he got to do with anything?'

Vicky sighed. 'Because he was supposed to have told you all about it, when he gave you the sword. Only, of course, obviously he didn't. Tell you, I mean. Or give you the sword, apparently, because didn't you just say the goblins gave it to you?'

'Yes. Or rather,' Paul added, 'it just sort of appeared. Fell out of thin air. I assumed it came from them—' He paused; something about the handle being wrapped in pink ribbon, and goblins are allergic to pink. 'Presumably,' he said, 'but—'

'Whatever. Fact remains, bloody Wurmtoter screwed up again. Nice enough bloke, quite cute, great bum, but about as reliable as a petrol-station watch. It was just like that while we were married.'

'Just a second,' Paul couldn't help interrupting. 'You were married to Ricky Wurmtoter?'

Another sigh. 'Don't rub it in,' she said. 'Yup, Ricky and me, we go way back. But that's none of your business. I was explaining,' she went on, 'about magic swords and other halves. But clearly I was boring you, because—'

'Sorry. Please go on. It's very interesting, really.'

'Well—' she began. But Paul wasn't listening. A memory was starting to bleed through the walls of his mind; a memory of himself and Ricky Wurmtoter sitting together in a very strange pub, not long after the conclusion of the whole Countess Judy business—

'Her name is Skofnung,' Ricky had told Paul, as he stared at the ferocious-looking sword that Ricky had just laid on the table in front of him. 'Used to belong to King Hrolf Kraki. Go on, take a closer look. Rather a nice pattern, I think.'

Paul remembered how he'd gripped the scabbard with his left hand and pulled the blade out an inch or so. To his surprise, it wasn't bright and shiny; the blade was dark brown, with intricate patterns of silver specks and whorls. 'Damascus steel,' Ricky explained, or at least Paul guessed it was meant as an explanation. 'You never find two the same, which makes it easier, of course.'

'Makes what easier?'

Ricky narrowed his eyes. 'Finding her, of course,' he said; then, 'I forgot, you obviously don't know. It's a living sword, right?'

'Is it? I mean, right, yes. Obviously.'

Ricky laughed. 'A living sword,' he said, 'is special because it has a life of its own – which is good, because it knows what it's doing when in use, so you don't have to. But it does mean that you have to find its other half before it's much good for anything, and,' he added, with a slight grimace, 'I have to admit, I never did find her. And without the other half, of course, it's pretty much useless.'

'Other half.'

'That's right. A living sword has a human counterpart, and once you find – oh, excuse me.' Ricky had stopped there and gone off to see someone he wanted to talk to, and he never had got round to finishing the explanation. For his part, Paul had just about managed to override the very strong instinct that had urged him to find a river or canal to throw the horrible thing into, because no doubt Ricky would be mortally offended if he ever found out. Instead, he'd taken it home and shoved it away out of sight under the sofa, and had never looked at it or thought about it since.

'I remember,' Paul said. 'Yes, that's right.'

'Excuse me?'

'I remember,' Paul repeated. 'I remember, I remember, I remember. There *was* a sword. Ricky Wurmtoter *did* give it to me, in a pub, just after—'

'Fine,' Vicky said, 'that's all right, then. You've just saved Ricky from a very unpleasant experience which would, just for once, have been entirely undeserved. I wish you'd remembered it earlier, saved me a whole lot of explaining, and—'

'That was it,' Paul said, 'the memory I knew I'd had but couldn't find, the one I was looking for. It was Ricky and me, in that pub.' He frowned; implications and logical conclusions and all sorts of other horrible things were swooping round his head like killer bats. 'In which case,' he said, 'how the hell did it come to be falling out of the air at the christening? It should still be on my floor, covered in dust and bits of fluff.'

'You mean you don't hoover regularly under the sofa? I'm shocked. What would your mother think if she knew?'

'And you're—'

'Hoo-bloody-ray, we finally got there in the end. Yes, I'm the other half Ricky told you about. He *did* tell you about that, didn't he?'

Paul nodded. 'He said he could never use the sword because – well, he never found you.'

'Arsehole,' Vicky said succinctly. 'Never bothered looking, more like. Anyway, there we are. And yes, you were right, at least as far as you went. You survived the christening party because my other half kept you real, because it transcends elements, as you so elegantly put it. Actually, you'd be amazed how many perfectly ordinary everyday objects do exactly the same thing, not just swords. Humdrum kitchen appliances that you take for granted, every bit as good; and the only reason Viking heroes weren't buried with electric kettles and fridge-freezers is that they hadn't been invented yet. But you're on the right lines at last; slowly, painfully, by incredibly tortuous routes, a bit like a second-class letter, but you're getting there. The only big question you don't seem to have addressed yet is, why didn't you pay attention in history and geography when you were in school?'

Oddly enough, precisely the same question had just crossed Paul's mind; and so remarkable was the coincidence that he broke his resolution and looked round at her – except she wasn't there any more. She'd gone, and he was alone on a bench in a small public garden with a mouldy old Victorian statue of an east-facing man on a horse.

East-facing. That was what mattered. Everything else – swords, mermaids, elements transcended or otherwise, goblins, decapitated TV anchormen and even Audumla the Great Cow of Heaven – was just trivia compared to the single joyful fact that the mouldy statue's horse's head, on which a rather disreputable-looking pigeon had just landed, was pointing due east rather than due north. *I'm back*, Paul thought. *Back from exactly where I am right now. Isn't that just the most amazing thing ever?*

His legs were weak and wobbly when he put his weight on them, and he staggered a few times before they started working again, but he took no notice. The first priority was to get the hell out of there, as far away from the mouldy old statue and the bench and the small public garden as he could go before his strength gave out and he fell over.

In the event, he found he'd underestimated himself; he contrived to stay upright as far as a bus stop and rested for a minute or so, hanging from the concrete stand. Then a bus seemed to materialise out of nowhere, and by some freaky chance it happened to be going to St Mary Axe. By some equally weird coincidence, the driver was a short, bald man with a perfectly spherical head resting on top of a minimalist neck and a wide slough of chins, like an egg in an eggcup.

Paul fetched up outside Number 70 on the stroke of two o'clock. Perfect. He'd escaped from wherever the hell it was that his insane curiosity had led him into, and he wasn't even late for work. He wasn't wobbling at all when he strolled through the door and past reception—

'There you are, at bloody last.' Mr Tanner's mum wasn't at her usual place behind the front desk. Instead, her son was standing in the doorway, with a scowl on his face that stripped away Paul's feeling of vague euphoria like Fairy Liquid cutting through grease. 'Where the hell have you been? We thought you'd skipped the country or something.'

Not fair, wailed Paul's inner child; so *not fair*. 'But it's just gone two, I'm not late,' he started to protest. But the words never got past Customs; because before he'd got as far as *just*, the front door slammed and four very large goblins stepped up behind him and twisted his arms behind his back.

Paul opened his mouth to yell at the pain, but fear muted out his voice. There was something very wrong here, far worse than sloppy timekeeping. Mr Tanner was staring at him as though he was trying to remove his liver and spleen just by looking. Not good at all.

'Well?' said Mr Tanner.

It took Paul a moment to remember how his mouth worked. 'Sorry,' he said, 'I don't understand.'

'You don't. Is that right.' Mr Tanner flared his nostrils; a goblin thing, Paul assumed. He could do it himself, sometimes, a bit. 'Well, in that case I'd better bring you up to speed. It's Dietrich Wurmtoter.'

Dietrich? Oh, *Ricky*. 'What about him?'

'He's dead.'

Dead. Dead what? Dead lucky, dead annoying, Vicky the non-mermaid had thought at some stage he was dead cute, but apparently not any more. Or could Mr Tanner possibly mean—?

'Dead?'

Mr Tanner lifted and lowered his head slowly. 'Dead. In his office.' His little round eyes glowed, with a flash of the genuine goblin red. 'He was murdered.'

'*Murd*—' Paul cut off the word before he choked on it. 'Did you just say—?'

'Poisoned,' Mr Tanner said. 'Absolutely no doubt.'

'But—' Paul couldn't move enough to gesture his disbelief, because of the goblins holding on to his arms. 'That's so – Have you got any idea who might've done it?'

'Oh yes, we know who did it, all right. And we've got all the proof we need'

Paul waited for a second, but Mr Tanner just carried on glaring at him, so he asked, 'Go on, then; who was it?'

Mr Tanner grinned, like an open wound. 'You.'

CHAPTER EIGHT

A ll the evidence they could possibly need.

'We have four witnesses who saw you with it,' Mr Tanner was saying. 'My mother, on reception when you came back; Christine and Benny Shumway both saw you carrying it with you on the way to Frank Laertides's room; and Frank says you were still carrying it when he sent you away. One custard slice, in an open-ended cardboard box inside a paper bag. The same custard slice that Ricky was eating when he suddenly collapsed, started screaming and died. He'd eaten about a third of it.'

'Custard slice?' Paul remembered: the coffee bar, the round-headed man who'd told him about leaving Manitoba because of the war. He'd made Paul take on a cup of coffee and another custard slice; and Ricky had bumped into him in the corridor—

'I was there when it happened,' Mr Tanner went on. 'Me and Cas Suslowicz and Sophie Pettingell, we all saw it. He took the cake out of the bag, mentioned that he'd met you in the passage and you'd given it to him. He said how generous you were, and wondered how you knew custard slices were his favourite. Then he dropped to the ground, and two minutes later he was dead.' Mr Tanner nodded at the four goblins, who tightened their grip on Paul a little. 'Just to make sure,' he went on, 'I had Frank Laertides analyse it; he's a fully qualified forensic sorcerer. He says there's enough arsenic in what's left of that cake to poison a small army.' Mr Tanner folded his arms. 'I wonder if there's anything you'd like to say at this point.'

'Yes, there bloody is,' Paul yelped. 'I didn't do it.'

Mr Tanner frowned. 'Anything apart from that,' he said. 'The truth, for instance.'

Paul knew better than to struggle, with four goblins holding on to him. 'It didn't happen like that, like you just said. Yes, I brought a cake back with me—'

'A custard slice?'

'Yes, a custard slice, in a box, in a bag, just like you said. And yes, I bumped into Ricky in the corridor. But I didn't offer him the bloody thing, he dropped these really heavy hints, about how custard slice was his favourite.'

'I see,' Mr Tanner said calmly. 'And then you offered it to him, and he took it.'

'No.' Paul scowled. 'Sorry, actually yes. But only because he made it obvious he wanted the stupid thing. What I mean is, I didn't bring it back on purpose to give to him.'

Mr Tanner's lips curled in an expression that was a smile the way a young, hungry lion is a kitten. 'I see,' he said. 'You offered him the cake, he took it, but it's nothing like what I just said. All right,' he went on, 'tell me where you got the cake from.'

'It was this little sandwich place,' Paul said. 'Kind of like a poor man's Starbucks, just a few yards down the road from the Waterpebbles where I got Frank – Mr Laertides's book.'

'Book.'

'That's right. Didn't Mr Laertides tell you? He sent me out to pick up a book he'd ordered in Waterpebbles.'

'Right.' Mr Tanner's scowl deepened. 'You're quite sure about that?'

'Of course. You just ask Fr—'

'Mr Laertides doesn't seem to remember it quite like that,' Mr Tanner said. 'He told me you vanished for a while, didn't say where you'd been when you got back, and you had a styrofoam cup of coffee and a cake box in a bag with yellow showing through. He didn't say anything about any book.'

'But it's there. On his desk.'

It hadn't been, of course. When Mr Tanner went to look,

there was no sign of a big book full of pictures of medieval Canadian illuminated manuscripts; and when Paul told him what he'd seen in the book, Mr Tanner just looked straight past him, as though he was pretending for Paul's own benefit that he hadn't heard it. He even sent Christine to see if she could find the sandwich bar; and needless to say she couldn't. No trace of it to be seen, she reported back. The location Paul had described, she added, was the lingerie department of Marks & Spencer, it wasn't even a separate shop.

Mr Tanner reported her findings to Paul in the strong room, where he'd been locked in, closely watched by the four large goblins. They hadn't said a word while he'd been waiting for Christine to get back, but they'd stared at him a lot, and two of them had mimed chewing food, and grinned. He really didn't want to think what they meant by that.

'So what are you going to do?' Paul asked, when Mr Tanner had finished telling him about Christine's expedition. 'Are you going to call the police?'

Mr Tanner almost sort of laughed. 'I don't think so,' he said. 'We prefer to deal with this sort of thing ourselves. Security, you see. Besides,' he went on, 'if we had you arrested for murder all they'd do is lock you up in prison for the rest of your life, and what good would that do anybody?' He sighed. 'Much better if we handle it our way – which we're fully entitled to do, of course, since we own you. That way, it's just an accountancy issue. Writing off a dead loss, as it were.'

Paul really didn't like the sound of that. 'But this is stupid,' he said. 'I didn't kill anybody, really. I went to that coffee-bar place—'

'The one that doesn't exist.'

'Yes, but lots of things don't exist where you lot are concerned, you know that better than I do. It was probably a magic sandwich bar.'

'Really.' Mr Tanner raised an eyebrow; if he'd been taller, faintly greenish and had had pointed ears, he'd probably have said, *Fascinating.* 'What's the difference between a magic sandwich bar and an ordinary one?'

'I went there,' Paul said grimly, 'and I had a coffee and a

custard slice. Then when I was about to go, the bloke said have another coffee, on the house; and another slice of cake. I said I had to get back to the office, he said I could have them to take out. I didn't want to hurt his feelings, so I said yes.'

'I see. And he gave you a poisoned cake. Any idea why?'

'No, of course not.'

'You hadn't upset him or anything?'

'No. At least, I don't think so. I asked him if he had a twin brother who ran a fine-art-and-toothbrush shop, and he said no, he came from Manitoba, he'd left there because of the war.'

'What war?'

Paul shrugged. 'The Canadian civil war, I suppose. Only of course—'

'Ah,' said Mr Tanner, 'that war. Before you follow this line any further,' he went on, 'maybe I ought to mention that in the sorcerer community we don't actually recognise insanity pleas as a valid defence to a murder charge. Just thought I'd tell you that, before you sprain your imagination.'

Paul drew a deep breath, because he'd need a lot of air if he was going to explain about Canada, and Miss Hook, and custard, not to mention swords and mermaids and various other related issues. But as he did so he caught sight of the look in Mr Tanner's eye and decided it could probably wait until later. Until after they'd had him ritually killed, for example. Instead, he said, 'Really, I didn't do it. Why would I want to do a thing like that, anyway?'

Mr Tanner shrugged. 'We were hoping you'd tell us that,' he said. 'We did sort of wonder.'

'Because,' Paul went on, 'there's absolutely no reason why I'd want to hurt him, let alone kill him. He saved my life once. Well,' Paul amended, 'he sort of saved it. And he took me out to lunch on my first day here, which was a really nice gesture. All right, he did kill me that one time, but that was a total misunderstanding, he thought it was all perfectly OK, and I didn't hold a grudge or anything.'

Mr Tanner frowned. 'He killed you? You've got that a bit arse-about-face, surely.'

'No, he killed me, with a crossbow.' Paul stopped short;

because, of course, Ricky Wurmtoter hadn't shot Phil Marlow with a crossbow, he'd shot Paul Carpenter—

The same penny appeared to have dropped in Mr Tanner's mind, though it bounced off in a different direction. 'A crossbow,' Mr Tanner said. 'I remember the late Paul Carpenter telling some sort of cockamamy story about Wurmtoter shooting him with a crossbow. Are you saying he shot you too? Because—'

'Sorry,' Paul said desperately, 'I was, um, mixing him up with someone else I once knew. So, please forget I said that. Red herring. The fact is,' he went on, 'I only actually met him for the very first time today, when he asked me for that bloody cake. Why'd I want to kill someone I'd never even met before?'

Mr Tanner shook his head. 'Lots of people do that,' he said. 'Soldiers, for instance. Also, more to the point, assassins and hired killers. Would that happen to be a sideline of yours, by any chance?'

That notion was so absurd that Paul started to laugh, but he didn't get very far. There was a look in Mr Tanner's eyes that soaked up laughter like blotting paper. 'No,' Paul said. 'No, it isn't. I never killed anybody in my life.'

'Until today.'

'Not even today,' Paul said; and as he spoke, he recalled the graceful arc the TV anchorman's head had described as it sailed through the air. 'I gave him a cake. That's different. Obviously someone wanted to kill me, and—'

'Right. And why would he want to do that?'

Paul shrugged. 'I already told you, I haven't got a clue. Maybe *he* didn't know the stupid thing was poisoned. Maybe it was all an accident or something, I don't know. Look, why don't you ask Mr Laertides? He'll tell you, I'm not the killing-people sort.'

'Frank Laertides told us about the cake,' Mr Tanner said quietly. 'He's as shocked and appalled as the rest of us. Blames himself, he said.'

That was a singularly nasty moment; because Mr Laertides was the only person who could corroborate the story about how Paul Carpenter turned into Phil Marlow. It had crossed Paul's mind several minutes ago that one way out of the mess would be to turn back. It'd be embarrassing, sure enough, and there'd be a lot of very awkward questions, but at least he wouldn't be a murder suspect. Phil Marlow would simply disappear, and Paul Carpenter would come back again, like a soap-opera character stepping out of the shower. But Paul wasn't at all sure that he could turn himself back without Mr Laertides's help; and now it seemed that either Mr Laertides believed he was a cold-blooded killer, or else he was trying to frame him . . .

'I think I've had about enough of you for one day,' Mr Tanner said. 'We're having a partners' meeting in an hour to decide what to do with you. Shouldn't take long. In the meantime, you'll stay here. You can try and escape if you feel so inclined, but then my third and fifth cousins here will rip you into shreds and eat you, and there's a remote chance that that'll be a nastier way to die than the one we decide on at the meeting. Up to you, really. I wouldn't want to influence your decision one way or another.'

The door snapped shut behind him. Paul could hear soft, muffled clicks as the wards of the lock dropped into place. Between him and the door stood the four goblins; they were watching him the way Hong Kong gourmets study the restaurant carp pool.

He wondered what on earth he was going to say to Mr Dao this time.

Probably it wouldn't be so bad, not once he'd settled in. What was it Mr Dao had said? *Nothing to hope for, nothing to be afraid of.* He had, of course, an incredible advantage over all other human beings who'd ever stared death in the face before; been there, done that, got the winding sheet. He knew exactly what was coming next; and sure, it was a swizzle that he'd miss out on the rest of his life, all the years he could reasonably have expected to live – the balance of his miserable, insecure twenties, followed by the stressed-out thirties, responsibility-laden forties, gradually dwindling fifties, over-the-hill sixties, decrepit seventies and so on, assuming he'd ever have made it that far. There would be spring, summer, autumn, winter that he wouldn't be there to see, and life would go on for everybody else. But, in all fairness, he couldn't really get terribly worked up about that, since he'd always have been Paul Carpenter, for whom life would always prove to be a parcel excitingly wrapped in brightly coloured Christmas paper, containing socks. The edge of the scythe is no big deal; it comes sooner or later, and once it's done its job, everything falls into a perspective so vast that none of it could possibly matter. People are mostly afraid of death because of the pain it'll bring to those who love and need them; but Paul had been to his own funeral, seen the dry eyes and the remarkably small amount of grief and misery his absence had caused. Nothing to hope for; nothing to be afraid of. It wasn't what he'd have chosen for himself, and on a fundamental level it was bitterly unfair, to the point where, if he'd had the time and the stationery, he might even have written to the papers or his MP about it, maybe even thought about starting up a pressure group – People Against Death, or the Anti-Mortality Network. But it could so easily have been a whole lot worse. Somebody might've given a damn.

He still couldn't decide on what to say to Mr Dao. *Fourth time unlucky* was a bit too flip; *I'm back* a trifle understated. He toyed with *You call this an awfully big adventure?* but there was the risk that Mr Dao wouldn't get the reference. Like it mattered, anyhow. Very soon there'd be nothing left of him at all, and in all conscience he couldn't see how that'd be a great loss to the universe. Or to himself.

The goblins were scowling at Paul, all fiery red eyes and pointy teeth. At any other time he'd have been scared stiff, but now there was nothing to be afraid of; and it was a bit dull, just sitting here. He looked at the biggest goblin and smiled.

'Hey,' he said, 'you. Turd-face.'

The goblin didn't like that; Paul could see him making an effort to control his temper. It was amusing, really.

'I'm talking to you,' he said. 'Here, you fancy a game of cards or something?'

The goblin sneered, baring further and sharper teeth. Paul shrugged. 'Screw you, then. You'd only have lost, anyway. I can tell just by looking at you that you're really, really stupid as well as incredibly ugly. Also,' he added after a moment's reflection, 'you smell. Not as badly as the other three, I grant you, but pretty bad nonetheless. Tell me, are you soluble in water or just totally slobby?'

The goblin just stood and stared, and Paul gave up. *We've got to stop meeting like this*? Nah, too clichéd. *Mr Dao, I presume?* A bit lacking in sparkle. Probably better just to smile politely and ask where the lavatories were.

'*Pssst.*'

He frowned. It was a goblin voice; sibilants through a mouthful of very long teeth are quite distinctive. But none of the four guards had said anything, and he was pretty sure it had come from behind him.

'*It's me. Don't look round.*'

Interesting. Maybe not interesting enough to stay alive for, but Paul's curiosity was piqued. Also, he didn't much feel like looking round anyway; he knew the strongroom – there was nothing on that wall apart from shelves and a few battered old tin boxes.

'*It's me,*' the voice repeated, '*Colin. Wanted to ask you; you still got those Van Spee crystals?*'

Colin. Colin, Colin. Oh yes; the goblin he'd met in the pub, who'd offered him four million pounds for the rest of the crystals he'd stolen from the jar in the professor's desk; also, the goblin who'd briefly replaced Sophie in St James's Park. Hence, presumably, the inquiry. Very slowly he lifted his head, then pressed his chin against his chest.

'*Swap. I rescue you, for the crystals. Deal?*'

Paul repeated the manoeuvre. One of the guards looked up, but only briefly. *Why not?* Paul thought. *They won't be any good to me where I'll be going if I don't get out of here quickly.*

'*Done. Stay still, don't move.*'

At last; orders he could obey to the letter. Annoyingly, the tip of his nose chose that moment to start itching, but he ignored it.

The light went out.

Cursing and clattering over in the direction of the doorway told Paul where the goblins were; also, low muttered bitching about which of them was supposed to have brought the torch. Assuming it was Colin who'd somehow doused the light (a single shadeless sixty-watt bulb, Paul remembered from earlier visits), he didn't see how it was going to help, since the guards were still very much in place between him and the door, which was the only way out. So: neat trick, but he was underwhelmed. He yawned slightly.

Then someone grabbed him by the sleeve and hissed, 'Come *on*!' in a rather frantic whisper. Paul stood up and allowed the invisible hand to guide him, until his shin banged into something hard and thin; his best guess was, the shelves on the back wall. Conclusion: Colin was taking him in the wrong direction. *Goblins*, Paul thought, with an unuttered sigh.

'*Now*,' the voice said in his ear. Before he could ask, '*Now what?*' or anything along those lines, a heavy boot kicked the backs of his knees, folding him up like a newly ironed shirt, and a solid hand in the small of his back shoved him forward, off balance. He grabbed for a support to stop himself going down flat on his face, but there wasn't anything to grab on to. He felt himself lurch forward. He was falling.

Squelch.

Even before he'd spat out the mouthful he'd unintentionally ingested, Paul knew what he'd fallen into, because it was practically inevitable. Soft, squidgy, and he was wallowing in the stuff. *So this is what it's like to be a prune*, he thought as he felt himself starting to sink. There are many terrible ways to die, and during his more morbid moments he'd speculated about quite a few of them, but drowning in custard wasn't a possibility he'd ever addressed. Short-sighted of him, he realised, bearing in mind just how lousy his luck could be.

Then a hand grabbed the collar of his jacket; there was an unspeakably vulgar slurpy-sucking noise, and he was out of the custard, back into the air. He tried to open his eyes, but they were gummed shut with the foul stuff, and by the time he'd wiped it out of the way with his knuckles he'd been stood upright again, like a toy soldier. He wobbled a bit until he got his balance back, and looked round.

Oh, for crying out loud, Paul thought, *I'm still in the bloody strongroom; that horrible little goblin's screwed up the rescue, and I'm back where I—* But then he noticed a couple of significant details. No guards. Oil light lit. Door open.

'There you go,' said Colin the goblin, slapping him offensively on the back. 'Piece of cake, no pun intended. Right, where are those crystals?'

'Hang on.' Paul turned until he could see the goblin, who'd

been standing behind him. 'Give me a moment, will you?' The goblin nodded. Paul took a couple of deep breaths and knuckled away a bit more custard from his eyes and face. Then, with a degree of speed and agility he didn't think himself capable of, he whirled round and grabbed Colin's throat in both hands.

'What the fuck—' Colin spluttered, and then found he was a bit short on air.

'Quiet,' Paul snapped. 'Right.' *First things first,* he thought. 'Thanks,' he said politely. 'For rescuing me, I mean.'

The rest of Colin's face was turning as red as his eyes, and he was gurgling like the last quarter-pint of water going down the plughole. Paul took that as meaning *'you're welcome,'* and nodded.

'Next,' he went on, 'if you ever do anything like that to me again, I'm going to squeeze your neck till your head bursts. Got that?'

Colin nodded a little; enough to be going on with. 'Sure?' Paul asked. Another nod, accompanied by a sort of wheezy snort. He let go, and Colin flopped to the ground in a messy heap.

'That's all right, then,' Paul said briskly. 'You bastard,' he added, 'just look at me, I'm all covered in bloody *custard.'* Replaying that one in his mind, Paul had to admit he was probably stating the extremely obvious. 'Now then,' he went on, 'how do we get out of here?'

'Door,' muttered Colin, and waved a claw.

'Yes, I can see that, thank you very much.' Paul sighed. 'I wasn't talking about the room, actually. I meant this – this whatever it is, where we are now. This dimension thing.' He shrugged. 'Custardspace, or whatever you want to call it. Only, I've been in it already once today, and I know how you get yourself into it, but not how you leave. Presumably you know the answer to that.'

Colin the goblin scowled up at him, his red eyes bright with loathing and terror. 'Yup,' he said. 'And there's no need to go strangling me when I've just saved your stupid life.'

'I didn't strangle you,' Paul pointed out. 'I just squashed your neck a bit. Quite a big difference.'

'All right, whatever. Now,' said Colin, getting to his feet (*he* wasn't covered in custard from head to foot, Paul couldn't help noticing), 'give me those bloody crystals, or you can stay here for ever for all I care.'

Paul smiled. 'Haven't got them on me, sorry,' he said. 'You think I'd carry something as valuable as that around in my trousers pocket? No, you want them, you get me out of here and I'll fetch them for you. Can't say fairer than that.'

Colin the goblin seemed to take the announcement very badly; his eyes widened, and he growled like a dog. 'Fucking humans,' he said angrily, 'no *principles*. No wonder our lot don't want to have anything to do with you people. Quite apart from the fact that you're all ugly as hell. You might've mentioned you didn't have the stupid things on you, before we started this.'

'Yeah, right,' Paul said. 'Because if I'd told you that, I'd still be in there. You wouldn't have rescued me if you'd known I hadn't got the stuff with me.'

'Absolutely right,' Colin replied crisply. 'For the simple reason that we need Van Spee's crystals to get out of here. Without them we're – what's the word I'm looking for, begins with an S? Screwed; no, but pretty close. Stranded, that's it. No crystals, we're here for ever.'

Oh, Paul thought. *Bummer.* 'You idiot,' he snapped guiltily, 'why the hell didn't you mention that before—?'

'Because I naturally assumed . . .' Colin the goblin waved his arms in the air in a gesture of wretched resignation; he looked like a very small, wizened actor performing Greek tragedy in semaphore. 'Serves me right for thinking one of you lot'd have the brains to figure it out. Van Spee crystals—' He sighed, and sat down cross-legged on the ground, like Rumpelstiltskin in a book of fairy tales. 'That's what they do,' he said sadly. 'That's why they're so incredibly valuable. They're how you get in here.'

Paul frowned. 'That's not right,' he said. 'You get in here by gorging yourself on custard. I proved it, by experiment. Or wallowing about in the stuff, apparently. But custard's definitely the key.'

Colin sighed again, longer, louder and sadder. 'That's where you're wrong. Custard's not the key, it's the door. Van Spee's

crystals are the key.' He frowned; allergic to metaphors, probably, unless the mental image of a custard door was doing strange
things to the inside of his head. 'Look,' he said, 'this is neither
the time nor the place for a magic-theory tutorial. Bottom line is,
guzzling custard on its own doesn't fetch you here, otherwise the
place'd be crowded out, standing room only. You need to have
swallowed the crystals first; they do something to you on the
atomic level, they sort of make it so you can slide in through the
mesh. Once you're in, though, you need another dose to get out
again. Otherwise—'

'Hang on,' Paul interrupted. 'That time in St James's Park.
Did you know all this back then?'

Colin shook his head. 'It was that set me trying to find out
about the stuff,' he replied. 'All I knew about it at that time was
how much it was worth. But I thought, if you'd gone to all the
trouble and risk of stealing so much of the stuff right out of the
professor's desk – well, I assumed you must know what it does,
or why nick it in the first place?'

Paul winced. Easy mistake to make; so was treading on a
landmine. 'This is the first I've heard of it,' he said heavily, 'what
you've just told me. I mean, I sort of figured a bit of it out from
first principles; like, how this place exists, kind of at right angles
to the real world, and how it had something to do with stupid
bloody custard. But I thought—'

'Whatever.' Colin shrugged. 'You write it up for the scientific
journals and send me a copy. Meanwhile, we're stuck in here for
ever and ever, so really it's not amazingly helpful agonising over
how we got here in the first place.' He scowled; then a look of
great bewilderment crossed his face. 'What did you say just
now?'

'Several things,' Paul pointed out. 'Which particular—?'

'You said,' Colin continued, 'you said this is the second time
today you've been in here.'

'Perfectly true, actually.'

'Great,' Colin said. 'So you know how to get out again.'

Paul couldn't help grinning. 'Absolutely right, I know precisely how you go about it, and not a crystal in sight. All you
actually need is the other half of a living sword.'

'A what?'

'Well might you ask. Me, I haven't got a clue. But it worked fine earlier on, that's all I'm saying.' With a long, dreary sigh Paul sat down on the floor, next to Colin. 'Look,' he said. 'It seems like we're in the shit so deep we need a pair of extra-long snorkels. How'd it be if we pigeon-holed stressing out and scoring points off each other for now, and tried to figure out a way of escaping? I mean,' he added, as Colin frowned at the bewildering novelty of the idea, 'you obviously know a lot of stuff about these things, clearly much more than I do—'

'A small cottage loaf knows more about magic than you do.'

'Very true,' Paul admitted, 'and the bit I know is a bit more than I'd like, believe me. On the other hand, your choice of people to cooperate with is rather limited right now, and you never know, I might come in useful. Also,' he added quickly, 'I've got that jar of crystals back home. If we get out of this in one piece, they're yours. No charge.'

A slight quiver of nose and ear told Paul that he finally had Colin's undivided attention. 'Well,' the goblin said eventually, 'I suppose it can't hurt; fool's luck and all that. And if getting out of here turns out to involve getting things down off high shelves, I guess you'd be better at that than me. All right, you're on.' He paused. 'Got any ideas?'

Paul shook his head. 'But I might have,' he added, 'if only I had just the faintest glimmer of a notion of what the hell's going on here. For instance: what's with this whole custard thing?'

'You mean you—?' Bewilderment, contempt, even a faint trace of amusement. 'Well, for pity's sake,' Colin said, 'everybody knows *that*. Even humans.'

Paul shook his head. 'Everybody except me.'

Colin stretched out his legs; cramp, probably. 'It's totally basic, really. The world is made up out of four elements, right? Earth, air, fire, water. Scientific types'll try and kid you into believing there's a whole load of other elements, with funny-sounding Latin names all ending in –um. You don't want to take any notice of that. There are only four elements, and everything else is just a mixture of them. Your lot have known that ever since the Dark Ages, but clearly you weren't paying attention in school or something.'

'Oddly enough—' Paul shrugged. 'Go on.'

'Well, that's it, more or less. Or it was up till about thirty years ago – for reasons that'll become clear, it's rather hard to pinpoint the precise date. The important thing is, there are now five elements: earth, air, fire, water and a sort of slimy sweet-tasting yellow gooey stuff.'

'Custard.'

Colin pulled a well-sort-of face. 'Actually, not custard,' he said. 'At least, not custard as we known it, Jim. Looks like it, smells like it, feels like it, tastes like it – but that's where the resemblance ends.'

'I see,' Paul lied. 'So, not custard.'

'But we *call* it custard,' Colin added, 'for convenience. Really, of course, it's the fifth element.'

'Fine. Glad we cleared that up.'

'Exactly.' Colin yawned. 'And, like I just said, it came out of nowhere not that long ago. Theo Van Spee invented it. It's what he's famous for.'

'You mean, he discovered it.'

Colin shook his head. 'No,' he said, 'invented. It's whatsits-name, synthetic. Artificial. Van Spee made it, cooked it up on a stove or something. Now, of course, it's everywhere, like Russian vine.'

'Then it can't be an element, surely.'

A pained look crossed Colin's face. 'Yes, it *can*,' he snapped. 'Because it *is*. You want to know how he managed it, you go ask him. Anyhow, there you go. The point is, things made out of the fifth element exist sideways to everything else; it copies anything it comes into contact with, you see, exact replicas. Only thing it can't copy is life. But inanimate objects – no trouble at all. And, if you swallow some Van Spee's crystals, you can sort of wiggle through, in and out of it. That's how the folding parking space works, and all the other stuff Van Spee's come up with over the years – such as the buildings that sit on top of each other, like Russian dolls except they're all the same size. You can see what a gold mine it is.'

'I suppose so,' Paul replied, his mind elsewhere. He was thinking of the circumstances of Ricky Wurmtoter's death; also about
the living sword that could transcend the elements. Some of it
was starting to make sense, but it was the sort of sense you can
see clearly at three a.m. when you've been drinking steadily since
six o'clock the previous evening. He wasn't sure it'd carry on
making sense in any other context but this. 'So,' he said, 'Van
Spee invented this stuff simply to make money.'

Colin looked at him. 'Well, I imagine so. Why else would you
bother?'

'I don't know,' Paul replied truthfully. 'Anyhow, thanks for filling me in. Of course, I still can't think of any way of getting out
of here, but at least I'm doomed but informed rather than
doomed and ignorant. That's progress, isn't it?'

'Not what it's cracked up to be, progress,' Colin replied. 'So,
what'll we do next? Noughts and crosses?'

Paul shook his head. 'I have a cunning plan,' he said. 'It won't
work, of course, because I'm missing something really blindingly
obvious, though I don't actually know what it is yet. Still, giving
it a try'll help pass the time, I guess. You up for it, or would you
rather stay here?'

Colin shrugged. 'Tell me what you've got in mind,' he said.

'Nah. You'll say it's too stupid to be worth trying.' Paul stood
up. 'You coming?'

'Why not?' Colin rose, winced a bit as he put his weight on his
feet (pins and needles, probably) and hobbled after Paul as he
headed for the door.

70 St Mary Axe was pretty much the same in Custardspace as
it was in real life, with the important and rather pleasant difference that they had the place to themselves. No armed goblin
guards, no partners, not even a single solitary spider in the nets
of cobweb up in the corners of the hallway ceilings. Annoyingly,
none of the lights worked (nothing electric worked, apparently)
but someone had thoughtfully left a couple of lit oil lamps on the
front desk.

'Up the stairs,' Paul said. 'Top floor.'

Custardspace stairs were just as steep, and there were just as
many of them. Eventually, they reached the door of Professor

Van Spee's office. Paul halted in front of it and caught his breath.

'This is one of the points at which this could go horribly wrong,' he announced cheerfully. 'Feel free to leave if you don't fancy the risk.'

'You don't get shot of me that easily.'

'Didn't want to. All right, here goes. Only don't blame me if we find Van Spee sitting behind the desk.'

The thought of that made Colin turn faintly green, but he kept his apprehensions to himself. 'Get on with it,' he said. 'I'll wait outside, in case anybody comes.'

Paul glowered at him scornfully. 'You're scared.'

''Course I'm bloody scared. That's Professor Van Spee's office you're about to break into. And you thought death was bad.'

Paul knocked, loudly, three times. Then he turned the door knob and walked in.

The office was uninhabited, to his great relief. Also, the desk was where it ought to be, exactly the same in all respects as its counterpart in realspace. That was what Paul had been hoping for. He slid open the second drawer from the top, and a surge of joy mixed half and half with amazement flooded through him. It was there, where he'd hoped it would be: a glass jar about the size of a soda syphon, three-quarters full of something that looked like coffee sugar.

Couldn't be that simple, could it?

But this was Professor Van Spee's desk in Professor Van Spee's office, and this was the very same jar Paul had burgled not so long ago, so was it so difficult to believe that these could be Professor Van Spee's famous patent crystals, as recommended by larcenous goblin pharmacists everywhere?

Yes, it was; because nothing was ever that convenient. Gobble a mouthful of these, and God only knew where he'd end up. What if they led him through to a dimension at right angles to this dimension? And if only he'd paid attention in school like every other bugger, he'd know if right angles to a right angle ended you up out in hyperspace or back where you started. But there: maths, the twelve-year-old Paul Carpenter had declared with the unassailable arrogance of youth, when am I ever going to need to know any of this stuff?

Paul picked the jar up, even got as far as fiddling with the lid, but he couldn't bring himself to take the risk. What if these crystals dumped him in yet another iffy dimension? Would there be a drawer in a desk containing a jar full of crystals, and what would happen to him if he munched a handful of them? It'd be like that old gag about being trapped in a room with mirrors on all four walls; he could finish up bouncing endlessly through time and space, like the misdirected luggage of an airline passenger. Shaking his head, he stooped to put the jar back where he'd got it from, and in doing so caught sight of a sheet of yellow paper, the sort JWW used for internal memos—

To: PAC
From: TVS
Your caution is both uncharacteristic and commendable; however, there is nothing to worry about. The crystals in this jar will return you to normal four-elemental space. Nonetheless, for your own safety you are advised not to steal from this jar again.
You have failed the fifth test. All is not lost; even so, one more failure will lead to regrettable consequences.

Bastard, Paul thought, though he wasn't quite sure why. He opened the jar, shuffled a handful of crystals into his palm, put the jar back and went out before he saw anything else that might upset him.

'Here,' he said. 'Now what?'

Colin the goblin looked at the crystals in his hand, then slowly up at him. 'You jammy git,' he said softly. 'Are those—?'

Paul nodded. 'Like falling off a log. Do we eat them, or dissolve them in water, or what?'

'Where'd you get them from? Are there any more?'

Goblins, Paul thought. 'Answer the question,' he said. 'What're we supposed to do with them now we've got them? Do we swallow them, or do they just—?'

He got no further, because Colin grabbed his wrist and buried his face in the pile of crystals in Paul's hand, licking at them like a dog. Then he vanished.

'I'll take that as a yes,' Paul said aloud to the space where

Colin had been; not such an unreasonable thing to do since, if he'd made sense of any of this stuff, Colin was still there, precisely where he'd been a moment ago, except in a different axis. Still, Paul felt a certain reluctance to put in his mouth anything that a goblin had just licked; so he carefully picked out a couple of crystals on the edge of the pile with his other hand and raised them to his lips, like someone taking a very small pill. Here goes, he thought—

Then someone screamed, right in front of him. He jumped, scattering the crystals everywhere.

'*Paul?*'

The shock had made him shut his eyes. When he opened them again, he saw Sophie standing where Colin the goblin had been, staring at him as though she'd seen a ghost. Which, of course, from her viewpoint she just had.

'Sophe?'

'Don't call me—'

'Sophie,' he snapped impatiently. 'It's all right, I can—'

She took a couple of steps back, and the wall got in her way. 'What are you doing here, Paul? I thought you were dead.'

He could feel his face adjusting itself into some stupid expression, an inane half-grin or something of the sort. It was the sort of expression that wouldn't have fitted on the strong, confident face of Phil Marlow; also, Sophie had recognised him. Clearly, Paul Carpenter was back in town. 'Depends on how you define—'

'*Bastard!*' She lunged forward like an Olympic fencer and smacked him round the face with her fist. Paul did the only honourable thing in the circumstances; he wobbled for a moment, folded at the knees and sat down on the floor, very hard. He also tried to apologise, but there was something not quite right about his jaw.

'I cried,' Sophie was yelling. 'I cried and cried, because I thought you were bloody *dead*, and here you are, still bloody alive, and what the hell am doing here anyway? Last thing I knew I was in the ladies' toilet, just about to—' She stopped and scowled at him. 'You *are* Paul, aren't you? I mean, you're not some stupid goblin in disguise, or anything like that?'

Paul nodded, then realised the gesture was ambiguous. 'It's ee,' he mumbled, and his mouth felt like it was full of razor-sharp flints. 'Eally.'

'Then why the hell does everybody think you're dead? And where've you been? And—'

'Oo eally kied?'

'What?'

'You really cried?' Paul said, painfully. 'Just because you thought—'

'Oh, for God's sake.' For a moment he thought Sophie was going to kick him. 'And why are you talking in that stupid voice?'

'I think you broke my jaw.'

'Good. And has this got anything to do with that other time? In St James's Park, with that other—' She stopped, and stared at him. Something uncomfortable was slowly taking shape in her mind, like a square egg inside a small chicken. *Of course*, Paul thought, *I could have explained all this really quickly and succinctly, if some dozy cow hadn't smashed my face in.*

'It's me,' he said. 'Yes, I died, but I, um, escaped. Like I did the other times, sort of. And yes, it's sort of like the St James's Park thing, though I don't actually know why it's doing it. Look, would it be all right if we did this explaining stuff later, because—'

He tailed off. A horrible thought had just occurred to him. Before, in St James's Park, Sophie'd gone away and Colin had taken her place. This time, Colin had gone away and here she was. Paul had a nasty feeling that it was something like those funny mechanical clocks you get sometimes in old churches and town halls and places like that: a little man comes out when it's sunny, and a little woman pops out when it's going to rain. As soon as one comes out, the other one's whisked back in, because that's how the mechanism works. If that was how it was and Sophie was somehow linked to Colin concerning exits and entrances in Custardspace, it had been Colin's escape that had drawn her here. Which was fine up to a point, provided there wasn't going to be a problem getting her back home again—

Or either of them, come to that. Paul had spilled all the crystals when Sophie had screamed, and the professor's memo had left him in little doubt about the risks incumbent on going back and stealing another dose. He winced a little. Quite apart from the nameless horror of being stranded in Custardspace for ever, it was yet another damn thing to explain, and no jaw to do it with.

'Because what?'

'Because my face hurts where you hit it, you—' He shut his eyes for a couple of seconds. 'Sorry,' he mumbled. 'I really can't talk any more. Really.'

Sophie muttered something about men in general that Paul didn't quite catch, then went on: 'Right, first things first. We'd better get you to a doctor, see if you've really hurt your jaw. Then you can explain— Why are you gawping at me like that?'

Resourcefulness had never been one of the qualities Paul would have attributed to himself, but if necessity was the mother of invention, extreme pain in the face was at the very least its aunt. Nodding his head to make Sophie follow him, he led the way down one flight of stairs, along a bit of corridor and into the room where the laser printer lurked. It was deserted, of course; but there was a computer station there, and the computer was switched on. He sat down and started to type.

It's like this, he wrote. *We're in a sort of alternate dimension. I was trapped here. You got pulled into it by a goblin called Colin leaving, I think, though I'm not sure. Trouble is, I don't know how we get out again. Also, going back wouldn't be a really good idea for me right now, since they think I killed Ricky Wurmtoter—*

'No, they don't,' Sophie interrupted. 'They think you're dead, remember? Anyhow, it was that creep Philip Marlow, they practically caught him red-handed. Oh, you don't know him, he was after your—' She stopped and scowled. 'Just a second. How do you know about that if you've been trapped in this whatever it is you called it?'

Oh for— Paul went back and deleted that. *It's complicated.*

'You don't say.'

You think Phil Marlow's a creep? I thought you liked him.

Sophie opened her mouth, then closed it again. 'Now you come to mention it,' she said, 'so did I. But not any more, apparently. Look, what's that got to do with anything?'

If only I knew a bit more about typing, Paul thought, I could set up *it's complicated* as a macro, and save myself a lot of work. *Later,* he typed. *Look, I'll explain everything later, I promise. Only now, I*

His fingers uncurled. Only now, what? By now, back in real-space, Dennis Tanner would have discovered that Phil Marlow had escaped from the strongroom; quite probably, also, Mr Laertides would have told everybody about who Phil Marlow really was. It definitely wouldn't be safe to go back, either as Phil or as Paul. Staying here, on the other hand, in an empty building, presumably an entirely deserted universe, didn't strike Paul as a good idea either. And even if he could get back somehow, if he risked Professor Van Spee's dire warning and stole some more crystals, there was the danger that Sophie'd be stuck here. It was all much, much too difficult, and he really wished it was happening to someone else, preferably his worst enemy.

Only now I haven't got a clue what to do next. Any suggestions?

And then Sophie did something completely unexpected, not to mention out of character. She smiled. It was almost a smirk, only Sophie didn't smirk, the way whales rarely tap-dance. 'Yes,' she said. 'Budge over. I need to get to the keyboard.'

A wave of blessed relief hit Paul like a large velvet hammer; because for what seemed like for ever, he had been very much on his own, having to cope with all manner of weird and terrible things, and now here was Sophie, pushing him out of the way in a manner that implied that she *knew what to do.* Paul had, of course, loved her since the first time he'd set eyes on her, but that had been his Pavlovian reaction to any girl who stayed still for five minutes and didn't stamp on his foot while wearing stiletto heels. He'd loved her like he'd loved all the others, back then, before he took the medicine. There hadn't been any reason (because Love, like other forms of psychotic behaviour, doesn't need a reason) and if he'd been called into the witness box, put on oath and asked why he loved her, he'd have had to admit that it was the same impulse that made people climb mountains, simply because she was there. Now, maybe for the first time, there was something he could love her *for;* because, after everything he'd had to go through on his own, right at the very furthest extreme of his rope, she was suddenly here, and taking charge. True, she'd also hit him very hard in the face, but nobody's perfect.

He glanced down at the screen. *Mail write*; she was typing fast, her fingers scampering across the keys like the legs of bald pink spiders. *To: dtanner@jww.net*. Then she hit the return key a couple of times, and typed in—

Help

– And, before Paul could reach down and stop her, Sophie hit the send button.

CHAPTER NINE

'O t the ell,' Paul tried to shout, 'id you oo at for?'
  Slight pause, while Sophie translated. 'I've sent an e-mail to Mr Tanner,' she said blithely. 'You see, I think I've figured out where we are. If this is really a different dimension, it's got to be the artificial one that Professor Van Spee made for himself. I've been working with him, you see, ever since you died – whatever. Anyway, he told me about it, it's how all his inventions work. And the thing is, although you can't get backwards and forwards you know, like physically, it's possible to send an e-mail, because theoretically it's all the same dimension, just phased differently because of the elemental resonances—'

'Yes, but *Tanner*,' Paul howled, ignoring the pain in his jaw. 'He's going to kill me. He thinks I murdered Ricky Wurmtoter.'

Sophie gave him her own special don't-be-so-silly look. 'Oh, we'll explain all that,' she said. 'Like, obviously it couldn't have been you, you wouldn't hurt a fly. I expect he was just, what's the expression they use, eliminating you from their enquiries—'

Behind them, the door flew open. Paul swung round to see who'd burst in, and saw someone who looked just like Ricky Wurmtoter – except that Ricky was dead, wasn't he? But it wasn't the new arrival's identity that was monopolising his attention. It was the long, shiny sword he was gripping in his outstretched right hand, so that the needle-sharp point was just bending the skin slightly under Sophie's chin.

'Apologies for the melodrama,' he said, and he sounded just like Ricky. 'You – stay absolutely still.'

It was one of those occasions when ambiguity was not your friend. 'Me?' Paul squeaked.

'Good Lord, no. You can move about as much as you like. Her.'

'But—'

'And before you make a complete arse of yourself trying to rescue her, you might like to know she just sent an e-mail to Dennis Tanner, letting him know you're here. Hence,' he added grimly, 'the trace elements of distrust and downright animosity clouding my otherwise sunny disposition.'

'I know,' Paul said. 'She was only trying to help.'

Sophie had been uncharacteristically quiet throughout all this; now she yelped, 'That's right!' in a tiny little voice. Something about it, probably the tininess, seemed to convince Ricky that she wasn't a threat. He pulled the sword back, and lowered it.

'Bastard!' Sophie screamed at him. 'And anyway, you're dead.'

'So's he,' Ricky replied reasonably, nodding towards Paul, 'and you're not yelling at him.'

'Yes, but she hit me on the jaw a few minutes ago,' Paul couldn't help pointing out.

'Maybe she just doesn't like dead people,' Ricky suggested.

Talking of which . . . Paul didn't have a sword handy, and he was pretty sure he didn't pack a mean right cross like Ms Pettingell; but there was a fat, heavy-looking book on the desk a few inches from his right hand. He picked it up and threw it at Ricky's head. Probably only sheer luck that it connected, because Paul had lousy hand/eye coordination and cleared pubs in seconds whenever he hefted a dart, but the effect was quite dramatic. Ricky tottered sideways, caught his foot in a coil of the spaghetti that spewed out of the back of the computer, and keeled over, dragging the monitor and the keyboard down with him. There was a rather satisfying crash, and even a few sparks.

'Bastard,' Paul said conversationally, echoing Sophie and rubbing his jaw. It was starting to feel much better now. 'And why aren't you dead, anyway? Tanner thinks you are. He thinks I killed you.'

'You bloody nearly did,' Ricky growled, gathering himself up off the floor. 'Talk about gratitude. Thank you so much, Ricky, for rushing down here to save me the moment you saw that e-mail on the office net; oh and by the way, here's a broken skull as a token of our appreciation.'

Sophie just glowered at him. 'You can't feel it, though,' she said. 'You're dead.'

'Oh, be quiet,' Ricky snapped. 'And now, if you two pinheads have quite finished, could we possibly go somewhere else, before Dennis and his horrible relatives find us? I've been to a lot of trouble to get out of the way for a bit, and I'd hate for it all to go to waste.'

Paul wasn't so sure about that. If Dennis Tanner came charging in and found him and a perfectly healthy (bruises aside) Ricky Wurmtoter, it would solve at least one of his major problems. On the other hand, there weren't any more big fat books handy, and he wasn't thrilled at the idea of stopping Ricky leaving if he wanted to go somewhere. If Ricky left and then Tanner turned up, it would probably be very bad.

'Please yourself,' he muttered. 'Where do you suggest, anyhow?'

'Closed-file store,' Ricky said. 'You know what it's like in there. Dennis won't set foot in the place unless he's absolutely got to, and that's the version in normal space. I believe the one over this side is a lot stranger.'

Hardly encouraging; but Ricky was already striding down the corridor. 'Might as well,' Paul hissed to Sophie, who nodded glumly and followed him.

'Hope you don't mind me borrowing this,' Ricky barked out as they scurried to keep up with him. It took Paul a second or so to figure out that *this* referred to the sword in Ricky's hand. Paul hadn't bothered examining it in any detail while it had been tucked under Sophie's chin. Now Ricky happened to mention it, however, he couldn't help noticing the glossy brown sheen of the blade, the extravagant pattern of silver whorls deep inside the steel—

A sword transcending dimensions, a living blade, the other half of Vicky the mermaid. Evidently that was how Ricky had got into Custardspace. It was also a way out, and not a Van Spee's crystal needed; which meant, presumably, no need for Colin the goblin to be inconvenienced as and when Sophie crossed back into Realspace. It was slightly unsettling to think that the sword was also, viewed from a certain perspective, fifty per cent of Ricky's ex-wife, but that really wasn't any of Paul's business.

'I suppose I owe you an apology,' Ricky went on, as he lunged off down a corridor that Paul wasn't sure he'd ever been in before. 'Framing you for my death, I mean. Sorry about that. Only I didn't realise it was you and not that Philip Marlow person till it was too late. Plans all made, you see, everything scheduled and timetabled, I had to press on and hope you'd find a way of coping, which obviously you did. I always knew you were the resourceful type—'

'Hang on,' Paul said. 'You knew it was me?'

The back of Ricky's head nodded. 'On the first floor landing. You were standing in front of the mirror, and it's an imp-reflector – you know, like the top of the table in the board room, it shows things as they really are, not as they appear to be. I caught sight of your reflection in it, and I knew straight away, for some reason best known to yourself you were back alive again and disguised as that Marlow bloke. Of course, I've never met Marlow, I only know what he looks like from his personnel file, so—'

'You knew it was me,' Paul repeated. 'And anyway, it doesn't matter. Even if it hadn't been me, even if it really had been Phil Marlow, what the hell do you think you were doing, making it look like he'd poisoned you to death?'

A slight shrug, as Ricky shoved open the closed-file store door. 'It was him or me,' he said. 'All right, it was *someone* or me, and I don't know this Marlow guy from a bar of soap, so the hell with it. If you've got to dump a million tons of horseshit on the head of an innocent man, it's better if it's a stranger rather than a close friend or valued colleague, right?'

'No,' Paul said. But Ricky wasn't listening. He'd clicked into full action-adventure mode, creeping stealthily along the walls and racks of shelving with the sword at the ready, carefully searching for hidden enemies and other lurking hazards. He carried on like that for a minute or so, until he tripped over a discarded electric fan, barked his shin on a shelf bracket, and gave the whole thing up as a bad job.

'I think we're safe here,' he said, limping back to where Paul and Sophie were waiting for him. 'For now, anyway. In theory, this being Van Spee's Dimension, there shouldn't be anything alive here apart from us, just inanimate objects. Some of the stuff that's got chucked in here over the years, though, it's hard to draw the line, if you know what I mean. In most offices, old bits of equipment get slung in the lumber room because they've died suddenly. Here, though, sometimes it's the other way around.' He paused and shuddered slightly. 'I particularly remember an old green filing cabinet that took to following people about, usually just after lunch. Finally we got it cornered, dragged it in here and bolted it securely to the wall, just over there—' He pointed to a patch of broken, crumbling plaster, where it looked as though something had yanked itself free with extreme force. 'Oh,' Ricky said. 'Bugger. Never mind.'

'You knew it was me,' Paul repeated for the second time. 'They were going to kill me. I was locked up in the strongroom with a bunch of goblins standing guard, while they had a partners' meeting to decide how to put me to death. And all the time—'

'It was *important*.' Ricky sounded angry and guilty, both at the same time. 'When you're up against someone like that, with your life on the line, you can't muck about. Sometimes one of the good guys gets hurt in the process. Can't be helped. I'm sorry.'

'You're sorry,' Paul said. 'Fine.'

'Hang on.' Sophie had that dangerous timbre in her voice that commanded attention. 'Something not quite right here. You said your life was on the line.'

Ricky nodded enthusiastically. 'That's right,' he said. 'It was.'

'So you thought, I'll cunningly cheat death by dying.' She

clicked her tongue. 'Couldn't you have just, I don't know, emigrated to Canada and grown a beard or something?'

Paul was impressed; he'd never seen anybody move so quickly. Ricky swung round, making a conscious decision at the last moment to belay the instinct to poke Sophie under the chin with the sword again. 'Canada,' he said. 'What the hell do you know about Canada?'

Sophie had backed away into the corner of a rack of shelves. 'All right, then, Australia. Or Papua bloody New Guinea. What I meant was—'

Ricky relaxed, from the soles of his feet up. 'Sorry,' he said. 'Private joke. And to answer your question, absolutely no dice. He's not someone you can run away from just by going somewhere very fast in an unexpected direction. That'd be like looking for a gas leak with a lighted match. That's why I had to come here, of course, to Speespace. It's the only place in this or any world where he can't come after me.'

'Excuse me,' Paul said in a quiet voice, 'but who's *he*, exactly?'

'What?' Ricky looked as though he'd just run through a locked plate-glass door without knowing it was there. 'You don't know – Oh, for crying out loud.' He sagged, leaning against a shelf unit. 'You mean, you haven't really got the foggiest idea what's going on around here?'

'No,' said Paul and Sophie at precisely the same moment. 'But you're going to tell us,' Sophie added savagely, 'or I will personally take that overgrown pencil-sharpener off you and stick it right up—' Then she screamed.

It was a full-blooded, extra-volume, super-high-fidelity rendition of the classic sci-fi B-movie scream, the sort of thing you'd expect to hear in any sleepy small Midwestern American community when the Martians or the Pod People blow into town. It wasn't the typical reaction of a sophisticated young urban woman faced with an everyday kitchen appliance. On the other hand, there has to be an element of give and take in these matters. People shouldn't freak out at the mere sight of fridge-freezers. Fridge-freezers, by the same token, shouldn't suddenly lunge out of the shadows and fling their doors open.

The different ways in which Sophie, Ricky and Paul reacted

to this sudden intrusion were, in many respects, illuminating. Sophie started yelling like a pig in a blender. Ricky, by contrast, sprang into action. He jumped up, landed perfectly poised on the balls of his feet, legs a shoulders' width apart, leaning slightly forward at the waist; his left hand grasped a chair, held out as an improvised shield, while he gripped the sword with his right in a coaching-manual-perfect high backhand guard. For his part, Paul stood rooted to the spot, staring at the white light pouring out of the open fridge door, which backlit its contents: a sad-looking lump of antique cheese and a milk carton. They looked very, very familiar –

'Hang on,' Paul said.

'Quiet,' Ricky hissed. 'It's confused, can't figure out which of us to attack first. That's our best chance, keep it off guard. So if you keep absolutely still—'

'No, listen,' Paul said. 'That's my fridge.'

'Don't be silly,' Ricky snapped at him. 'What'd your fridge be doing here, stalking us? Now, on the count of three—'

'It is,' Paul insisted. 'It's my fridge. And that's the pint of milk I bought in the seven-eleven on the corner of Ascot Terrace ten days ago. Look, it's still got the little sticky price tag with their name on it.'

'Actually, he's right,' Sophie broke in. 'I remember it now, from the flat. It's got that scratch, look, down at the bottom, where you bashed into it that time with the Hoover.'

'On the count of three,' Ricky repeated loudly, but he'd forfeited their attention. Rather huffily, he straightened his back and put the chair down, though without entirely relaxing his grip on the sword. 'All right,' he said, 'so it's your fridge, you deal with the bloody thing. Give it a carrot or blow up its nose or something, whatever it is you usually do when it goes berserk.'

Paul frowned. 'It's never done anything like this before,' he said. 'I've had it for ages, it's never been any bother.'

'Sod it,' Ricky said. 'I'm a Knight of the Holy Grail and an honorary lieutenant colonel of the Riders of Rohan – I'm buggered if I'm going to be backed into corners by a poxy fridge.' He strode forward, reaching out his hand to give the fridge a shove. As soon as he was within range, the fridge swung its door at him with appalling force. Ricky flew across the room like a cricket ball middled by a cover drive, slammed up against the wall and went to sleep.

'Idiot,' said the fridge contemptuously. 'Anyhow, that's him out of the way for a bit. Didn't want to talk in front of strangers, obviously. Now then, where were we? As I recall, Utgarth-Loke had just stolen the Great Cow of Heaven from the gods—'

His memory, Paul suddenly realised, was a jigsaw, and there'd been a piece missing for quite some time, only he hadn't noticed that it wasn't there. 'You talked to me,' he said. 'That night after I came back from the pub and all the fuses were blown. You were telling me all sorts of weird shit about gods and stuff.'

The fridge sighed. 'This is what you get,' it said sadly, 'for trying to be user-friendly. Burning bushes don't have to put up with this sort of apathy. But here I am, making a real effort not to be scary or intrusive, and you can't even be bothered to remember what I told you. It's in one ear and out the other with you people. All right, here we go again. In the beginning—'

Sophie, meanwhile, appeared to have had about as much as she could take. She jumped up and stood in front of the fridge (though, Paul noticed, just slightly more than a door's width away from it) with her hands on her hips. He couldn't see the look on her face, and reckoned that that was probably just as well.

'No,' she said. 'Shut up a minute. I want to ask you something.'

The fridge clicked some internal component, probably a valve. 'I remember *her*,' it said. 'Bloody door-slammer. Please don't tell me you've made up and she's moving back in, I don't think my seals could stand it. Anyway, in the—'

'*Quiet.*'

The fridge door might have quivered for just a moment; if so, the fridge thought better of it. 'That's better,' Sophie said. 'Now, I want answers. If you're the fridge from the flat, what're you doing in here? And how come you can talk, anyway?'

'I was just about to tell you,' the fridge answered stiffly, 'only you started shouting at me. I hate that.'

'Oh.' Sophie shrugged. 'Fine. Carry on.'

'Thank you so bloody much. Right, as I was saying. In the beginning—'

Sophie practically flickered with rage. '*Fridge—!*'

'It's a long story,' the fridge protested. 'He's heard a bit of it already, but he's forgotten, and you've got to hear all of it, or none of it makes sense. Look, do you want me to explain or don't you?'

'Explain,' Sophie repeated. 'You can do that?'

'Yes.'

'Really?'

'Of course I can. I can explain the whole bloody thing from start to finish, if only you clowns give me the chance. Maybe you haven't got your thick skulls round this yet, but I'm not your bog-standard run-of-the-mill food-storage unit. I exist simultaneously in all known dimensions and I transcend the elements like a rainbow bridge. I know all that was, all that is and a fair old chunk of what will be. The tiny, trivial footnote to history you're concerned with is only the smallest fraction of— All right, don't pull faces at me, and stop bobbing up and down like that, it makes me dizzy.'

There was a moment in which the immovable object reached breaking strain; and then Sophie said 'Sorry' and sat down on the floor. 'I won't interrupt any more,' she said. 'Promise.'

'Splendid,' said the fridge. 'Finally, here we go. In the beginning—'

That was as far as it got, because Ricky Wurmtoter, who'd woken up from his concussed sleep while their attention had been elsewhere, suddenly surged to his feet and, in one smooth, seamless movement, grabbed the sword, hop-skip-lunged across the floor and drove the blade into the fridge's works. A bang, a cloud of foggy gas, a brief shower of sparks; Ricky dragged the sword out of the gaping hole it had made, and water gushed out as the fridge slowly keeled over and crashed sidelong to the floor. Ricky howled with savage triumph and swung the sword over his head in a barbaric gesture of victory, inadvertently clobbering the lampshade so that contrasts of light and shadow danced round the room like Tinkerbell running for a bus.

'Ricky,' said Sophie, in a soft, deadly voice.

'Eat dirt, fridge,' Ricky snarled, as he reached up to steady the lampshade. 'You try pushing the Graf von Wurmtoter around, you get what's—'

'Ricky,' Sophie repeated. 'You total idiot. What the hell did you do that for?'

'It hit me,' Ricky replied, a wounded look on his face. 'Bastard thing slammed me against a wall. You got to take a hard line with these things, or next thing you know—'

'You killed it.'

Ricky had lowered the sword by now; he was looking ever so slightly embarrassed, in an utterly defiant sort of way. 'Don't anthropomorphise,' he said. 'It's a fridge, fridges are machines, you can't kill a machine. You can bust it,' he admitted. 'You can bust it real good,' he added with relish, 'as a lesson to any other arrogant son-of-a-bitch barrowload of valves that reckons it can shove a Grail Knight around and get away—'

'You know what I think?' Sophie said, ignoring him completely. 'I think you just murdered old Mr Wells.'

The look on Ricky's face was really rather impressive. Commission any of the greatest artists in history and tell them to depict a blend of horror, guilt, fear, disgust, disbelief, embarrassment and very, very profound annoyance using just a nose, two eyes and a mouth. Ricky did it better than any of them, unpaid and without even having to think or consult a mirror.

'What makes you say that?' he mumbled.

'Think about it,' Sophie said. 'Nobody's seen him in ages, right? And it's a known fact, as soon as the poo hits the ventilation system around here, what does old Mr Wells do? Turns into something. First he was that stapler thing, for years and years; then, when Countess Judy was on the rampage, he turned himself into a bad cold and hid inside people's heads till it was safe to come out. And now, with all this weirdness going on, you dead and Paul being hunted for murder, quite suddenly a talking fridge pops up out of nowhere and says it'll explain everything.' She clicked her tongue. 'Naturally I hope I'm wrong, but if not—'

Ricky said something under his breath that rhymed with Luck. 'Stupid bastard,' he added bitterly, 'why didn't he say

anything, let us know what he was up to? Of all the inconsiderate . . .'

Paul wasn't listening to any of this. He had no idea why, but
he was on his knees beside the fallen fridge. If there were tears in
his eyes, it may have been that once, long ago, he'd kept onions
in it, and the powerful chemical still lingered. After a long time,
he looked up at Ricky, and his expression wasn't friendly. 'You
arsehole,' he said. 'You stabbed my fridge. Now look at it.'

Ricky scowled at him. 'Look, I said I'm sorry. I'll get you a
new one. I'll get you a bloody *Zanussi*. Right now, that's the
least of my problems. If she's right, and that's really Jack Wells in
there—'

'Oh, shut up,' Paul commanded; and to his surprise, Ricky
did as he was told. 'I remember,' he went on. 'Back home, at the
flat. I came in late one night, and it started telling me stuff;
about what happened in the beginning, Utgarth-something and
the Great Cow of Heaven. Seemed to think it was important.'
He frowned in Ricky's direction. 'And now,' he added thoughtfully, 'you've killed it.'

'All right,' Ricky protested, 'all right, I get the message. My
bad, I'm very, very sorry. Next time a piece of electrical equipment uses me as a punchbag I'll turn the other bloody cheek.
Nothing we can do about it now, though, so I really think we
should stop stressing and do something practical.'

'Really,' Sophie said. 'Such as?'

Awkward silence.

'Sorry,' Sophie went on, 'I forgot. You're a man of action, and
long words bother you. All right, here's a suggestion. First, you
tell us both exactly what you're up to, and why you framed Paul
for killing you. And then you can find a way of getting all three
of us out of here, so you can go to Tanner and make it absolutely
clear that you aren't even the teeniest bit dead. And then—'

'Excuse me.' It was hard to associate the tiny, whimpering
voice with Ricky Wurmtoter. 'Slight problem there. You see, I
can't leave here and go back to Realspace.'

'Oh, really? Why's that?'

'Well,' Ricky said reasonably, 'I'm dead. Over there, anyhow.
No, honest, I am. It's just here that I'm alive. That's why I came

here, you see. I have—' He paused and bit his lip. 'Reasons.'

Sophie's mouth flopped open. 'You're kidding.'

'Alas, no.' Ricky's mouth folded into a sad smile. 'Wish I was, but I'm not. And the fact of the matter is, I *am* dead, back home anyway, chock-full of arsenic, and he *did* kill me. Not on purpose, obviously,' he added quickly, 'but the bitch of it is, I did a really bang-up job of making it look like poor old Paul here murdered me, and there's absolutely no way he could ever possibly prove otherwise. And in Trade circles, that thing about innocent till proven guilty is actually sort of the other way around.' He grinned weakly, which couldn't have been easy for a man whose chin made Kirk Douglas look like a parsnip. 'What happened is, you see, I really did die back there, it was real arsenic in the custard slice, I know because I put it there myself, while poor old Paul here was mopping coffee off his crotch. I was dead for a bit, but my old mate Mr Dao at the Bank owed me a favour, in return for worming his three-headed dog one time, and he let me stash a spare body and a quart of AB negative in a safe-deposit box. I came here through the door in Benny Shumway's room – obviously there's one in this dimension, same as in Realspace – and I was just on my way out when I saw Sophie's e-mail; so I dashed off and collared the sword, which was a piece of cake because it exists in all five dimensions simultaneously, the way swords do, and here I am. I'm afraid Paul and I are both stuck here pretty much for the duration. You're not, of course, you can go back any time. But not us. Sorry.'

'But that's—' Sophie shot him a look of pure cold fury. 'You've ruined everything. Our whole lives, everything. You—'

'Just a second,' Paul interrupted.

'Bastard,' Ricky said, with a hint of impatience cutting through the guilt. 'Yes, I know, I think we've established that point already. But be practical, for heaven's sake. I mean, if you can suggest anything we can do that'll put things right then, yes, I'm up for it, no worries. Unfortunately, I can't think of anything. Can you? I'm open to suggestions.'

'Just a *second*,' Paul insisted, so loudly this time that both of them turned and looked at him. 'Sorry to interrupt,' he went on, 'but what did you just say? Not you. Her.'

'Oh, I was just explaining to muscle-head here,' Sophie growled, 'about how he's made a complete bitch of everything, and it's all his fault, and—'

'You said *our*,' Paul interrupted. 'Our whole lives.'

'Yes, that's right. And it's no good him standing there like two yards of concentrated pillock saying there's nothing he can do about it, because—'

'No, hang on,' Paul insisted. 'There's something I want to get straight before we go any further. When you said *our* whole lives, you meant you and me, right?'

'Well yes, of course. I couldn't give a flying fuck about *his* life. Assuming,' she added acidly, 'he's still even got one.'

'That's what I thought you meant,' Paul said. 'Only, sorry if I'm being a bit slow, but why would him and me being stuck here for ever ruin *your* life, particularly? Because—'

'Because I love you, you moron,' Sophie snapped. Then she paused, as though she'd only then realised what she'd just heard herself say. 'Oh,' she added, and frowned thoughtfully.

Paul didn't notice, but Ricky was looking at them both. First bemused amazement, as though it had just started raining badgers; then a brief uncontrollable spurt of anger, followed by a rather more self-conscious radiant beam, as he clapped his hands together with a resounding crack and boomed, 'Congratulations, kids! I always knew it'd work out between you guys. And you see, it's an ill wind—'

'What did you say?' Paul asked quietly.

'I said it's an ill wind that blows—'

'Not you. Her.'

Ricky shrugged, grinning, and started to walk away. If he thought he was off the hook, however, owing to a sudden outbreak of moonlight, laughter, love and romance, he'd underestimated Sophie's apparently limitless reserves of fury. 'Not so fast,' she snapped, 'we haven't finished with you. The explanation.'

'But Sophe,' Paul put in, and was ruthlessly shushed for his trouble. 'Oh well,' he mumbled under his breath, and went back to kneeling beside the fridge. He wasn't quite sure why, but he knew that his place was still at its side.

Meanwhile, Ricky was getting glowered at. 'The explanation,' Sophie repeated. 'The one you were about to give us, remember, when the fridge appeared?'

'Ah,' Ricky said. '*That* explanation. Well, I think we've more or less covered all that, really.'

'No, we *haven't*.' Sophie didn't stamp her foot, but her knee quivered. 'You said there was someone after you, some *him* who could follow you anywhere except here; and presumably that's why you staged your own death and got us all in this God-awful mess in the first place. So, who is he? Well?'

Ricky sighed. 'It's embarrassing.'

'Embarrassing!' If Sophie had been a kettle, the room would have been full of steam. 'You're dead, he's the most wanted man in Europe, and you're *shy*? Oh, for—'

'All right.' For a moment, Ricky snatched back a little of his old, arrogant authority. 'If it means so much to you, I'll tell you, if you'll just shut up for a moment.' He took a deep breath and sat down on the edge of a shelf, leaning forward, the sword across his knees. 'It was all a long time ago,' he said. 'A matter of honour, I guess you could call it. There was – well, let's say there was a very bad man, back in the old country. A magician, goes without saying. He was being a real pain, beating up on my family and friends, I was young and just getting into the hero biz. When you're that age, of course, you think you can do any bloody thing. So I challenged him to a duel. Holmgang,' Ricky went on, shaking his head slightly. 'Sorry, technical term. The two of you go to an island out in one of the big fjords, and only one of you comes back. It's a pretty big thing, very solemn, absolutely no cheating and absolutely *absolutely* no running away. Anyhow, we rowed out to the island in a little boat – didn't talk much, naturally, I rowed and he sat there hating me, it was all a bit fraught – and then we started fighting. And – well,' Ricky said, turning his head away, 'he was winning, there was nothing I could do, so I ran. Not very far,' he added, 'because it was a small island. After that, I swam. The point is, I broke the rules and earned undying dishonour. Also,' he added bitterly, 'I lost. I *hate* losing. And that's it, basically,' he said, 'except that the other guy, the very bad person, didn't like me running out on him like that. He came after me. I kept running.' Long sigh. 'I still am.'

Sophie looked at him for a moment or so. 'And that's why you came here.'

Ricky nodded. 'I was sure I'd finally got shot of him,' he said. 'It'd been, well, a very long time, I hadn't seen or heard anything, I was starting to think he'd given up, got a life, died. But no, there he still was, waiting for me, bloody lurking. And this time, he nearly got me, I was just an inch or so away—' He stopped, shivered. 'I knew this time I had to do something a bit clever, because I've run out of places to hide over the years. So, I figured: he wants me dead, fine, give him what he wants. Sooner or later, once he knows I'm dead, he'll pack it in and go away; and then, after a really long interval, I can come out again, make a new life for myself, all that. Actually,' Ricky said, with a slight grimace, 'that's one detail I haven't quite got sorted yet, because when I say *make a new life*, that's exactly what I'm going to have to do if I ever want to get home without dropping dead the moment I cross the interface. But what the hell, one problem at a time, and I always knew I'd be stuck here for a good long while. It'll give me something to occupy my mind while I'm waiting.' He breathed out, closed his eyes, as though he'd just escaped from some oppressive burden. 'And that's it,' he said, 'the whole sorry story. And really, I do regret most sincerely having to involve you two, but in my place, what would you have done?'

Sophie looked into Ricky's eyes for quite a long time, five seconds at least. Then she said, 'I think you're an unmitigated shit, Mr Wurmtoter.' Then she stamped on his toes, quite hard, and walked away.

'Ow,' Ricky yelped. 'What did you want to go and do that for?'

'Fun,' Sophie replied without looking round. 'Also because you just killed old Mr Wells. And even if you didn't, you still smashed up Paul's fridge, and he can't afford a new one. Mostly, though, because I don't like you very much.'

A look of profound bewilderment and distress crossed Ricky's face. 'You don't?'

'No.'

'Oh.' He hesitated; you could practically see the crumbling ruins of his cosmos tumbling about his shoulders. 'But that's – Everybody likes me,' he pointed out. 'I'm a very pleasant, affable sort of guy.'

'Affable,' Sophie repeated. 'Really. Well, let me tell you, Mr bloody Wurmtoter, I wouldn't aff you if you were the last man left alive in the whole world.'

Ricky was starting to get annoyed. 'That's so tight,' he said. 'Look, you don't know what he's like, this very bad person. If he was after you, I'm telling you, there's nothing you wouldn't do to get away from him. All right, so I set up ferret-features here. Big deal. I knew how incredibly resourceful and clever he is, I knew he'd be OK. I mean, he's been dead twice – correction, three times – and hardly turned a hair. That's how it is with best mates; you know you can do stuff and you can trust your best mate to guard your back, do what's got to be done, look after himself. It's a sign of respect, really.' He turned to Paul. 'And we're mates, aren't we, Paul old chum?'

Paul looked at him. 'No.'

'Yes, we fucking *are*.' Ricky's knuckles were white around the sword's hilt. 'Look what I've done for you. Your first day with the firm, I bought you lunch. Looked after you, took you under my wing, taught you the pest-control biz—'

'No, you didn't, that was Benny Shumway. You weren't there. You'd been captured by Countess Judy, remember. And if it wasn't for me—'

'Yes, but I saved your life.'

'You shot me with a crossbow,' Paul reminded him. 'It *hurt*.'

'Balls. Death was instantaneous. You never felt a thing.'

'It *felt* like feeling something.' Paul shrugged. The conversation was getting tedious, as far as he was concerned. 'Truth is,' he said, 'I don't like you either.'

'Big deal.' Ricky breathed out through his nose. 'So we've had our ups and downs,' he said. 'So what? It's been more ups than downs, that's got to count for something. Didn't I give you a magic sword?'

'What, the one you've got there in your hand? Besides,' Paul pointed out, 'I didn't want it. I stuck it under the sofa where I didn't have to look at it. I tried chucking it out once, but the nasty thing's so sharp it went through the bottom of the bin liner so fast that it nearly pinned my toes to the floor.'

'Yes, but it's the thought that—'

'No, it *isn't*,' Paul snapped, unexpectedly loud. 'The thought doesn't matter a toss. What matters is the terrifyingly dangerous mess you get people into. Now, will you please shut up? I'm trying to figure out an escape plan, and you whingeing away in the background isn't making it any easier.'

When Ricky Wurmtoter shrugged his mighty shoulders, it was like watching two herds of bison walking towards each other. 'Suit yourself,' he said. 'For the record, I don't like you much, either. I've never liked you, not from day one.' He edged round on his shelf until he was facing away from Paul and toward Sophie. 'Ungrateful bastard,' he said. 'I really went out of my way for him, you know – well, of course you do, you were there. And anyway,' he added, chivvying a smile onto his face, 'he's just a bit upset right now, it's making him want to lash out, say stuff he doesn't mean.'

'Really?' Sophie said sweetly. 'Such as?'

Ricky sighed. 'Right, fine,' he said, holding up his left hand. 'Look, I think we're all getting a bit over-tired and overwrought here. Best thing, if you ask me, would be a nice, sociable, relaxing drink, followed by a good rest, maybe a couple of hours' sleep. Just so happens,' he added, reaching inside his jacket, 'I've got a bottle of premium Estonian vodka here in my inside pocket. The good stuff, two hundred and eighty-seven proof. Any takers?'

Instinctively, Paul and Sophie looked at each other. 'Two hundred and what?' Sophie asked, in an awestruck voice.

'Eighty-seven. Distilled and bottled in Kohtla-jarve, Dragon Snot brand. One sip of that, you'll be amazed how much cheerier things'll look.' Ricky pulled out a fat square bottle, and shook three shot glasses out of his sleeve. Remembering the night the fridge first spoke to him, Paul shuddered and looked away. Sophie, on the other hand, was plainly interested in spite of herself.

'Funny name,' she said.

Ricky grinned, filled a glass and handed it to her. 'Traditional,' he said. 'Like, you know the Polish stuff, it's called "buffalo-grass" because they put a blade of special grass in it to give it that special flavour? Well, same principle.'

Sophie, who'd just swallowed her dose of the stuff, immediately turned green. Then she burped. 'Actually, she said, 'izzen bad. Gimme nother.'

'Pleasure.' Ricky refilled her glass. 'Sure I can't tempt you?' he asked Paul, who shook his head and swallowed hard. 'Here's health, then,' he said, picking up his own glass and holding it a few inches from his nose, as though savouring the bouquet. 'I always carry a bottle with me, for just this sort of situation. Butterfingers,' he added, as Sophie's glass, now empty, slipped through her fingers and rolled across the floor. 'Well, you're a convert, obviously,' he said to her.

'Sgreat,' Sophie muttered. 'Funny taste, mind. Reminds me of something.' She pulled a deep, thoughtful face, eyebrows scrunched up, lips pouting. 'Ackshly, reminds me of—' Then, with a long, sweet sigh, she flopped onto her back like a carpet unrolling, and went to sleep.

'Is she all right?' Paul asked sharply.

Ricky turned to him and grinned. There was a look in his eyes that wasn't reassuring. 'Oh, she's fine,' he said. 'Absolutely fine. In about twenty minutes or so, she'll wake up, and about five seconds after that, she'll be happier than she's ever been before. Life for her will be one sweet song, for ever and ever.'

A forty-watt bulb lit up in the back of Paul's mind. 'Oh yes?' he asked mildly. 'Why?'

Ricky laughed. Not quite a full-blown villain's laugh, but it had nothing to do with seeing the funny side. 'Because what could be better than being young and in love?' he said. 'Well, different in your case, obviously, because you'll never get the girl, even if they start hiding them in the bottoms of cereal packets. But in twenty minutes' time, dear sweet little Sophie's going to open her puffy little eyes and gaze at the face of the man she's going to love for the rest of her life. Now,' he went on, standing up and flipping the sword nonchalantly round in his hand, 'that face belongs to one of the two men in this room. Another hint. It's not you.'

The click of bits of information falling into place in Paul's mind was as deafening as a tap-dancing contest on a galvanised-iron bridge; all too late, unfortunately. 'The drink,' Paul mumbled, 'the whatsitsname vodka. It's not that at all. It's that bloody love-philtre stuff.'

'Got there in the end,' Rick sighed. 'Took you long enough. That's right; mainstay of JWW for over two centuries, never fails, satisfaction guaranteed or your life back. You may have noticed,' he added, edging forward a step or two, 'that I didn't drink mine. No offence, because I know you're soft on the stupid bitch, but really, she's not my type. Doesn't matter, so long as she loves me. That's all that's required for the job in hand, and there's no point over-egging the pudding, as my old granny used to say.'

Paul backed away. Pointless, because he knew he was no match for Ricky Wurmtoter in reach, speed, skill or agility. 'Bastard,' he said. 'You vicious bastard, why—?'

Ricky sighed melodramatically. 'I wish people'd stop calling me that,' he said. 'For someone in my line of work, I'm pathetically sentimental. For starters, I ought to kill you right now, it'd solve a lot of problems. It'd solve *everything*.' He breathed out impatiently, as though chiding himself for his weakness. 'But I can't,' he said, 'not unless I have to, self-defence or whatever. Partly it's the old code of chivalry stuff, partly because—' He shrugged. 'Anyhow,' he said, 'that's not relevant. You'll be relieved to hear, I'm not proposing to kill you, or even hurt you. Except,' he added, 'I need to give you a tiny little tap on the head, just enough to put you to sleep until after Sophie wakes up. Attention to detail is ninety-nine per cent of the heroism business, and I don't want any possibility of you being around when she wakes up, so you're going to have a pleasant nap in the stationery cupboard. I may even come and let you out again, if I remember.' He stepped forward again, and somehow he seemed to have covered far more than a single stride of carpet; he was looming over Paul like an unfriendly Alp. 'I'll ask you to keep still, if you don't mind,' he said. 'I'm pretty good at precision knocking-out, but there's always a very slight element of risk, and we don't want you ending up with a smashed skull and permanent brain damage.'

Ricky's left hand closed into a big fist. 'Look,' Paul said, 'you can bash me up all you like. You can kill me, if you feel you really must. But can't you let her alone, for crying out loud? It's not fair, and she's never done you any harm.'

'That's all you know,' Ricky snapped. 'For your information, that bloody woman—' He pulled a stern face. 'Tell you later,' he said, 'maybe, if you're good and hold still. But just in case I never get another opportunity, I'll tell you this. There's a whole lot more to Sophie Pettingell than meets the eye, and if you think what I'm doing to her is a bit nasty and mean, you don't know the half of it.' He paused, then laughed harshly, like a dog barking. 'No pun intended. Okay, hold still. There may be some slight discomfort.'

He raised his fist, and Paul looked away. Accordingly, he saw the door start to open a split second before Ricky did, and a tiny little scrap of self-preservation instinct that had been hibernating in with all the cowardice and freezing-with-terror stuff at the back of his mind ever since he'd been born suddenly blossomed into action. He jumped sideways; Ricky's fist crashed into the angle-iron shelves behind him. Ricky yelled with pain and started to make predictions about Paul's immediate future, which wasn't, apparently, terribly promising. He didn't get very far, however, because the door was open now and someone was charging into the room.

Ricky saw him, yelped with terror and sprang back. He landed in a perfect high forehand guard, sword held out, knees slightly bent, and his face was as white as soap-powder-commercial laundry. That would've been remarkable enough, in any other context, but Paul noticed it in passing and immediately dismissed it from his mind as trivial when compared with the other remarkable thing on display at that precise moment—

Namely, a tall, slim young man in chain-mail armour, holding a round shield in his left hand and a long, dark blue sword in his right. His whole body radiated purpose and quivered with pure aggression, and you could've barbecued shish kebabs over the fire burning in his eyes. He was terrifying, clearly extremely competent in the use of edged weapons, palpably afraid of nothing in this world or the next, and his face was exactly what Paul would expect to see when he looked in a mirror.

CHAPTER TEN

It's probably the same for the policemen who stand duty at football matches. On the pitch in front of them, twenty-two highly paid experts are putting on an exhibition of the very greatest science and skill that the game affords, pulling off shots that extremely boring people will discuss in pubs for the next twenty years. But the policemen aren't interested; they probably don't like football, hate standing around in the open air for hours on end, and wish they were back home with a nice cup of tea watching the ballet on Channel Four. Completely wasted on them, the whole show.

So with Paul. Even he sensed that the display of swordfighting of which he was a very unwilling spectator was something quite out of the ordinary: the jumping, ducking, prancing, swishing about, blade-clashing, flying sparks and bad language were all evidently Olympic standard and then some. Paul, on the other hand, just wished they'd go away and do it somewhere else, where there'd be less risk of a careless backhand slash slicing him in two. He'd have followed his instincts, shut his eyes and curled up into a little hedgehog-style ball on the floor if it hadn't been for the extreme surrealism of the thing, which gripped his attention in spite of everything. No doubt about it: utterly improbable as it might seem, the tall skinny bloke giving Ricky Wurmtoter such a very hard time out there was unquestionably Paul Carpenter.

It was a curious feeling, watching himself fight. It wasn't an activity he'd ever had the slightest desire to indulge in, and his knowledge of it matched his enthusiasm. But there he was, plain as the nose on their mutual face, hacking and hewing and slashing, to the point where Ricky Wurmtoter (who was presumably pretty good at that sort of thing) was starting to look decidedly harassed. *That's me*, Paul thought, as another shower of sparks blossomed out of the collision of the two blades. *I'm doing that.* It surely added a new penumbra of terror to the proposition that he'd always been his own worst enemy.

Ricky was getting tired. He was sweating, his movements were growing jerkier and more desperate, he was puffing like a fat man on an exercise bicycle, and he was trying all those stunts that Kirk and Errol and Burt pull off in the movies but which don't actually work – jumping up on the furniture, weaving in and out of shelf units, ducking behind free-standing lampstands. *Any minute now*, Paul thought; and sure enough, Ricky ducked out of the way of a lunge with micromillimetres to spare, sprang up in the air and grabbed for the light fitting, presumably with a view to swinging across the room over his enemy's head towards the door and safety. But of course there are things that Errol and Sean and even Mel and Pierce can get away with on the silver screen, but which you should not try at home. For a split second Ricky hung in mid-air, an electric flex stripped of its insulation in one hand, a steel sword in the other. Then he dropped like a dead spider and thudded heavily on the floor.

Immediately, Swordfighter Paul was standing over him, sword raised for the kill. Real Paul couldn't bear to look. He turned his head to the wall, waiting for that tearing, slicing sound he'd only heard in butchers' shops, and instead heard a piercing female yell. He looked up, and saw that his other self had inadvertently trodden on Sophie's outstretched ankle.

Shit, he thought. Even she couldn't sleep through that.

And when she woke up—

Swordfighter Paul hesitated, the sword still hanging in the air above his head, and that was all the reprieve that Ricky needed. In the time it would take a camera to snap a picture at noon on a hot summer day, he'd scuttled between Sword-boy's legs and shot away behind a bank of file stacks. Sword-boy lunged after him like a pouncing cat, with the result that, at the precise moment when Sophie's eyes opened, the first person she saw wasn't Ricky, or even the ninja doppelganger. Before Paul could look away or do anything, their eyes met, and you could practically see the pink filter come down behind them, like the safety curtain in a theatre.

Though they were too far away to hear it, a nightingale sang in Berkeley Square; and Paul gazed deep into the eyes of the only girl he'd ever really loved, saw in them the deep glow of the same fire that burned so fiercely in his soul, and thought: *Balls, shit, fuck, bugger.* Because only a few minutes ago, Sophie had told him that she loved him; and now she still loved him, almost certainly a whole lot more, but entirely because she'd just drunk a tumblerful of J. W. Wells's world-famous, infallible, all-conquering love philtre. Which meant, of course, that he was now ineffably screwed.

Sophie didn't seem aware of the ear-splitting bangs, crashes, thumps, clangs and scrunching noises issuing from behind the file shelves. She only had eyes, and ears, for him. She gazed at him, her lips trembling. 'Paul,' she said huskily.

'Shh,' Paul hissed back.

'Sorry, darling.'

Shit, Paul thought. *Créme de merde in diarrhoea sauce with a tossed salad.* 'Look,' he said desperately, as a wild thought crossed his mind, 'we've got to get out of here. Right?'

'Anything you say, darling.'

That was when the file stack collapsed. It had every right, given that Ricky (wouldn't you just know he was a B-movie buff?) had just kicked it over under the misguided impression that it would help matters. It didn't, of course. All it achieved was an avalanche of alphabetically ordered buff folders, which engulfed Sophie like the lava stream from a volcano. A moment later, Ricky and Psychotic Paul fell on top of the pile. Both of them had lost their swords. Ricky had hold of his opponent's wrist, while Psycho Paul was trying to skewer him with a long knife, with every prospect of success. Not that the real Paul really gave a damn, one way or the other. But if they weren't careful where they rolled and thrashed about, Sophie was going to get squashed like a fly on a windscreen, and he wasn't having that.

'Excuse me,' he said.

Predictably, they took no notice: all wrapped up in each other, like a pair of amorous teenagers. Paul tried clearing his throat loudly, but that had no effect. So he got up, strolled round the back of the trashed file stack, looked around till he found the two discarded swords and picked them up.

'Excuse me,' he repeated; then he slammed the flat of the sword in his right hand across the shoulder blades of his mirror self. That was a rather weird feeling, too, but he hadn't been able to bring himself to hit Ricky – partly because he was so obviously losing, partly from some lingering vestige of respect or fear – whereas beating up on himself was, after all, something he'd been doing for years, in one way or another.

That got through in a way that mere words couldn't. Sword-boy clearly had all the right instincts for someone in his line of business. As soon as he became aware of the potential danger he didn't muck about yelling or turning round. Instead he shot forward, using Ricky's face in roughly the same way that a sprinter uses the starting blocks, landed on his feet, and threw the big knife in his right hand as he turned.

Paul watched it coming straight at him for a very, very long fraction of a second. He had time to think about the nasty mess he was in and even analyse the various wrong turnings and mistakes he'd made that had fetched him up here. *If only*, he concluded, *I'd paid more attention in school; I could've got better exam results, decent qualifications, right now I'd be sitting behind a desk doing grossing-up calculations for advance corporation tax, not watching a dirty great knife spinning through the air right at me. Miss Hook told me I'd regret it. Wonder how she knew—*

The knife missed.

Odd, that. Alternative Paul didn't look like the sort of man who was capable of missing a fairly straightforward shot like that, even if he'd wanted to. Maybe he was having a bad day (*Makes two of me*, Paul thought sourly), or maybe deep down he still had a shred of the Carpenter decency and reluctance to shed blood. Or not; a moment later, Alt. Paul had jumped over Ricky like the cow in the nursery rhyme, grabbed the sword out of Paul's left hand, and driven it hard into the floorboards, in the spot that Ricky's head had just vacated. Ricky, meanwhile, was on his feet and hurtling towards the door. Alt. Paul howled something in a language Paul didn't recognise, and went after him, close on his heels as a very angry shadow. He didn't bother closing the door after him; clearly, good manners, as well as regard for the value of human life, was something he didn't share with his identical twin.

Paul sat down on the only unsmashed chair, dropping the other sword on the floor with a clang. He had no idea what the hell all that had been about, but at least it appeared to have gone away, for now anyway, and that was one of those small mercies he was always being urged to be grateful for. He took a couple of deep breaths to steady himself, and turned his head to look at the mountain of dislodged files under which, presumably, Sophie was fast asleep.

Fine, he thought. *Now comes the difficult bit.*

After a good long rummage, Paul found Sophie's shoulder. He recognised it by feel: thin, bony. He shook it. 'Sophe?'

'Don't call—' She sat up, files tumbling off her like snow from the branches of a tree. 'Darling,' she said.

Oh well, Paul thought. There'd been a tiny spark of hope in the back of his mind; she'd wake up, and the bash on the head would have cured her of the effect of the philtre, or something like that. No chance. 'Jesus,' she added, in a slightly less soppy voice, 'my head hurts. What the hell's been going on?'

'Several things,' Paul replied economically. 'Tell you later. Right now, though, we need to leave. Turns out that Ricky's a baddie after all –' As he said them, the words didn't sound right. Not a baddie as such; if Psycho Boy caught up with Ricky and succeeded in chopping him into slices, you wouldn't find the words *really evil* printed all the way through, like seaside rock. An arsehole, yes, the sort of really unpleasant person who'd dump all over any number of harmless bystanders in order to save his own skin, but that was about it, and most people could end up like that, given a thoroughly horrible set of circumstances.

But not me, Paul realised with a jolt. *Apparently not me. Well, there you go.*

'My God,' Sophie was saying. 'That's terrible. Did he try and hurt you, darling? I'll kill him.'

Paul shook his head. 'Don't bother,' he said. 'There's another nutcase on the loose, trying to do just that. Hence,' he added, indicating the trashed room, 'the make-over. They've buggered off, but they may come back. I think we should leave before they do.'

Sophie nodded vigorously. 'Of course,' she said, and took his hand to help herself get up. She was probably a bit absent-minded from concussion or something, because she forgot to let go of it once she was on her feet. 'Who was the other man, do you know?'

Excellent question. 'No idea,' Paul said. 'Like it matters. Let's get out of here.'

'Right. Where to?'

Where indeed? Oh, for a portable door or something of the kind—

He looked down at his left hand, which was still full of sword. In particular, he noticed the satin-brown gleam of the blade, the sparkle as the light played on the silver patterns set deep in the heart of the steel. *Well,* he thought, *why not? It worked before—*

So did helicopters, and Harrier jets, and space shuttles; but it helped if you knew how to make them go. Paul looked at the sword, just in case there was something helpful written on it in very small letters, but if there was he missed it. Quite possibly, using a living blade to skip across dimensional interfaces was yet another useful piece of knowledge they'd covered in Miss Hook's class, only he'd been too busy making paper aeroplanes to listen. Vicky knew, he assumed. Probably Mr Laertides, Mr Tanner, maybe Mr Tanner's mum; Professor Van Spee undoubtedly knew, and so did Ricky Wurmtoter. Quite possibly everybody in the world except him—

Everybody?

'Sophie,' he said. 'You wouldn't by any chance happen to know how to use a magic sword to transcend the elements, would you? Only—'

She nodded eagerly. 'Funny you should say that, because I

was tidying Van Spee's desk for him and there was a photocopy of an article about it. Actually, it's really, really simple, all you have to do is get the sword and do a sort of sideways swish, like this—'

'Here,' Paul said. 'Show me what you mean. You can use this one, if you like.'

'All right, but you'd better stand back. I don't want to cut you in two accidentally. There was a diagram, it's like a kind of rising sideways—'

The sword glittered for a split second, then vanished, taking Sophie with it. Paul sighed. At least she was safe for now and he wouldn't have to worry about her getting caught in the crossfire while he (*Why me?* he demanded of the universe at large. *Why fucking me?*) did what little he could to straighten things out a bit.

Paul frowned. He'd forgotten something. Not that it was terribly important, but good manners always mattered, regardless. He smiled.

'Hi, Colin,' he said.

'Fuck you,' Colin the goblin replied, scrambling up off the floor. 'Look, I'm getting sick and tired of this. You and your girlfriend want to play virtual revolving doors, find some other poor sod.'

Paul sighed. He no longer had a sword, but he had a severely frayed temper; and Colin was, after all, shorter than he was. Grabbing the goblin by the shirt-front, he heaved. To his great surprise, he actually managed to lift him an inch or two off the floor.

'Be quiet,' he said.

Colin started, as though he'd just been gored by Bambi. 'Sorry,' he mumbled. 'Only, would you mind putting me down? Heights make me dizzy, see.'

Paul sighed, and let him go. 'You'll have to excuse me,' he said, 'I'm having a rather trying day. Did you get them?'

'Get what?'

'The crystals.'

Colin wasn't a very good liar. 'Um, no,' he said. 'Didn't get round to it, sorry. At least, I went and had a good rummage round in your desk drawers, but—'

'Hand them over.'

'All right.' Colin fished the bottle out of his pocket. 'Only you promised—'

'I only want a tiny bit,' Paul reassured him. 'You can keep the rest.'

'You sure?'

Paul took the bottle out of his hand and unscrewed the lid. 'One other thing,' he said. 'You'll have to stay here for a bit, until I've sorted things out. We apologise for any inconvenience.'

'Hey—'

'But,' Paul went on, 'if my theory's correct, this dimension or whatever it is contains all the inanimate objects in the world, and no people. So it occurs to me that a dishonest person could probably find ways of occupying his time, if he got stranded here for a while. That's no comfort to you, of course, but I thought I'd mention it, purely out of interest.'

Colin went all quiet and thoughtful for a moment. 'Well,' he said, 'I can see why you want me to stay here, so your lady-friend won't get pulled across when I leave. And what the heck, I can sit and read a book or something, right?'

Paul clamped his hand tight around the pinch of crystals he'd taken from the bottle. 'That's very considerate of you, Colin. Now please go away.'

'Anything you say.' The goblin waddled towards the door, then stopped. 'I don't suppose you've got such a thing as a jemmy or a pair of bolt-cutters on you, by any chance? Only, sometimes you get a book where the pages have got all stuck together, and—'

'Goodbye, Colin.'

'Cheerio, then. See you around.'

Left alone, Paul sat cross-legged on the floor and tried to think. His mind was so full of weirdnesses that concentrating was like trying to drink with chopsticks, but gradually he began to patch together a plan of action. It wasn't exactly wonderful, but it was the best he could do, and as such a marginal improvement on bugger all.

He stood up, found a piece of paper – a single sheet of A4, a copy of an invoice (*To Mr D. Grey, in respect of cleaning and restoring one portrait*) – and folded it neatly around the crystals, forming a small envelope which he tucked into his top pocket.

It was perfectly simple. All he had to do was find Ricky Wurmtoter, challenge him to a duel to the death, and kill him. Once he'd done that, everything would gradually unravel, and the rest of his day would be his own. Either that, or he'd be seeing Mr Dao again very soon, and maybe he'd be in time to enrol in the flower-arranging evening class, though he had an idea it'd get boring after a while. Only so many things you can do with lilies, after all.

With this aim in view, Paul set off to find his prey. Tracking him turned out to be pretty straightforward; all he had to do was follow the trail of hacked doors, trashed computer terminals, lacerated soft furnishings and viciously mutilated office furniture. There was, of course, the rather nasty thought that he'd be too late. When last seen, Ricky had barely been holding his own against the other Paul Carpenter, and that had been some time ago. If Ricky was already dead, Paul was probably screwed. Alternatively, if Ricky had somehow contrived to kill the other Paul – He didn't want to think about that, the ramifications were practically two simultaneous quadratic equations, and maths was yet another subject he'd let slide past him during his early youth. He quickened his step a little, occupying his mind with a selection of small, trivial practicalities, such as what he was proposing to use as a weapon, now that Sophie had taken the living sword back with her to Realspace.

Thus diverted, Paul wasn't paying much attention to where he was going. He turned a corner and walked straight into something chunky. It turned out to be a small, bald man with an almost perfectly spherical head.

'Hello, Paul,' he said.

It was as though the collision had physically jolted a component part of his mental jigsaw into place. He stared at the man for a moment, then blurted out: 'You're not human.'

'Never said I was, Paul.'

'You're—' Now he came to mention it, he still didn't have the faintest idea what the bald man, was, only what he wasn't. 'You're a friend of Mr Laertides,' he said.

'More than a friend,' the man replied, grinning. 'You're a smart kid. Well, no, you aren't. But you got there in the end.'

'It was you, though,' Paul replied doggedly. 'I kept meeting you everywhere, and I thought I recognised you, but each time you were someone different. And then,' he added, 'you gave me the custard slice. The one with the poison in it, that killed Ricky, back on the other side.'

'Guilty as charged.' The round-headed man grimaced. 'Sorry about that. But yes, essentially you're on the right track. I can't be human, because this place is uninhabited apart from a few trespassers who've somehow got hold of Van Spee's crystals. Is that what you were about to say?'

'Something like that.'

'Ah. In that case, seven out of ten. Now listen,' the man added, taking Paul by the elbow in a wholly unthreatening manner. 'I just popped across to give you something.' He stuck his fingers up his left sleeve, like an elderly lady reaching for her hanky, and teased out a perfectly ordinary blue toothbrush. 'It's the one I sold you, back when you came in my shop in Aldgate. Frank feels it might come in handy when you run into Dietrich Wurmtoter.'

Paul took the brush from him and looked at it. 'Thanks,' he said. 'Just what I need. Now I can club him senseless with the butt end and floss him to death.'

The bald man considered that. 'I suppose,' he said. 'But it's a bit on the elaborate side, if you ask me. You'll probably do better if you just tap the handle in the palm of your hand three times and think of Christmas cake.'

'Christmas—?'

'Well, it's what I do. Really it's just to clear your mind. Go on, try it.'

Feeling rather silly, Paul did as he'd been told: tap, tap, tap, *dark brown cake the consistency of firebrick, pebble-dashed with hard nuggets of petrified currants and glacé cherries. Yum.*

The toothbrush twitched slightly in his hand, and morphed into an assault rifle.

'There you go,' the bald man said. 'Swords and stuff are fine if you're a top-flight fencer, but for the novice you can't beat a plain old M-16.'

'M-16,' Paul repeated. 'That's the one that goes from Goole to Rotherham via Doncaster, right?'

'If you say so,' replied the bald man tolerantly. 'Now, to make it work, you press that bit there. The bullets come out of the end with the hole in it – that's quite important, so be careful. If you pull the trigger and nothing happens, your best bet is to run away, whimpering. All right?'

'I guess so,' Paul said. 'Thanks,' he added. 'Um, are you sure it works against, well, heroes and the like? I mean, don't they have special magic stuff that means the bullets just bounce off?'

The bald man looked up, pursed his lips. 'You know,' he said, 'now that you mention it, I believe they do – some of them, anyway. On the other hand, not many of them know that, so you may be able to bluff your way. See you later,' he concluded. 'Maybe,' he added.

'Just a second.' Paul called him back. 'Suppose I do kill Ricky Wurmtoter, what happens then?'

'Well, for a start, you can nick his stapler and Sellotape dispenser. Probably you'll have to cover at least part of his workload till they get a replacement, but I expect Benny Shumway will do most of the complicated stuff. Otherwise—'

Just what I need at this point, Paul thought sadly, *a comedian.* 'Thanks, anyway,' he said. 'I don't suppose you'd consider telling me who you really are?'

The bald man smiled. 'Sure I'll consider it. There, done that. No. Be seeing you.'

Surprising himself with the speed of his own reactions (three years of compulsory tennis at school and he'd never actually hit the ball once; apparently he'd improved since then) Paul grabbed for the bald man's windpipe. But his fingers closed on empty air, and a thoroughly unpleasant buzzing sensation ran down his arm as far as his elbow: something like an electric shock. Well, it was an answer of sorts. He lifted the rifle in his left hand and looked at it with mild distaste. It was lighter than he'd expected, rather tinny and plasticky and cheap-and-nasty-look-ing, and he didn't really trust it not to go off of its own accord if he bumped into something or dropped it. On the other hand, it was the only friend he had in this dimension, as against two extremely hostile and athletic enemies.

'Here's looking at you, kid,' he muttered.

As if he didn't have enough to put up with, Paul also had a vague but alarming feeling that he was lost. Edging along the corridor (sketchy memories of how Starsky and Hutch used to do it; but he couldn't have remembered right, because he kept tripping over his feet) he came to a fire door; he nudged it open with his foot and charged, just as the automatic door-closer brought it sharply back onto the tip of his nose. He dropped the rifle and hopped about on one foot for a while, then went back, opened the door properly and went through. He found himself in a passageway that he couldn't recall having been in before. Nothing new there; 70 St Mary Axe belonged to the Tardis school of architecture at the best of times, as he'd found out on a number of occasions when late for a meeting or an appointment. There was nothing overtly threatening or weird about this passageway. It was carpeted in hard-wearing beige Axminster, the doors were plain white with aluminium handles, and there were framed prints of the Lake District on the walls. But it seemed to go on for rather a long time, straight as a Roman road, windowless. At last he decided he couldn't take much more. He stopped, chose a door at random and went in.

The room Paul found himself in was small, window-deficient and empty, apart from a plastic stacking chair, a rather battered old desk, a telephone and a waste-paper basket. There was a thin layer of dust on the desktop; Paul was something of an expert where dust was concerned – at home, he could sit and look at it for hours, and often did – and, in his considered opinion, the desk hadn't seen the fighting surface of a duster for about a month.

Fine, he thought. *Just an empty office, no big deal.* Anyhow, he wasn't going to find what he wanted here. He turned to leave, and found that the door wasn't there any more.

Don't you just hate it when that happens? Paul had been in this situation before, not long after he'd joined the firm; he'd been trapped in his own flat for an indeterminate length of time, though nothing like as long as the two clerks who'd been marooned in the same flat for over a century. In the end he'd managed to rescue them both, and one of them was now married to Mr Tanner's mum, so the situation wasn't inherently hopeless. Even so.

He picked up the telephone. No purr or buzz; it didn't work or wasn't connected, which didn't surprise him at all. He put it down, sighed, and sat in the chair, staring at the patch of wall where the door had once been. He hadn't forgotten that he still had the pinch of Van Spee's crystals in his top pocket; they could get him out of this dimension, back to Realspace, but there was no guarantee that that would be much help. If, as he'd been led to believe, Custardspace was identical in every respect to the real thing except for the absence of life forms, if he gobbled the crystals and went back he'd still be trapped in a disused office without a door. Briefly he considered shooting a hole in the wall with the rifle, but he didn't like the idea much. Knowing his luck, either the wall would take no notice, or else the whole building would come down round his ears.

'Hello,' said a voice about nine inches from his ear. 'Who're you?'

Paul didn't jump or even flinch; he was getting used to unexplained, unexpected voices. He looked round to see who'd spoken, and saw—

Later, he realised what it reminded him of: the colouring books he'd been given as a child, where there'd been black and white outlines of things and people, which he'd filled in with his crayons and felt tips. The woman was just such an outline; he could see the opposite wall through her, but he could also see her shape quite clearly – a head, arms, body, down to the waist where she disappeared behind the desk. With a big box and crayons and enough time, he could colour her in and then she'd probably exist.

'Hello,' Paul replied. 'Are you a ghost?'

She laughed. 'I suppose I am,' she said, 'though actually it's a bit offensive calling me that, not terribly PC.'

'Sorry,' Paul said. 'What ought I to call you?'

'The preferred term,' she replied gravely, 'is consultant. Not that any of them use it. Dennis Tanner calls me spiritware, or at least that's how I'm described in the accounts; though I'm down in the books as a fixed asset, which can't be all bad. Humphrey Wells calls me *that bitch*, but we never did get on. Judy doesn't call me anything, wild horses wouldn't drag her in here. Cas Suslowicz calls me Miss du Guesclin, he's always very polite and proper. Dietrich Wurmtoter calls me Toni, which I really don't care for very much. You can call me Antonia if you like. Who are you?'

'Paul Carpenter,' Paul replied. 'Um, pleased to meet you.'

Antonia smiled; at least, two thin black lines in thin air curved. 'Likewise,' she said. 'Who are you? You're a bit young to be a partner. Are you a clerk?'

Paul nodded. 'Junior clerk,' he said. 'At least, I was. Don't know what I am now. I was working for Mr Laertides, as his assistant, but that's all a bit complicated, really—'

'That's all right,' she said. 'This is friendly small talk, not a police investigation. You don't know who I am, do you?'

Paul shook his head. 'But don't read anything into that,' he added, 'because I've only been here less than a year, and I've never even been down this corridor before.'

'Well, of course you haven't. You don't know what the corridor is, either, do you?'

'Actually, no.'

'This,' Antonia said, 'is Death Row. No, don't worry, it's not like that. It's just a sort of nickname. This is where all the ex-partners have their offices, you see.'

'Ex-partners,' Paul repeated. 'Um, if that's an explanation, I guess I must be too thick to understand it.'

Antonia giggled. 'Quite all right,' she said. '"Ex" is just a polite way of saying dead. You see, when you get made a partner in J. W. Wells, you have to sign a partnership agreement, and the terms and conditions are pretty, well, strict, really. Basically, unless the others decide to throw you out on your ear for stealing money or something, once a partner, always a partner. And they don't let you off the hook just because your body eventually wears out and you die. You just get moved to a smaller office. Like this one.'

Paul frowned; then he opened his mouth and closed it again.

'Other firms have sleeping partners,' Antonia went on. 'That's where you don't do any work but you still get a share of the money. We've got the opposite; we don't get paid, but the contract says we still have to work. So they shunt us up here, in Theo Van Spee's artificial dimension, where the rules aren't quite the same; and that, by the way, is why you never found this part of the building before, if you've only been here in ordinary space. It's all rather clever, really,' she said, with just the very faintest hint of bitterness. 'At the time, when you sign on, you think gosh, that's wonderful, it's as good as being immortal. But after a while—' She sighed. 'My speciality is applied numerology; that's doing magic with numbers, which is just another way of saying I'm an accountant. And you don't have to be alive to be an accountant, in fact in many ways it's a positive drawback; so here I am, thirty-seven years after I died, still plugging quietly away.'

Paul stared at her for a while, then said, 'Oh.'

'That puts it very neatly,' Antonia replied. 'Actually it's not that bad. Before, you see, my friends all used to say to me, "Come on, Antonia, get a life," and it always used to make me feel just a little bit guilty, because I was always so busy, never had time to get around to it. But now there's just work, and nobody gives me a hard time about working evenings and weekends and holidays and Christmas any more, and mostly it *feels* the same, except I don't get hungry or cold or tired, and my feet don't go to sleep when I've been sitting still for hours on end. In a way, I suppose it's an improvement; for an accountant, death is a form of evolution. At least,' she added sadly, 'that's what I tell myself sometimes. The rest of the time, I sit here and do the numbers.'

'That's', Paul said, and left it there. There was only so much you could say in words.

'Anyhow,' Antonia said briskly, 'that's enough about me. What are you doing here? Did Theo send you to fetch something?'

Paul shook his head. 'It's a long story,' he said.

Antonia clapped the outlines of her hands together. 'Splendid,' she said. 'Start at the beginning and go very slowly, it'll make it last longer.'

'Actually,' Paul said awkwardly, 'I'd rather not. A lot of it's quite embarrassing, and most of the rest of it I don't understand.'

Antonia grinned, in between the lines. 'Here's the deal,' she said. 'You tell me the story, and perhaps I can explain some of the bits you're confused about. No promises, mind, but I've been here a very long time, and I *was* a partner, after all. Go on,' she added. 'If you're in a tearing hurry, I can stop Time if you like; then you can tell me the whole thing and you won't be late for whatever it is you've got to do. How's that?'

Paul thought for four seconds. 'Actually,' he said, 'I'd really like that. You see, I've been living in this horrible weird place for nearly a year and there's never been anybody I can talk to about it – well, apart from Sophie, but that was awkward at the best of times, and then she left me, because of Countess Judy, and—'

'Oooh, that sounds good. Start at the beginning,' Antonia said firmly.

So Paul told her, the whole story; everything from the interview right up to escaping from the strongroom with Colin the goblin, and watching his alter ego swordfighting with Ricky Wurmtoter in the closed-file store. It all came tumbling out, every weird, baffling bit of it, all the frustration and resignation and despair, the pain of losing Sophie, the even greater pain of being himself. As he talked, steadily getting faster and less controlled, Antonia listened, not saying anything, occasionally nodding to show that she was listening and following the narrative; from time to time the outline of her hand moved across the desktop, as if she was making notes on invisible paper with an invisible pencil. As he approached the end of the story he glanced up, and probably it was just fatigue or his imagination, but he fancied that the insides of her outline, the places where the colour would go, were starting to get just a little opaque; the view of the wall or the desk through her was very slightly blurred, like the faintest trace of mist on a mirror.

'And that's about it, really,' Paul said at last. 'I was poking about looking for Ricky Wurmtoter, I wandered into this room, and now I'm stuck. Pretty silly way to end up, don't you think?'

For a second or two, Antonia didn't reply. Then she looked at him – her eyes were just a sketch in empty air, but he couldn't meet her gaze for long and had to look away – and said, 'I think that, by and large, all things considered, you've made a pretty reasonable fist of it, Paul Carpenter. I mean, yes,' she added, 'you've done a few bloody stupid things along the way; and, yes, you have the emotional development of a walnut and what you understand about how women think could be written on the point of a needle and still leave room for an infinite number of dancing angels. That aside, though, you've done a good deal better than a lot of people would've done in your shoes. Not that it matters much what I think,' she added, 'but I thought I'd mention it, anyway.'

'Thanks,' Paul said. 'It helps.'

'You're most welcome.' Perhaps she flickered slightly; it was hard to tell. 'It sounds like you've had a rough life, all things considered.'

'Me?' Paul thought about that. 'Well, yes, I suppose. Or at least, well, no. I mean, I've always had enough to eat, and clothes and somewhere to sleep, and it's not like I've spent my life dodging the storm troopers or having rocks thrown at me in the street. It could've been a lot worse.'

'And a lot better.'

Paul shrugged. 'I think it could always be better, no matter how lucky you are. And it can always be worse, unless you're dead . . . No offence,' he added quickly. 'I mean—'

'You mean, look at me: dead, and still an accountant. Perfectly valid point. But you shouldn't have interrupted – I was providing moral support, making you feel better about yourself.'

In between the lines, Antonia was now almost grey, as though he'd coloured her in with the dirty water he'd once cleaned his watercolour brushes with. 'Yes,' he said, 'you were. Kind of you.'

She shrugged. 'Nothing better to do with my time. But you were telling me about your life.'

Paul managed not to frown; because, yes, up to a point he had, but not all of it, only the nasty, smelly JWW bit. The entire biography was a different matter, and somehow he wasn't sure that any amount of support and sympathy really entitled her to that. 'You were going to explain the stuff I don't understand,' he reminded her.

'So I was, yes. But in order to do that, I need more data. More of your life story.' Antonia smiled again, and this time he could see more than just bare, thin lines. Grey swirls of half-digested colour were coagulating in between them, like steam in a glass tube. It wasn't a face yet, not by a long way, but Paul had the oddest feeling that, when it turned into one, he might well recognise it. 'For background, you see, to understand you better. I have the feeling that not many people have ever tried to understand you properly.'

He shrugged. 'Why would they want to? It's not like I'm anyone interesting or anything.'

'There you go, putting yourself down.' The grey was just beginning to blush pink in places, rather like the grey bits on the edges of grilled salmon. 'Obviously, if you go through life saying, "I'm boring, I'm not worth bothering with, you don't want to waste your time on me," eventually people are going to start taking you at your word. But it's not true. You aren't just some dull, grey, featureless thing in a suit, you're a unique, different individual. Of course you aren't boring. You're fascinating.'

'Thanks,' Paul said, 'but I don't think so. Nobody's ever found me fascinating in my whole life.'

'I do.' Not just her face and hands; on the desk between them, Paul thought he could see things – a stapler, a dictating machine, one of those page-a-day tear-off calendars, a couple of photo frames. That was – well, odd, because they certainly hadn't been there before. Maybe it was a case of his eyes adjusting to the light. 'Mind if I sit down?' he said.

'Go ahead,' Antonia said cheerfully. 'Make yourself comfy. Do you mind if I tell you some things about yourself, Paul Carpenter? Frankly, and without pulling any punches?'

'Sure,' Paul mumbled. 'Go ahead.'

'Good. Pin your ears back and listen carefully, because this is all good stuff.' Antonia's eyes flashed slightly; they were green. 'You want to know what your trouble is? You're a scaredy-cat. You're afraid of going out there and seeing what life has to offer, because you just might get caught up in something you want to

244 • Tom Holt

be a part of, and then you'll have to stick around, you won't be able to scuttle back to your skanky little flat and your warm little nest of self-pity. You know what people see when they look at you for the first time?'

Paul thought for a moment. 'Big ears?'

She shook her head, and her hair flowed round her shoulders. 'Not big ears, Paul Carpenter. Not a thin, beaky nose or goggly eyes. They see what you want them to see, the face you put on in front of the mirror each morning. It's just that old effective magic – you ought to know all about that by now. But what they didn't tell you is, everybody can do it, a little bit. Everybody does it all the time, without thinking, without realising. You do this magic thing where you barricade yourself in behind a few aspects of your appearance, and you're damned if you're going to come out, not if they lob in tear gas and stun grenades. Shakespeare said, whoever loved, that loved not at first sight? Absolutely, totally correct, it's all in that very first eyeful, and all the rest's just rationalisation, interpreting at your leisure the little bits of information that you took in subconsciously the first time you saw her. Hence your Maginot ears, Paul Carpenter, and your carefully crafted half-witted expression. Anybody can make themselves look like a total dork; the handsomest man, the prettiest woman, if they stand in front of the mirror and pull faces for long enough they can come up with something that nobody could ever want to love. But that's not what they want, so they don't do it. You, on the other hand—'

Antonia flung out a hand in a theatrical gesture and knocked down one of the picture frames. Paul picked it up and stood it upright.

'You, on the other hand, *want* to be a clown,' she went on. 'You want every female you meet to take one look at you and say, "No, not him." It's what we all do, isn't it? Every time we meet someone new, at that first moment of encounter we look at them and there's a little voice in our heads saying, "Is it him, is it her, the one?" It's only a teeny-tiny moment, and then, nine hundred and ninety-nine thousand, nine hundred and ninety-nine times out of a million, the voice says "No," and we forget all about it. And you put on the face that'll make them say no, because that's what you want. And why the hell do you do that? Because deep in your fuzzy little brain, a million times out of a million, that little voice's saying yes. But you can't have them all, you know that perfectly well, so you've fixed it so you won't ever get any of them, and that takes care of that. I'm right, aren't I?'

Slowly, Paul shook his head. Of course he was listening to what she was saying, every word of it, but right then his attention was mostly fixed on the framed photo he'd just put back on the desk. It was blank, of course; just a white piece of card surrounded by a gilded frame. 'I don't think so,' he said. 'No disrespect and all that. But I can prove it; because, you see, I really did love Sophie. *Do* love her, except—'

'Except that now, you can actually have her,' Antonia went on harshly. 'For ever and ever, no doubts, no insecurities, it's a chemically guaranteed dead certainty, thanks to the love philtre. Which is why, suddenly, you'd do anything to get out of it. It's so blindingly obvious. If you really loved her, even one little bit, you'd be so thrilled she'd drunk the stuff you'd be dancing on the ceiling. If you really love her, you'd know she's just right for you, and you're just right for her. All the philtre does is make sure that nothing can go wrong this time round. You do see that, don't you?'

'Sorry?' Paul looked at her as if he'd just woken up. He was sure there was something about the photo, something he'd already seen, but he couldn't quite figure out what it was. 'No, you're missing the point,' he said. 'Drinking the philtre's ruined everything, it's every bit as bad as when Countess Judy blanked out those bits of her mind, it's—'

As soon as he said the name, the last piece dropped into place. Quickly he glanced down at the blank card in the frame. But it wasn't blank. No picture; but there was handwriting: flowing, squiggly, flashy sort of handwriting, the kind that looks really elegant and classy, but you actually have to squint to read the words. And the words were—

Happy birthday, sis!
Love, Judy.

He looked up at her again; and now all the lines were coloured in, flesh and hair and eyes, everything except the very tip of her nose, which was still faintly translucent. Now that he knew, of course, the family resemblance was unmistakable.

'Excuse me,' Paul said, 'but are you one of the Fey?'

Every vestige of expression drained out of her face. 'Yes,' she said.

'And is Countess Judy your sister?'

Antonia nodded. 'My kid sister, actually,' she said. 'And didn't it ever take you a long time to figure it out. Luckily,' she added, with a slight curl of the edge of her mouth, 'long enough. Thanks a lot, by the way, I couldn't have done it without you. And gorgeous irony, of course. You murdered my sister, but you've brought me back to life. Even Stevens, you might say.'

She stretched out her hand, lifted up the picture frame and put it straight. There was a picture in it now, of course.

'Back to life,' Paul repeated. It wasn't a question; rather, it was the syntactical form known to philologists as a statement implying the term *Oh shit*. 'You really were dead, and now—'

'That's right,' Antonia said. 'And in just a moment, I'm going to stroll out through a door that'll magically appear in the middle of that wall, and you'll be stuck in here for ever and ever, all on your ownsome with nothing to read. Honestly,' she added, 'there's naive and trusting, and there's going down on bended knee and *begging* to be snared and drained. Soon as you came in, I knew that a little scrap of sympathy and under-standing'd have you by the balls. All I had to do was make it sound like I gave a toss, and out it all came, gushing like a Scouser's vomit: your whole heart and soul, every last drop of you.' She stood up. She was very tall. 'Get a life, they said to me when I was working here. And I have, haven't I? Not what I'd have chosen, of course,' she said. 'In fact, slumming it would be putting it mildly. But beggars can't be choosers, and it'll do to get me out of here, till I find something better. Actually, I think you're such a pathetic loser that you might actually prefer it in here; in which case, enjoy. I'll be going now,' she said, and at once the outline of a door began to glow sky blue on the wall in front of her. 'Any last request, by the way? Just as long as it's something easy and trivial that won't put me out at all.'

Paul looked at her. That last bit, the tip of her nose, was almost perfectly solid, but not quite. 'You're alive again,' he said.

'That's right. Actually, *again* is a bit misleading; not strictly accurate where the Fey are concerned. Right now, though, I'm most definitely alive.'

'And human?'

'Human as you are,' Antonia replied jauntily. 'Were, at any rate. So, any small favour I can do for you?'

The door was swinging open; it was ajar, it was yawning, and light was streaming through. 'There *is* one thing,' Paul said.

'Well?'

Paul swung the rifle up from under the table and pointed it at her head. 'Say hello to Mr Dao for me,' he said, and pulled the trigger.

Antonia screamed as the colour drained out of her. Paul fired again, and the noise hit him like a hammer. The door began to swing shut; Paul closed his eyes, dropped the rifle and hurled himself at her: into her, through her – and through the open door.

He hit the floor of the corridor just as the door clicked shut behind him. When he craned his head round, there was no trace that it had ever been there.

Instinctively, he put a hand to his face and felt his nose. It was different. Smaller. He collapsed to his knees and threw up.

On the other hand, he thought, once he'd finished regurgitating, she'd been right about one thing.

He wiped his mouth on his cuff. *Bloody fucking Fey*, he said to himself, *why can't they just leave me alone? And now they've gone and made me kill someone. I really didn't want to do that, not ever; not even someone who's dead already.*

On the other hand—

Paul stood up slowly, positively relishing the sensation of movement. 'That,' he said aloud, 'was for implying I'd make a good accountant.'

On the other hand, she *had* been right, he could see that now: about the barricade, the Maginot ears, the not wanting to come out and play in case the other kids were nasty to him. He'd sort of guessed it while he was being Phil Marlow, but he'd been able to explain it away because Phil had the looks, the bone structure, the easy smile. But it had all been simple effective magic, and Mr Laertides hadn't actually taught him a single thing he hadn't already known, that day on the train. It had taken the full malevolence of the Fey to make him admit it to himself, to force him to acknowledge that life was worth taking a flying leap through his deadliest enemy for.

Appropriate; Antonia had tried to steal him from himself. And hadn't he always been his own deadliest enemy?

Till now.

Shame, though, about his nose. Paul wondered what it looked like. Was the very tip missing, snapped off like a carrot? He tried to picture himself with a truncated snout. If only she could've taken a quarter of an inch off each ear, she'd have been doing him a favour.

The fire door, he noticed, was a foot to his left. In which case, he was just up-corridor of the ladies' toilet; where (because there's a grain of truth in even the most offensive gender stereotypes) there was bound to be a fully operational mirror. Normally, of course, Paul wouldn't have dreamed under any circumstances whatsoever of walking into a ladies' toilet; but he was still in Custardspace, wasn't he, and he had it on the very best authority that the whole dimension was completely uninhabited, apart from a few trespassers and associates of Theo van Spee. In which case, he'd probably be fairly safe—

He pushed open the door, and somebody screamed.

Not just any old scream, either; it was like having the inside of his head rasped and sanded. Paul jumped back, slammed the door and mumbled 'Sorry' several times in a row.

'Paul?'

Of all the toilets in all the offices in all the world . . . He froze, caught like a rabbit in the headlight glare of her small beady round red eyes. Too late now to make a run for it, anyhow. She'd seen him, and that was enough. 'Um,' he replied. 'Yes.'

'*Paul?*' The door flew open, and Mr Tanner's mum came

bounding out like a stack of cans collapsing. 'You *bastard*,' she screeched, 'I thought you were dead.'

'Well, I'm not, all right?' Churlish, yes, but he really wasn't in the mood to explain anything right now. 'And yes, I'm sorry if you got upset thinking I'd died, but—'

'*Upset!*' She fired the word at him like a harpoon shot at a whale. 'You arsehole, I went to your funeral. I *cried*.'

'I know, I saw you. But I assumed you were upset' – he emphasised the word deliberately – 'because I thought you were afraid of getting sued. I mean,' he went on, ignoring the look of fury on her face, 'if you didn't like me being dead, maybe you shouldn't have bloody well had me killed in the first place.'

'I explained all that,' she roared. 'And you weren't killed. You escaped just fine. I saw you that evening, remember, when you got back. So don't go blaming me for what happened to you.' Mr Tanner's mum paused, righteous fury disputing for possession of her mind with unbearable curiosity. 'So what happened to you, then?'

Paul sighed and thought, *Well, why not?* 'It's a long story, but the gist is, Mr Laertides taught me how to change how I look.'

She frowned. 'What? He gave you fashion tips?'

'Taught me how to remould my bone structure, shorten my nose, deflate my ears, all that stuff. So I did. You've been seeing me round the place every day for weeks.'

'But—' She stopped dead. 'Philip Marlow. You turned yourself into Philip Marlow.'

Paul nodded. 'Got there in the end, then.'

A slight sway of the torso, rolling of the right shoulder, forewarned Paul of the coming punch, just in time for him to take one step to the side, one step back. Her balled fist swung through the patch of air he'd just vacated. 'You rotten, callous, thoughtless, self-centred shit,' she snarled. 'And hold still while I'm hitting you. You can do your shoulder in, hitting hard into empty air.'

'No way,' Paul replied. 'Holding still, I mean. I didn't ask you to be unhappy or anything. I kept telling you, no offence but I'm just not interested that way.' He could feel himself starting to go beetroot colour round the ears – an unfortunate effect, he couldn't help thinking, given the outstanding size of the bloody things. Probably he looked like a portable sunset. 'Anyhow,' he said sharply, 'I'm not dead, so that's all right, isn't it? Look, you can shout at me all you like, but would you mind dreadfully if we did it later? Because I'm actually really rather busy right now, and—'

Mr Tanner's mum made an ominous creaky growling sort of noise, like a huge iceberg calving. 'You know what?' she said. 'I think I liked you better when you were dead. Yes, all right, subject closed. For now, anyway.'

'Good,' he said briskly. 'Right then. What the hell are you doing here, anyhow?'

'Me?' She frowned. 'Our Dennis asked me to. I'm part of the posse, hunting down Phil Marlow for killing Ricky Wurmtoter. Actually,' she added, 'I'm the *whole* posse, on account of the rest of them thinking they could skip over here using a pentangle, an athame and a packet of Bird's custard powder. Told them it wouldn't work, and I was right.'

Paul clicked his tongue. 'So how did *you* get here, then?'

'Guess. Oh, all right, then. I used the Door.'

'Door?' Then something clicked in his mind. 'The Portable Door, you mean.'

'Of course. Borrowed it off little Paul Azog, I knew he wouldn't begrudge his dear old mum. Needn't have bothered, need I, if that Phil Marlow doesn't even—' She hesitated, frowned. 'Hang on,' she said. 'If you were Phil Marlow all along, did you murder our Ricky?'

'Oh, for crying out loud,' Paul snapped. 'No, I bloody well didn't. Nobody did, he's over here, alive and kicking and—' Pause. 'At least,' he added, 'he was last time I saw him. But that was a while ago now, and things may have changed a bit since then. Anyway,' he added decisively, 'screw him. If you've got the Door with you, we can both of us go back through it, right? That's wonderful, it'll solve everything.'

'Like hell,' Mr Tanner's mum replied. 'Haven't you been listening? Our Dennis has got every goblin in the building out looking for you. Wanted, dead or alive. And saying that to goblins is a bit like asking you, "Do you want your tea hot or cold and full of worms?" Now if Ricky really is here, we can grab him and take him back with us, and just maybe that'll convince our Dennis that maybe it's not such a watertight case against you as he thought. But you know him – I wouldn't bank on it. Otherwise, you'll just have to stay here.'

'No, I won't.' Then he thought, *Yes, I will*; because Colin the goblin had told him that Mr Laertides had let Mr Tanner in on the secret, and Tanner knew who Phil Marlow really was. 'Fine,' he said wearily. 'Let's go and find Ricky Wurmtoter, then, shall we? As a matter of fact, I was just going to look for him myself. Actually,' he remembered, 'I was sort of planning on challenging him to a duel. But if we've got the Door, I won't have to, which is nice.'

'You were going to—' She stared at him. 'What the hell would you want to go and do a stupid thing like that for?'

'It's complicated,' Paul sighed wearily. 'Really, really complicated. It's a load of crap about living swords and stuff, and I think custard and early Canadian history come into it somewhere, and Vicky the mermaid and a small, bald bloke with a round head like a melon. But with the Door, I don't have to do any of that stuff, I can cheat. Well?'

Mr Tanner's mum shrugged. 'Whatever. I take it you're imploring me for my help, because you know you haven't got a politician's chance in hell on your own.'

'What? Oh yes, right. If you're not busy or anything.'

Suddenly she grinned. 'Anything for you, sugar muffin, you know that. All right, where was Ricky when you saw him last?'

Where was Ricky? Well, he was being hunted down by a carbon copy of me armed with a living sword and hell-bent on slicing him into little thin strips, but I got sidetracked gunning down a dead Fey in cold blood, so they could be anywhere by now.

'Um,' Paul said.

CHAPTER ELEVEN

Actually, the trail wasn't that hard to pick up and follow, consisting as it did of trashed furniture, doors hacked down and drooping sadly from their hinges, banister rails chopped into firewood, shredded curtains, disembowelled filing cabinets and other subtle clues. It led from the closed-file store along the corridor, through the laser-printer room (which no longer contained a functional laser printer), up the stairs, over the landing, down the stairs to the strongroom (apparently not as strong as all that), back up the stairs to the third floor, in and out of half a dozen offices, back down the other staircase into the front office, sideways into the post room, and along the corridor straight back to the closed-file store from the other direction.

'Which suggests—' Paul started to say.

The closed-file store no longer had a door in any meaningful sense, but there were just enough splinters still hanging on to the hinges to provide a screen of sorts. They paused and listened; sure enough, from the other side of the doorway came bangs, crashes, thuds, the clash of steel and what Paul took to be some very rude words indeed in Old Norse.

'I think they're in there,' he whispered.

Mr Tanner's mum nodded. 'Fine,' she said; then she asked, 'And one of them's our Ricky. So who's the other one, then?'

'No idea. Sorry.'

She looked at him and grinned. 'You want me to go first, don't you?'

'If it's no bother.'

Her grin spread a couple of inches, like an oil slick. 'This would be a good time for me to name my price,' she said. 'How about dinner at my place, followed by – shit, I was only kidding. Come back here.' She grabbed his shoulder and pulled him back. 'If they kill me,' she said, 'the Door's stuffed down the front of my knickers.' She leered at him. 'You just help yourself, all right?'

'Come back safe,' Paul replied, with feeling.

'Spoilsport.' Mr Tanner's mum took a deep shouldered aside the tattered fragments of the door, and bundled through. Paul heard a crash, a chunky sort of sound, another noise which could conceivably have been two skulls colliding with great force, and Mr Tanner's mum yelling 'What the *hell*—?' Then silence.

'Mr Carpenter.'

Paul swung round so fast that he almost lost his footing. Behind him stood Professor Van Spee. He looked pretty much the same as always – long, thin, little wispy white beard, old but best-quality dark grey wool worsted suit, watery pale blue eyes – apart from the custard pie on a paper plate that he held in his right hand. That was a new one on Paul, and he wasn't quite sure he liked it.

'Please take one step to your right,' the professor said. 'Thank you.'

Well, Paul thought, *why not? It's not as though I'm particularly attached to this square foot of carpet.* Naturally he wasn't in the least bit scared of an old man with a custard pie, of all things. Absolutely not. Ridiculous. No, he just fancied a very small spot of exercise, change of perspective, fresh carpet squares and pastures new. He moved.

'Thank you,' the professor repeated, and with his left hand he pointed at the door frame and the mangled remains of the door. There was no flash of brilliant blue light, shower of sparks, ripple effect; but the doorway sort of healed up, rather quickly, until there was nothing to show that it had ever been there.

'Just a minute,' Paul said. 'There's people in there.'

The professor nodded. 'Correct,' he said. 'Dietrich Wurmtoter, Mr Tanner's mother and—' He sighed, apparently with genuine regret. 'You,' he added. 'It's very disappointing. I had hoped that this time, matters could have been arranged rather more efficiently, and with a minimum of suffering. Unfortunately not. Naturally, I accept all the blame myself. I should have done better. I—' He hesitated, like someone bracing himself to pull a plaster off his arm. 'I am sorry,' he said.

That didn't sound good at all. 'What did you just do?' Paul demanded. 'Can they get out?'

The professor shook his head. 'Sadly, no,' he replied. 'Not even by using my Portable Door, which for some reason Mr Tanner's mother has seen fit to insert inside her underwear. It can bring you back from the Land of the Dead, as you know, but it will not work where they have gone. Indeed, where the whole room has gone. Demolish that wall, and you will find yourself out in the street. Most unfortunate.'

Paul stared at him for a moment. 'They're dead, then,' he said. 'You killed them.'

'In a sense.' The professor frowned slightly. 'Mr Carpenter, you have seen yourself what I can do: how I can shift the course of comets, calculate the effects of such alterations hundreds of years in the future. I can do most things, in fact. I can build worlds,' he added, in a mild, almost apologetic voice, 'such as the one we are presently occupying. It is certainly not beyond my capabilities to end two lives, either practically or in terms of having the determination to do such a serious thing. They no longer exist, and I have brought that about. I suppose you could interpret that as an act of killing.'

'Right,' Paul said. 'Glad we got the semantics sorted out. Why?'

'Ah.' The professor sighed. 'That, Mr Carpenter, would be a very long story. You wish to hear it, but you are also very angry, and also rather afraid. You are speculating as to whether you can escape from me, or whether you would be able to overpower me, possibly do me bodily harm. Part of you believes that you ought to want to harm me – a duty to exact revenge, to punish me for what I have just done. Another part of you abhors the thought of violence, and has not yet come to terms with the killing of Antonia du Guesclin, even though that was done in self-defence and would be considered entirely justifiable in virtually all legal jurisdictions. You are also tired, confused, hungry and painfully thirsty, and you have pulled a muscle in your neck.'

'Fuck you,' Paul said.

'Anger.' The professor nodded slowly, like a wine buff acknowledging an adequate burgundy. 'An admirable piece of engineering, in its way. Anger is both a lubricant and an anaesthetic. Evolution requires that we retain it in our genetic matrix because it makes it possible for us in moments of great stress and danger to override various restraint mechanisms – fear, for example, and ethics – in order to do something necessary but unpleasant.' Slowly and carefully, he put the custard pie down on the floor. 'Anger at an injury, to ourselves or to one of our own, makes it possible to retaliate, to avenge, thereby preventing or making less likely a repetition of the original injury. It is as useful as any other tool, but it is in essence a very simplistic reaction. It is possible to control it, even in the most extreme circumstances, and I would urge you to do so in this case. It will not help, and it is likely to make things worse for you. However,' the professor added, 'if you feel you absolutely must, you may proceed.'

Paul thought about it. Absolutely must he? *Well*, he thought, *yes*. He took a big step towards the professor, until he was about two feet from his nose, then swung back his right fist and punched as hard as he could.

He missed. At first he assumed that the professor had ducked, but now he came to think of it, he'd maintained eye contact all the time and the old bastard hadn't moved at all. He'd just missed, that was all.

'You may try again if you wish,' the professor said, 'but the outcome will be the same. In case you feel belittled or humiliated by your failure to harm me, I should point out that thousands have tried it and no one has ever succeeded. It can't be done.'

'Like hell,' Paul snapped, and lashed out with his leg. He felt something go in his knee and hobbled over to the wall for support. 'Ow,' he complained.

'A very slight sprain,' the professor said. 'There should be no lasting impairment. Can we consider the experiment duly carried out?'

Paul nodded. 'Bastard,' he said. 'So, are you going to kill me too?'

This time the professor frowned, as though what Paul had just said didn't make sense. 'But I already have,' he said, inclining his head in the direction of the patch of wall where the door had once been. 'Further action would therefore be superfluous, and a pointless waste of resources. However,' he added sternly, 'I'm afraid I shall have to ask you to leave this place. Your presence is frankly disruptive, and as you must by now appreciate, matters are coming to a head. You do not know where to go, of course, and I must confess that I cannot help you to reach a decision. However, it is of little importance, all things considered, either to you or to me.' He paused and looked at Paul with a curious blend of annoyance and compassion. 'You do not understand,' he said. 'Perhaps it would be a kindness to explain, after all. I have not done so before on the grounds that the parts of the story that concern you would cause you undue alarm, and the parts that do not are none of your concern. However, in spite of everything I am and always have been primarily a scientist; intellectual curiosity is my besetting sin, and I find it hard to deny it in others. If you wish to hear the whole story, Mr Carpenter, I will tell it to you. Then you must leave. Is that acceptable to you?'

Paul shook his head. 'No,' he said. 'But tell me, anyway.'

The professor smiled. 'You only wish to learn in the hope that the knowledge will better equip you to fight,' he said. 'If you were not involved, you would prefer not to know. But nevertheless, I will tell you. Perhaps it will make me feel better if I tell you. On balance, I believe that is the true reason. No matter.' He blinked, and a deep, snug-looking armchair appeared out of nowhere. Rather to his surprise, Paul discovered that he was sitting in it.

'You are sitting comfortably,' the professor said. 'I shall begin.'

In the beginning (said Professor Van Spee) there was darkness and emptiness and confusion. The creator of all things brought light and order and understanding, and the universe began. He divided everything into four elements: earth, air, fire and water. He held them in place by the force of his will, arranged them in time so that one thing followed another, confined them in space so that each of them had form and structure and was separate from the rest. That is how it was meant to be, and it was a satisfactory arrangement. Unfortunately, I saw fit to interfere. With hindsight I regret having done so. However, I had very little choice, as you will see.

As I mentioned a moment ago, I am a scientist. All I ever wanted to do was to understand how things worked, what made the universe behave as it does, the properties of materials, the effect of processes, the nature of time. Accordingly I studied long and hard, and eventually I learned everything, the answers to all the questions that I have just referred to. I knew and I understood, and there was nothing left to find out.

I was, therefore, at something of a loss. When, as a young man, I had set myself to my task, I had assumed, perhaps foolishly, that it was impossible, that I must inevitably die before I could complete it. But, in the course of my researches, I discovered simple techniques for the unlimited extension of life, the arrest of entropy and decay; death no longer applied to me, neither did sickness or disability. I had also assumed that my frail human intellect would not be able to grasp the vastness of the concepts that I had set myself to address. In that, too, I was wrong. In due course, therefore, I reached the point where I had accomplished the purpose of my existence, but in doing so I had made it impossible for that existence to come to a natural end. I could only cease to exist if I took steps – difficult, complicated steps involving lengthy and tedious procedures – to destroy myself. Quite apart from an instinctive reluctance, I felt that to destroy such a complete and unique work of scholarship as I had become would be the most unpardonable act of vandalism. I could not do it. But I had no purpose. I had nothing to do.

I was bored.

It then occurred to me that, since I had complete and perfect knowledge of the universe as it existed, I might find a worthwhile occupation for my time in creating another universe, an artificial one if you wish to call it that. Compared to my original task, this would be a trivial matter, an amusement, a diversion; I couldn't hope to learn anything from it, since by its very nature it would contain nothing that I didn't already know and understand. But you must appreciate that hitherto, I had been passive, a mere consumer of pre-existing information. It would make a pleasant change, I felt, to be active, to create rather than merely to observe. And, as I have said, I had nothing better to do with my time.

Immediately I found that my choices were restricted by the nature of the materials available to me. There are, as I have told you, only four elements from which the universe is made up. At once, I took a fierce delight in the challenge; the contrariness of my nature rejoiced to find something that apparently I could not do, and I was grimly determined to do it, for that very reason. I resolved to create – more accurately, to synthesise – a completely new element. And, in my arrogance, I made up my mind that it should not only be new, but *better* than the original four. I would create my new element, and my entire self-made universe would be built from it alone. By virtue of that, it would be different, to a greater or lesser extent, from the natural universe. In those differences might lie new things to learn, new mysteries to explore. You might say that I was in the position of a detective who, having solved all the crimes in the world, must resort to committing new crimes of his own in order to have something to investigate. The analogy is, of course, imperfect, but I offer it for what it is worth.

In order to create my new element, therefore, I stole the Great Cow of Heaven—

'You what?' Paul interrupted.

'I beg your pardon?'

'Did you just say,' Paul elucidated, 'the Great Cow of Heaven?'

'Correct. Her name is Audumla, and from her milk the Creator of all things—'

'Fuck a stoat sideways up a palm tree,' Paul said. 'Sorry, I interrupted. You were saying.'

★

I stole the Great Cow of Heaven (continued Professor Van Spee) and drew off a sufficient quantity of her milk into a standard opaque Mortensen chamber. Having skimmed the milk in the usual way I added cornflour, eggs and a small quantity of the material commonly known, I believe, as Van Spee's crystals – precisely the same material, I may add, as the sample you have in a twist of paper in your top pocket. I then subjected the resultant compound to intense bombardment with zeta-six radiation – I believe you would call it alchemical fire, although it is not properly speaking fire in the sense that you would use the term – until it was completely denatured, whereupon I froze it in a medium of transubstantiated gold alloyed with mercury and a pinch of baking soda. The result was a glutinous yellow semi-liquid with a slightly sweet taste, bearing a striking resemblance to ordinary confectioner's custard. When subjected to all the standard tests, however, the substance satisfied all the criteria of a new element. It also, as I subsequently discovered, had some remarkable and unexpected properties.

Although an element in itself, it could both permeate and penetrate the other four; and in doing so, inevitably, it moulded itself to the shape of any given object, so as in effect to create an apparently identical copy of it, existing in parallel to it both in time and space. I will say that again, in case you have failed to appreciate its significance. When brought into contact with any inanimate object made up of earth, air, fire or water, a quantity of the element will form itself into an exact but detached replica. I was not able to find a way to duplicate living matter: organic matter once dead could be replicated as easily as stone or plastic, but nothing alive. To date, in all the projects I have attempted, this has been my only failure. I regret it bitterly, but then, nobody is perfect. And I still have time.

Initially, I was held back by the problem of access. Although I could prove beyond any question the existence of my replicas, I couldn't actually get to them; nor could I see, touch, hear, taste or smell them. I was forced to conclude, therefore, that they existed in a separate, dedicated dimension – they had, in effect, slid through the object they were copying and out the other side into what I could only describe as Somewhere Else. This problem naturally reduced the usefulness of my creation somewhat, since all I could do with it was to enjoy the intellectual satisfaction of knowing it was there. My solution, elegant in its simplicity, was the artefact you know as the Acme Portable Door. A surprisingly basic mechanism, it allows travel backwards and forwards through time and space at will, including access to my synthetic universe. However, I soon realised that, although an efficient solution, it carried with it certain highly undesirable possibilities. In essence, it meant that I was no longer supreme ruler and sole inhabitant of my creation. Anybody coming into possession of a Portable Door could enter or leave my universe without difficulty. Naturally, that was unacceptable. Accordingly, I recalled and destroyed ten of the dozen Doors that I had constructed. One I retained for my own use; one, regrettably, went missing, and I have only recently discovered what became of it. Suffice to say that it should no longer pose a threat; it was in the possession of Mr Tanner's mother when I sealed up the closed-file store just now.

In my search for a substitute for the Door, I now at any rate had a lead that was previously not available to me. Using the one remaining Door I could, in effect, conduct my search on both sides of the interdimensional barrier; and sure enough, it was on the other side, in the synthetic universe, that I found the answer. Quite simply, Van Spee's crystals will, if taken internally, pull you back from the synthetic universe to the natural one. Once you have made that transition, ingestion of crystals will enable you to cross between the dimensions at will. Provided that your first crystal-facilitated crossing is from synthetic to natural, in other words, the process is as simple as blinking. It was then a simple matter of travelling to the synthetic universe through the Door and coming back by means of the crystals. Once I had done that, I was able to lock the Door away in a vault in the Bank of the Dead, whence it could never be removed without my express permission, and use crystals exclusively in order to commute between universes.

(*Now there*, Paul thought, *is a coincidence*. Or maybe just logic; after all, the only sane thing to do with something as massively dangerous as the Portable Door would be to stick it somewhere nobody could ever get at it. Hardly rocket science; so maybe it wasn't such a big deal that he'd had the same thought as the professor. It also meant, of course, that killing the professor extremely dead, a not unattractive idea if it turned out to be actually feasible, wouldn't really achieve a great deal, since he could use his Door to escape, just as Paul had. *Bummer.*)

I have been telling you all this (the professor continued) as if you were a fellow scientist, someone who understands the trials and frustrations of the academic life. I doubt whether that is the case. You simply don't know. In order to carry out research, one must have equipment, facilities, time; in other words, money. In theory, that is what governments are for, to provide support for learning and achievement, because what other possible justification could there be for them? In practice, of course, one must find one's funding where one can. Throughout my researches, I financed my work as all scientists must, if they lack sufficient private means. I invented things, spin-offs from my real work, and I sold them. Fatuous trifles, all of them; you can judge for yourself from the fact that my most lucrative single invention, for which I am best known in the world at large, is the portable car-parking space, which you can fold up and put in your pocket when not in use. It is, of course, merely a little piece of my synthetic universe – twelve feet by seven of my personal space, endlessly duplicated and sold over and over again, a tragic prostitution of my work but necessary nonetheless. It has paid for most of my greatest achievements. That is, of course, the way of things. Nobody will pay you money for defining the universe, and the patentee of the Black and Decker Workmate gets more in a year in royalties than the combined lifetime earnings of Newton and Archimedes. When I first invented it, needless to say, there was no call for it: no cars, no tarmac roads, in fact hardly any cities. But I foresaw that one day there would be a demand, particularly if I took steps to create one. It's ironic, don't you think, that I laid all the foundations for the invention of the internal combustion engine, indeed the whole Industrial Revolution itself, simply in order to create urban gridlock, a shortage of car-parking spaces, and a lucrative demand for what I had to sell. Transmitting the profits back in time through a series of offshore, off-world and off-dimension intermediaries was a simple enough matter, a diversion for a rainy afternoon. As always, I was in control. I knew what I was doing.

But the scope of the synthetic-universe project meant that I had to keep on inventing, making money; accordingly I resigned my academic post and joined this firm of money-grubbers. Here I could pursue my research in quiet and peace, interrupted only by the undemanding requirement of my partners that I should make them unimaginably rich. This I have done. Trifling jobs of work were assigned to me, and I dealt with them. One such insignificant little job led to all this trouble, and threatens everything I have worked for, everything I have achieved and become. That is perhaps the greatest tragedy and the greatest irony of all.

It was, on the face of, it an entirely undemanding commission. About thirty years ago a Canadian banking cartel, unhappy with changes in the corporate taxation system, decided to do something about it. They looked into the feasibility of over-throwing the government by armed force, but concluded that it wouldn't be cost-efficient. Then they consulted me. It had occurred to them that, if in 1776 the Canadian colonies had joined in the Revolutionary War, they would now be trading under American law and paying American taxes, which would save them a significant amount of money. Could I, therefore, adjust history accordingly?

Having considered the matter, I told them that such a rearrangement was entirely feasible, but that they had made several grave errors in their calculations, and that if I did as they asked, they would turn out to have been unable to compete with the US banking sector in the 1950s and been forced out of business by 1962. They were, understandably, rather disappointed, and asked me (as of course they should have done in the beginning) if I could recommend a better course of action. I did some simple arithmetic, and explained to them that if Canada had been successfully settled by Europeans in the early Middle Ages, a sufficiently powerful Canadian banking industry would have been in place by, say, 1917 to enable them to see off any threat from the US banks in the second half of the century and go on to establish a highly lucrative monopoly of the entire American continent by 1999. They were delighted by this prospect, as you can imagine, and instructed me to proceed without delay – a rather fatuous enjoinder, given the circumstances, but that's businessmen for you.

It was easy enough to pinpoint the decisive moment in history at which the fate of the earliest European settlement in Canada failed. As you may know, Vikings from Norway and Iceland under the leadership of Leif Ericson established a small colony on the coast of Labrador around the year AD 1000. History attributes their failure partly to harsh weather, crop failure and the hostility of the indigenous Amerindian population, but mostly to the sheer extent of their lines of communication and supply. They were, quite simply, too far from home to be supported, given the technological and cultural status of Viking Scandinavia. In order for the colony to have succeeded, therefore, I had to advance the civilisation of tenth-century Norway and Iceland by several centuries, so that they would be capable of maintaining a colony across three thousand miles of open sea. Once I had established that that was the prerequisite, I was able to search for and locate my hinge, my turning point; and in due course, I found it.

The precise moment when the world changed was 17 August AD 722, on a small island off the coast of Norway's Ranrike province. There, two petty chieftains fought a duel to decide which of them would rule south central Norway. In the event, King Hring of Rogaland defeated and killed King Hroar of Vestfold – you have no idea where Rogaland and Vestfold are, but it makes no difference whatsoever – and the consequences ensuing from that victory are what we know as history. Had King Hroar been the winner, however, things would have been quite different. Hroar, a visionary and social reformer, would have gone on to weld the whole of Scandinavia into a single monolithic nation, dominant in Europe for the next five centuries. The heirs of King Hroar would have possessed both the resources and the will to make a success of the Norse discovery of the New World. By the beginning of the thirteenth century,

Canada would have seized its independence; by the fourteenth, it would have grown to be the second most powerful Western nation, after France. There would have followed the usual round of religious and social conflicts, culminating in a bitter civil war somewhere around 1972, during which my client's bank would have sided with the winning faction, thereby ensuring their financial supremacy in the New World until the sun eventually goes cold and the planet ceases to be habitable. Beyond that I did not care to speculate, since the extinction of all sentient life on the planet introduces variables into the calculations that I cannot reliably extrapolate from. All I had to do, therefore, was to ensure that Hroar, not Hring, came back alive from the duel on Bersa Island in the early evening of 17 August 722.

I need not overtax your limited concentration span with technical details. It was a fairly simple matter to go back in time, using the Portable Door, and engineer a chance meeting with the two combatants en route to the island. Very occasionally, I enjoy disguises, dressing up, a little amateur acting. I played the part of an old peasant hedge-wizard living in a miserable hovel on the shores of the fjord. By the simple expedient of permitting King Hroar to save me from drowning – it did not occur to him that it was extremely unlikely that a seventy-year-old man who'd lived beside the water all his life would be unable to swim; Hroar had many sterling qualities, but intelligence was not one of them – I was able to gain his unquestioning trust. He was a basically good-hearted man, stupid, egotistical and emotionally immature but highly appreciative of what he believed was the sincere gratitude of a simple old man saved from a watery grave. Accordingly, when I offered him a gift of enormous value as a token of thanks, he accepted it without question. A wiser, more cynical man might have been suspicious, particularly since the gift was a sword. Only a fool would undertake to use a sword that he'd never handled before in a crucial and politically significant duel, a weapon given to him by a perfect stranger under circumstances of extreme melodrama. Fortunately, for me and for him, Hroar was just such a fool, since the sword I gave him was Skofnung, the most powerful of all the nine Living Blades forged by Weyland himself, a weapon that effectively guaranteed victory to anyone who wielded it. I had already been to some trouble to locate and acquire Skofnung; I eventually tracked it down in the vaults of the Petersen Collection in Oslo. That, however, was the easy part. Considerably more difficult was the task of locating the young woman who constitutes the sword's other half, without whom Skofnung is simply three feet of laminated steel. How I found her, and how I induced her to assist me, is another matter entirely, and something that I would prefer not to go into at this time.

My plan, then, was running smoothly. Once I had seen King Hroar safely aboard the boat, I made my own way to Bersa Island to watch the contest. I did so only out of curiosity, as I had no doubt whatsoever concerning the outcome. My researches had revealed that, for the duel, Hroar's opponent King Hring had chosen the axe Battle-Troll, a fine weapon of the very highest quality and one with which he was most proficient. But it was no match whatsoever for a living blade. However, I had never actually seen a Viking duel, and my scientific interest was piqued. Rendering myself invisible by means of a simple Sobieski's Glamour, I made myself comfortable and waited for the fight to begin.

It was only when King Hring unloaded his equipment from the boat that I realised that something was badly wrong. The goatskin sack was the wrong shape for an axe; somehow, he had acquired a sword instead. Nor was it just any sword. As soon as the cover was removed, I recognised it as Tyrving, another of Weyland's living blades.

As the fight began, I knew intuitively that I was not the only one seeking to meddle with history that day. Furthermore, I realised, as Tyrving parried Skofnung with an ear-splitting peal of harmonics, the substitution of Tyrving for the axe could only represent a counter to my own act of interference. Someone had figured out what I'd done, and was seeking to redress the balance. Furthermore, whoever it was lacked my knowledge and insight – to a disastrous degree. It is a property of the living blade that it never gives up; once it has begun a fight, it must inevitably finish it and achieve victory, even if it means that the fight lasts a thousand years. However, the two swords, Skofnung

266 • Tom Holt

and Tyrving, were exactly matched. Neither could overcome the other. In consequence, neither Hroar nor Hring could possibly win the fight; they would be condemned to fight it out for all time, their lives indefinitely extended, while the entire history of Canada, the New World and therefore, by implication, all humanity would be suspended – on hold, to use the modern expression – until the duel was over. In other words, thanks to the incompetent bungling of some wretched meddler, I had unwittingly brought about a temporal paradox of the greatest possible magnitude.

I was appalled. I simply could not understand how such a thing could have happened, for the simple reason that nobody except myself could possibly have known what I had been intending to do. Naturally I had taken the very greatest precautions to ensure security, both at the time and retrospectively. In fact, there was only one possible explanation; and although it was so hopelessly improbable that the very thought revolted me, I had no alternative but to accept it. Since nobody but myself could possibly have known that King Hroar would be wielding Skofnung that day, nobody but myself could have arranged for King Hring to wield Tyrving. The criminally incompetent bungler could only be me.

The professor looked at him.

'By "Um", Mr Carpenter,' he said, 'you mean to imply that it would surely have been impossible for me to have made such a mistake, knowing as I quite obviously did that arming King Hring with Tyrving would not rectify my interference but would in fact turn it into an insoluble disaster.'

Actually, that wasn't what Paul had meant at all. What he'd been trying to express, but they didn't make words big enough, was a subtle combination of 'I don't understand a word of this' and 'The other one's got bells on.' He couldn't be bothered to explain, though.

'You are,' the professor went on, 'essentially correct. I couldn't have made such a crass error; not unless I had, at some point in the interim, forgotten what I'd done originally, or unless I had some reason, albeit hopelessly bizarre and far-fetched, for *wanting* to create a catastrophic temporal anomaly. Neither explanation, however, applies. This is the twenty-first century; if I'd forgotten something back in the eighth century, I would by now have remembered forgetting it. As to the other hypothesis, all that needs be said in that regard is that there are penalties for making disgusting messes in Time, and those penalties are rigorously, even sadistically enforced by an individual of whom even I am afraid. But—'

I am getting (the professor said) ahead of my story. At the point when you interrupted me, I was watching the opening stages of the duel, standing open-mouthed with horror at the scenario unfolding before me. I knew that immediate action was called for. I had no viable options to pursue at that time. My only hope lay in prevarication, delay and obfuscation. Also, I panicked.

The duel could not, I decided, be allowed to continue. Accordingly, I caught hold of the nearest combatant to me – by chance it happened to be King Hring – and dragged him with me through the Portable Door, away from the eighth century and into the twentieth.

Even as I did it, I knew that unless I was extremely careful, this initiative could only make things worse. Both living blades, Skofnung and Tyrving, had been unlawfully cheated of their victory. Accordingly, neither sword would rest until the duel was resumed. Once that happened, the duel could never end, since neither sword could beat the other. Until the duel was resolved – not only that, resolved *in the eighth century* – the history of Canada would be in a state of flux, with both alternative versions existing simultaneously in real time and real space.

The implications of these things were clearly both infinite in number and monumental in scope. Only one of them, however, commanded my immediate attention at that point. By causing the anomaly I had, as I mentioned just now, broken the most basic laws of my craft and thereby made myself liable to a most unattractive series of punishments at the hands of the only entity in all time and space that I have reason to be afraid of. Clearly, then, my first priority was my own safety. I had to run, and then I had to hide. But where?

It was at this juncture that a mystery that had puzzled me for some time suddenly became clear.

Just now I glossed over, in a rather facile manner, my motives for creating my synthetic universe. I suggested to you that it was mere idleness and intellectual curiosity; that it was, in essence, a good idea at the time. I had been asking myself that question for several centuries – because idleness and intellectual curiosity were by no means a sufficient reason for undertaking such a monumental task, and accordingly I was entirely unconvinced. Now, quite suddenly, I knew the answer. I had built my synthetic universe as a place of refuge in anticipation of this very crisis. Somehow I had known – retrospectively, I can only assume – that one day I would need a place where nobody, not even my deadly enemy, could reach me.

I couldn't help but take a certain degree of pride in the fore-sight that I would one day have already exhibited. It would have been helpful, I admit, if at the same time I could have transmitted to myself a warning or some simple instructions, but I realised that it would have been extremely hazardous to do so, and that I would have been and would in the future be entirely justified in having complete confidence in my own ability to figure out the chain of causalities, if need be from first principles. That I have not yet done so is no reflection on my intellect or abilities. All I need is a little more time, and perhaps one or two clues which I am certain I have left for myself, secreted in some safe place where I will be sure to find them.

'Um,' said Paul again.

This time the professor raised his eyebrows. 'Excuse me?' he said

'I'm sorry,' Paul said, 'but I still haven't got the faintest idea what all that's got to do with me. Or why I'm here. Or why I just saw myself beating twelve kinds of shit out of Ricky Wurmtoter with a bloody great sword. Was I not paying atten-tion, or haven't we got to that bit yet? And also,' he added, as the professor opened his mouth to answer, 'is there really a

Great Cow of Heaven, or was that bit just, you know, symbolic and stuff? Because if it turns out that the universe – the real one, I mean – is really made out of yogurt, I think I'd rather go and join Mr Dao's bridge club right now, and screw the lot of you.'

The professor gave a long, sad sigh, plaintive as gypsy violins and rich with sincerity. 'That,' he said, 'is probably just as well. Strange as it may seem, Mr Carpenter, in one respect I envy you. There is one place where you have been and I have not. You have seen what lies beyond death. Of course, I know all there is to know about it, but only second-hand, from report and rumour carefully scrutinised and analysed using the finest protocols of scientific scholarship. You, by contrast, were little more than a tourist. But you have been there and seen it, and that is a different matter entirely. And very soon,' he added, with an almost wistful expression, 'you will be there again, except that this time you will not be coming back. To answer your question: there is indeed a Great Cow of Heaven. She most closely resembles a Jersey/Charolais cross, but with a faint suggestion of Hereford around the jawline and upper shoulders. And yes, I suppose that in a sense the universe is in its most basic form made up of – not yogurt precisely, but dairy products of a sort. You should not, incidentally, place too much confidence in Mr Dao when he leads two no trumps or one club. Frequently he bluffs, with unfortunate consequences for his partner. If you are ready, we may as well proceed with your termination.'

Too many long words can make your head spin. It took Paul maybe as long as half a second to translate 'termination' into his kind of English, by which time the professor had pulled a pin out of the lapel of his coat and was just about to stick it into Paul's arm.

With a yelp like an ironed dog, Paul jumped back, or tried to. No dice: his feet stayed where they were, as though they'd been set in concrete by a very discreet gangster. The professor frowned. It was the sort of frown Paul had come across when he was a kid, and terrified of injections. *This won't hurt*, the professor's expression was telling him. *Don't be such a cry-baby. It's for your own good. You'll like it once you get there.*

'Just a fucking minute,' he heard himself whimper. 'What harm did I ever do you?'

'I could of course explain,' the professor replied. 'But what would be the point? Please keep still. I have a great many things to do once I've finished with you, and a little cooperation would be most welcome. Nothing you can do could possibly alter the outcome, and it's churlish to cause inconvenience for others simply for the sake of being difficult.'

The pin. How many angels could dance on the head of it, and would any of them survive if they tried? Paul tried wriggling out of the way, but his arms and legs didn't seem to be working. Just a pin: what possible harm could it do? The Chinese have used them for acupuncture for thousands of years. Above all, it probably wouldn't hurt. Would it? And did he really want to waste any more time in a universe where there could possibly be such a thing as a Great Cow of Heaven? Seen from that angle, Mr Dao and his evening classes seemed positively inviting.

Of course, he'd miss Sophie quite a lot.

The professor jabbed at Paul with the pin. He swerved – a touch of flamenco dancing, rather more of the unexpected beetle down the back of the neck – and the point missed him by fractions of a millimetre. The professor tutted, as though he'd caught him passing notes in class. Would he be required to do a hundred lines before he was killed?

'One last thing,' he gasped (breath was being rationed, apparently). 'What exactly is it with that needle thing? Is it poisoned, or what?'

'Does it really matter?' the professor said wearily. 'You may safely assume that it is sufficient for the job in hand.'

'Oh, come on,' Paul said. 'Don't be such a misery. Besides, I think I've got a right to know, especially if it's poison. I might be allergic, or something.'

Maybe it was simply the sheer reverse swing of the logic in that last statement. In any case, the professor hesitated, frowned. Quite possibly, after all those years associating with the finest intellects in history, he simply couldn't cope with a mind like Paul's. 'Since you insist,' he said, 'it is not poison. Now, if you'd be so kind as to stop wriggling.'

'In a second,' Paul said firmly. 'So, if it's not poison, what is it?'

The professor was starting to look downright grumpy. 'Magic,' he replied. 'Really, Mr Carpenter, I must insist.'

'Magic?'

'That's right.'

'I thought you said that you're a scientist.'

Just the tiniest patch of raw nerve, apparently. 'I believe I have established my credentials quite adequately, Mr Carpenter. Now, unless you stop prevaricating in this blatant manner, I shall have no option but to sedate you.'

'How?'

'I beg your pardon?'

'How do you reckon,' Paul said, and it took a lot of his remaining stamina, 'on doing that? Injection? No offence, but you don't strike me as all that hot when it comes to needle-work.'

The professor paused, his brow furrowed. 'I shall cause the entire area to be flooded with anaesthetic gas,' he said. 'That would be a perfectly simple operation.'

'Quite,' Paul said. 'Fine. By all means. Go ahead.'

Ting! went the falling penny. If the professor filled the place with gas, he'd zonk himself out too. 'Alternatively,' he said, 'I can conjure a rope to tie you up with.'

'Bet you can't.'

'For heaven's sake, Mr Carpenter. I can adjust the trajectory of a comet to within a sixteenth of a minute of angle. Conjuring ropes—'

'Ought to be child's play, fine. Except, I don't think you can. Otherwise, you'd have done it already. I think you're too, what's the word I'm after, you're too highly specialised. It's like hiring a brain surgeon to pull a tooth. Admit it, you're screwed.'

'Certainly not. All I have to do,' said the professor, as though persuading himself, 'is wait until you fall asleep, as you inevitably must. However, since it would prolong the traumatic experience of waiting for the inevitable, I would prefer to dispense with futile attempts at resistance.'

Paul dredged up a grin from somewhere. It was a bit soft

round the edges and it had that forced air you get in old photos where the sitters have had to keep exactly still for ten minutes, but it was the best he could do. 'Nah,' he said. 'You'd fall asleep first.'

'I most certainly would not.'

'Says you.' Paul sniggered. 'It's whatsisname, subliminal suggestion. The moment I started talking about you falling asleep, your eyelids suddenly started getting heavy. Any second now, you'll be zizzing away like a buzz-saw. You want to be careful you don't stick yourself with your own pin while you're at it. Or are you immune to, er, *magic*?'

He partnered the last word with a sort of ultra-snide sneer, with lots of top lip in it. The professor shook his head again, but this time there was rather more energy in the gesture. 'You are playing for time by seeking to engage me in fatuous arguments and discussions, hoping that something will intervene and distract or incapacitate me. Such a strategy is doomed to failure. Your left shoelace is undone, and your television licence expires today. Let me put you out of our mutual misery, Mr Carpenter. Both of us will feel better for it.'

There was an urgency in the professor's voice that Paul hadn't ever heard before; also a very reluctant admission of uncertainty, just as if God had paused in the middle of handing down the Ten Commandments to ask if Moses had the right time. *He needs my permission*, Paul suddenly realised, in a flash of intuition that didn't come from anywhere inside him. *He needs my permission before he can kill me.*

'Get stuffed,' he said, forcing his eyelids apart. 'Look, you may be a partner in the firm and the cleverest man who ever lived and practically immortal and who gives a shit what else, but you can't hurt me. Not here,' he hazarded, trying to sound as though he had the faintest idea what he was talking about. 'Anywhere else, but not here, not unless I give in. Isn't that right?'

'No,' the professor snapped. He was a pathetic liar.

'Yes,' Paul corrected him. 'It's because there's no such thing as death here, isn't it? That's how come you're nearly immortal here, and why I couldn't bash your face in earlier when I tried.

There's no such thing as death or getting hurt here, not unless—'
He hesitated. Sophie had given him the most terrific smack
round the face earlier; he'd been convinced she'd cracked his
jaw, because it had hurt so much. But a few minutes later it was
perfectly all right again, and he hadn't given it a moment's
thought since. All right; when Sophie had thumped him, he'd
believed; therefore his mind had provided him with the pain he'd
expected to feel. Then he'd got sidetracked, the purported
busted jaw had slipped his mind, and now it was completely
better. And if that wasn't good enough, what about Ricky and
the psychotic athlete with the uncanny resemblance to P.
Carpenter? Lots of hacking and slashing with big scary swords,
completely one-sided fight, but not a drop of blood anywhere.
Maybe Ricky didn't know the rules, which was why he'd been
fighting back instead of just standing there sticking his tongue
out while the blood-crazed loon carved him like a virtual
Christmas turkey. Nevertheless. 'Not unless,' Paul repeated,
'you're dumb enough to believe you can be hurt. Like, say, if I
was to give up and hold still so you could jab me with that stupid
pin thing. If I really thought it could kill me, it would. But I
know better, so it can't. Right?'

The professor smiled; at least, a thin crack opened up
between his nose and his chin. 'Would you care to put that
hypothesis to empirical proof, Mr Carpenter? If so—'

'Sure,' Paul said; and suddenly he could move his arms and
legs quite freely. He held out his hand, palm upwards. 'Go
ahead,' he said. 'But it won't do you any good, because I don't
believe in fairies any more. Well? I'm waiting.'

Such a look of sheer cold hatred he'd never seen before; it
glowed through the professor's eyes like candlelight through a
Hallowe'en pumpkin. 'How annoying,' the professor said. 'How
vexing that you should choose this moment to discover your
latent intelligence. A few weeks earlier, and you could have been
of such great use to me, as my assistant in my work. That you
should pick this time to evolve is most—' He shook his head
sadly. 'Most unfair,' he said. 'In case you're interested, this is the
first major setback I've encountered in over three hundred and
twenty-five years.'

'Whooppee,' Paul said grimly. 'Do I get a prize, or a badge or something?'

'Hardly.' The professor took a step back. 'Nothing so agreeable. I shall leave you now, and take a trip through the Portable Door to 16 November 1980, disguised,' he added with a very mild smirk, 'as a Jehovah's Witness of unparalleled eloquence and persistence. I regret having to do it, of course; such a blunt, brutal approach is practically an admission of defeat. However, I have to say, you have nobody to blame but yourself. Goodbye, Mr Carpenter. It was hardly a pleasure having known you, but most certainly an education.'

He was backing away through the wall, as if he was a ghost or the wall wasn't really there. As Paul watched him go, he was counting frantically on his mental fingers, just to check he'd guessed right. November, December, January, February . . .

'Quite right,' the professor told him, as his ears vanished into the plaster. 'Eight months and twenty-six days before you were born. On the night in question, your mother wasn't really in the mood, your father had been drinking a little. The arrival of a Jehovah's Witness who refuses to be shooed away—' Suddenly the professor broke off. He was staring at Paul, his mouth slightly open. 'Good heavens,' he said. 'Remarkable, quite remarkable. In that case—' He pulled himself together with a visible effort. 'In that case, I shall no doubt see you again soon enough, at which point we can resolve all the issues between us. I hope so. I—' Just the tip of his nose was sticking out of the wall now, and a few wisps of eyebrow. 'I just don't know any more.'

As soon as he'd definitely gone, Paul sagged like share prices in an oil crisis. To have fought off Professor Van Spee, on his own turf – Brave. Definitely brave. Brave, he couldn't help thinking, as two short planks. He didn't know the professor all that well, but you don't have to be on best-buddy lawnmower-borrowing terms with someone to get the impression that they don't give up quite so easily. Apparently the threat to see to it that Paul would never be conceived (*a Jehovah's Witness*, he thought, *that's just so diabolical*) wasn't going to be carried out; it was almost as though Van Spee had fast-rewound to that moment in his mind, and found there something he really hadn't been expecting . . .

That set up a whole gallery of images in Paul's mind, none of which he wanted any part of. He shook himself like a wet dog. Time, he really felt, he wasn't here.

Talking of which: before Van Spee had bubbled up out of nowhere and started prattling about living blades and Great Cows of Heaven, he'd been about to try and do something. What was it? Ah, yes. Ricky Wurmtoter. He tried to remember: was he going to kill him, or just place him under citizen's arrest?

Well, looked like killing him was a non-starter anyway, here where death didn't work unless you wanted it to or the whole audience clapped or something. So that just left—

Paul remembered. He pictured Mr Tanner's mum charging into the room, and then the room ceasing to exist, with her and Ricky and whoever that was with the face and the sword, all trapped inside. He remembered the stunned, blank feeling when he'd been sure that they were all suddenly dead, or at the very least never coming back. He remembered feeling angry enough to want to smash in the teeth of a partner in JWW and former professor emeritus in the University of Leiden.

Odd that he should have forgotten that. It had seemed so very important before he got chatting and let the professor distract him with Great Cows and opt-in death threats.

Think, Paul urged himself, like a horse led to water. *No harm can come to anybody here; but it looks like he's sent them somewhere else.* But where else was there? Realspace: dodgy old place, but not necessarily fatal. Custardspace, which was here. There wasn't anywhere else. Was there?

Anyway. To answer the question: that just left rescue. Because, Paul reasoned with a strong why-the-fuck-*me?* feeling going right down into the marrow of his bones, if Van Spee wanted rid of them, he pretty much had to get them back, or else he'd be screwed. Why this was inevitably so he wasn't quite sure. He just knew, that was all.

Deep breath. Then he tried very hard to picture in his mind the doorway that Van Spee had caused to disappear. Somehow he was convinced that it was still there somehow, if only he could get a grip on it, a fingernail under the very edge so he could prise off the lid . . . *How nice it would be, he thought, if right now I had the gift of being able to do magic. I could perform a really neat reveal-ing spell, or a dead cool opening charm, or maybe crackly green fire would leap from my fingertips and blast a bloody great big hole in the wall. Or maybe a kindly old voice would whisper in my mind's ear,* Use the Force, Luke, *and I'd just be able to do it, like wiggling my ears.*

But I can't.

Staring at the wall wasn't doing any good, so Paul sat down with his back to it instead; because in all those movies, that was how the hero accidentally found the hidden lever that opened the secret passage. But that was just another kind of magic that didn't work.

Maybe they really were gone for ever.

Quite possibly they were; but he wasn't giving up, mostly because he was stuck here with nothing else he particularly wanted to do, so he might as well persevere as get out a pen and start playing noughts and crosses with himself on the plaster-work. But there was nothing he could do, right?

Wrong. Paul felt in his top pocket, just to make sure it was still there, and it was. There was something he could do, some-thing magical and JWW-ish, which was very good except that it was the wrong thing. He could still do it, of course. It wouldn't help, it'd quite probably make everything a whole lot worse, but yes, he could do it.

He considered that for a moment. *Bloody stupid idea, but on the other hand it's the way this country's been governed for the last fifty years.* He took out the little paper packet containing Van Spee's crystals, pulled it open and spilled its contents onto the palm of his hand. He could eat these, he thought, they were supposed to make him able to travel back into Realspace from here. But what if he scoffed them while leaning on the bit of wall where a door used to be, one that used to open into the closed-file store but which now apparently led to somewhere quite other?

Indigestion, probably. Or he'd end up back in the genuine 70 St Mary Axe, where he'd be arrested by Mr Tanner's goblins for killing Ricky Wurmtoter, who wasn't going to be able to stand up and admit he wasn't dead really, because now he possibly was—

Aargh, Paul thought, *too bloody complicated for me.* He closed his eyes, opened his mouth and gulped. For a moment, absolutely nothing; then the wall began squidging out between his fingers, as though he was leaning on, say, custard.

The Great Cow of Heaven, he thought, *for crying out loud.* Then he fell over.

Paul woke up, and lifted his head off his hands.

'I said,' growled a horribly familiar voice behind him, 'wake up.'

Every muscle in Paul's body stiffened, and he swung round in his seat, in doing so barking his knee against the leg of the desk. Behind him stood Miss Hook, just the same as when he'd last seen her. Suddenly it seemed terribly important that he should remember exactly how long ago that was. Good question, actually. It was either eleven years or three minutes, but he wasn't quite sure—

'You were asleep,' said Miss Hook, with that ominously soft tone of voice that always meant extreme danger. 'You were asleep and making funny noises.' Giggles all around him. Paul didn't dare break eye contact with Miss Hook, but he could dimly see rows of desks, faces behind them. 'You were dreaming,' she went on. 'Rather an interesting dream, by the sound of it. Perhaps you'd like to share it with the rest of the class?'

CHAPTER TWELVE

hit, Paul thought. Out of the corner of his eye he could just see his sleeve. He remembered that loathsome shade of navy blue, the shine of daily-worn gaberdine. Away to his right, he could just make out one of the grinning faces: Demelza Horrocks, age about eleven.

It couldn't be, he told himself. Surely not. Not even in his worst nightmare—

And then the full impact of what Miss Hook had said hit him like a falling building. He'd been asleep. He'd been dreaming, but he was awake now.

He'd been dreaming—

'*No!*' he yelled; he tried to get up, but banged his knee on the underside of the desk and froze with the pain. 'That's not—' The words died on his lips, as the unspeakable truth ground itself into his mind. 'Um,' he said.

'Sleeping in class,' said Miss Hook, her voice full of savage delight. 'How do you expect to learn anything if you can't even stay *awake*?' She shook her head. 'I don't come in here every morning for the good of my health, you know. I come here to try – heaven help me, to *try* to ram knowledge into your thick head, teach you the things you're going to need to know in later life. One of these days, you're really going to wish you'd paid attention, and then it'll be too late. All right, on your feet. Headmaster's office. Come on, don't just sit there. *Move!*'

Paul's legs were wobbly and defective. It took him three goes to get out from behind the desk, and all the other kids were laughing at him. 'Please, Miss Hook,' he pleaded, as he turned for the door. 'What was today's lesson about?'

Roar of laughter from the other kids; a cocktail of anger and contempt in Miss Hook's eyes. 'The rest of the class,' she said, 'has been learning how to escape from a synthetic universe without accidentally finding yourself trapped in something even worse. But, of course, you won't ever need to know that, will you? Headmaster's office, Carpenter. And no running in the corridor.'

He'd taken this walk so many times he'd have known the way blindfold: down the passage, past the library, past the assembly hall, up the stairs, past the closed-file store (but they'd shut it at the end of last term, bricked up the doorway), down the stairs, past the science labs, up two flights, turn left, you couldn't miss it. In a way, it reminded him of somewhere else, but that was just an illusion. At some stage last term, the rest of the class had learned that all buildings are in fact the same building, made over and seen from slightly different angles, like a reused film set; but Paul had been gazing out of the window, and so had missed it. Subconsciously, he therefore misrationalised, he must've modelled the floor plan of the fantasy office building in his dream on the school. Just the sort of thing you do in dreams.

And here he was—

Theodorus Van Spee
Head Teacher
Do NOT enter until told to do so

Yeah, yeah; he knew the drill by now. He knocked, stood back, waited. No answer, so he'd just have to stand there and wait until the old git was ready for him. He hated that.

Such a vivid dream, he could have sworn it was all real. But now he was awake he could see just how ridiculous it had been. Magic, for crying out loud. A whole bunch of grown-ups making their living doing magic, right here in the late-twentieth century; and for a while back there, he'd actually believed in it. How stupid could you get?

What was he going to tell the Head?

No mileage whatsoever in trying to lie to Van Spee; he had this horrible knack of knowing exactly what you were thinking, what you'd just done, what you'd been just about to do, it simply wasn't *fair*. Sometimes Paul imagined he was living in a world that was made and run by Van Spee, the way nerdy kids built huge dioramas for their model-railway layouts.

So, he'd have to tell him the truth; he'd fallen asleep in Miss Hook's class, he'd been having this really weird dream – no, he didn't want to tell *anybody* about that, it was too freaky, they'd drag him away and lock him up in a loony bin. But if he went in there and had to face Van Spee, trying to keep it secret'd be a complete waste of time. Van Spee would hook it out of his mind like a bogey. They'd come and take him away in a big white van, just like they'd come for Ricky in Year Twelve last month.

I can't go in there, Paul thought desperately. *I daren't. If I go in there, I'll never get free again. Not ever.*

In his dream . . . He had to stop thinking about it – nothing but a bad dream, a nightmare. Dad said bad dreams were just because you'd eaten sweets and stuff just before you went to bed. But in his dream, this room would've been *Professor* Van Spee's office, and you weren't allowed in there unless you were told you could go in—

'Next,' said a voice from the other side of the study door.

His hand was on the door handle. He paused, used his right hand to pry open the fingers of his left. Obviously there was no way of knowing just by sight, or by feel, or anything like that. A door is just a door; the fundamental things apply.

When is a door not a door?

'Next,' the voice repeated. It wasn't happy.

Answer. It came at him like King Harold's arrow, so fast and straight and sudden that it could've taken his mind's eye out. Answer: a door isn't a door when it's one of *those* doors, the sort that seal up behind you and won't let you out again. And it hadn't been a dream. It'd been *real*.

Fine; but what was he supposed to do next? Even if it had been real, and he was a twenty-two-year-old clerk in a magicians' office in the City rather than an eleven-year-old schoolboy, and this was indeed one of those doors, leading to the place you couldn't go to unless you were allowed to go there, and where you couldn't get back from ever – Knowing all that was one thing, but what was he supposed to *do* about it? Miss Hook's words were still ringing in his ears. How to escape from a synthetic universe without accidentally finding yourself trapped in something even worse. One of these days, you're really going to wish you'd paid attention, and then it'll be too late.

Well, since he'd been asleep and missed all that useful stuff, he was just going to have to figure it all out for himself, from first principles. As bloody usual.

(*Rule Forty-Six: no mental swearing in the corridors. Stay behind after school. Permanently.*)

The best place to start, Paul resolved, would be not going through this particular door. Try another one instead. He looked round, and saw a door that he couldn't remember having seen before. It was only a few yards down the corridor from the Head's study, and it was pink. Even so.

He stood in front of it. Getting there had been awful, like squelching through thick mud, the sort that sucks your boots off and swallows them, but he was there now. He reached for the door handle.

'What do you think you're doing?' He cringed; Mr Tanner, the maths teacher, horribly strict and bitterly unfair, was standing next to him, looking just like a goblin out of a story book.

I was just about to go in here, sir.

'You can't go in there, Carpenter.'

Sorry, sir. Why not, sir?

'Because it's the girls' changing room.'

Balls, sir, and by the way, you don't exist. Mr Tanner obligingly vanished, and Paul opened the door.

It was, indeed, the girls' changing-room; but it was empty, apart from a few battered old lockers and an ancient but familiar-looking fridge-freezer. With a sigh of relief, Paul stepped over and pulled open the door. The light came on.

'What kept you?' asked the fridge.

'Don't start,' Paul replied. 'All right: first, is it true? Is there really a Great Cow of Heaven?'

The light blinked, which Paul assumed was a yes. 'Her name,' said the fridge, 'is Audumla, just like I told you but you wouldn't listen. Do you know who I am?'

Paul shook his head. 'At least,' he added, 'I have a vague sort of idea, but I bet it's a long story,' he said, 'so you'd better tell me later. Right now, I need to know some things.'

'Please yourself. There may not be a later.'

'There will be,' Paul said firmly. 'Question one. The next door down on the left. That's Van Spee's secret place, isn't it? The place only he can get into or out of.'

Agonising pause. 'Very good,' said the fridge. 'Correct. When I came looking for him, to punish him for his crime, he built it as a last hiding place, somewhere I could never find. I'd figured out how to break into his synthetic dimension, that was easy, but however hard I try – and believe me, these last fourteen hundred years, I've *tried* – I can't find that one small room. Oh, I know where it is, it's just a few yards down the corridor on the left, but I can't *find* it—' Silence for a moment, as the fridge fought back its rage. 'Do you know why?'

Paul nodded. 'It needs a key,' he said. 'And the key's not a bit of metal with a frilly end, it's a person.' He took a deep breath, because if he was wrong, this was going to sound so stupid. 'It's me, isn't it?'

Long pause; then the fridge seemed to shimmer, like heat haze on the road, until it turned into Mr Laertides. 'Very good indeed,' he said, 'I knew you had the right stuff, deep down inside where nobody but me could see it. That's quite right, you're the key. Though there's a bit more to it than that, of course.'

'Oh,' Paul said. 'Right.'

'It's a long story,' Mr Laertides replied, with a grin, 'and I'll be happy to tell you all about it later. But right now I need you to open a door for me.'

'Yes,' Paul said, 'but there might not be a later.'

'There will be.' Mr Laertides looked at him. 'I promise.'

Paul looked back at him. On one level, the idea that he'd trust a partner in JWW ever again was about as likely as the Swiss army invading America; and a very good level it was too, as far as Paul was concerned. But there was a look in Mr Laertides's eye, just a faint glow, as of something buried gleaming through, that was so different from anything he'd seen before that he could just about imagine himself believing in it. Not that that counted for much, given that Laertides was a self-confessed master of glamour and illusion; if he wanted to, he could have every US coastguard ship from Anchorage to San Francisco yelling into their radio sets, '*The Swiss are coming, the Swiss are coming!*' And he'd said it himself, he needed Paul to do a job for him, a factor which in itself gave him the credibility of Bill Clinton trying to sell someone Mexico.

And yet.

'Why can't *you* do it?' Paul asked. 'If I show you where it is.'

'I *know* where it is,' Mr Laertides snapped. 'I just can't find it, that's all. Come on, it's not exactly difficult, and it'll only take a moment of your time.' He paused, calming himself down so obviously that he practically changed colour. 'Or don't you want to save Ricky Wurmtoter and Mr Tanner's mother? I thought they were your friends.'

Bastard, Paul thought. 'Ricky Wurmtoter drugged Sophie with the love-philtre stuff,' he said. 'He completely screwed up my life. Why the hell would I want to save him?'

Curiously, Mr Laertides found that extremely amusing. 'Why indeed?' he said. 'But you do. Admit it. OK, it's not so much wanting to as feeling you're obliged to, conscience and all that malarkey. One of these days, I might even find time to tell you exactly why you feel under an obligation to him. But anyhow, let's forget about Ricky. Rosie Tanner, now. She's your friend, right?'

Paul looked away. 'She had me killed,' he said sullenly. 'By goblins. Goblins jumping out of a cake, for crying out loud.'

'Yes, but you know she didn't mean anything by it. Come on, Paul, there's no point lying to me, I know exactly what you're thinking. You've got to save them, you don't have a choice. It's who you are. You're the hero, see.'

'Balls,' Paul replied with feeling.

'Absolutely not. Ever since you joined the firm, it's been one heroic deed after another. Saving lives. Rescuing people. Standing up to Countess Judy and the Fey. You're twenty times more of a hero than Ricky. He just does stuff for money. You can see the difference, can't you?'

But Paul shook his head. 'You're wrong about me,' he said. 'Surprising, really, a smart bloke like you. I'm not doing it. Go and find your own bloody door.'

'Good Lord,' Mr Laertides said softly. 'You mean it, don't you? Even though it'll leave Ricky and Rosie stranded in there for ever and ever.' He frowned, then grinned. 'It's because you're not sure, right? You can't figure out who's the real bad guy here, Theo Van Spee or yours truly. You think that if you open the door for me and I turn out to be the arch-villain or the Dark Lord or something, the universe'll suddenly be knee-deep in the smelly stuff and it'll all be your fault. Yes?'

Paul looked down at the ground. 'Something like that,' he mumbled.

'You prat,' Mr Laertides said, but there was the faintest trace of pride in his voice, as if he'd been hoping that Paul would turn out to have the moral fibre to refuse. 'All right, then, here's the deal. Sophie drank the love philtre, right? She's now inalienably besotted with you for ever and ever.'

'Apparently.' Paul winced. 'Don't they have tact where you come from?'

'No, actually. Here's what I'm offering. If you open the door for me, I'll put it right. I'll take the love spell off Sophie, and I'll make her permanently immune to it. What do you reckon? Tempted?'

It was one of those moments that made Paul realise that, nine times out of ten, Life really is doing it on purpose. Suddenly, everything seemed to narrow down into a very small, tight place, where two alternatives confronted him, and both of them meant losing the girl he loved; and without her, what was the point of anything? Without her, he'd have to go on being the same old Paul Carpenter, Cupid's labrador, always running after the arrows and bringing them back in his mouth. He could see the rest of his life stretching away in front of him, the long dark road you have to walk when you've fallen asleep on the last bus home and ended up at the terminal. Being himself, for ever and ever. But that seemed to help, in a way; because if he gave up on himself as a bad job, there could only be one logical course of action.

'Deal,' he said.

'Excellent.' Mr Laertides grinned, like a suitcase unzipping on three sides. 'You've always managed somehow to be a decent bloke, Paul. Half-witted, annoying, thick as a stack of railway sleepers, but when the chips are down you've always done the right thing. Hasn't done you much good, of course, but I'm proud of you anyway. Now then. Lead the way.'

'Not so fast.' Paul folded his arms; he meant it as a gesture of steely resolution, but he had a nasty feeling that it just made him look as though he had an upset stomach. 'First you sort out Sophie.'

'Already done,' Mr Laertides replied. 'Magic,' he explained. 'And no, you can't go back and see for yourself because I haven't got the time or the energy to run a bus service across the inter-dimensional void. You'll just have to trust me.'

'I thought you'd say that,' Paul replied glumly. 'Sooner or later everybody says that to me, and I always do. Probably explains a lot about how I keep ending up getting comprehensively screwed.'

'Ah yes,' Mr Laertides said, 'but this time it's different. This time, it's me saying it.'

'That makes a difference, does it?'

'Yes. It's the only difference between a lie and the truth, actually. And you can trust me on that, too.'

'Oh well, in that case,' Paul said. But apparently Mr Laertides didn't do irony, either. 'This way. Just follow me, it's not far.'

'Oh, I know where it is,' Mr Laertides said. 'After you, though. Might as well do it properly, I guess.'

Out into the corridor, turn left. Paul walked a few yards, then stopped. 'It's around here somewhere,' he said. 'Only I can't be more specific than that, because—'

'No problem,' Mr Laertides said. He reached out with his left hand, and where the tips of his fingers touched the wall they seemed to soak into it, like ink into blotting paper. They flowed, sideways and down, defining a thin black rectangle about the size and width of your average door frame. 'This is just a guess and God forbid I should presume to lead the witness, but would it be sort of near here, perhaps? Warm?'

'Burnt to cinders,' Paul replied. 'Now what?'

Mr Laertides took a step back. The rectangle stayed where it was. 'After you,' he said.

Paul looked at him. 'You want me to go in first?'

'Essential,' Mr Laertides said. 'The door won't open for me. Just give it a push and toddle in, there's a good lad.'

'I'm not sure, I—' Paul didn't get any further, because Mr Laertides booted him hard on the backside. He hit the wall bang in the middle of the rectangle, and fell forward.

He was home.

Which was ridiculous, because the house he was standing in no longer existed. When his parents moved to Florida, they'd sold the house that Paul had grown up in to a developer, who'd razed it to the ground and built a block of flats. But here, apparently, he was again, kneeling on the living-room rug trying to figure out who'd just kicked him so hard.

Paul stood up. *Home*, he thought. *Not that I was ever desperately fond of the place. This must be symbolism or some such shit; in which case, it probably doesn't matter too much that I'm wearing my shoes in the house.*

Unnaturally quiet. Back home, either the TV or the radio was on all the time, a permanent background drone, like the voices of the Furies in his head. Other things were missing, too: no smells – furniture polish, air freshener, recently cooked cabbage, stale cigar smoke, elderly and evil-scented dog. Without them it couldn't really be home; in which case it was a construct, a set, contrived deliberately for his benefit by someone. No, he could be more precise than that. By Professor Van Spee. A password, maybe: as soon as you came in here, it morphed into your own personal space. Or, more likely, a defence mechanism – whenever someone broke in, it turned itself into the environment in which the intruder felt most uncomfortable. That made rather more sense. It'd explain the school set Paul had just come from, too. What a particularly nasty mind the professor had, to be sure. But it was a great comfort, practically overwhelming, to know that it wasn't actually real, and he wasn't about to be thirteen again. He'd managed to put up with a lot recently, including death, but he wasn't sure he could have coped with another dose of adolescence.

So, if it wasn't real . . . 'Hello?' Paul called out. 'I'm here. Now what?'

Mr Laertides materialised beside him, a shimmering column of black dots like a newspaper photograph, rapidly coagulating into apparent solidity. 'About time,' he said. 'I was afraid you'd got lost or something.' He looked round, practically quivering with excitement, like a dog about to be walked. 'So this is it,' he said, 'I'm finally here. You have no idea what it's been like, waiting on the doorstep for thirteen hundred years but not being able to get in.'

'I'm sure,' Paul muttered. 'All right, where's Ricky Wurmtoter and Mr Tanner's mum? We're going to rescue them, remember?'

Mr Laertides nodded. 'It's all right, I hadn't forgotten. And don't worry – as soon as I've nailed Theo Van Spee they'll be sent straight back to Realspace, no messing. How many times have I got to tell you? Just trust me.'

'I wish you wouldn't say that,' Paul replied. 'It doesn't help.'

'Oh, you.' Mr Laertides grinned. 'Anyhow, I can take it from here. You don't have to hang around if you don't want to. If you like, I can send you back right now.'

That got Paul's attention. 'You can?'

'Of course. There's practically no limit to what I can do – hadn't you figured that out by now? And to think,' he added, 'all this time you were keeping milk and old mouldy bits of cheese in me, and you never knew I was one of the five most powerful entities in the universe. You want to go back? I can send you straight to the photocopier room if you want, it's no trouble.'

'Why would I want to go there?'

Another of those horrible grins. 'Because that's where your Sophie is, right now. Cured,' he added. 'Back to normal, or as close as she ever gets to it.' His eyes (composite, like a spider's, now Paul came to think of it) twinkled. 'I don't want to spoil any surprises for you, but this would actually be rather a good time. And you've helped me out here, rather a lot, so why shouldn't you get something out of it?'

Paul didn't say anything; but if he'd had movable ears, like a cat, they'd have been flat to the sides of his head. He stayed exactly where he was.

'Fine,' Mr Laertides said. 'You can stay here if you like, makes no odds to me. It'd be good if you could stay back out of the way, just in case there's any crossfire. I can guarantee your safety about ninety-six per cent, but beyond that you're on your own. Make your mind up, one way or another. I don't think I can wait any longer.'

'You don't want me here, do you?' Paul said.

Mr Laertides looked away. 'Nothing personal,' he said.

'Fine. I'll stay.'

'Whatever. At your own risk, though.' Mr Laertides closed his eyes and took a deep breath. 'Wish me luck,' he said. 'Even I need it, you know; for the missing four per cent, if you follow me. Ninety-six per cent is pretty good odds, but I like dealing with gilt-edged stone-cold certainties. Like, for example, the last time I was this close to nailing Theo Van Spee, the odds were ninety-nine point six per cent in my favour, and that was thirteen hundred years ago.' He took a step forward, then stopped as though he'd bumped into an invisible wall. 'Word of advice for you,' he said. 'Never believe in any god who reckons he's omnipotent. If the small print on the stem of the burning azalea says *Guaranteed 99.78% omnipotent*, you're probably OK. But not a hundred. There's no such thing.'

'Thank you,' Paul said. 'I'll bear that in mind. Look, can we get this over with, please? Only all this standing about—'

'Fine,' snapped Mr Laertides irritably. 'Here goes nothing, then.'

He moved very suddenly – like the place where the film's been badly edited, and five or six frames have been cut out. Before Paul knew what was happening, Mr Laertides had grabbed him; left hand covering his mouth, right hand digging a knife into his neck, almost but not quite hard enough to break the skin.

'Sorry about this,' Mr Laertides whispered. 'But it's, you know, the old omelette/egg causality nexus. Real bitch, but there you are. Theo!' he shouted. 'I know you're here somewhere. If you make me do it, I'll snuff the kid. You know you can trust me on that, Theo.'

A sigh. Quite a clear, audible noise: disappointment, regret, contempt, annoyance. 'There is absolutely no need for violence,' said Theo Van Spee, walking out of thin air as if he'd just been standing behind a curtain. 'Just as you know that if you kill him, we will all be lost beyond any hope of recovery.'

Paul could feel Mr Laertides's shoulder shrug; an instinctive translation of the slight increase of pressure behind the knife-point. 'Broad as it's long to me, Theo, you know that. Which is it to be? If you really do want a thousand years of utter chaos either side of now—'

Van Spee laughed coldly. 'You have never even begun to understand me,' he said. 'No wonder you have failed so wretchedly up to this point. To hunt something, you have to understand it perfectly. But you are the sort of hunter who closes his eyes and shoots arrows into the forest at random. Eventually you will hit something, but it will take you a very long time.'

'Whatever, Theo. Right now, I've got your nuts in a mole wrench. Whichever way you choose, I'll have you this time. All that's left is how much damage you want to do to the scenery, and that makes no odds, as far as I'm concerned. Either way, your choice.'

'You clown.' Van Spee's voice was quiet and utterly contemptuous. 'You claim to be the guardian of all that is good in the universe, but you have the heart and soul of a policeman. Very well; we will let them fight it out. Will that satisfy you?'

A deep sigh from directly behind him; Paul could believe it was thirteen hundred years' worth of frustration drifting away into the air. 'Perfect, Theo, that'll do just fine. I've got mine right here; you got your two handy?'

'As you know perfectly well.' Van Spee lifted a finger, and that same curtain of invisibility lifted off Ricky Wurmtoter and Mr

Tanner's mum. They stood quite still, but looming slightly, like heavily sedated elephants. 'And of course,' he added, 'the weapons themselves.'

Two bright flashes in the air: a sword and an axe landed on the floor with a clatter, like the loose, rolling hubcaps so dear to the hearts of film directors. Paul didn't need to look closely in order to know that the sword was a shiny brown colour, with cute spirally silver patterns. Only it wasn't; more a sort of dark steely blue.

'Sorted,' said Mr Laertides. 'No, fuck it, where's she got to? Daft bloody tart. *Heel!*' He snapped his fingers, and Vicky materialised a couple of feet away from where Paul was standing. 'There you are,' he said. 'What kept you?'

'All right,' Vicky snapped back. 'I was drying my hair, actually. Came as quick as I could.'

'You were drying your hair. Anyhow,' Mr Laertides said, 'you're here now. Let's get this over and done with, Theo, before you figure out some other way of making trouble. You're a clever bloke, but you change your mind more often than a tart changes her knickers. Ready?'

Van Spee shrugged. 'Of course.'

'And no cheating. Promise?'

A mild click of the tongue from the professor. 'Even now you wilfully refuse to understand anything. All I wanted to do was prevent the fight. If that objective is lost to me, the outcome is a matter of complete indifference. In fact, I would prefer not to watch. I would rather read a book, if that is acceptable to you.'

Mr Laertides laughed. 'Sure,' he said. 'If you want to improve your mind, go ahead. It's the last chance you'll ever get.'

'Then I most assuredly shall not neglect it,' Van Spee replied mildly. From his pocket he produced a battered black paperback; he picked out a bookmark and began to read.

'"Heart and soul of a policeman",' Mr Laertides muttered under his breath. 'You're going to have a long, long time to regret saying that. All right,' he barked, letting go of Paul so that he stumbled forward. '"let's finish up and then we can all go home. Your majesties.'

Ricky came to life with a shudder, walked forward, stooped,

and picked up the axe. He was staring at Paul as though there was nothing else visible in the room.

'You what?' Paul asked.

'You and him,' Mr Laertides said. 'Fuck me, I was just trying to be polite. Oh, for pity's sake,' he added. 'You still haven't got it, have you?'

'Is this necessary?' the professor said mildly, without looking up from his book. 'All that is required is that they fight, not that they understand.'

'Wrong, smartarse,' Mr Laertides snapped back. 'Got to know what they're fighting for, or it's not a fair re-enactment. Motivation, see? All right,' he went on. 'Time for some introductions. In the blue corner, King Hring of Rogaland, armed with the two halves of the axe Battle-Troll.' Ricky Wurmtoter smiled weakly; Mr Tanner's mum, face expressionless, dropped a tiny curtsey. *Old battleaxe*, Paul thought; Viking humour was clearly no better than goblin humour, in fact marginally worse. 'And in the brown corner – that's you, Paul, sorry – King Hroar of Vestfold with Tyrving.'

There was an interval, maybe three-sixteenths of a second, during which Paul just stood there thinking, *What's the stupid git talking about?* Then it hit him like a falling tree.

'Me?' he said.

'You,' Mr Laertides confirmed. 'After one thousand, four hundred years, so I guess you could call it a grudge match. Well, don't just stand there like a prune. Get your sword.'

'Like hell,' Paul replied with intense feeling. 'I'm not fighting any stupid duels.'

Mr Laertides nodded over his head to Vicky; she swept past Paul, snatched the sword up off the ground and thrust the hilt end into his hand. He managed to grab hold of it just before it could slip through his fingers and skewer his foot. 'You're pathetic, you,' Vicky hissed at him. 'And don't even think of trying to throw the fight, because if you do—' The sword bucked suddenly in his hand, wriggling like a live fish and sweeping round, nearly carving off his chin. 'Do I make myself clear?'

'Crystal,' Paul muttered anxiously.'Only, I'm not terribly good—'

'Oh, for God's sake,' Vicky sighed. 'That's the whole point, you don't need to be. Just don't drop me – leave the whole thing to us, it's what we're for.'

'She's right,' Mr Laertides confirmed. 'In fact, it's best if you don't try and participate at all, just let Vicky here take control. Vicky, by the way, isn't short for Victoria.'

'Huh?'

'Victory,' Vicky explained irritably. 'Now, can we *please* get started?'

Paul tried to step backwards, but something felt wrong. To be precise, wet. Stepping backwards, he was walking into water.

'Which is why they had their duels on small islands,' came Mr Laertides's voice, now apparently far away in the distance. Mr Laertides himself was nowhere to be seen; nor were Vicky, Mr Tanner's mum nor the professor. Just Ricky, standing in front of Paul, very still. 'On a small island,' the voice continued, 'there's not a lot of scope for creative running away. Means you either stand and fight, or you drown. Unless you're a really good swimmer, of course.'

Paul tried to move his feet, but they seemed singularly lacking in bones. He wobbled and had to use the sword to prop himself up. Ricky was apparently doing deep-breathing exercises; at any rate, he seemed uncommonly reluctant to start the fight, which struck Paul as rather odd until he remembered the spectacle of his alter ego, Psycho Boy, only just failing to slice Ricky into pastrami. Except—

Except nothing. There was, of course, no way in Hell that Paul could even begin to make sense of all this. But it was beginning to dawn on him that the vicious and extremely competent swordsman he'd watched earlier had, on some level at least, been himself, Mrs Carpenter's little boy, the one who'd always been picked last when they chose teams at school. It was therefore quite possible that Ricky knew quite a lot more about what was going on here than Paul did himself. If Ricky was – dear God – *scared* of Paul, he was bound to have his reasons. Scared of him, scared of the sword . . . That at least struck him as reasonable. If he'd understood the living-blade business correctly, he was there as little more than a sop to the laws of gravity, a hand for the sword to sit in while it did its stuff; basically a base of operations for the loathsome thing, a *main à terre*. And hadn't someone told him at some stage that Vicky was Ricky's ex-wife?

No wonder the poor bastard was sweating.

Even so; there has to be a limit. There comes a point where the reasonable man, even if he's a born coward, has to draw the line against the insweeping tide of weirdness and say, *That's it, that's my lot, I will humour you no further.* Paul had been killed by goblins, sent halfway across the country to look at trees, been patronised by fridges, framed for murder, stranded in an alternate universe apparently made out of custard and forced to believe in the existence of the Great Cow of Heaven. Participating further would simply be encouraging them, and he wasn't going to do it.

He glanced over his shoulder at the calm blue sea behind him. Theo Van Spee had made it, and presumably controlled it, and Theo Van Spee didn't want the fight to happen. It was worth the risk, even if he wasn't what you'd call a human fish. Van Spee's synthetic ocean wouldn't let him drown, it was more than its job was worth. 'Bye, then,' he called out to Ricky, who stepped back and winced. Then Paul dumped the sword – getting rid of it was like ditching chewing gum, it really didn't want to leave his fingers – and ran down the beach into the water.

Just for once, he reckoned as the sea welled up under him and took his weight, he'd guessed right. The water cushioned him like a lilo, and somehow each successive wave got out of the way of his face so that he didn't get a mouthful of brine. He began to doggy-paddle, and soon had enough weigh on him to tow a water-skiing Barbie doll. *Screw Mr Laertides and the rest of them,* he thought; somewhere, all this wet stuff had to have a dry edge. All he had to do was keep on sploshing about until he reached it. Elegant in its simplicity, though he said it himself. ·

An arm shot out of the water eighteen inches from his head. The shock made him flounder; he should have panicked and gone under, but the sea pushed him firmly back, like a mother trying to convince her toddler that the noisy, scary party was actually fun. The arm sliced through the water at him, shark's-fin-style. He tried to avoid it, but no dice. Its hand – he knew it from somewhere – grabbed itself a generous handful of his hair, and yanked him back.

'Ow,' Paul wailed, and then the sea fed him a mouthful of salt water, like an impatient mummy cuckoo feeding its young. The hand in his hair dragged harder, pulling him under with a level of force that was beyond the power of doggy-paddle to resist. As the waves closed round him, he shut his eyes tight and breathed out through his nose, to keep it from filling up with sea.

'Say you're sorry,' Vicky hissed.

Never mess with a mermaid in a maritime context. Paul opened his mouth to comply, but it flooded before he could get further than 'So—' Luckily, Vicky seemed happy with that, and let go of his hair. He bobbed up, spitting out brine, and she punched him in the eye.

That sort of broke Paul's concentration, and the world went rather vague for a while. When he came round he was lying on the beach on his back, with Vicky leaning over him, looking worried. He looked up at her and groaned.

'Context,' he said. 'I hate context.'

'What?'

'Think about it.' Paul felt his jaw; like a Bedford van, it wasn't perfect, but it worked. 'I'm not allowed to leave, right?'

Vicky nodded. 'Now get up and fight,' she said.

'Or what? Or you'll hit me again?'

'Yes.'

He grinned. 'And if I do as I'm told, Ricky's going to kill me. Gosh, tricky one. I may have to think it over for a whole millisecond.'

'Don't be so feeble.' She grabbed his wrist and yanked hard; Paul yelped and scrambled to his feet. As he did so, he noticed that there was something sticking to his right heel; automatically he reached down and pulled it off. It was a dark green leather bookmark. Without thinking, he stuffed it in his trouser pocket.

'Nice game plan,' he grumbled. 'Dislocate my sword arm, inspirational stuff. You should get one of those hooded fleeces with "coach" on the back.'

'For crying out loud, stop whining,' Vicky replied. 'And how many times have I got to tell you, leave everything to us, don't interfere and we'll be fine. We've been waiting thirteen hundred years for this, remember.'

'When you say *we*—'

She stuck the sword in Paul's hand, closed his fingers round the hilt and shoved him in the small of the back. He stumbled forward, and by the time he'd got his balance back, he was standing no more than three feet away from the cutting edge of Ricky's axe.

'Hello,' Ricky said unhappily. 'So here we are again.'

'Again?' Paul shook his head. 'You may be, I'm not. Look, there's obviously been the most colossal balls-up, but if you and I just chill for a moment, talk it over, sort it out like rational human beings—'

Ricky swung at him with the horrible axe. Paul felt the edge, sharp as a needle, trace a line across his forehead. 'Fuck!' he shouted. 'That hurt.' But then his own arm jerked out straight, as if the sword was a huge, boisterous dog wanting to be walked, and he watched in horror as the cutting edge grazed Ricky's cheek, shaving a small patch of his designer stubble.

'Jesus, sorry,' he gasped, 'I really didn't mean—'

Ricky lunged. Paul felt himself sway out of the way – actually, it was like being batted in the stomach with a large invisible pillow – and his annoyingly wilful arm swished a fearful horizontal blow at Ricky's neck. Just as he thought he'd killed the poor bastard, Ricky's axe-head got in the way, and there was a noisy clang of steel on steel. Paul tried to jump back out of the way; his body tried to obey, but his feet stayed planted. Fortuitously, his failed attempt coincided with a furious sweep from Ricky, which turned it into a perfectly judged evasive manoeuvre.

'Ricky,' he yelled. 'Stop it. This is *stupid*.'

'I can't,' Ricky grunted back, avoiding a murderous downward slash by the thickness of a cigarette paper. 'It's not up to us, don't you see?'

Paul saw all right, but there wasn't a lot he could do. Each time he tried to lower his sword, step back or turn around, Ricky's axe would dart past him, converting his move into an appropriate response. That, he couldn't help thinking, was insult to injury with insult sauce. Meanwhile, his poor abused arm was putting up one hell of a fight; even Paul could tell it was hot stuff, and considerably better than the show Ricky was putting on. When Ricky was a fraction of a second late with a high parry, and the edge of Paul's sword nicked his shoulder with a revolting chunky snicking sound, it was almost more than Paul could bear. *Sure*, he told himself, *dying won't be fun; it'll be back to that horrible dark place with no walls or floor, and Mr Dao's bridge club and gradually fading away, like the end of a song.* But one of these days, sooner or later, he was going to die anyway; it was inevitable, and there was nothing he could do about that. Killing Ricky, on the other hand, was something he didn't have to do, not now or ever, and if there was any way he could avoid it, he would.

Paul did his best. He tried letting go of the sword hilt, but it stuck to his hand like chewing gum on a shoe. He tried holding still when the sword wanted him to move, but the sword kept winning. He tried yelling out what he thought the sword was about to do, so Ricky could dodge or parry or counter-attack, but he didn't know nearly enough about swordfighting and just made things worse. He tried jamming his foot down on a large stone, hoping he'd turn his ankle over and go crashing to the ground, but all he succeeded in doing was kicking the stone into Ricky's face, nearly knocking him off his feet. It was hopeless; any moment now a cut or a thrust was going to get past Ricky's fragile-looking guard, and there was nothing Paul could do to stop it, because every deliberate mistake he made got forcibly converted into brilliant defence or remorseless aggression. *It's not fair*, he howled at himself. *The only time in my life I'm really good at something, and I don't want to be.*

And then, in the tiny interval between Ricky's feeble counter-cut and his own ruthless feint, leading inevitably to an opening in Ricky's guard on the left-hand side of his chest, Paul figured it out. The sword, it seemed, could predict his attempts to throw the fight and could transform them into winning moves. It didn't trust him, obviously, and was wise to the few half-baked ploys that made up his entire repertoire, itself a vague collage of images remembered from watching Mel Gibson in *Braveheart*, before he fell asleep halfway through. But what if he deliberately tried to win? Would the sword stop him and make him do the fight its way, or wasn't it devious enough for that?

If he did nothing, Ricky would be dead meat in about thirty seconds.

Screw it, Paul muttered to himself, and launched an all-out attack on Ricky's head. He swung the sword and hacked as hard as he could. Just as he'd hoped, Ricky dodged the cut easily, then drew back his arm for the counter-attack. *About time, too*, Paul told himself, and waited for the sharp steel to slice into him. At least it'd be quick, and then he'd have nothing to worry about apart from some dead guy trumping his best cards on a bid of two clubs redoubled.

Ricky didn't attack. Instead he stood there, his left hand clamped to his right wrist, his teeth gritted with strain, Dr Strangelove with a huge meat-cleaver. He was trying desperately to say something, but he couldn't get his mouth open wide enough to make himself understood. Paul was pretty sure it ended in *-un*, but that was the best he could do.

'Fun'? At any other time, maybe, but Ricky didn't look like he was enjoying himself much. Not 'gun', because they were both using more basic instrumentation; or was Ricky trying to tell him to pull his gun out from his shoulder holster and blast him while he was still able to keep the sword from doing its stuff? Or 'bun', perhaps, referring to the poisoned custard slice. Sun, pun, nun—

'Forfuckssake' exploded from Ricky's mouth. '*Un!*'

Tun, spun, shun, my kingdom for a rhyming dictionary, *run*. 'I can't,' he whimpered, 'this fucking stupid sword won't let me. I wish I could, but—'

'Uck,' Ricky said with feeling, as his right hand forced itself down half an inch. 'Ill. Ill *now*.'

Me too, Paul was about to say, but he figured out the context just in time. *Here we go again, playing Scrabble in the jaws of death*. Bill, fill, spill, mill, nil—

Kill.

'I can't,' he whispered. 'Sorry.'

'*Ill!*' Ricky shrieked, as his left fingernails gouged out bloody

298 • Tom Holt

furrows of skin from his right wrist. His eyes were screwed shut. Paul could feel the unbearable pressure of Ricky's will-power concentrated on him, ordering him to stick the sword into his opponent's chest. 'Please.'

Well, it'd solve a lot of problems.

No. Couldn't be done. Paul couldn't send someone else down there, where he'd been. He could feel his own arm dragging at its socket, the tendons ripping away from the bone, the muscles tearing, but it was still his arm, and he could make it do as it was told; because even magic couldn't achieve the impossible, and killing Ricky was, quite simply, something he was incapable of doing. A pity, really, because one of the two of them wasn't going home, and Miss Hook had managed to hammer enough basic arithmetic into Paul's skull to make the implications of that appallingly clear. If he couldn't kill Ricky, he himself was going to die. In about three seconds.

'Tell Sophie I love her,' Paul said. 'All right, she knows that, but tell her anyway. Oh yes, and could you see to it that someone picks up my grey suit from the dry-cleaners and takes my library books back? That's about it, I think.'

'Alls,' Ricky sobbed, and his right hand tore free. Paul watched the blade come straight at him, most of the way.

CHAPTER THIRTEEN

They'd put up a banner. It was big and white, slung between two poles, and it read –
WELCOME BACK, PAUL CARPENTER.
There was also a brass band, and an honour guard of spectral warriors in full dress uniform, and a thin, shadowy crowd, and the grey outline of a little girl who presented him with a bouquet of insubstantial flowers, while the onlookers applauded, soft as an echo, and the band played a Souza march. And, of course, there was Mr Dao, who came out from the crowd and stood there and looked at him and said, 'You again.'

'Yup.' Paul nodded.

'And are you planning on staying this time? Because I don't like to complain, but some people treat this place like a hotel.'

'I'm staying,' Paul said firmly. 'You can count on that.'

'Right,' said Mr Dao, and the crowd, brass band and banner vanished into dark grey swirls. 'No offence, Mr Carpenter, but I must express my relief. Your various comings and goings have caused us, let's say, a degree of administrative difficulty. Made all the worse, of course, by the fact that I was not at liberty to tell you the whole truth, in case it prejudiced the outcome.'

Paul frowned. 'The whole— Oh, you mean that stupid duel thing. It was really that important?'

Mr Dao looked at him solemnly, then nodded. 'Very important

indeed,' he said. 'Without exaggerating, it was a matter of life and death. Come here and I'll prove it to you.'

Nothing better to do; so Paul followed him, a hundred paces or so over, under and through nothing, until they reached a doorway. There was no door to go in it and no wall for it to fit into; just a doorway, and screwed onto it a brass nameplate, such as you see outside posh offices.

THE BANK OF THE DEAD
(A wholly owned subsidiary of the Allied Toronto & Winnipeg Banking Corporation)

'Oh,' Paul said. 'Is that a good thing?'

Mr Dao almost smiled. 'That word and its antonym have no meaning here. It is just a thing, neither good nor bad. But until it was sorted out, we found it hard to know what to do. Who do we report to? Do we pay out the profits to the shareholders, or to ATWBC Head Office in St Lawrence? Now, at last and at least, all that has been resolved and we know who we are. And of course,' he added, with a slight smirk, 'the world above has been changed for ever out of all recognition. Fortunately, that is none of my business, or yours. You're free from all that now. You see, there *are* benefits.'

'You told me,' Paul said. 'The bridge club.'

'And the evening classes, and the experimental theatre group, and the quilting circle. There used,' Mr Dao added sadly, 'to be nine quilting circles, but we've had to cut back. But we now have a chess tournament and a flower show. No flowers,' he added, 'except a few lilies. But we have plenty of time, and a certain degree of ingenuity. We will adapt.'

Paul shrugged. 'What you told me last time,' he said. 'I'll just sort of seep away fairly soon, won't I? Until there's nothing left.'

Mr Dao nodded. 'It's for the best,' he said. 'Living people make the mistake of believing that death is somehow a malfunction, something that's wrong with you, an illness. It's not. It's perfectly natural. People have been dying for well over a million years now, it's an intrinsic part of the way of things. Quite a few of our guests here will tell you it's the best days of their lives.'

'Whatever,' Paul replied. 'Look, it's really very kind of you to take the time to make me feel at home and see that I'm nicely settled in and everything, but really, I just want to get on with the fading painlessly away. Looking back over my life, I find the words *no great loss* seem to fit pretty nicely, and I think I'd like to be rid of it as soon as I can.'

Mr Dao made a deprecating gesture. 'As usual, you're being too hard on yourself,' he said. 'Consider your case objectively. You were the victim of the most appalling circumstances, yet you acted with honour, decency and compassion. At the end, you willingly gave your life rather than kill another. Unfortunately,' he added with a mild sigh, 'that doesn't actually count for anything; you don't get a better room or preferential treatment or even a badge. But since this is the last time you'll ever be aware of yourself, it's only reasonable that you should part from yourself on good terms, free from any misconceptions.'

'So,' Paul said with a hint of impatience. 'I did all right, then.'

Mr Dao thought for maybe a moment longer than was tactful. 'In some respects, anyway,' he said. 'And the other aspects of your existence no longer matter; in a hundred years, nobody will care or even remember. And a hundred years, here—' He shrugged. 'There is no harm in my telling you that you did all right, and if it'll make you feel better, by all means believe it. You did well. We're all very proud of you. Now—'

Paul shivered, though he wasn't feeling cold, or anything at all. 'I don't want to go,' he said.

'You will. Would it help if I pointed out that there's a twenty-foot-high statue of you on the edge of the main car park of Vancouver airport? Or that your portrait is on the current ten-dollar bill? It's not a wonderful portrait – in fact it makes you look rather like a chipmunk – but you can rest assured that your name will be remembered for as long as there's a People's Democratic Republic of Canada.' Mr Dao frowned. 'You don't seem very pleased.'

'I'm not, actually. I've never even been to Canada, and if I had I'm sure I wouldn't have liked it.'

'Well.' Mr Dao clicked his tongue. 'It doesn't actually matter. Nothing does, here. I imagine you'll find that a great relief. Just think. Nothing will be your fault ever again.'

But Paul shook his head. 'But it never was,' he said. 'I just thought it was, but I was wrong. I thought I was solely responsible for my life being a great big heap of poo, but lots of it – most of it, really – was other people playing silly buggers with me.' He scowled, but there was nothing left of his face except unreliable memories. 'You know what?' he said. 'That's not fair. That's not fair at all.'

'Correct. And now, if you'll excuse me, Mr Shumway will be here soon with the day's receipts, and I really should be getting ready for him. Of course, there is no time here, so I don't actually need to do anything, but it's nice to pretend.'

He didn't grab Paul by the elbow – Paul no longer had an elbow to grab – or beckon to him, or anything like that. He stood, slightly to one side, making it clear that Paul should lead the way. A polite gesture, like opening a door or giving up a seat on the Tube. Polite, and very, very final.

'I don't want to go,' Paul repeated.

'Nobody ever does,' replied Mr Dao. 'It's like those awful children's parties when you were young. Your mother promised you that you'd enjoy it once you got there, and of course she was right—'

'No, actually. I used to hang around by the door, waiting to be collected.'

'Well, then,' Mr Dao said, with a hint of impatience. 'A life like that. You'll be happier here. Many of our guests are happier once they've got rid of themselves.'

Paul had no head to shake, no feet to take a step back with. 'I don't want—'

'Like it matters.' Mr Dao frowned. 'I'm sorry, I don't mean to be insensitive. But this was always where you were going to end up, the rest was just a matter of time. Your name went on the list as soon as you were born, like rich people putting their children down for Eton. Come with me now, please. There's nothing left to say.'

'No, wait.' Where the defiance came from, Paul had no idea. At first, he wondered if it was the thought of Sophie, of true love, of the normal or sort-of-normal-ish life that had always been just out of reach, like a hand stretching down from the air to pull him up off the cliff ledge but never quite reaching. But it wasn't that, because a normal life is just a life, and Mr Dao had convinced him that it really didn't count for much in the long run. That realisation made him falter; he could feel the emptiness pulling a him, like a big, boisterous dog tugging on its lead. He felt it, but somewhere deep inside him, a little voice said, *No. No, why should I?*

'Mr Carpenter.'

Why should I? It wasn't my fault.

'Carpenter.' Mr Dao flickered for a moment and became Miss Hook, stern and inevitable as divine justice, standing over Paul with that look on her face. 'It was you. Now, unless you own up before I count to ten, I'm going to have to keep the whole class in after school.'

— And that's what's happening to me, Paul thought; *maybe I'm being kept in after life, as a punishment. Maybe it's because there's something I've still got to do, only I'm buggered if I know what it is—*

'Now.'

But Paul shook his head (and, he realised with a faint jolt of hope, that he once again had a faint vestige of a head to shake). 'I can't,' he said. 'Sorry. No, really, I've got something I need to do, up there. I'll be back just as soon as it's done, I promise.'

'*No.*' Mr Dao was back, and his usually grave face was contorted with some strong emotion that Paul couldn't quite identify, maybe because it seemed so out of place there. 'I really am terribly sorry,' he said. 'But there it is. No choice. No second chance. No alternatives. No deal. You have to come with me, that's all there is to it. I really don't want to call security, but I will if I must. You must see that. The rules apply. There's nothing anyone can do.'

'I'm not going.'

'Mr Carpenter.' Still that unplaceable something in his eyes. 'I shall count to three. Please don't make this any more distressing than it has to be. I don't enjoy this, you know.'

'Fine,' Paul said. 'One, two, three.' He paused. 'Your go.'

Nothing happened. It was almost as though Mr Dao was having to work hard just to stay there, as though something was tugging at him now. Paul, on the other hand, felt strangely exhilarated: breathless (well, obviously) but strong, in a way he'd never been before. Any second now, he predicted, Mr Dao was going to start pleading.

'Please?'

'No,' Paul said. 'When did you say Benny Shumway was due? I'd quite like to see him, I think.'

'Time has no meaning here.'

'You know,' Paul said – he almost drawled, though his mum had told him not to when he was nine. 'I don't think that's true, somehow. Otherwise, why are you in such a hurry to get me to come with you? Surely you've got all the time in the world. We could stay here for ever and ever chatting like this, and it wouldn't matter a damn.'

'Mr Carpenter—'

'And besides,' Paul went on, 'if you're telling me the truth, you don't need me to come with you, because I'll just evaporate and blow away, whether I like it or not. That should have happened by now, but it hasn't. Something's wrong, isn't it?'

'Of course not. Nothing is ever wrong here. That's the point. There's nothing that can go wrong, because there's nothing. I thought I'd explained all that.'

'You did. But it's not true. You can't touch me. I'm different.'

'*Fuck*.' Mr Dao closed his eyes, screwed up his face into a snarl and jumped up and down. 'Fuck, fuck, fuck, *fuck*. Yes,' he went on, immediately resuming his usual calm, 'you are, of course, quite correct. The rules do not apply in your case, which is why you are the only person ever to leave this place. The fact that you have done it on more than one occasion is, I must confess, something of an embarrassment. One does not care to have one's shortcomings highlighted, even here, where failure is as irrelevant as everything else. But you are right, Mr Carpenter. Death has no jurisdiction over you. Which means,' he added, with the very faintest of sighs, 'that you are free to leave.'

'Am I?'

'Yes. It was – interesting. We shall not meet again.' Mr Dao paused, and shrugged. 'Never thought I'd hear myself say that, but there you are. Three impossible things before breakfast, and all that. Goodbye.'

Mr Dao started to walk away into the shadows, but Paul

yelled, 'Stop!' Mr Dao paused, then walked backwards, as though he was being rewound, until he was exactly where he'd been a moment ago. 'Well?' he said.

'For crying out loud,' Paul shouted. 'You can't just tell me I'm different and death's got no jurisdiction and all that stuff and then walk away.'

Mr Dao smiled, and Paul saw just a trace of salvaged satisfaction. 'Actually,' he said, and vanished.

Paul looked around. There was still nothing; in fact, if at all possible, there was even more nothing than there had been a moment ago. Just by being there, Mr Dao had defined a tiny area; where he'd stood there had been at least a suggestion of something for him to stand on, and just enough light to see him by. Now he was gone, and there was nothing at all.

Nothing, that was, except Paul Carpenter.

Maybe, he thought, *this is the sting in the tail. Maybe I really did die and go to hell, and this is how hell is for incurably self-centred people; a universe where nothing exists except me. In which case, it probably serves me right. But.*

But. But nothing.

Exactly. The whole point.

Paul thought about that for just over four seconds. Then he dropped to his knees and started yelling, 'Help!'

He yelled for quite some time, except (he could picture Mr Dao in his mind, grinning insufferably) time had no meaning here; there was no time, no space, there was just Paul, a whole universe full of him. A bad place. Very bad. *I don't like it here*, Paul thought. *I want to go home.*

'*Yes, but if you do that, you'll have to go and deal with people. You were never any good at that. Stay here, this is where you belong. Besides, we never really liked you anyway.*'

'I want to go home,' Paul tried to say. (But there can't be any words where there's nobody to hear them except yourself.) 'I didn't mean to do any harm. What did I do, anyway?'

'*It's never what you do, it's what you are.*'

Bullshit, Paul thought, *that's just not true.* And then he thought: *I don't believe that, in which case I can't just be talking to myself. Therefore—*

Who are you?

He waited. Nothing.

And then there was a sound. Coming through the total absence of anything, it was rather like the creation of the universe, except that in the beginning there wasn't the Word. There was, in fact, the Moo.

'Sorry?' Paul yelped, startled.

'Moo.'

Moo, he thought; and then, *Oh, for crying out loud.* 'Moo?'

'Moo.'

And there she was, ambling towards him with that utterly relaxed, laid-back look about her that only cows can manage. She was smallish for a cow, a sort of light sandy beige, with big eyes, little pointy horns and a bell on a collar round her neck. She looked like something out of a butter advertisement.

'Excuse me.' Many, many times before, Paul had felt an utter fool, but never more so than now. 'Excuse me,' he repeated, 'but are you Audumla, the Great Cow of Heaven?'

She nodded, and her bell tinkled softly. 'Moo,' she said.

'Ah, right. I've, um, heard of you.'

'Moo,' she replied, with the faint air of good-natured boredom of any celebrity stopped in the street and told who they are. Her vast brown eyes surveyed him as thoroughly as a billion-dollar research project, and blinked once. She swished her tail. She looked unspeakably cute and friendly and cheerful and, what was the concept he was groping for, ah yes, *Swiss.* Now there was a thought: could a Swiss cow possibly have created the universe? That would account for the precision mechanism of the seasons, the perfect timing of comets, the fact that two blades of grass picked at random are exactly identical. But the Swiss, even the bovine Swiss, could never have created people. Too messy.

'God, I'm glad to see you,' Paul said; and then he stopped and wondered, *Yes, but why? It's a cow. Why on earth should I be so pathetically relieved to see a cow?*

'Moo,' said Audumla; and Paul thought, *Here we go again,* because if only he could understand Cowspeak, he was sure that she'd just answered his question. The answer, and he'd missed it – just like being back at school.

'I see,' Paul said. 'Thanks. Look, can I get out of here? Can you help me get out?'

'Moo.'

Paul closed his eyes and opened them again. 'Is that a yes moo or a no moo?'

'Moo.'

There was a proverb about that, he reflected. 'Sorry,' he said, 'just to clarify. Nod for yes and, um, swish tail for no. Can you help me—?'

'Moo.' Audumla nodded her head, and the bell tinkled like all the church bells that ever were. Then she started licking her left front hoof.

'That's fantastic,' Paul said. 'Um—'

She looked at him. He waited. She looked at him some more.

'Sorry,' Paul said. 'But, um, can we be a bit more, you know, precise. Like, how can you help me get out of here?'

'Moo.'

'Oh Christ,' Paul said wretchedly. 'Just my luck, just my bloody rotten luck. Here I am dead, and I bump into a cow who knows how to get me out of here, and the sodding thing can't speak English.'

'Of course I can speak English, silly,' said the cow. 'I was just being annoying.'

Ninety per cent of Paul wanted to dance around in circles rejoicing. The other ten per cent wanted to force-feed the Great Cow of Heaven her cowbell. Fortunately, Paul was a democracy.

'Please,' he said. 'Please can you tell me—?'

'How to get out of here, yes.' Audumla shook her head, as though dislodging a notional fly. 'Piece of cake. Actually, you know what to do already. At least, you ought to, if you've been paying attention.'

Aaargh, Paul thought. 'Let's assume,' he said, 'for argument's sake, that I haven't.'

'All right.' The cow licked her lips with an insole-sized pink tongue. 'Professor Van Spee told you about the other Portable Door, the one he made for himself. Yes?'

Paul nodded. 'Now you mention it,' he said.

'He told you it's here, in the bank, in a safe-deposit box.'

Audumla turned her head to nibble a tuft of hair on her knee. 'That's your way out. Told you it was simple,' she added.

Fuck, Paul thought. 'That's not actually a lot of help,' he said. 'You see, I've sort of pissed off Mr Dao rather a lot. I don't suppose he's going to be in the mood to leave his keys lying about accidentally on purpose where I can find them.'

Cows can look at you the way no other living creature can. They have a special, cows-only bemused gaze that says, 'Why are you doing that, you very strange person?' in a way that mere words never can.

'Well, if I can't get the keys,' Paul said, 'how'm I going to open the safe-deposit box? Unless you just happen to have a stick of dynamite stashed away somewhere.'

But they don't do irony. 'No,' Audumla said. 'And anyway, if you blew up the box with dynamite, it'd damage the Door. But you don't need a key.'

'I don't?'

'Of course not, silly. The boxes aren't locked. Why would you bother, down here?'

Paul thought about that, and realised that he'd been missing the point with all the futile diligence of a blind machine-gunner. 'All right,' he said, 'fair enough. But I can't just wander into the Bank and rob it. And anyway, how'd I know which box it's in?'

'Number 18873446229D,' Audumla replied promptly, 'third shelf up on the right as you go in the door, they're in number order, very neat and tidy. And Mr Dao won't catch you, he's busy with your friend Mr Shumway, doing the paying-in and the petty cash.' She lowered her voice just a little. 'Entirely between you and me, but Mr Dao's been fiddling the books, embezzling. From your firm.'

'Get away,' Paul replied. 'Really?'

The cow nodded. 'For the last six years.'

'Um, has he embezzled a lot?'

'Oh yes.' Audumla flicked her ears and chewed for a moment; Paul realised that, for lack of fingers, she was counting on her teeth. 'Six pounds and forty-seven pence. I believe he plans to use the money to buy up newspapers, radio stations and TV companies, like that nice Mr Murdoch. Eventually,' she added.

'But don't tell on him, will you?'

'Wouldn't dream of it,' Paul replied. He hesitated. 'Well, I'd better go, then. Before Mr Dao comes back.'

'Yes.'

Paul turned to go, but found he couldn't; something was pinning him down, like a great weight. 'Um,' he said, 'excuse me, but you wouldn't happen to know what it is about me that means death has no jurisdiction over me?'

'Oh yes.'

Pause. Silence. 'Can you tell me what it is?'

'No.'

'Fine.' Paul waited, then went on. 'Why not?'

'It's better that you don't know. Trust me.'

Well, put like that— 'One last thing,' Paul said. 'Are you really, *really* the Great Cow of Heaven?'

Audumla looked at him, great big round cow eyes. 'Moo,' she said. 'Mind how you go.' Then, without a crack or a hum or a blur or any visible or audible accompaniment (because, apart from the bewildering storylines and the cheesy sets, real life isn't a bit like *Star Trek*) she vanished; and there was nothing to show that she'd ever been there, apart from a small, slightly steaming brown pile.

'Moo,' Paul said. 'Brilliant.'

He had, of course, forgotten to ask her how to get to the Bank from there, wherever 'there' was. But that was just sloppy thinking, of course. He walked in a straight line, and ten yards or so from the cow-pat he came to the Bank's main gate. There was nobody to be seen in any direction. Well, of course not. Mr Dao was talking to Benny, and the rest of them, the hundreds of thousands of billions of dead people – probably away somewhere playing bridge, or practising German irregular verbs, or learning how to weave baskets.

Moo, he thought, as he barged his way through a revolving door that hadn't been there the last time. And why on Earth would the Great Cow of Heaven approve of Rupert Murdoch? He shrugged. Somehow, involuntarily, more by luck than judgement, he'd solved a fair few of the fundamental mysteries of the universe lately. It doesn't do to push one's luck.

Today the Bank only had one room, and fortuitously that room happened to be the safe-deposit vault. Paul had no trouble at all finding the box, and of course it wasn't locked. Inside there were just two objects: a roll of thin plastic sheeting, spitting image of the one he'd owned for a little while, and a half-empty tin of Bird's custard powder. As simple as that; but maybe everything's simple when you've got the Great Cow of Heaven on your side.

Fine. All he had to do now was find a wall, spread the Door across it, and step through.

No wall.

It came as something of a surprise at first, but when Paul stopped to think about it, why should there be a wall? Not needed here, after all. He retraced his steps, and there, sure enough, was the revolving door he'd come in by; but it was free-standing. No wall.

Bugger.

'I could have told you,' Mr Dao whispered urbanely in his ear. 'Never trust a ruminant. Anything with that many stomachs is bound to have its own agenda.'

'Go away,' Paul said.

'There's no call for hostility,' Mr Dao replied. 'I'm trying to be sensitive. You were having problems coming to terms with the situation. That is, of course, perfectly understandable. In such cases, we find it's best to allow the subject a moment of hope, usually triggered by the manifestation of some apparently supernatural agency or object of faith. We noted that you seemed to believe in the existence of divine dairy cattle, and accordingly framed the illusion in the form that you would be most likely to accept. You believed; you did as you were told, came here, took the Door, only to find that there is no wall to place it against. As is only to be expected, here in the middle of nothing. I trust you have learned the lesson: all hope is illusory. It has no place here. We try to exclude all harmful and misleading influences, for the good of the community. Hope isn't a good thing, Mr Carpenter. Hope is a parasite. It dupes people into soldiering on, forcing themselves to keep going through pain, trauma and misery, until finally they can go no further and end here, where all things end. Ignore hope, and you get here quicker, with less distress and anguish. Now you know the truth about hope, having experienced its bad effects for yourself. Now, perhaps, you will come quietly.'

It was as though there was a fish-hook lodged in every part of Paul's body, each one tugging at him, drawing him away. *Really*, said every instinct, *there isn't any point, you're just being embarrassing. Stop making trouble for everybody. Go in peace.*

'Last time,' Paul said, and his voice seemed to come from somewhere else. 'Last time, there was a wall. There was a wall, and I got away.'

'That was because it wasn't your time,' Mr Dao explained patiently. 'Now, it's right and proper that you should be here, and so there is no wall. Give me the Portable Door – you shouldn't really have taken it and I have responsibilities. Give it to me and let me end all this for you. Please.'

'There was a wall,' Paul whispered. 'There *is* a wall. Get the fuck out of my way and I'll go and find it.'

'Indeed.' Mr Dao was smiling. His face was so calm it was beautiful. 'And where exactly do you propose looking? This—' he waved his arms at the encircling darkness. 'This is all there is, this is everywhere. You can see it all from here. No wall.'

Paul tried to look round, but he had no way of knowing whether his eyes were open or closed. Didn't seem to make any difference. Where all places are one place, why bother?

'Moo.'

'*Fuck*,' Mr Dao snapped. 'Piss off, you stupid bloody cow. Go and chew something.'

'Moo,' replied the Great Cow of Heaven, and Paul wasn't sure if that was a reply, an explanation, a rebuttal, an insult, an act of forgiveness or all of these things simultaneously. What he did know was that it was also an invitation. He sprang forward, fumbling to unroll the plastic sheet, and slapped it against the cow's broad flanks. It stuck, and he trembled as he smoothed out the folds and wrinkles, like a passionate paperhanger.

'This is your last chance, Carpenter,' Mr Dao was yelling. 'If you leave this time, that's it. Don't ever try and come back, do you hear me? If you leave, it's for keeps, you can never come here again. Think about that, will you? Think about it.'

There was the door handle, solid as solid could be. 'I've thought,' Paul said. 'Cheerio.'

He squeezed the handle as though he was trying to strangle it, and turned it half a turn to the left. The door opened. 'Home,' Paul said aloud, and stepped through.

There was a door in his kitchen wall, one that hadn't been there before. Paul stepped through it, fell forward and landed painfully.

'Bloody hell,' he mumbled, and looked back over his shoulder. Apparently, God only knew how, he'd just walked out of his fridge.

The fridge light wasn't on; it was dark inside. He scrambled up – sharp tweak in the ankle – and peered inside. *Oh*, he thought.

No milk in this fridge: no mouldy cheese, furry tomatoes, time-expired pots of yogurt. Instead, through where the back of the fridge should have been, he could see an endless absence of anything at all, except for the distant tiny figure of an elderly Chinese gentleman in a silk robe, shaking his fist at him and yelling something he was too far away to catch. Quickly he slammed the door shut, counted to ten slowly, and opened it again.

The milk was off, and the cucumber he'd bought on a vague whim several weeks ago hadn't made it. But there was a light. No darkness, no absence. Paul shut his eyes and sank to his knees, as the fridge door slowly swung shut. There was a gentle pop, as the seals met.

'I did it,' he said aloud. 'I escaped.'

No reply. Not even a faint lowing of distant cattle. Once again Paul was alone. The difference this time was—

The difference was, he didn't have to be. If he wanted, he could go outside. He could go to the shop on the corner, and there'd be people there. He was alive.

He thought about that. 'Good,' he said.

He stayed there, on the floor on his knees, for quite some time; how long he wasn't sure, because he wasn't quite used to time having any meaning; a bit like jet lag, only much, much more so. He wasn't entirely sure where he was, of course, which universe he was in, whether things outside were what he'd think of as normal or whether he was living in a world where Canada had a monopoly of the international banking sector and more medieval cathedrals than the whole of Europe put together. Like, he decided, it mattered. He had nothing against Canada. Live and let live, that was his motto. Especially the live part.

I'm alive, Paul told himself. *I was dead, and now I'm alive again. Thank God. Or thank Cow. Whatever.*

'What I'd like now,' he said, still aloud, because it was so wonderful to be able to make a noise that existed outside his own head, 'is a nice cup of tea. And a sandwich.'

He paused and thought about that. Not a drop of drinkable milk in the place, of course; ditto edible bread, butter, and ham. All such things would have to come from outside this room, and maybe he was just being silly and overcautious, but he wasn't quite sure if he was ready to go opening any more doors quite yet, for fear of what he might find on the other side. Every door opened was a risk, after all.

'But I'll settle,' he decided, 'for baked beans and tinned peaches.' He knew that he had some of them, because he'd seen them in the lower kitchen cupboard a few days ago. He pulled out the cutlery drawer, found the tin-opener, then opened the cupboard door.

It was dark inside, and there were no peaches. No baked beans either. No anything, just nothing.

Very quickly indeed, Paul slammed the door shut and leaned his full weight against it. Not good, *not* good. Very bad, in fact. Obviously, it was better being here in his kitchen than back there with Mr Dao and absolutely nothing else; but he couldn't very well stay here for ever and ever. There was also the singularly disturbing question of where *here* was.

Paul had a nasty feeling that custard might enter into it, somewhere.

Then he realised how very, very tired he was. Of course, sleep and food and stuff were only significant factors if you were alive, and arguably he hadn't been, not for quite some time. He'd been dead; and before that he'd been in Custardspace, and before that – he couldn't actually remember that far back with any degree of precision. He had vague recollections of sword fights and Van Spee's crystals and goblins that appeared out of thin air and a lot of other stuff like that, but none of it seemed to want to stick, as though the inside walls of his mind were coated with Teflon. Instead, he remembered what it felt like to be drifting away into nothing, and the great big round eyes of the Great Cow. This wasn't, he couldn't help thinking, the way he'd have liked his life to turn out, if it had been up to him.

No good, Paul told himself sternly. *Might as well still be there, in fact it'd probably be better: bridge club and flower-arranging classes and first steps in conversational Spanish.* But it was all very well being brave and grimly determined and never saying die; the plain fact was that he had every reason to believe that he was marooned here, a desert island with walls and doors instead of sea. *Hopeless.*

Whereupon the phone rang.

It took him a moment, one full beep-beep and then a single beep, to realise what the sound actually meant; then he dived at the phone like a hungry seal and knocked it off the table onto the floor.

'Hello?'

'Hello,' said the voice at the other end. 'Is Janet there, please?'

Janet. Janet. *Janet?* 'Sorry?'

'I said, is Janet there, please?'

Paul closed his eyes. One theory of Creation has it that God only made the human race so that He could have a straight man. 'Sorry,' he said, 'I think you've got a wrong number.'

The voice apologised and rang off. Paul tried to move but he couldn't, so he stayed where he was, on his knees with a phone pressed to his ear. *Bugger*, he thought. *Bloody stupid. At the very least, I could've pretended to be Janet – it'd have been better than nothing.*

Of course he tried putting the phone back and picking it up again, tapping the little plastic spur thing (presumably it had got a name, an arcane technical term used every day of the week by telephone engineers), hoping for a dialling tone. Zip. Nothing. That old thing again.

Eventually he gave up, dropped the phone back onto its cradle, and sank into a heap of arms and knees, like a pile of discarded laundry from which he'd carelessly forgotten to remove himself. His eyes closed, because there wasn't really any reason why they should bother staying open. Days and nights of frantic activity, fear, disorientation and other fun stuff caught up with him like the ground catching up with someone who's fallen a long way. And, since Paul had nothing much to gain from staying awake, he fell asleep.

He was dead. Apparently Mr Dao had just been kidding, or he'd changed his mind, because he was quite definitely dead, and they were carrying him in his coffin, and in the distance he could hear the mournful tolling of bells; ring, ring-ring, beep-beep –

Beep-beep?

Paul sat up and snapped his eyes open. The phone again. He threw himself at it like a prop forward and stuck the receiver in his ear.

'Paul?'

'Yes. *Yes!*' He paused. 'Sorry, who is this?'

'Paul? Are you all right?'

Memories flooded his mind like the flushing of great celestial toilets. 'Sophie,' he said.

'Yes. Look, are you OK? You sound really weird.'

Ah yes, but that's because I am *really weird.* 'I'm fine,' he said. 'Except that I think I'm sort of trapped here, in the flat. Like, all the doors, when you open them they don't go anywhere. Except the Land of the Dead, of course. How are you?'

'Oh, I'm all right. What do you mean, the doors don't go anywhere? That doesn't make sense.'

'No, it doesn't. Where are you ringing from?'

'Me? The office. Mr Tanner asked me to give you a call. He wants to know why you haven't come in today.'

He wants to know why— Because I died. Because I only just managed to escape from a bunch of goblins who were going to execute me for a crime I didn't do. Because last time I was in the office I wasn't even Paul Carpenter, because Paul Carpenter died –

316 • Tom Holt

'Excuse me,' he said, as calmly as he could manage, 'but what day is it today?'

'Thursday, you idiot. Same as it was this morning. Look, what's wrong with you?'

Paul knew the answer to that one. 'I'm immature and self-centred and I have real problems relating to people, mostly because of my appallingly bad self-image, the result of a near-abusive family environment. What I meant was, what's the date?'

'The date?'

'Which day of which month of which year.'

'Paul.' He knew that tone of voice only too well. 'This really isn't a good time, we've got to finish photocopying all those leases for Mr Suslowicz, not to mention Countess Judy's filing and that bloody great big stack of Mortensen printouts. Trying to skive off work by pretending you've gone barking mad since five o'clock yesterday is like so childish, and I'm buggered if I'm going to do all this lot on my own.'

'Sophe—'

'Don't call me that.'

'No, but for fuck's sake *listen*, will you? What did you say about filing?'

Short, bemused silence. 'I didn't – Oh, you mean all those letters and reports and stuff we've got to file for Countess Judy. She's getting really pissy about it, I promised her we'd have it done by Wednesday and she's not the world's most patient—'

Countess Judy. If Countess Judy was still a partner, still in a position to order junior clerks about, then she wasn't permanently banished to the Isle of Avalon, where Paul had sent her just a few months ago—

'Sophie,' he said. 'I want you to do something for me. No, just shut up for a second and listen. Have you got your chequebook handy?'

'*Paul*—'

'No, please, it matters. I want you to look at it, and tell me what's printed on the cover. *Please.*'

Long, ominous silence. 'I'm not happy about this, Paul. I don't think you should be screwing around with my head like this, at this stage in our relationship. I mean, presumably you think it's a big joke—'

'Just read the fucking chequebook!' Paul yelled; partly to emphasise the message he was trying to get across, partly to drown out the echoes of that word *relationship*. 'Really, I need you to do this for me. I'll explain, I promise. Please?'

'Oh, for— All right. It says, *Imperial Bank of Canada, a wholly owned subsidiary of the*—'

'Thank you,' Paul said. 'That's all I needed to know. I'm feeling much better now. Oh, by the way. Has Ricky Wurmtoter dropped by the office today?'

'Who?'

'Doesn't matter. I'll be there as soon as I can. I'll get a taxi or something.'

'Paul—'

He put back the receiver, and breathed out until his lungs were completely empty.

Not Custardspace, because if it was Custardspace he'd be alone. But Sophie's chequebook said the Imperial Bank of Canada, and she was in love with him, and Countess Judy was still there, and there was no Ricky Wurmtoter. Which meant—

Paul took a moment to marshal the evidence, examine the implications. Because, in this version, King Hring had beaten King Hroar (or was it the other way around? Like he cared), the Vikings had settled permanently in Canada and founded banks, and the world was slightly different. Ricky Wurmtoter had died thirteen hundred years ago. Countess Judy obviously hadn't made her bid for world domination yet. He was still a junior clerk, so no Mr Laertides – no need for Mr Laertides, whose sole purpose in existence had been to put right Theo Van Spee's offence against time and space. And Sophie – he and Sophie hadn't split up yet.

Let's have that one more time, please. He and Sophie—

Hadn't split up, because Countess Judy hadn't hijacked Sophie's mind and wiped out her love for him; and now, because he knew the other version, he could make sure that it never happened. All right, so the world had changed, and presumably the gnomes lived in Montreal instead of Zurich, and lots of big stuff wasn't the way it should be – or the way it used to be, more like, because who was to say this version wasn't every bit as good as the other one, or maybe even better? Actually, it was much, much, much better as far as he was concerned, and fuck the big stuff. This version was *right* – it had to be, surely, because what Countess Judy had done to Sophie was wrong, about as wrong as it was possible to get, so if changing the world had changed that, surely it had to be better, an improvement. And true, Paul hadn't met a lot of Canadians, but the few he'd come across, or to be precise the one Canadian he'd met briefly at a party two years ago, had been perfectly pleasant and nice, a bit boring maybe, not the sharpest knife in the drawer, but very polite and well mannered, definitely the sort of person you'd want running the world, particularly if it meant he could have Sophie back –

Just like the love philtre?

No. Not even a teeny-tiny bit like that.

Paul slumped on the floor, his forehead pressed to the kitchen tiles. There was, after all, the fact of Mr Laertides. He'd said, hadn't he, that he was some kind of supernatural umpire or referee, who'd been sent here to fix the terrible fuck-up caused by Theo Van Spee's synthetic dimension, and the postponing of that stupid fucking duel on the island all those hundreds of years ago. And he, Paul, had made the duel happen, at last, eventually; he'd made it so that there was a definite outcome, by allowing Ricky Wurmtoter to kill him. As a result, the world had changed. Fine. Mr Laertides's mission had been a success, which implied that everything that had gone wrong was now put right, as a result of which Sophie was now in love with Paul. What the bloody hell could possibly be wrong about that?

Well?

On his hands and knees, Paul shuffled over to the nearest kitchen cupboard, and opened it with all the energy and vigour of a man pulling the pin from a grenade inside a small, sealed room.

Furniture polish. Cif. Scotchbrite pads. Two tins of peaches. Loads of stuff. No trace of eternal nothingness or the Land of the Dead. Excellent.

Next he went to the front door and opened it just a tiny crack, through which he could see the top of the stairs. Every indication seemed to suggest that some kind person had put the world back. It was OK. All he had to do was jump in a taxi and go to work, and forget about the other version of the world, and everything would be absolutely fine. Happy ending, here he came. It was perfect. It was his just reward for putting things straight and giving his life for others and all that crap. He'd have to be barking not to be happy with a deal like that.

Except –

It was a very small voice, so small that he could easily have ignored it, if only it had come from outside his head. He did try. Quite hard –

Except –

Paul tried humming. He didn't know many tunes, but he hummed them all, one after another. He tried counting up to a hundred. He recited a poem he'd been made to learn at school, something about daffodils.

Except you can't, really, can you? It wouldn't be right.

And when he'd run out of tunes and numbers and scraps of half-remembered poetry, he tried reasoning with it. He explained, carefully and patiently, that it wasn't his fault, it hadn't been his idea, he'd been press-ganged into it, it had all turned out to be for the best, it had all been arranged by people who were much cleverer than he was, people who knew about these things, and if they reckoned it was all right, then who the hell was he to argue? He pointed out that, quite apart from the wider implications, this neat and elegant solution would secure not just his happiness but that of the girl he loved – and what on Earth could be more important than that? And sure, Ricky Wurmtoter wouldn't be around any more, but that was all perfectly proper because he should have died thirteen hundred years ago, and all Paul had done was put straight a ghastly mess brought about by the greed and arrogance of the loathsome Theo Van Spee. Even if he had the faintest glimmer of the vaguest penumbra of a clue about how to undo what'd just happened, it'd be a crime against humanity past, present and future to put things back how they were, with Van Spee triumphantly profiting from his evil interference with time and space. *Call*

320 • Tom Holt

yourself a conscience? Paul shouted into the foggy depths of his mind. *You don't know jack about right and wrong, you haven't got a clue—*

It's not on, you know. Really, you've got to do something about it. You know I'm right. Don't you?

'Yes,' he mumbled, very quietly. 'I suppose so.'

Well, there you go, then. Glad we got that sorted out.

'Yes, but—' Yes, but what the hell was he supposed to do? How could he even start putting it right, whatever it was, when he didn't even know how it worked? And why him, when everybody else in the whole world knew everything about everything, except him—?

The little voice cleared itself and said nothing. He gave in.

'All right,' Paul said aloud. 'All *right*. Just leave it with me, and I'll—' He tailed off. He'd what? He didn't know. He didn't know *yet*. In which case, he was going to have to find out. Which meant figuring it all out for himself, from first principles. He could do it on the bus, on the way to work. *Ha.*

So he thought about it: at the bus stop, on the bus, walking from the bus stop at the other end to the office, and by the time he reached the front door and the reception desk, he still didn't have the faintest idea where to start looking for a clue, let alone what it might look like once he'd stumbled across it. Break back into Custardspace – but since Theo Van Spee's crime had never happened, there wouldn't be any Custardspace, because Van Spee had never invented it. Without Custardspace, how was Paul supposed to get from this dimension or alternative reality or whatever the hell it was he was in, back into the real one? Magic sword, maybe? Fine, except he had no way of knowing where to find one; if the duel had taken place, they could be anywhere, buried in a grave mound or tucked away in some museum or long since crumbled into flakes of red rust. He couldn't ask Mr Laertides, because if the duel had taken place, there hadn't been any breach in spatio-temporal continuity, and Mr Laertides wouldn't have been called into being to deal with it. Theo Van Spee? He might conceivably know, but he'd be the last person in the universe who'd want to tell him, because in this reality Van Spee was innocent of any crime, whereas in the real version he'd be the most wanted man in history. It was just imposs—

'You're late,' said the reception girl. He looked down. He recognised her. The hair.

'Vicky?'

She gave him a look. 'Don't stare,' she said, 'it's rude. You look like you've seen a ghost.' She frowned. 'No, actually,' she went on, 'you look like you've just seen your best friend eaten alive by elephant-sized pink ferrets. What's the matter? Hangover?'

Paul shook his head. 'Can I ask you something?' he said.

She scowled. 'If it's anything to do with my plans for my spare time at any point in the next sixty years, forget it.'

'It's not like that,' he said. 'Look, this probably sounds a bit odd, but have you got an other half?'

If the American government could have bottled the look on her face and dropped it out of helicopters, they might well have won the Vietnam War. 'Yeah, right,' Vicky said. 'Weren't you listening just now? I wouldn't go out with you if—'

'No, not like that. What I mean is, are you the other half of anything?'

From revulsion to bewilderment in one flicker of the eyelids. 'What, you mean like a pantomime horse or something?'

Well, it had seemed like a good idea at the time. 'Obviously not,' Paul said. 'Sorry, please forget I said any of that stuff. It's, um, a project I'm working on for Professor Van Spee, much too complicated to explain. I'd better be getting along, I'm late enough as it—'

'Yes,' she said.

'Fine. Well, if anybody asks if you've seen me—'

'I mean,' she said, 'yes, I have.'

Paul pulled a long face. 'Sorry,' he said, 'I'm getting confused. Yes, you've seen me, or yes . . .'

'Oh, for crying out loud. Yes, I've got an other half.'

'Ah, right.' Getting somewhere at last.

'And if he catches you trying to chat me up again, he'll break your neck. Understood?'

Sigh. 'Sorry,' Paul said. 'It's not like that, really. Look—'

Then Vicky scowled at him and stared hard at the desk, as someone walked past. Paul caught a glimpse of red lipstick and shoulder-length blonde hair, and a rather nice voice called out, 'There you are. Hurry up.' Before Paul could turn his head, she'd gone.

'Who was that?' he asked.

Vicky lifted her head and stared at him. 'What did you just say?'

'I asked who that was.'

'That?' Vicky took a deep breath, then blew it out through her nose. 'That, you complete arsehole, was your wife.'

CHAPTER FOURTEEN

Down the corridor, sharp left turn, along the passageway; Paul caught up with her just outside the small interview room. She turned and smiled at him. It was a dazzling smile, white teeth and full red lips and cornflower-blue eyes. He'd never seen her before in his life.

'Oh,' he said. 'You.'

'Darling?'

'It's you, isn't it?' he said, in a weary voice. 'Pretending.'

'I don't know what you mean,' she said, but she spoilt it rather by grinning. Paul shut his eyes, leaned back against the nearest wall and groaned.

'What's up, lover?' asked Mr Tanner's mum. 'You look like you just ate a slug kebab.'

'Vicky,' Paul said. 'That girl on reception. She just told me we're married.'

Mr Tanner's mum frowned. 'What, you and her? That's—'

'No, no, no.' Paul banged the wall with his fist. 'Me and you. Us. Is that right?'

Mr Tanner's mum rolled out another smile, even dreamier than the last one. 'I can hardly believe it myself,' she said. 'Sometimes I have to stop and—'

'Oh, for God's sake.' Paul felt his knees fold, as though the cartilage had turned to wet cardboard. He slid down the wall

324 • Tom Holt

and squatted on the carpet. 'It's you,' he repeated. 'Mr Tanner's mum. You're a bloody goblin.'

Silence, just long enough to blow your nose in. 'Oh,' she said. 'You found out. Somebody told you.'

'No.'

'Well, you can't have figured it out for yourself, and I don't suppose it came to you in a dream. It was that bitch Vicky, wasn't it? I'm going to wring her skinny neck.'

'It wasn't her,' Paul muttered. 'Nothing like that. Long story. Really, can't be bothered telling you now.' He opened his eyes, sat up a bit. 'How long?' he asked.

'How long have we been married?'

'Yes.'

'Three months,' she replied. 'Three glorious, wonderful—'

'Fucking snot,' Paul yelped. 'You're kidding.'

'No, I'm not,' Mr Tanner's mum said irritably. 'Whirlwind romance – you swept me off my feet, you tiger, you. Then three weeks' honeymoon in Marrawatta Ponds—'

Paul lifted his head. 'Where?'

'Marrawatta Ponds. In Australia. New South Wales. You must remember our honeymoon.'

'No. And please,' he added quickly, 'don't tell me why it was unforgettable, because I really don't—' He frowned. 'Australia,' he said. 'Let me guess. Right in the heart of bauxite country, yes?'

'Well, yes, actually. At least, I did hear somewhere they'd found large, previously undiscovered bauxite deposits quite near where we were. But—'

'And we used to go for long romantic walks in the evening, out in the desert? Forget it,' he added quickly, before she could answer. 'It doesn't matter, really. This is awful. It's—'

He paused, rewinding back through what Sophie had said to him on the phone, back in the flat. '*I don't think you should be screwing around with my head like this*, she'd said, *at this stage in our relationship.*' As soon as he'd heard the R word, Paul had jumped to the obvious conclusion like a tree frog trying to win Olympic gold – because it was the conclusion he wanted to jump to, presumably, or something like that. But someone like

Sophie – the R word, he remembered, did tend to figure quite heavily in her vocabulary. Bloody useless sloppy language, English; you could have a relationship with someone that didn't involve love, kisses, choosing cushion covers and arguments about washing-up rotas. You could have a working relationship with a colleague, for example. Or—

'Excuse me,' he said. 'Can I ask you something?'

Mr Tanner's mum blinked. 'Sure.'

'I mean,' he went on, 'you're a pretty observant sort of person, and I don't suppose much gets past you, right?'

'I suppose so, yes.'

'Fine. Am I having an affair with Sophie Pettingell?'

There had been times in the recent past (but in another dimension, so maybe it didn't count) when he'd have betted good money that nothing in the known universe could ever leave Mr Tanner's mum at a loss for words. Typical, of course; you finally see the thing you thought you'd never see, but by then you don't give a toss any more.

'What did you just say?'

'I asked you a question,' Paul replied briskly. 'Come on, it's not exactly rocket science. Am I having it away with Sophie Pettingell, or not?'

'Well, I—' She opened and closed her perfect rosebud mouth a few times, then shrugged. 'I don't know,' she said. 'I'd have thought you'd have known, but maybe it slipped your mind or something. You'd better ask her. And if the answer's yes, I'll see to it personally that what's left of both of you gets buried in separate graves, a long way apart. Paul, are you feeling all right? Something tells me you aren't quite yourself today.'

Couldn't help laughing at that. 'To put it mildly,' he replied. 'Who I quite am right now is a bloody good question, but I haven't got time. Listen. No, just this once, shut up and *listen*, will you? Thanks. Have you still got the Portable Door?'

She flinched, just a bit; so that when she said, 'What's a Portable Door?' he knew she was lying. 'The Portable Door,' he repeated. 'Plastic thing like a picnic mat, with a door drawn on it. You slap it on a wall, and then you can go places. Have you still got it, or not?'

Maybe she really did love him; because when he looked at her, all stern and fierce, she sort of wilted, and nodded her head. 'Who told you about that?' she said. 'That cow on reception?'

For a moment, the word *cow* threw Paul quite badly. 'No,' he said. 'Nobody told me. Well, *you* did. But that's another long story. In fact, it's a bloody epic. I need it.'

'What?'

'The Portable bloody Door, of course.' He calmed himself down; took some doing. 'I need to use the Portable Door for something,' he said. 'It's very important. I promise you, I'll give—' He checked himself; for some reason, he felt it was important to be precise in his use of words. 'You'll get it back,' he said, because, after all, that had already happened. 'Promise. But I really do need it, right now.'

Mr Tanner's mum looked at him, and he could see that she was desperately worried about something. Another time, in another place, he'd have had real problems with that look. 'Paul,' she said, 'what do you want it for?'

'Trust me.'

'About as far as I could fart you. What do you want it for? Is it because you've just found out I'm really a goblin?'

It was nice to be able to tell the truth sometimes. 'No,' Paul said, 'absolutely not. Got nothing at all to do with that, I swear.'

'Oh.' She frowned. 'Is it a work thing, then?'

You could say that. 'Yes,' he said. 'Just work, really. But I do need it, desperately. Go on,' he added, though he knew it wasn't fair. 'Please?'

Even then, she hesitated a full half-second. 'Oh, go on, then,' she said. 'But I do want it back.'

'Guaranteed,' Paul said. 'It's as good as done.'

It was, of course, in the strongroom, in a tatty-looking black tin box on the top shelf. Paul's hands shook slightly as he smoothed it out on the wall, and it wasn't just the cold.

'Thanks,' he said. 'I'll make it up to you. Soon.'

Mr Tanner's mum looked at him, and there was that worried expression again; and for just a split second he thought, *Actually, she's very pretty, and nice too, apparently, and I think she likes me, and so what if she's a goblin, I'm a bloody goblin too, partly* – But it wouldn't be right, or fair. Somewhere else, somewhere where he belonged, there was a mess that had to be put right, and if he didn't do it, nobody would, and then everything would be wrong for ever, and this time it really *would* be his fault. Also, he couldn't help but reflect, he didn't really want to find out how Mr Tanner felt about having Paul as a father-in-law. 'Thanks,' he repeated. 'You're – you're really quite nice, actually. Some of the time.'

'Paul?' she said. But by then he was halfway through the Door, and thinking, *Back—*

Paul stepped out through the doorway, and a large clawed hand clamped itself around his shoulder.

'Got you,' said a voice; and quite a few of the liberal, open-minded, non-judgemental things he'd been thinking about goblinkind in general a few moments ago got deleted with extreme prejudice.

'Ouch,' Paul said. 'That hurts.'

'Good,' replied the goblin. 'How about that?'

'That too,' Paul replied truthfully. 'Look, would it help if I promised to come quietly?'

'No.'

'Fine.' *Ouch ouch OUCH*, he thought in advance, then he shut his eyes and deliberately fell backwards.

Just as he was about to land heavily across the threshold of the Portable Door, he tore his thoughts away from the excruciating pain of talons clenched into his shoulder, and concentrated hard on a date, a time and a place. The goblin hit the deck first, of course, but he hoped very much that he was too preoccupied with Paul resisting arrest to fill his mind with anything that might contradict what Paul was thinking.

'Ouch,' screamed a goblin voice underneath him, as he landed. 'Fuck! Look where you're going, can't you?'

'Sorry,' Paul said, as he scrambled to his feet. 'Did I hurt you?'

'Yes,' snarled the goblin; but Paul was standing up, hastily shutting the Door and rolling it up. Only then did he turn round.

Perfect. He was standing in his office; there was the calendar on his desk, and the date was wonderfully, beautifully *right*. He helped the goblin up.

'What the hell am I doing in here?' the goblin asked. 'We aren't supposed to come out till half-five.'

Paul shrugged. 'Sorry,' he said. 'Can't help you there. I'd get back to the cellars quick if I were you.'

'Too bloody right,' the goblin muttered, and bolted, leaving Paul finally, blissfully alone.

Joy, he thought. *Absolute bloody joy.* He'd taken himself back to his office on the day of Mr Tanner's mum's baby's christening party. He hadn't yet killed Ricky Wurmtoter, or metamorphosed into Philip Marlow, he hadn't been killed yet, not even once. Furthermore, he resolved grimly, he wasn't going to be, not if he could help it. Which he could.

Just to make absolutely, absolutely sure, he took out his wallet and looked at his bank card. He read the words printed on it, and grinned.

'Sorry, Canada,' he said aloud. 'Nothing personal.'

Paul glanced at his watch, but it had stopped, and he couldn't find it in his heart to blame it. Anyway, there was a perfectly good clock on his office wall, and it told him the time was 10.35. Perfect.

Down the corridor, up one lot of stairs, down another, along more stupid passageways, fuck this horrible bloody building for being so *big* – He stopped just round the corner from Benny Shumway's office, caught his breath and waited. A second or so passed; then Benny came out, with a file under his arm, and disappeared round a corner. Great. Paul sneaked up to the office door and slipped in.

There, leaning against the wall, was the sword. If he remembered right, its name was Skofnung, and it was a magical, transdimensional, self-motivated pain in the bum. It was also, unfortunately, essential to his plan –

(*A plan. Whoopee. Here I am, alone against the universe, but I have a plan. So that's all right, then.*)

He picked it up and, very carefully, drew it out of its scabbard. It looked horribly sharp, and the way the light glinted on the blade was depressingly sinister, like the grin on the face of a goblin. *Loathsome bloody thing*, he thought. Then he turned to face the door in the wall, the one Benny used when he did the daily run to the Bank. Any moment now—

Someone was bashing on it, from the other side. Of course, Paul had seen that, and heard it, before. Last time round, it had scared him out of his wits, because he'd naturally assumed that whoever or whatever was out there wasn't going to be his friend. Actually, he hadn't been far wide of the mark, at that, because (according to all his relatives and friends) the bloke on the other side of the door had been his worst enemy for the past twenty-three years.

Instead of slamming back the bolts, he drew them. Then, as soon as there was a lull in the hammering and bashing, he turned the knob and pulled the door open.

'Come on,' he said. 'And stop making that bloody racket.'

A head and body flopped through he door, like an exhausted salmon eventually making it to the top of the waterfall. 'Thanks,' said the newcomer, 'I'd almost given up—'

The newcomer stopped short. He was staring.

'Yes, all right,' Paul said impatiently. 'It's me. Us. Long story, another time. Now, here's what we've got to do—'

'*Fuck!*' the newcomer yelped; and of course, the newcomer was Paul himself. To be precise, the Paul who'd died at Mr Tanner's mum's christening party, slaughtered a virtual TV anchorman, and sprinted across the empty plains of the Land of the Dead after Benny Shumway, only to arrive just as the door was bolted. He could remember the despair he'd felt as he'd pounded on the door with his fists until they ached, and nobody had heard him, nobody had rushed to help him. In fact, as he knew better than anybody, some bastard on the other side had shot all the bolts and wedged the door shut with a filing cabinet. His own worst enemy indeed.

But the other Paul, the one he'd just let through the door, wouldn't have that memory. The way he'd remember it would be bashing on the door and yelling, and the door opening, and seeing *himself* standing there on the other side, looking all stressy and tense. Also, this sucker had only died – what, three times? Once by his own hand, once by a bolt from Ricky's crossbow, once stabbed to death by goblins. A mere novice when it came to dying, a mortality virgin.

'You might at least pretend you're pleased to see me,' he said. 'I've been to a lot of trouble on your behalf. The least you could do is simulate a little gratitude.'

'Sorry,' said the other Paul instinctively.

'And shut that bloody door, will you?'

'Oh, yes. Right.'

Paul leaned past his other self and made sure all the bolts were shot home and all the latches were dropped. 'Come on,' he said. 'Time we weren't here. Benny could be back any moment, and it'd be really, really embarrassing if he sees the two of us.'

Where to go, that was the question. Awkward. He hesitated for a moment—

'You've got the sword,' said his alter ego.

'What?'

'That sword I got at the christening party. I thought I'd lost it, back in there.'

'You did,' Paul said. 'You're careless as well as feckless, but fortunately I'm here to tidy up after you. Closed-file store,' he added. 'Only logical place. Come on.'

Luckily they made it to the closed-file store without meeting anybody. Paul closed the door, then wedged it shut with the sword. 'Sit down,' he said. 'And don't interrupt, because this is going to be complicated, and I know you've got the attention span of a goldfish. Ready?'

'Um. Yes, I suppose so.'

So Paul started to explain, and his identical twin listened. Interesting study the other Paul's face made: first, of course, utter bewilderment; then the gradual dawn of understanding; then a very intense, almost fierce concentration; then the effects of a rather nasty set of implications, starting as a tiny glimmer of doubt and spreading into a pall of gloomy acceptance. Watching himself listening to him, Paul was actually rather impressed: a bit more stoicism, courage even, than he'd have expected from himself under such circumstances. He never knew he had it in him.

'Any questions?' he concluded. The other Paul shrugged.

'Not really,' he said; then a pause, then (not really very hopefully): 'I don't suppose there's another way, is there? I mean, another approach we haven't considered yet. One that doesn't involve me getting—'

'No,' Paul replied. 'Sorry. But look at it this way. One, by rights you shouldn't be here at all. The goblins killed you, fair and square. Two: all right, it's not looking good as far as you're concerned, but look on the bright side, with any luck I'm going to make it; and you're me and I'm you, so really it's all as broad as it's long. Right?'

'I guess.' The other him didn't sound totally convinced, but he was trying his best, bless him. 'And I suppose, if one of us has got to—'

'Quite,' Paul replied. 'And the simple fact of the matter is, I'm the real me and you're just some sort of anomaly, so—'

'No way. I'm the real me and you're the bloody by-product . . . Sorry.' The other Paul shook his head. 'It doesn't actually matter, does it?' he said. 'It's got to be me, you're right. Only, isn't it just fucking typical, it's always me that loses out. Even against my bloody *self*.'

Paul tried to think of something to say; something comforting, something ennobling, something that'd help his tormented alter ego find some degree of inner peace in the face of the horror that lay ahead of him. 'Oh well,' he said. 'Never mind. You ready?'

'As I'll ever be.'

'You'll need this, of course.'

The other Paul took the sword; unwillingly, as if it was something slimy and horrid. 'Thanks,' he said.

'Our biggest mistake,' Paul told him. 'Well, one of our biggest mistakes, anyhow. Not figuring it out sooner.'

'I wouldn't know,' the other Paul replied peevishly. 'I wasn't there at the time.'

'Fine.' Paul frowned. '*My* mistake, then. Only, I should've known when Vicky told me she and Ricky had been married. Bloody great big hint, went right over my head like a flock of migrating geese. Still, I got there in the end.'

'We got there,' replied his other self, and Paul couldn't be bothered to point out the inconsistency. 'Well,' other-Paul went on, 'I'd like to say it was a pleasure meeting you, but . . .'

'But lying to yourself is a mug's game, right.' Paul stood up. 'Look, if it's any consolation, this is all for the best, and I think what you're doing is actually pretty cool. So—'

'Yes, well. You would, wouldn't you?'

No pleasing some people. 'You coming,' Paul snapped, 'or what?'

'What do you think? Of course I'm coming.' Other-Paul trailed wearily to the door, then paused. 'One bright side to all of this,' he said. 'I can't wait to see the look on bloody Wurmtoter's face.'

Paul grinned. 'Me too,' he said. Then he stopped and pulled a face. 'Idiot,' he said. 'Not you,' he added. 'Me.'

'Pretty much academic, surely?'

'Oh, be quiet. Sophie,' he added. 'We need Sophie, or it's not going to work. Only—'

'Only there's two of us,' his other self said. 'Which is going to freak her out no end. Still, can't be helped. Omelettes and eggs.'

Paul sighed. 'I guess so. I suppose I'll just have to explain it all to her later.'

Other-Paul grinned. 'Rather you than me, chum. All right, I'll stay here, you go and fetch her. Okay?'

He found Sophie, eventually, in the photocopier room; she was running off something like a thousand copies of a big fat document, sorting, collating, stapling. He came in quietly and she didn't hear him over the whirr and clatter of the machine (which had once, of course, been the younger Mr Wells, but there wasn't enough space left in his mind for side issues that size). He looked at the back of her head and thought, *Only you, you and no other*; and then he asked himself, *Why, for pity's sake? What's so special about her, as against, say, Vicky or Demelza Horrocks or even, within certain firmly defined parameters, Mr Tanner's mum?* Paul thought about that for two, maybe two and a half seconds, and realised that he didn't know, that there wasn't an answer; just as there's never any answer to those simple but incredibly difficult questions you ask when you're four years old, and the grown-up just looks at you all cross and embarrassed and says, 'Just because, that's why.' (And, of course, that's the only real, true answer to that kind of question; there are long-winded ways of saying the same thing, involving lengthy digressions and background materials and abstruse and nebulous concepts, but they're just another way of saying that same old thing.)

Why? Because. And that's how you know it's true love. If you love someone for or because of something, it doesn't count; it's admiration, appreciation or the recognition of some resource she's got that you can exploit to your own advantage. Unless it's just Because, it can't be unconditional, instinctive, involuntary. Doesn't count. No good.

'Sophie,' he said.

'What?' She turned round, banged her elbow against the machine's dust cover, dropped a sheaf of pages, swore, scowled at him. 'Oh, it's you. What?'

'Oh, nothing,' he said. 'I just wondered if you were busy right now, that's all.'

She gave him that oh-for-crying-out-loud look he knew so well. 'Do I look busy?'

'Yes. Fairly.'

'Fine. No need to ask, then, was there?'

'Sorry. Only I need your help with something. Won't take a moment.'

'No. Look, I've got to do this stupid copying for Mr Suslowicz, then there's a bloody great pile of filing for Mr bloody Tanner, and then—'

'Really,' he said, 'it won't take ten seconds. And you're so busy already, one more little thing's not going to make any odds, is it?'

'Paul.'

'Yes?'

'No.'

'Oh.' He took a step back, as though a real door had just been slammed in his face. 'Please?'

She sighed. 'Can't you get someone else to help you?'

'Not really.'

'Why? What is it you want me to do?'

'It's—' There's never a word around when you need one, is there? 'It's complicated. Take longer to explain it than actually do it, if you follow me. Look, it really would be very kind of you if you could just spare me two seconds.'

'Paul.' It was a sort of combination half-scowl, half-grin. 'Did anybody ever tell you, you're really annoying when you're being pathetic?'

He nodded. 'And really pathetic when I'm being annoying, yes. Actually,' he added, 'I think it was you.'

'Mphm. Sounds like the sort of thing I'd say.' She frowned. 'All right, but you've got to promise you'll do the Mortensens for me, tomorrow morning. All right?'

'Sure.' No problem at all promising that. 'All right, so that's settled, is it?'

'What do you want, a signed contract?'

They didn't say anything to each other on the way to the closed-file store. When they got there, he lunged past her, pulled open the door and darted in, saying, 'This way,' or something equally pointless. As he'd devoutly hoped, there he was, the other him, waiting.

'Paul? Look, what's—?' She stopped just inside the door, for once completely speechless. The two Pauls smiled feebly at her, and Paul said, 'Hi. It's us.'

A moment of deep silence; then, 'Paul, what the *fuck*—?'

'Long story. Very long story. Think Robert Jordan and multiply by three. Meanwhile, it's very important that you see this. Here, look.'

The other Paul drew the sword out of its scabbard, knelt down and laid it carefully on the ground. She looked at it and said, 'Paul, what the hell's that got to do with—?'

And stopped.

'Oh,' she said.

Other-Paul stood up and got out of the way quickly as Sophie crouched down and looked at the sword. Her hair, falling forward from behind her ear, brushed the gleaming brown-with-silver-swirls blade. She looked up.

'I don't understand,' she said. 'It's like I know this. Like—' She pulled a face, angry and frightened and confused. 'Like it's,

I don't know, *family* or something. Paul, what the hell's going on?'

He knelt down beside her. 'I don't really know,' he said. 'Not all of it. But apparently this is some kind of magic sword, and the way it works is, it's in two parts. There's the actual sharp metal thing, and then there's a human that sort of goes with it. Its other half. And—' He stopped, taking on board a small but vital moment of understanding that had eluded him till now. 'The thing is,' he went on, 'neither of them works without the other. No, that's not it. Neither of them is *right* without the other. What I mean is, you can't use the sword unless you've got the girl too. And—' He looked away for a moment. 'And vice versa,' he added. 'And I've actually had this stupid thing for months now, it was under the sofa, Ricky gave it to me, but I hadn't actually figured out the rest of it. You see, all this time I'd got the idea that the other half of this sword was – well, someone else. But now I've finally got it straight in my mind, that part of it anyway. It was you, all along, and I was too stupid to realise.'

Pause. 'Me?'

Paul dipped his head slowly. 'That's right. You're this thing's other half. So . . .'

'Vice versa?'

He nodded again. 'I think it sort of explains a lot of stuff. About, you know, us. Only it *wasn't* us, it was stupid bloody magic, getting in the way and screwing us around, as usual. And—'

'So who's he, then?'

The other Paul might have muttered 'The cat's mother' under his breath, or not; he wasn't helping matters, and Paul ignored him. 'That's a different story – well, part of the same story but way, way off at right angles. The thing is, unless I fight a duel to the death with Ricky Wurmtoter – not here, somewhere else, which reminds me, we need a goblin called Colin – unless we have this stupid duel, the whole of history for the last thousand-odd years is going to get really screwed up, and it's all Van Spee's fault but I'm the only one who can sort it out. Actually, it's a real bugger. That's why I need you to help me.'

Sophie scowled at him. 'You said it'd only take two seconds.'

'I exaggerated. But I will still do the Mortensens for you.'

'After you've saved the world, you mean?'

Paul nodded. 'Sure,' he said. 'Assuming there's a world left tomorrow, no problem.'

She thought for a moment or so. 'I'd still like to know exactly what you meant by vice versa.'

'Look—'

'And anyway,' she went on, 'you and me breaking up, it wasn't about magic. Well, not all, anyway. Partly it was because you're shallow and emotionally retarded and completely self-centred and inconsiderate and—' She stopped.

'Yes? Go on.'

'Actually.' A deep, thoughtful frown on Sophie's face. 'Yes, you're all that stuff, but that wasn't it. I mean, that's the kind of thing you have endless rows and tears and yelling over, but it's not why we split up. I don't know why we split up, do you?'

Paul smiled. 'Because.'

'What?'

'Because of Countess Judy,' he said. 'It really was just because of her, doing horrible things to your mind. And also this sword stuff too, that was something to do with it. But whatever it was, it was just all magic crap, all JWW and work and nothing to do with us. That's why—'

Sophie raised a hand. Miss Hook used to do something just like that, Paul remembered, when she wanted to shut the class up. 'Forget it,' she said. 'We'll talk about it later. A lot. For now, though, what're you actually going to do with that – thing?'

'Like I said,' Paul replied. 'I've got to fight Ricky Wurmtoter.'

'But you can't do that. He'll murder you. You don't know spit about swordfighting and stuff.'

Paul shook his head. 'Not important,' he said. 'The sword sees to all that sort of thing, I've just got to, like, be there. And you too, of course. And . . . shit,' he added. 'There's something I've forgotten.'

Sophie rolled her eyes. 'Paul,' she said.

'No, it's all right, really.' He turned to his other self. 'Vicky,' he said.

'What about her?'

'We'll need her too, or it won't work. Look, can you go and find her and bring her here?'

'What did your last slave die of?' the other Paul grumbled, and left the room.

That made a difference. The presence of a third party, even though it had been the second party in duplicate, had made things a bit tense, but also easier, in a way, because they couldn't really discuss – well, personal stuff – in front of someone else. Now they could talk, and they had nothing to do for five minutes or so. No reason not to. *Bloody hell*, Paul thought, and cleared his throat.

'Sophie,' he said.

'Well?'

Christ. 'I don't know how to put this,' Paul said with transparent sincerity, 'but I think – well, I think we ought to give it another go. If you'd like to, I mean.'

She looked at him. 'Not really,' she said.

'Oh.'

Bugger, he thought. It was one of those horrible relationship moments where it was your fault for not being a telepath and knowing exactly what she was thinking so you could say the right thing. He could see Sophie waiting, with imperfectly disguised impatience; she wasn't actually tapping her foot or looking pointedly at her watch, but absolutely the next best thing. And he couldn't think of anything to say to *Not really.* Which was odd, because twice now, or was it three times – he'd lost count – he'd faced down death and made it go away just by refusing to accept the unacceptable. The difference was, of course, that he couldn't give a shit about death's feelings.

'Not really,' she repeated, 'because if we did we'd be right back where we started and it wouldn't be right for either of us because I can't ever be me so long as you're afraid to be you, and it'd all just get fraught and horrible again and I wouldn't be able to breathe, and anyway you're just about to trot off and get yourself killed by Ricky bloody Wurmtoter, so where the hell would be the bloody point?' Whereupon (and this was rather worse than facing Mr Dao against a backdrop of nothing whatsoever) Sophie started to sniffle, and a tear leaked out of the corner of her eye, like oil from a knackered gasket, and of course that was all his fault too –

'No, I'm not,' he said.

'Yes, you are.'

Great, Paul thought, *panto time.* 'No, I'm *not*,' he said briskly. 'That's what *he's* for.'

Sophie cut off the snuffles abruptly in mid-sniff. 'What?'

'Him,' Paul said. 'The other me. I'm not going to fight Ricky. He is.'

'But that's—'

'Yes,' Paul said savagely. 'I know. But someone's got to do it, and I'm sick to the teeth of dying. I figure it's some other bugger's turn. Besides, he's dead already, so it's not like it'll put him out or anything.'

'Paul.' Her I'm-warning-you voice. He ignored it.

'I was in Benny Shumway's office,' he said. 'It was a strange morning. I'd died, you see. None of this has happened yet, by the way,' he added helpfully, 'and it's not going to, either, if I have anything to do with it, but I'm drifting off-topic. Where was I? Sorry, yes. What should happen, you see, is this: tonight, I go along to Mr Tanner's mum's christening party—'

'Is that tonight? Hell, I'd forgotten all about it.'

'Tonight,' Paul repeated. 'And I've said I'll be the godfather, right? What I don't know is, the role of godfather in a goblin christening is, um, sacrificial. They killed me. Bloody goblins jumped out of a cake and stabbed me to death.'

Sophie was staring at him. Probably she was just shell-shocked by his reckless disregard for tenses, but at least he had her attention. 'Anyway,' Paul went on, 'I died, and you remember me telling you about Mr Dao, from the Bank? Well, he was there. And I won't bore you with the details, but I sort of escaped, and I ran like hell, and I reached the connecting door in Benny's office just as he was shutting it behind him. I stood there banging on it and yelling, but of course nobody answered. And then I figured out another way of escaping, so that was all right; but a couple of days later, when I'd come back to life – sorry, am I going too fast for you or something?'

'No, no,' Sophie said, in a quiet, stunned voice. 'Go on.'

'Like I said,' Paul continued, 'it was being a really weird morning, but what the hell. Anyway, I had to go into Benny's office to get something, Benny wasn't in; and then I heard this terrible banging and shrieking coming through the connecting door. Well, naturally, I got out of there as fast as I could; but afterwards I got to thinking, and I realised. It wasn't some hideous undead fiend trying to get through from the other side that was making all that racket. It had to have been me.'

She was looking at him again. 'OK,' she said. 'Let's say for argument's sake—'

'And then the next time,' Paul went on, 'the next time I died and there was Mr Dao waiting for me, he tried to take me away but I didn't want to go, and guess what, it turned out that he couldn't. He couldn't, because he didn't have any jurisdiction over me, that's what he said. But that didn't make any sense, because I'm not immortal or anything; unless, of course, what he meant was, I can't die because I'm dead already. He couldn't take me away again, because he'd already got me. And that,' Paul concluded, 'was what made me think of whatever it was on the other side of the door in Benny's room: it had to be another me, the one who's already dead. And of course, all the fuck-ups can't be sorted out till Ricky and I have our duel, and obviously I'm not going to survive it; but it won't matter a toss, because it won't be me he slashes to bits, it'll be the other me, the dead one—' He paused. 'You see what I'm getting at, don't you?'

'No.'

But it didn't matter, because the door opened and the other Paul came back, and Vicky was with him. She took a couple of steps into the room, saw Sophie and the sword, which was lying on the floor, and screamed. Then, very quickly indeed, Vicky punched the other Paul in the mouth and tried to get to the door. Much to the real Paul's surprise, the other Paul was too quick for her; he grabbed her by the wrist and yanked her back, as though she was an overexcited dog on a lead. For a moment Vicky looked as though she was going to make a serious fight of it; but then she just drooped, and flopped back against the wall.

'That's not fair,' she said. 'You're pathetic, all – all *three* of you.'

Paul stepped forward, trying to be reassuring. 'It's all right,' he told her, 'it's not like that. Really. What we're going to do is, we're going to find Ricky now—'

'Just a minute,' Sophie interrupted, and there was something in her voice that suggested breaking strain. 'What did she mean, all three—?'

'You,' Paul said, 'and the sword, and me. That's right, isn't it?'

Vicky gave him a nasty look, and nodded. 'You're all right,' she said to Sophie. 'You've got your other half, so if we fight now, you'll win and it'll all be over. But it'd be cheating, and . . .'

'Oh, for pity's sake,' Paul protested. 'Why doesn't anybody ever *listen*?' Sophie and Vicky turned and both of them scowled at him instead of at each other. 'Sophie,' he said, 'it's like this. In this duel I've got to have with Ricky, both of us, him and me, we've got to have these stupid magic swords, right? I've got one of them, and you're the other half of it. Ricky's got the other, and—'

'And the other half of Tyrving is me,' Vicky interrupted. 'And Ricky thought he could break the spell by marrying me – No, let's not beat about the bush. First, he got that bitch Countess Judy to wipe out my memory so I wouldn't know who and what I am. *Then* he married me. Thank God Frank Laertides found out about it and made Countess Judy put it right.'

'Anyway,' Paul said firmly. 'Vicky thinks we've tricked her here without her other half, the other magic sword, so we can cheat by killing her. That's what she thinks,' he added, 'because she may be a supernatural being of exceptional power and able to transcend the elements at will, but she's got the common sense of a small beetle.'

'Hey,' Vicky protested, but it didn't do her any good; and Sophie, in spite of herself, giggled.

'What we're actually going to do,' Paul went on, 'is cross over into Custardspace, which is where Ricky's hiding right now—'

'Into *where*?' Sophie demanded.

'And we're going to have the duel, and that'll be that.' Paul turned to Vicky. 'All right?' he said. 'Will that do, as far as you're concerned?'

Vicky looked a bit doubtful, but nodded. 'Fine by me,' she

said. 'Of course, if you could spare an extra ten minutes or so, first we could grab hold of him and hold him down and smash his face in with a baseball bat and *then* have the duel, but I can see you're not keen on that idea. Pity.'

'Yes,' Paul said, 'it is, but I don't want to risk screwing things up. I mean, what if we broke his arm or sprained his thumb or something, and he couldn't fight in the duel? Then everything'd be all to cock again, and all the chequebooks'd have English on one side and French on the other. No, you'll just have to be magnanimous and forgive him. Right?'

'I'll forgive him,' Vicky said pleasantly, 'provided you promise faithfully to chop his arms and legs off in the duel and make him eat them with a salsa dip. Well,' she added, 'his legs and his left arm. He'll be needing the other one to kill you with.'

'Or,' Paul replied after a brief, fraught pause, 'you can carry on hating him to bits, I don't care. I mean, I'd like it if everybody was friends and we all laid aside our differences and tried to get along, but it's no big deal. And I suppose if we're all going to be fighting to the death—'

Vicky grinned. 'How charmingly naive,' she said. 'Your trouble is, you don't think things through. I mean, I'm assuming you've figured out that Ricky is actually King Hring, which means he's over thirteen hundred years old. Yes?'

Paul nodded glumly. 'Been trying not to think about that,' he admitted. 'Too weird for me. But yes, I suppose if you're going to take it to its logical conclusion, that's who he's got to be. I suppose he's been hanging around ever since, trying to keep out of everybody's way—'

Vicky shook her head. 'Not everybody's,' she replied. 'Just *that's*.' She nodded curtly towards the sword lying on the floor. 'The thing about a living sword is,' she said, 'once it's drawn in anger, it's got to finish the fight, otherwise it can't rest easy. Now everything was fine until Theo bloody Van Spee interfered: we'd had the duel, Ricky and I lost but that's the rub of the green, and at least the fight was over. But then Theo stuck his oar in. The duel was interrupted, he whisked Ricky away from the island by magic, brought him here, even got him a job as a junior clerk; and Ricky worked hard, eventually got made a partner. All completely wrong, of course. It left both of us – my sword, and hers – stranded, marooned in mid-obligation. We had to finish the fight; but Ricky didn't want to – for obvious reasons: he was the one who was supposed to lose – and his opponent . . .' Suddenly she grinned without the slightest trace of levity. 'What do you suppose came of his opponent?'

Paul sighed. 'That'd be me, right?'

'That'd be you, yes.'

'*What?*' Sophie yelled. 'You mean to say *he*'s thirteen hundred years old too?'

'In a sense.' Paul had a nasty feeling that Vicky was enjoying this. 'What actually happened was, as soon as the duel was interrupted there was a breach in normality, for want of a better word. Stuff had gone wrong, and that called into existence an avenger. It's automatic, it just happens that way. It's like the screw-up comes to life and turns into a person.'

Paul took a deep breath. 'Mr Laertides.'

'Excellent.' Vicky clapped her hands together, like a little girl. 'Frank Laertides. Of course, the timescale is completely screwy. The duel happened thirteen centuries ago; but Van Spee chose to fuck everything up thirty years ago. So, he went back thirteen hundred and seventy years from his own time, did the screwing-up, substituted Tyving – that's me – for that stupid clunky old axe – Rosie Tanner – and came back home. Meanwhile, thirteen hundred years ago, the screw-up makes Frank Laertides suddenly come to life. But he can't just fast-forward through thirteen centuries to catch up with Theo and kick his arse. No, Frank had to go the long way round. More than that; in order to fix Theo's fuck-up, he had to restage the duel, and of course that would be difficult if Ricky's opponent, King Hroar, had conked out from extreme old age back in the early ninth century AD. Which means, not only did Frank have to wait around kicking his heels for thirteen hundred years, he had to bring King Hroar with him.' She smiled, almost affectionately. 'Just as well, really, that Frank's a very resourceful guy. Or you wouldn't be alive now, for one thing.'

Long, long silence. 'You mean,' Paul said slowly, 'he brought *me* with him?'

'That's right.' Vicky nodded gravely. 'Now you're getting it. And yes, that does mean that technically, you're thirteen hundred and something-odd years old. There's a word for it—'

'Well-preserved?' Paul suggested.

'Undead,' Vicky corrected him. 'Which accounts for a lot of things that must've seemed a bit odd to you, come to think of it. Like, how you've been able to pop in and out of the Land of the Dead like a commuter catching the bus; why you found the Portable Door when you first arrived here; why Ricky shot you with a crossbow a few months back—'

'No, that was an accident,' Paul protested. 'Well, a misunderstanding—'

'Balls,' Vicky replied. 'Deliberate; he wanted to kill you so you'd never be able to fight the duel, and he could make it look like it was a misunderstanding, all part of the Countess Judy fiasco. But you didn't die, because you're undead. Was Ricky pissed off, or what? It also explains,' Vicky went on, 'how come your mother and—' She frowned. 'How your mother and father were able to sell you to the firm to pay for their retirement. I'm surprised you didn't wonder about that, because strictly speaking, selling people isn't all that legal these days.'

Paul shrugged. 'I assumed it was, well, magic and stuff, so the rules didn't apply.'

Vicky shook her head. 'Not at all. The rules didn't apply because they only cover living human beings; a category,' she added sweetly, 'into which you do not fall. Now then,' she went on, 'I hope that makes everything lambently clear?'

Paul tried not to snigger, but with indifferent success. 'Absolutely,' he said. 'The good thing is,' he went on, 'I'm getting to where I can just ignore a lot of this stuff, at least in the short term. So, I'm undead, and presumably Wurmtoter is, too.'

'Yes.'

'And let's get this absolutely straight. If we go back to that island and fight a duel to the death, your stupid magic sword against mine, things will go back to how they're supposed to be, and it'll all be all right again?'

'Yes. Well,' Vicky said, with a slight frown, 'not entirely.

Strictly speaking, if two of the Undead fight, it's a duel to the Undeath. But in real terms—'

'Fine.' It was as though someone had just switched Paul on at the mains. He jumped up, and the other him moved simultaneously, like a semi-detached shadow. 'Let's do it, then. No time like the present, right?'

'Well, again, it's not actually the—' Paul pulled a horrible face, and Vicky stopped herself. 'All right,' she said. 'I get the message. The finer points are completely wasted on you, aren't they?'

'Yes.' Paul waited for a moment, then said: 'All right, how do we get there? I mean, I'm assuming that it's something to do with living swords transcending the dimensions, and no, I really don't want a lecture on the theoretical basis of how it works. Do I have to press a button, or pull a lever, or what?'

'No need.' Vicky smiled at him; and behind her, a flock of startled ducks clattered noisily off the misty surface of the water and flew away, their resentful quacking echoing back from the rocky cliffs of the distant fjord. 'We're here.'

CHAPTER FIFTEEN

'Hello, Paul.'

Paul swung round. Ricky Wurmtoter was leaning against the pointy end of a small boat, drawn up on the beach. In his right hand, he held a long, slim sword that glittered blue in the uncertain light. With his left he was raising a cigar to his lips.

'Not terribly good for you, apparently,' he went on, having blown a stream of blue smoke out through his nose. 'But I thought, in the circumstances, what the hell.'

'You used to smoke them in bed,' Vicky put in, over Paul's shoulder. 'That's so revolting.'

Ricky frowned. 'Clint Eastwood does it,' he said. 'And he's a hero.'

Vicky's eyes flickered upwards, just for a second. 'Of course, there's no hurry,' she said. 'Time has no meaning here, blahdy-blahdy. It's just that if I'm around Ricky for more than three minutes, I tend to throw up. So, if we could get to the sword-fighting—'

With a frown, Ricky straightened up. Maybe it was a trick of the light or the terrain, but he'd never looked taller, broader, more intimidating or (as he did stylish little backflips with the living sword) more annoying. He had the languid grace of a panther, and his hair was perfect.

Paul, on the other hand – 'Just a moment,' he said, and

glanced round for his other self, who wasn't there. Ricky, Vicky and Sophie, all present. Also, holding the swirly brown sword, himself but not in duplicate. Someone had blundered.

'Just you and me,' Ricky said. He sounded bored, as though he was playing himself in repertory, his hundredth Wednesday matinée. 'Let's finish this,' he added inevitably.

'Excuse me.'

Three of them looked round and stared at the fourth: Sophie, who was scowling. 'Excuse me,' she repeated, 'but nobody's finishing anything till someone's told me exactly what it is I'm supposed to do. Only, apparently I'm essential to all this crap, and I've got this sick feeling that this is the moment my whole life's been leading up to, but nobody's had the simple good manners to tell me—'

'Nothing,' Vicky snapped. 'You don't have to do anything – just shut your face, stay still and don't interfere. Just being here's enough, that's all.'

'Oh, really?' Sophie seemed less than convinced. 'And I should believe you, the enemy. Right.'

'She's telling the truth, actually,' Ricky put in. 'All that's needed is for the two halves of the sword to be present at the same time, and that sets the magic going.'

'That's it?' Sophie sounded almost disappointed. 'So, I could be reading a book, doing the crossword—'

Ricky nodded. 'Sure,' he said. 'It's totally straightforward. All it takes is for the guy to have the sword, and the girl to be there, in a direct line of sight. And she's got to be in love with him, of course, but—'

Sophie protested loudly; Vicky yelped and threw a piece of seaweed, but missed. Ricky, smirking, did a triple over-the-wrist backflip and rounded it off with a little flourish. The other Paul still wasn't there.

'Let's start,' Ricky said.

'No, but—' Paul got no further. The sword in his hand was tugging at his fingers, like a small child who's just sighted chocolate. He wanted to stay exactly where he was, wait a bit, give his alter ego a bit more time to show up, but apparently he didn't have that option. Unfortunate. He heard Sophie behind him insisting 'I am *not*—' and then his left foot plunged forward, his right foot slid across, and he was advancing, purposeful, menacing and for some obscure reason sideways, like Tyson reincarnated as a crab.

Ricky was doing much the same sort of thing, though ever so much more convincingly. 'Sorry,' he muttered. Then he darted forward and swung his sword from the shoulder, his arm shooting out like a hinged flail.

Whatever happened next – Paul was rather foggy about it, partly because he had his eyes shut a lot of the time – seemed to go on for absolutely ages. As for Paul, dragged along behind the sword as it lunged, cut, parried, riposted, counterthrust, he felt a bit like a small, frail policeman trying to arrest a huge, drunk Marine in the middle of a fight. Luckily, nothing he did seemed to matter in the slightest. The sword knew exactly what it wanted to do and seemed to regard him as an annoying but trivial handicap. It was bewildering, humiliating, exhausting and scary, and the closest thing to it in his narrow range of experiences was using Windows for the first time.

Not for one moment, however, did Paul have the slightest doubt as to how it was going to end, magic sword or no magic sword. Sooner or later – he tried to think back and remember, the last time, the time before that, whether dying had hurt very much. Part of him still hadn't given up hope yet; Mr Dao's voice in the back of his mind, death has no jurisdiction. The rest of him could point out to their shared heart's content that that had obviously been a reference to the other Paul, the one he'd let in through the door in Benny Shumway's office, the one he'd planned to bring along here so that Ricky could kill him, only that had gone wrong somehow. He tried consoling himself with the thought that at least one of him was probably going to make it, and that in that case it was all as broad as it was long, surely. The trouble was, though, that he knew himself too well to be able to lie to himself convincingly. But it didn't matter, not now, and for all he knew he might turn out to be a born bridge player, or very good indeed at basket-weaving, assuming Mr Dao forgave him and let him join in after all.

In the middle of all this, he heard someone talking to him. He was rather surprised to discover that it was Ricky Wurmtoter.

'This isn't working,' Ricky was saying.

'Excuse me?' Paul panted, as his sword passed within a millimetre of Ricky's jugular vein.

'Not bloody working,' Ricky gasped back. 'Too evenly matched. Cancelling each other –' Ricky lunged, Paul sidestepped and hacked at his collarbone as he sailed past; Ricky's sword somehow got there in time to parry '– out. Completely screwed. We'll be doing this for ever and ever. *Really* ever and ever. Don't you understand?'

'Why start now?' Paul replied. But, wretchedly, he could see what Ricky was driving at. It was the swords' fault; they seemed to have forgotten all about the poor miserable life forms dangling off their hilts, as they worked out thirteen hundred years of pent-up frustration. The fight had subtly changed in the last few seconds. The swords weren't trying to cut flesh any more, they weren't aiming themselves at Ricky's head or Paul's guts. Instead, they were slamming into each other, edge to edge, flat to flat, in a series of savage parries, each sword trying to batter the other one to death; only, Paul intuitively recognised, that was a mug's game, because neither of them was capable of being broken or even scratched. An internal review board inside Paul's head delivered its minority report: *This is silly*. But nobody who mattered wanted to know. Vicky had been right after all; a fight to the undeath. Give him Mr Dao and infinite nothingness any day.

'Ricky,' he muttered.

'What?'

'Think of something.'

'What?'

'You're the fucking professional. Think of something.'

Ricky shook his head. 'Can't,' he said. 'Mind's a blank, sorry. How about you?'

A shower of sparks fell across Paul's cheek. They stung. 'Nothing' he replied. 'I think we're stuck like it, just like my mum used to warn me.'

'Theo Van Spee,' Ricky grunted, as the feedback from a particularly violent clash vibrated right down Paul's arm into his elbow. 'He might be able to do something. But he wouldn't. He must be laughing like a drain right now.'

'Why?' Paul said, as his sword slammed itself against the other sword's cutting edge and bounced off like a squash ball. 'I thought—'

'We're here. Stuck. In the bloody past. He's back home, in our time, and nobody's ever coming back to sort him out, because we'll be here for ever. He's won.' Ricky pulled a horrible face, his clean, sharp, aftershave-commercial features contorted into something both inhuman and surprisingly ordinary. 'You have no idea how much I hate him, the bastard. It's all been his fault, right from the—'

Paul wasn't listening; because he understood. It had all dropped into place, like the last bit of the jigsaw, which you thought all along was a bit of left-hand sky, but when you turn it over you realise it's the last chunk of right-hand sea, or the sky tricksily reflected in the surface of the pond.

Well, *all* was an exaggeration, but he understood a lot of it, even including Audumla the Great Cow of Heaven. Annoyingly, there simply wasn't time to digest most of it – he could see it all, like the view from a tower, but he only had a microsecond or so, the fragment of time while the sword was recoiling sideways after a savage but fruitless hack, so he concentrated on the most relevant bit.

Of course the fight could end; Ricky was being dim, or deliberately not taking the point. It just needed—

'Ricky,' he said.

'What?'

'Do you trust me?'

– A great leap of faith, on the part of both of them. The swords belted each other, bounced. Sparks flew. Paul's elbow hurt like buggery.

'Yes,' Ricky said. 'Yes, actually I do. You and about two other people, and one of them's dead.'

'Great,' Paul said. 'Now listen. Next time the swords bash into each other—'

Well, not the next time, because they were at it again, pounding into each other like two seas meeting. The time after that.

'The next time,' Paul repeated, 'let go. All right?'

'What?'

Another opportunity missed. This time, Ricky's sword tried to chop off the crosspiece from Paul's hilt. No dice. *Boing.*

'Just let go of the fucking sword, all right? And I'll do the same. If we aren't holding them, they can't fight. Or if they can, we can leave them to it and go home. Looks like they don't really need us, anyway.'

Crash, bounce, sparks. 'You sure that'll work?' Ricky, a thirteen-hundred-year-old professional dragonslayer (and lieutenant colonel of the Riders of Rohan) asking him if he thought it'd work. That was the funniest thing yet.

'Yes,' Paul said, and then he repeated, 'Trust me. OK?'

'OK. On three.'

A glittering curve slicing through air, as the sword Skofnung and the sword Tyrving raced towards each other, edge to edge. 'Three,' Paul shrieked, and let go.

In that moment, there was a great deal he wanted to say. He wanted to apologise: to Sophie, for leaving her, now that it was pretty well settled that she loved him too, without philtre, without outside interference, possibly because of the sword and thirteen centuries of carefully seeded destiny and Custardspace and related dogshit, but completely and for ever. And to Ricky, of course, because when he'd said, 'Do you trust me?' he'd been plotting Ricky's death, cold-blooded and calculating as any accountant figuring out how to reduce a tax bill. And possibly to a wide selection of other people whom he'd generally let down, disappointed, not done the right thing by: his mother, Uncle Ken, possibly Mr Tanner's mum though that was pushing it a bit. And to himself, of course, because he'd just thrown away his life in a quixotic gesture, only for the sake of fixing some fuck-up in the space-time continuum that he couldn't even understand. Quixotic? Absolutely the right word for it. Quixotic as two short planks.

Meanwhile, Ricky's sword slipped through Ricky's suddenly relaxed fingers and flew through the air towards Paul who watched it come at him. At the same time Paul watched his own sword hurtling straight at the little hollow where Ricky's neck snuggled down onto the collarbone. For some reason (Newton or Einstein would know why; possibly also Galileo) Skofnung got there first, winning the race by a nanosecond, and Paul watched the needle-sharp steel disappear into Ricky's throat, just south of his Adam's apple. So; did that mean Skofnung had won the fight, and if so, what implications would that have for the Canadian banking industry? *Fuck*, Paul thought, *I can't remember which way round—*

Then he remembered, that thing he'd forgotten about whether dying hurts. Yes, but not for very long.

'You,' said Mr Dao, 'have got a fucking nerve.'

Paul grinned feebly into the darkness. 'Not any more,' he tried to say, but it came out in italics, without the quotation marks. *Not that I was ever a great fan of the central nervous system. Pain, for one thing. Hell of a lot of grief just to tell you not to do something. A little flashing light'd do just as well, and no –*

Mr Dao wasn't amused. Mr Dao also wasn't there; Paul couldn't see his broad, calm face, or hear his deep, refined voice. Instead, the words passed through Paul's mind, out of nowhere, going nowhere. 'I thought I told you,' Mr Dao said, 'don't you ever come back. But here you are.'

Yes.

'Marvellous. And this time—' A deep sigh; and because Paul couldn't hear it, or see the accompanying facial expression, it was somehow even more poignant, pure grief and frustration and annoyance without the ice cubes and slice of lemon. 'What did I tell you? I said, death has no jurisdiction over you.'

Ah, well. Everybody makes mistakes.

'Not me. That's the whole point. Infallible. Me and taxes.'

Actually, that's inevitable, not infall—

'Infallible.' Mr Dao clicked his tongue. 'Until now. So,' he added grimly. 'Here we are again. Only this time—'

I know. And I'll come quietly. You'd better show me where I'm supposed to sit, and what it is you actually do. Presumably you've got to sort of poke one bit of stick in and out of the other bits.

'What?'

Basket-weaving. And isn't there some tool called a rapping-iron? Is that for patting down the bits of stick so they lie straight?

'Basket-weaving?'

That's right. And contract bridge, and conversational Spanish. I'm all ready, and I promise I'll join in and not stand about sulking like I used to do at the other kids' birthday parties. I know it's for keeps this time, because the only way we could end the duel was if we both died. There wasn't any other choice. A nasty thought struck Paul; highly unlikely, but you never knew. *Ricky is here, isn't he? He did die?*

'Wurmtoter?' Mr Dao laughed icily. 'Oh, he's here all right. Beat you down here by a fifty-thousandth of a second. I can only put it down to his instinctive competitive streak, always got to win at everything. But you—'

Born loser, Paul said. *Always have been. I remember one Sports Day, the teacher saying—*

'You aren't dead.'

Time had no meaning there, so it must've just felt like a very long, awkward silence. *Excuse me?*

'You aren't dead. No basket-weaving for you, sunshine. Like I keep telling you but will you bloody listen? Over you, death has no jurisdiction.' Mr Dao sighed again, raw emotion, unbearably bitter and sad. 'Either of you,' he added.

You what? Only this time Paul could hear himself saying it. 'You what?'

'I mean,' Mr Dao replied, suddenly visible, 'one of you's not enough, oh no. Now I've got two of you cluttering up the place, unsettling the other guests, monopolising my time-which-has-no-meaning-here when there's a million and one things I ought to be doing. Over there, look.' Mr Dao nodded into the surrounding darkness. 'Just sitting there, like an overgrown doorstop. Sulking.'

Paul peered, but no dice. 'Where? I can't see him.'

'What, are you blind as well as annoying? Over there. Talking to Theo Van Spee.'

Oink? Paul thought. 'What did you just say?'

'Theo Van Spee,' Mr Dao repeated. 'He showed up a second or so after you two. You three,' he added wretchedly, 'though of course in real time, that was thirty-odd years earlier. But screw the details, death's too short.'

Not the time, Paul felt, to go wandering off the point. 'Professor Van Spee is *dead*?'

'Oh yes.' Mr Dao laughed grimly. 'Quite definitively, after what that Frank Laertides did to him. Thunderbolt,' he explained casually. 'Right on the spot, too. Zap, aargh, and a bit of a burning smell. No, he won't be going anywhere, ever again.'

'Oh.' Paul felt a shudder running up his spine. 'Well, I suppose—'

'He had it coming, too right. Custardspace won't help him now. Not that Frank wasn't doing him a favour, in a sense, because at least it was very, very quick. I'd have hated to have been in Van Spee's shoes when the Canadians caught up with him.'

Paul looked in the general direction where he thought Mr Dao had been pointing, but he couldn't see anything. It took him a moment to realise that that, of course, was the point. In the Land of the Dead, you can't see the dead people, just as you can't see individual raindrops in the ocean.

'Oh,' he said.

'Anyway.' Mr Dao was letting bygones go by, though it was clearly costing him an infinity of effort. 'There you are, all sorted. I expect you'll be wanting to go home now,' he added, with the subtlety of a pink elephant.

'Will I? I mean, yes. Yes, please.' Paul struggled to find the question he knew he needed to ask, but it was like trying to tickle trout with numb fingers. 'Um, how do I—?'

'Oh, for pity's sake,' Mr Dao said –

– And Paul opened his eyes, and saw the most beautiful thing he could possibly imagine. It was white, it was sort of rectangular, and it hummed very softly. He got up from the floor, crossed the lino and opened its door. Inside he found a pint of needled milk, a bit of translucent yellow cheese rind with green bits on it, two vintage yogurts and a very, very old carrot.

'Hello, fridge,' he said.

The fridge didn't say anything back, but it beamed clean white light at him, like a smile.

Paul backed away and looked round. He was in his kitchen, back at the flat. Through the window he could see the street: the street lamps, parked cars, the sad, dead plane tree installed some time ago by the government with a view to turning Outer London into a green and pleasant land. Carefully, he opened a cupboard door; to his overwhelming joy, he found washing-up liquid, a packet of Daz, some cans of soup, but no short cut to the existential void.

'Well,' he quoted, 'I'm back.'

But –

Temporal paradoxes or no temporal paradoxes, Paul hadn't been born yesterday. He went back to the fridge and looked at it for a while, waiting for it to make the first move. Then he folded his arms and said, 'I know you're in there.'

The fridge made a sort of clanking noise, and turned into Mr Laertides.

'Hello yourself,' he said. His left arm was stuck out at an angle, just as the fridge door had been. He lowered it. 'Any chance of a cup of tea?'

Paul shrugged. 'If you like,' he said. 'I wouldn't have thought that you drank tea.'

'I don't,' Mr Laertides replied. 'Actually, I don't drink anything, except to be sociable. However, in human society the sharing of hot, milky drinks creates a relaxed ambience conducive to better understanding. Bung the kettle on.'

'All right,' Paul said. 'And then you can start at the beginning.'

'Sure,' replied Mr Laertides. 'If that's what you really—'

'At the beginning,' Paul repeated firmly. 'Even if it means the Great Cow of Heaven.'

Mr Laertides perched on the edge of the kitchen table. 'Milk and two sugars,' he said. 'You ready?'

'As I'll ever be.'

'Then I'll begin.'

In the beginning (said Mr Laertides) was me.

'Let me stop you there for just a second,' Paul interrupted.

'Sure,' Mr Laertides replied, sipping at the tea that Paul had just handed him and pulling a face. 'Milk's off,' he said.

Paul scowled. 'Whose fault is that?'

'Sorry.' Mr Laertides grinned. 'Guess I had other things on my mind than being the best fridge I could possibly be. Which is understandable but not acceptable. Here.' He reached into the top pocket of his jacket and produced a two-litre plastic carton of milk.

'Thanks,' Paul said, adding some to his own tea. 'But what you just said. In the beginning was you.'

'That's right,' Mr Laertides said. 'And pretty dull it was too, waiting around for the others to show up. When you're floating around in the presubstantial void, playing "I Spy" doesn't help much, either. Something beginning with N.'

Paul shuddered. 'Been there,' he said.

'Ah.' Mr Laertides nodded. 'But that's the void at the end, which is rather different. Also very dull, but also rather depressing and sad. The void at the beginning is just – well, boring, really. So I decided to fill it up with stuff.'

Paul narrowed his eyes. 'Bang?'

'*Big* bang, yes,' Mr Laertides said, with a chuckle. 'I suppose it's the childish side of my nature, but I've always had a thing about loud noises, explosions and so on.'

'So that makes you—'

'I had help, of course,' Mr Laertides continued smoothly. 'From Audumla, the Great Cow of Heaven. Where she turned up from I have no idea, but suddenly there she was, big cow eyes, going *Moo*. Nice to have on your side, though. Anyhow, that was all pretty straightforward.Now I'd like to fast-forward a bit –'

A few hundred million years, give or take (Mr Laertides went on). Can't be more precise than that. Time really does fly when you're having fun. Which, in my case, consists of delegating responsibility, taking on more of a consultancy role, putting my feet up and managing not to get involved. Let them get on with it, I said to myself. After all, they're only humans, how much damage can they actually manage to do?

Silly me.

Enter your friend Theo Van Spee. He wasn't calling himself

that back then, of course, because a name like that'd have stuck out like the proverbial sore thumb in the primeval Dark Ages. So he said his name was Utgarth-Loke, and he was there to do a bit of routine maintenance to the structure of time and space; and since he was wearing overalls and carrying a toolbox and a clipboard, everybody believed him.

Of course, it's easy with hindsight. But I wasn't around, in fact I was fast asleep; and back then, thirteen centuries ago, nobody'd heard of time travel or alternative realities or trans-dimensional shift. Instead, they had gods; and if a bloke turns up who looks like a god and acts like a god and starts jacking acroprops under the Sun and unscrewing the stars, you aren't inclined to ask for any ID. Not if you're sensible.

We know better, you and me. We know Theo Van Spee had gone back in time, using his stupid bloody Custardspace, to cheat history by making King Hring – or is it King Hroar, I get them muddled up – win the duel, so the Canadians could inherit the Earth.

Like I just said, I was fast asleep at the time. Actually, that's a bit misleading, because it makes me sound bone idle and uncaring. But you've bumped into the Fey; so when I tell you I was asleep and dreaming, you'll know that I was hard at it, busy-busy, creating new worlds and new civilisations, populating them with truly unpleasant people like the late Countess Judy di Castel' Bianco, boldly zizzing where no man had zizzed before. Not a good thing, in retrospect, but then, quite a lot of what I've done over the years has turned out to be good ideas at the time. Anyhow, the first I knew about Theo Van Spee's scam was when I woke up – and I'm not a morning person, I freely admit that – in my office at 70 St Mary Axe, in the guise of Frank Laertides.

I hate it when that happens. I only exist, you see, where I'm needed. Sort of goes with the territory. It cuts out a lot of the hanging around in between jobs, but it means you have to get into the habit of hitting the ground running. Anyhow, I woke up; and as soon as I opened my eyes, I knew there had to have been a major fuck-up somewhere and somewhen in the vicinity, because otherwise why would I be there? That was just over thirty years ago, and Theo Van Spee had just activated Custardspace for the first time.

Unfortunately, by the time I kicked down the door of his office and barged in, it was too late. He wasn't there, and I was just in time to see his stupid Portable Door thing closing behind him and vanishing. I knew something was badly wrong, I could feel it in my bones, but at that time I didn't know exactly what it was, so I couldn't take the appropriate action. I had to go back through history, year by year, event by event, every damn thing from wars and plagues and the elections of popes down to minor cart accidents and butterflies flapping their wings in the rainforest, till I figured out what had gone wrong. By then, of course, Theo Van Spee had done his worst, and I was screwed. It was up to me to put it all right, but Van Spee was safely hidden away in his special secret hiding-place in the heart of Custardspace, where nobody could get at him, not even me. So I had to go back to the drawing board, so to speak, and figure out a cunning plan.

Which is where you came in.

'Me?' Paul objected. 'But I wasn't even born thirty years ago.'

Mr Laertides grinned. 'Of course not,' he said. 'It takes time setting these things up. First I had to fix it for your mum to meet your dad: dinner, flowers, all that sort of thing. Then the whole wedding to arrange. You have no idea how much planning goes into one of those things. In comparison, creating the universe was a piece of cake.'

Paul breathed in slowly, then out again. 'You arranged for me to be born.'

Mr Laertides nodded. 'That's right,' he said. 'Me and your Uncle Ernie, actually, on the two-birds-one-stone principle. He needed someone to stop Countess Judy, I needed someone to bring down Theo Van Spee. It stood to reason that anybody called into existence to be used, basically, as a weapon was going to have a pretty sad, confusing and miserable life; so we thought, hey, why make *two* people unhappy? And so we created you.'

'I see,' Paul said. 'Right.'

'Don't look at me like that,' Mr Laertides said. 'I mean,

millions of people are born into sad, confusing, miserable lives every day, and they don't have heroic destinies to make sense of it, they've just got to bash on with nobody to blame but themselves. You, on the other hand, have the satisfaction of knowing that the thoroughly shitty time you've been having all these years has served a noble and worthwhile purpose. Not to mention the fringe benefits, which I'll come to later.'

'Why not now?' Paul asked.

'Later,' Mr Laertides repeated. 'Otherwise I'll lose my thread. We created you—'

We created you (Mr Laertides went on); and, as you know, Ernie had his own agenda and I had mine. Now, as a rule, creating a human being from the ground up is a really difficult, messy, rather dangerous business – no, scratch that. Creating a human being is fatally easy, a couple of careless teenagers can knock one up, so to speak, behind the bike sheds in five minutes, or five minutes and nine months. Easy if you're human; but I'm not. I had to do it the *other* way. Because if you do what comes naturally, sure enough you get a human being; but you get one at random, if you follow me. I wanted a specific human being. I wanted you.

You're giving me that half-witted stare again. Come on, you should be happy. Finally, after all these years of being a redundant loser on the fringes, suddenly you find out you're practically the Chosen One. Hey, screw practically, you *are* the Chosen One, because I chose you. I designed you, and since I'm damn good at everything I do, you came out perfect, a hundred per cent up to specification. You see, you had to have various essential qualities. You had to be able to do magic, you had to be able to walk in dreams, for the Countess Judy thing, you had to be a fearless warrior who'd willingly give his life for the cause of right – I said a fearless warrior, Paul, and that's what you are, you just proved that. You don't have to be any good at swordfighting to be fearless. Anyhow, more than all of that, you had to have just the right combination of personality defects, neuroses and insecurities to drive you along the path we'd mapped out for you, as precisely as a champion lab rat with a connoisseur's nose for the right cheese. You had to be a complete fuck-up; not just that, you had to be a fuck-up in exactly the right way. Because we needed you like that. We had to put, if you like, the mess in the Messiah. And didn't we do well, your Uncle Ernie and me? Goes without saying, we're really proud of you. Well, I am, anyhow. I think Ern got a bit ticked off with you when you condemned him to death everlasting, but he always was prone to be judgemental.

So there you go. If ever you've stared wretchedly into a mirror – and of course you must've done, every day of your life – and wondered, why oh why couldn't I have been just a bit less of a total and unmitigated disaster area; well, now you know. Even then, we had to be on our toes every minute of every day while you were growing up. Luckily we had help. Like Miss Hook, for instance, at your school. She let us hex you into a trance so that you'd be staring gormlessly out of the window whenever the rest of the class was learning the really important stuff, the things we couldn't allow you to know. Have you ever wondered about that? Thought you had. You're thick, see, but not that thick. I mean, you couldn't be that thick, or you'd never be able to remember to breathe.

Now at this juncture I expect you may be feeling just a trifle resentful and upset, on the grounds that you've never had a proper life, you've been used and manipulated and it's just not fair. To which, Paul, all I can say is yes, you have. Sorry about that, but it's basically an omelettes-and-eggs situation. And, if it makes you feel any better, you aren't the only one. See, all along, ever since you were born – here's a clue. When is Sophie's birthday?

Paul opened his mouth to speak, then hesitated.

'I don't know,' he said. 'That is, she did tell me once – several times, actually – but I kept forgetting. Then she'd get all quiet and hurt about it and it was obviously not a good subject, so I didn't go there.'

Mr Laertides grinned infuriatingly. 'You forgot,' he said. 'Actually, you have a better than average memory, it's just that I keep punching holes in it. Paul, Sophie was born at the same time on the same day in the same year as you were, and that's not a coincidence. So, you see, the two of you have something in common. Like, if I was an artist and signed my work, you'd both have the same scrawly writing on the small of your backs.'

Paul gazed at him for quite some time without speaking. 'Oh,' he said eventually.

'Oh' is right (Mr Laertides continued). I created her too, or at least I manipulated her. But she already existed, because she was the other half of Skofnung, the living sword. My job was to reincarnate her, for want of a better word, as your counterpart and prospective soulmate. Which was bloody rough on her, as you can appreciate; in fact, she's probably had an even rougher deal than you have. Just think: being engineered from the moment of reconception to be the only girl in the world for you. Ghastly, or what?

But that's by the way. Actually, it's not, it's tangentially relevant; because we did roughly the same with you as we did with her. See, you too were already around when we were setting the project up. Of course you were; you were fighting a duel to the death on Bersa Island with Ricky Wurmtoter. We took you and reincarnated – no, I hate that word, we *recycled* you into Paul Carpenter. And that accounts for something which I know has been bugging the hell out of you for the last few days: namely, how come Mr Dao says that death has no jurisdiction over you? And why did the other Paul Carpenter who you let in through the door in Benny Shumway's office suddenly vanish when you reached the island?

Second question first. He vanished because, of course, he was already there. Had always been there, for the last thirteen centuries. Creating you wasn't an act of reproduction so much as duplication. If this was science fiction rather than prosaic fact, I'd call it cloning. I made a copy and sent it to live in your mummy's tummy for nine months. Which is why, you see, you can't die, or at least not for any meaningful length of time; because you've been there, done that, been dead for well over thirteen hundred years.

Oh, stop gawping at me like a brain-damaged goldfish and

think about it for a moment. You know the answer already, you just haven't made the connection.

Just now, you figured out what should have happened in the Bersa Island duel: King Hroar and King Hring killed each other, and everybody else lived happily ever after. But that was thirteen hundred years ago. Now, that's what should have happened; now, thanks to you, that's what *did* happen, and history's been put back on the right track. We have the almighty US dollar rather than the almighty Canadian dollar, and that means – yes, you're getting there, slowly but surely like a snail working for the Post Office – that means that you've been dead all that time. One of you, anyway. Which means the other of you – the *you* you – can't snuff it, since where you're concerned it has been conclusively snuffed for a very long time. Which is what I was banging on about just now when I mentioned fringe benefits. Congratulations, Paul, you can't die. You're an immortal.

That was too much.

'Fuck you,' Paul yelled.

'What?' Mr Laertides actually had the gall to look hurt. 'Sod it, Paul, I thought you'd be pleased.'

'Pleased' Paul could hardly find words. 'You bastard. You just said how really shitty it is being me. Now you tell me I've got to go on being me for ever and bloody ever.'

Mr Laertides laughed. 'Oh, I see,' he said. 'I get your point. Well, it's not like that. You see, that's the good thing about human beings. One of the good things, anyhow. In point of fact, there's four good things about being human, and this one's number three on the list. Human beings change, Paul. They don't have to stay the same. You don't have to go on being a pathetic little creep for ever and ever if you don't want to. No, really. Trust me on this. You can change. You can gradually grow to be less pathetic. You can mature, grow as a person, get a life.' He frowned. 'By my calculations it'd be your third, but we don't begrudge it to you. The labourer is worthy of his hire, and all that.'

Anyway (Mr Laertides said) there we are. We'd created you,

and Sophie as well, and programmed you, wound you up like a
couple of clockwork mice, ready to be turned loose to do your
bit in the struggle against chaos and Theo Van Spee. Everything
was set up nicely, the time was right, everything poised like a
coiled spring and tickety-boo. Just one last detail remaining.
Before I could get any further with fighting Theo, I had to find
him first. An essential ingredient, I hope you'll agree.

But not easy. You managed it, of course. You showed me the
way, as I knew you would. You flushed out Theo's extra-secret
hiding place in Custardspace. But it took a long time, and it was
touch and go at times. Ricky Wurmtoter nearly screwed us at
one point, as well: when he tricked you into poisoning him so
that he could escape to Custardspace, and then very nearly got
Sophie to drink the philtre and fall in love with *him* – in which
case, he'd have had the other half of your sword, and the whole
deal would've been off. But we got there in the end, thanks to a
lot of good luck *and* good judgement. And thanks to me, mostly.
Come on, I deserve some of the credit, after all those centuries
of unremitting hard slog.

How can I explain this? All right, think of a computer screen;
and somewhere on it there's an icon you can click on to open the
program you need. Only it's hidden. It's under something or disguised as something, and you can't find it. So all you can do is
go over the screen, millimetre by millimetre, clicking on everything until at last you get lucky and there it is.

That's you, Paul. You were my mouse. And all that really
bizarre crap I had you doing, going to weird places and doing
really stupid things, buying toothbrushes and standing under
trees – well, let's just call it camouflage. What I really needed was
for you to be in certain places at certain times, going click, to see
what'd happen. Eventually, by trial and error – oh, by the way,
did you really think that all that sticking your finger on blown-up
photographs was actually prospecting for bauxite? Really? God,
you're slow on the uptake. No, you were scrying all right, but not
for bauxite. For custard.

Anyhow, by trial and error, I narrowed it down to the right
place and time, and then I sent you there. With Sophie, because
she had to be there too, to set off the program, as it were.

Unfortunately, you two contrived to piss each other off – a hint for you, Paul: never, ever laugh at a girl who's wound her own hair into a forkful of spaghetti, because, well, it's a female thing and we all know how unbelievably alien and strange their mindset is, but they just don't like it, okay? You contrived to piss her off, just when the search was coming together nicely, and by some ghastly fluke of really bad luck, when I sent you back to have another try, who did you pick to take with you but the other half of the enemy's living sword, namely, bloody Vicky?

And that was where things started to get a bit screwed.

It was a bit, Paul decided, like being a sock inside a tumble-dryer. All around him the world, his whole life, everything he'd ever assumed or thought he knew, was swirling, spinning, not to mention chucking him about and bashing him into things. He was immortal; he was thirteen hundred years old, or he'd been alive thirteen centuries ago, he wasn't quite sure which; he'd been designed and built, like a barn conversion, to serve some grand design, except that its grandeur consisted of putting right a cock-up caused by a dirty little financial scam. Not just him but Sophie too; and the worst part of it (no, not in the least the worst part, but beyond all question the part that hurt him the most) was that Sophie—

Mr Laertides was still blathering on, but Paul tuned out, struggling to build up the scattered Lego bricks of fact into a coherent structure. Sophie was the other half of this stupid sword, so she'd been around thirteen centuries ago too. But it was necessary, for the stupid grand design, for her to be Paul's – his *whatever*, because he couldn't bring himself to drag even the word for what he felt for her into this disgusting mess; and so she'd been dragged through time, reborn, remodelled, made over like a Victorian end-of-terrace on the Isle of Dogs, so that he'd have no choice but to love her, and she'd have no choice but to love him back—

No choice.

And when he thought about how messed up he'd been over her drinking the stupid philtre, because then it could never be the real thing . . .

If anything ever merited the term obscene, this had to be it. Paul jumped up, and with a degree of speed and agility that he'd conspicuously lacked when he was dangling off the hilt of the stupid magic sword, he reached out and clamped both his hands round Mr Laertides's throat.

As I was saying (Mr Laertides went on, and Paul felt his fingertips meet in thin air) that was when things started to get a bit screwed. Would you mind not doing that, by the way? It doesn't bother me in the least, but if you go on like that you'll hurt yourself. See? Told you.

Right. Now you're sprawling comfortably, I'll continue. It was just as well that I'd taken the precaution of dosing you with the anti-falling-in-love stuff, because otherwise you'd have gone to the pictures with Vicky and you'd have been Cupid's pincushion while they were still showing the trailers. But my foresight and attention to detail won the day – I've already told you, that doesn't work, and don't blame me if you sprain your wrist trying – and we got away with it. Bit of a blow for Vicky, of course. Actually, she's a nice kid, for half a sword. It was a mean trick our Ricky played on her, using Countess Judy's secret Jedi mind techniques to wash out her memory, then turning on the old Wurmtoter charm and nagging her into marrying him. Clever, though; because Ricky – well, he knows as well as anybody that no woman on Earth could be married to him for more than a week without ending up hating him beyond all measure; and if she hated him, then he could never have both halves of Tyrving, his magic sword; and then that'd be a key ingredient missing, and so it'd be impossible to recreate the Bersa Island duel. Neat; only Ricky overreached himself, got careless. It was his feud with Countess Judy, you see. When you got rid of her, it broke the spell that Ricky had put on Vicky. Straight away she was able to figure out what he'd done, and the net effect of all his ingenuity was to get her so mad at him that she was determined that the duel was going to happen. It'd be her way of getting even with him, you see. So, although none of us realised at the time, Vicky was actually on our side all along.

When Ricky realised that, of course, he freaked out completely; which was why he had to try his last and wildest shot, getting you to kill him with the poisoned custard slice. It wasn't real poison, of course; it was custard laced with half an ounce of Van Spee's crystals, the effect of which was to zap him across the interdimensional doobry like a rat up a conduit. Theo helped him, of course; he arranged for the crystals to be put in the custard slice. That was dead clever, actually. But I'm getting ahead of the story.

'You are?' Paul said.

'Yes,' Mr Laertides replied, as Paul tried, without success, to smash in his head with the heel of his left shoe. 'Before we deal with that, let's go back to the night when you came reeling home from the pub, pissed as a battalion of newts. Remember?'

'I was not—'

'You bloody were. You fell over in the kitchen.'

'That,' Paul pointed out, 'was only because all the fuses had blown. You did that, presumably.'

Mr Laertides shook his head. 'Not guilty,' he said. 'That was Theo Van Spee. He'd found out somehow or other that I'd been standing guard over you all along in my aspect or avatar as your fridge. You were getting awkwardly close to becoming a nuisance; but he couldn't attack you at work, because I was there all the time, so it'd have to be at home, where he could neutralise me without being too obvious about it. So he sent a freak power surge down the electric mains and tried to fry me. Nearly worked, too; I really thought I'd had it that time. Which was why I tried, with what I reckoned just might be my dying breath, to explain things to you: the whole deal, Utgarth-Loke and the Great Cow. Only,' he added reproachfully, 'you fell asleep. And then I found I wasn't mortally wounded after all; but I wasn't going to hang about and let Theo have another crack at me, so I tidied the place up a bit and went away. That's why, you may remember, when you woke up there was a brand-new fridge – a Zanussi, no less – and it had fresh milk and eggs and bacon and stuff in it, instead of all the decaying grunge I had to put up with.'

'Fine,' Paul said after a while. 'So we've covered that bit. Get back to when I killed Ricky with the poisoned cake.'

Well (said Mr Laertides, apparently completely unfazed by Paul's fruitless efforts to poke his eyes out with a broken biro) it was really very clever. The custard slice, you see, wasn't poisoned when it left the sandwich-bar place. It was a perfectly good custard slice, I know that because I gave it to you myself—

What, you hadn't worked that one out for yourself? All those identical little bald round-headed guys with obscure-sounding names, Mr Palaeologus and Mr Porphyrogenitus and what have you? They were all me. Of course. Who else did you think they were?

I gave it to you myself, in order to make sure you'd overdose on custard and fall through into Custardspace, so you could sniff out Theo's secret lair. But when Ricky bumped into you in the corridor – spilt your coffee, if you recall, all down your front – well, while you were mopping coffee off yourself and generally fussing about and not paying attention, he quietly sneaked the massive dose of crystals into the custard slice, which he then proceeded to beg off you and eat. Now believe me, I hold no brief for the guy, he's – he *was*, rather – an annoying, pompous little toad most of the time, but you've got to concede, he was resourceful, and he was cool under pressure. He slid neatly out of the wreck of the let's-assassinate-me-and-then-you scenario, and straight into this Plan B, where he escapes to Custardspace and frames you for his murder. Extra cunning, of course, because he had a fair idea that Colin the goblin – remember him? – as soon as Colin the goblin found out that Tanner had you under armed goblin guard in the strongroom pending execution for murder, he'd realise that he had to rescue you or else lose out on any chance of getting his sticky claws on your stash of Van Spee's crystals. And, of course, he knew all about that unfortunate business whereby Colin the goblin and Sophie got linked up. Perfect, as far as he was concerned, because it solved his biggest problem – how to get Sophie into Custardspace too, so that he could dose her with philtre and so neutralise your magic sword and thereby prevent the Bersa

Island rematch. Simple: Colin gets you through, then goes back to collect the crystals so that both of you can escape from Custardspace. But as soon as Colin goes back, Sophie comes through. Bang! All set, everybody exactly where he wanted them to be. Clever boy, that Ricky. Shame he never amounted to anything in the end.

'He's dead, then,' Paul said.

'What, Ricky?' Mr Laertides nodded enthusiastically. 'Oh yes, you betcha. And not just dead but *really* dead. Right now,' said Mr Laertides, consulting his watch, 'he'll have finished an aerobics class and be just about to start his third session of conversational Esperanto.' He grinned. 'Let you in on a little secret,' he added. 'Your mate Mr Dao doesn't like Ricky very much.'

'I'm sorry,' Paul said, after a moment. 'I'm sorry he's dead. I liked – at least, I *thought* I liked him, a bit. I thought he was on my side, some of the time.'

'He was,' Mr Laertides said, 'just so long as you were being useful. Like, in the Countess Judy business, he was on your side then, when it suited him, and he probably decided he liked you, because it'd be more convenient that way. But first and foremost he was what he was. You don't get to be management in a firm like JWW if you aren't what Ricky was.'

'Oh?' Paul said. 'And what would that be?'

'Totally and unalterably self-centred,' Mr Laertides replied. 'Like me, for instance; all I've ever cared about, from the moment I woke up thirty years ago, is getting the job done, nailing Theo, putting history back together again. As a result, I caused you all this grief, and Sophie, and everybody else who had the bad luck to get sucked into the mess. Or like Theo Van Spee. Oh, sure, he wasn't in it for the money, like Tanner or Humph Wells. He was more your sort of Werner von Braun type, he went somewhere he could carry on his work, and screw loyalties and principles and, of course, other people. And Ricky, of course; all he cared about was keeping clear of me. That,' he added, with a sweet smile, 'and money. He liked money a lot.'

'Oh,' Paul said. 'I'm still sorry, though. I killed him.'

Mr Laertides frowned. 'He killed you, though. Twice.'

'So what? I shouldn't have done it; only I had to. But that doesn't make it right.'

Mr Laertides looked at him for an uncomfortably long time. 'You know,' he said eventually, 'when I designed you for this operation, I did a bloody good job. For which,' he added, 'for what little it's worth, I apologise most sincerely. I had to do it, though, same as you. But that didn't make it right.'

Paul was silent for a while, then he shrugged. 'Forget it,' he said. 'I'd probably have turned out a complete mess even if you hadn't—'

'Oh for crying out loud,' Mr Laertides said.

Anyhow (Mr Laertides went on) that's about the long and the short of it. Not the most edifying and uplifting of tales, I grant you. It'd have been far better if Theo Van Spee had been some kind of Dark Lord hell-bent on ruling the world, rather than just an obsessive academic with rather twisted priorities; and it'd have been far more satisfying for you if you'd been on a quest, battled the enemy to a standstill and chucked a ring down a crack in a volcano instead of basically just doing as you were told, once you'd finally managed to figure out what it was you were supposed to be doing. But it wasn't like that, I'm afraid. Theo doesn't fit the mould, for one thing. He was never cut out for Dark Lordery, mainly because – well, in this context, *dark* is usually just another way of saying *not very bright*, you've got to be as thick as a whole timber-yard of short planks to try that kind of gig, and whatever else Theo was, he wasn't that. And you—

'He's dead too, then,' Paul interrupted.

Mr Laertides grinned. 'Yes,' he said. 'You can take my word for that. I won't nauseate you with the details.'

'Thank you,' Paul said. 'I—'

'Don't tell me,' Mr Laertides groaned. 'You feel guilty about that, as well.'

But Paul just shrugged. 'He was someone I knew. It's always unsettling when someone you know dies. It feels odd, like the engine's been taken to pieces and put back together again, only a bit's been left out and it doesn't quite run right. But guilty,' he added, 'no. Well, not really. Actually, I'd much prefer not to have to think about it at all.'

Good idea (said Mr Laertides). There's a whole lot of stuff in this life that's not nearly as big a pain in the bum as it could be, just so long as you don't think about it. It's there, of course, but if you made a point of fixating on every damn thing that's wrong or bad or unfair in this universe, you'd come to a pretty bad end. You'd turn out all screwed up, bitter and warped and inhuman. Like me, in other words. Not a good idea. Don't go there.

But I was just saying. Theo wasn't an evil overlord type, and Ricky wasn't, either – he was more your basic resourceful idiot – and that just leaves you. The hero. And the bit that nobody's ever got right, not in fifty thousand years of storytelling, is what to do with the hero once the story's over. Oh, there's happily ever after, but you're not a fool, you don't believe in that for one minute. And killing off the hero at the end, that's good from a closure point of view, but we've already established, no go in your case, over you death has no jurisdiction. But you were designed, built, raised and programmed specifically for the purposes of the story, and now it's finished and you're left over at the end. So what do we do with you?

'Well?' Paul asked, after a long silence.

'Well what?'

'Was that a rhetorical question,' Paul asked, 'or do you really want suggestions?'

'Oh, I see,' Mr Laertides said, his face relaxing out of a slight frown. 'You want to be consulted, you want input. Well, why not? Your life, I suppose, or at least it is now, after we've all finished with it. All right, then, Paul. What do you want to be when you grow up?'

Paul thought for a moment. 'Rid of you,' he said.

Mr Laertides raised an eyebrow. 'Me specifically? Or—?'

'You specifically for starters,' Paul replied, 'and all the rest of you as well. To put it another way, I'd like for everybody I've come into contact with, ever since this whole horrible J. W. Wells thing started, to fuck off and leave me in peace.'

'Really?'

'Yes.'

Mr Laertides nodded. 'Okay,' he said. 'And that'd include Sophie, of course.'

Some moments can take a ridiculously long time. To begin with, Paul had assumed it was just a trick, a word game; and he'd been about to say, 'No, of course not Sophie'; but then the thought came wriggling into his mind that everything there might or might not be between her and him was a lie, a contrivance, every bit as untrue as if they'd both drunk the stupid bloody philtre. In fact, it was worse than the philtre, because at least she'd offered to drink it of her own free will, after Countess Judy had wiped the love out of her mind. But of course she'd offered, because her own free will was nothing of the kind. She'd been set up from birth, just as he had. He couldn't accept love like that, because it was as real and genuine as a three-pound note. Sure, he loved her and probably always would, but it wouldn't be fair on her, wouldn't be right . . . and the only reason he had these stupid high moral principles, couldn't bring himself to do something that he knew was wrong, was because Mr Laertides had seen to it that he'd been made that way.

So he took a deep breath and said, 'Including Sophie, yes.'

'Oh.' Mr Laertides looked at him, shrugged, and said, 'You don't mean that.'

'Yes, I do. You know I do.'

'But that's—' Mr Laertides thought hard, hunting through the recesses of his mind for a word apt but unfamiliar. 'That's silly,' he said. 'The two of you go together like, well, adolescence and acne.'

Paul sighed. He was fed up with this conversation. 'I know,' he said. 'You made us that way. And I want rid of everything you made us be. Can you understand that, or do you need me to draw you a Venn diagram?'

'No, it's all right.' Mr Laertides was frowning. 'Fine, if that's what you want,' he said. 'I can fix it, sure, no problem.'

Double take. 'You can?'

'Of course.' Mr Laertides grinned. 'Me, the master of the universe, I can do pretty much anything I like, now that Theo Van Spee's been dealt with.' He yawned and glanced at his watch. 'What I think you're getting at – though it's hard to be certain since so much of what you say is pure drivel – what I think you're getting at is that you're pissed off at the idea that I made the two of you what you are, because that was necessary for the job in hand. What you'd like, therefore, is to be someone else. For both of you to be someone else, presumably, since you care more about her than about you – which is kind of sweet, in a really dozy, half-baked sort of a way. Am I right?'

'Well,' Paul said slowly, 'yes. Yes, I suppose so.'

'OK.' Mr Laertides shrugged cheerfully. 'Any particular person you'd like to be, or are you happy taking pot luck like everybody else? No, of course, you don't hold with predestination and outside influence, so you'd want it to be totally random. You just want to be – let me guess – somebody *normal*. Yes?'

'Sophie and me both,' Paul replied. 'Yes. You can do that?'

'Well, it's hardly rocket science. You're sure?'

'Sure.'

'Sure-sure or just a bit sure?'

'Look, just get on with it, will you?'

'Fine,' Mr Laertides said. 'And—'

And then, everything was different. And, shortly after that, everything was pretty much the same.

CHAPTER SIXTEEN

'Well?' Paul said.

Mr Laertides shrugged. 'All done,' he said.

'That's it?'

'That's it. I now formally pronounce you no longer Paul Carpenter. Well,' he added, 'you're still called Paul Carpenter, because it's a lot more fuss changing someone's name than it is changing their personality; I mean, you've got to write to the DVLA and the Inland Revenue and the Council Tax people and the electricity board and all that, and frankly I haven't got the time or the patience. But I did what you asked. To all intents and purposes, you're now someone completely different. So's Sophie. Don't say thank you, will you? If there's one thing I can't stand, it's tears of snivelling gratitude.'

Paul thought for a moment. 'I don't feel any different.'

'Well, duh,' said Mr Laertides kindly. 'That's because you've completely forgotten what it was like to be the old Paul. Otherwise – well, you get the point, I trust.'

Put like that, it made sense. 'All right,' Paul said. 'And the rest of it; I mean, all the other crap from the past. Like, I don't have to go on working for JWW any more if I don't want to.'

Mr Laertides nodded. 'Do you want to?' He smiled. 'In case it has any bearing on your decision,' he added quietly, 'now that both Ricky and Theo are dead, they'll be needing two new partners: pest control and applied magic. Probably I shouldn't be telling you this, but Dennis Tanner's going to drop by here soon after lunch to ask you if you'll be the new pest-control partner.'

Paul blinked. 'Really?'

Mr Laertides nodded. 'Really. Dennis has always thought very highly of you, ever since you joined the firm. He likes your drive, your commitment; let's face it, your ambition. And there's no denying the fact, you've really taken to the pest-control stuff. Absolute flair for it, particularly the killing aspect. Even Ricky had to admit, you're the best assistant he ever had.'

Well, Paul thought, *that's only fair.* 'In that case—' he said.

'And after he's done that,' Mr Laertides went on smoothly, 'he's going to find Sophie Pettingell and offer her applied magic.'

'What, that stupid, soppy, fat-arsed—?' Paul was suddenly livid with rage. Ever since he'd joined JWW, he'd cordially loathed Sophie Pettingell and everything about her: her big cow eyes, her little-girl smile, her giggle . . . All an act, he'd known that since he'd first set eyes on her, and how a normally sensible person like Dennis Tanner couldn't see through it, he had no idea. Actually, he knew perfectly well: it was absolutely basic, beginner's-level effective magic, a bog-standard glamour. But when applied by small, pretty blonde girls to middle-aged men, it was one of the strongest forms of magic there was. 'Bloody hell,' he sighed. 'But she's useless. And annoying.'

'You should hear what she says about you,' Mr Laertides replied.

'But that's so unfair,' Paul protested loudly. 'I mean, I've worked my arse off for this firm, and what's she ever done, apart from float about wearing tight skirts and lip-gloss? I've killed bloody dragons for JWW, I've slaughtered demons, duelled with dark wizards, evenings and weekends too, and all she's done is stuff her face with expense-account lunches and gone to awards ceremonies.'

'It's not right,' Mr Laertides murmured.

'You bet it's not bloody right,' Paul growled. 'Well, we'll see about that. I mean yes, she's got Dennis Tanner eating out of the palm of her pudgy little hand, but I know for a fact that Cas

Suslowicz doesn't really like her very much, and you'll back me up, I know, so really it's just a case of getting Jack Wells on our side—' He hesitated. 'Talking of which,' he said, 'where is Jack these days? Haven't seen him around for a while. He's not off pretending to be something again, is he?'

Mr Laertides shook his head. 'He's been on holiday, remember? Every year he goes to the Isle of Man to watch the TT races. He only got back yesterday.'

'Oh, right.' Paul frowned. 'Only there's something in the back of my mind, and I can't quite – something about a fridge getting killed.'

'That was *me*, dumbo,' said Mr Laertides indulgently, 'and anyway, I wasn't killed, was I? But fancy you remembering that.'

'Remembering what?'

'You tell me,' said Mr Laertides.

Paul thought for a moment, then shook his head. 'Nope,' he said. 'Whatever it was, it's gone. Anyhow, if I can't talk Jack Wells round, I don't deserve a job sorting Mortensen printouts, let alone a partnership. We'll beat the bloody cow, just you see. We'll have her out of here inside a month.'

'That's the spirit,' said Mr Laertides pleasantly. 'No prisoners, right?'

Paul nodded. 'Absolutely. No prisoners.' As he looked round he happened to catch sight of the clock on the opposite wall. 'Hell's teeth, is that the time? Only I'm having lunch with that redhead from the Credit Lyonnais, brain the size of a lentil but legs up to her chin.'

'Don't let me keep you, then,' Mr Laertides said softly. 'Only, Paul,' he said.

'Yes? What?'

'Is this what you really want?'

Paul stopped. 'What a strange question,' he said. 'If you mean the partnership, well, yes, of course it is. To be the youngest-ever partner in JWW; it's what I've always wanted, all my life. It's what I was born to do.'

'Fine,' Mr Laertides said. 'Just checking.'

'And if that sad bitch Pettingell thinks she can spoil it for me—'

Mr Laertides tapped the glass of his watch. 'Your lunch date,' he said. 'Can't keep true love waiting, can we?'

Paul laughed. 'Yeah, right,' he said, and left the office.

That night, Paul had a strange dream, as he lay on his back with the leggy redhead from the Credit Lyonnais snoring open-mouthed beside him.

He dreamed that he was someone else, and it wasn't much fun at all. This someone else he was being in his dream was the most appalling loser ever: a junior clerk in the scrying department, staring gormlessly at bauxite photos and filing Mortensens and occasionally running errands for the grown-ups. That was a pretty bad dream, the sort you'd expect if you'd stuffed your face with lobster and pickled cucumber followed by half a Stilton cheese ten minutes before getting into bed. But there was worse. In this dream – and he wondered what dank, fog-wreathed swamp in the black recesses of his psyche this bit had oozed out of – he was in love. And if that wasn't bad enough, he was in love with, wait for it, Sophie Pettingell.

And then it got even worse; because in his dream, the Pettingell bitch wasn't even a bit pretty. In fact, she wasn't even *blonde*. In his dream, she was small and thin and dark and bony, like some kind of female brunette Gollum; she cleaned out her fingernails with a biro cap and wiped her nose on her cuff, and whined on about her feelings and relationships and commitment and all sorts of other New Age feminist women-are-from Venus crap. And his dream wanted him to believe that he – Paul Carpenter, for crying out loud – he was in love with this *object*.

Even while Paul was dreaming the dream, he was seriously considering the practicalities of suing his own subconscious for slander. It was obscene, there was no other word for it. Oh, there was more besides: in his dream, he hated working for JWW, he hated Dennis Tanner (he had a soft spot for Mr Tanner's mum, which could have been a step in the right direction; but no, it was as Platonic as a wet weekend in North Wales and he only liked her when she was being a goblin, and that was just *sick*) and anything at all to do with the firm's business, with magic itself, gave him the creeps right down to his toes. Under normal circumstances, that on its own would've had him sitting up in bed screaming so loud that the neighbours would've called the police; but since it shared the dream with the degrading and perverted Sophie Pettingell fantasy, he hardly noticed it.

Time is funny in dreams; it stretches and flollops about like fondue. In Paul's dream, it started as a day at work, and there he was in the unspeakably grotty clerks' office, the one on the ground floor with no windows, and he was working his way slowly through a huge stack of those stupid aerial photographs of slices of Kalahari desert. And then it was lunchtime, and he was happy, because he had a lunch date; but the date was with the bloody awful Pettingell cow, and apparently his idea of a really wild time was nibbling a stale ham roll in that crummy Italian sandwich bar round the corner from the office—

(At this point in his dream, Paul was aware of the leggy red-head from the Credit Lyonnais squirming in her sleep and dragging the duvet off his shoulders; and normally he'd have dragged it back off her and given her an elbow in the ribs to remind her whose duvet it was, dammit. But he was too weak and too numbed with horror to move.)

– And while he nibbled at his stale ham roll, the Pettingell monstrosity was bleating at him in her quiet, annoying voice, which was the sort of voice you'd expect to hear a lot up on the Yorkshire moors if sheep could talk, and she was giving him all sorts of dumb-assed half-baked reasons why it'd be a really bad idea at this stage in their (yuck, that word) relationship for her to move back in with him—

For the first time that Paul could remember, he felt himself agreeing with Sophie Pettingell; in fact, as he lay there, the corner of his mind in which he was awake and watching this ghastly nightmare unfold was shouting, 'Yeah, absofuckinglutely, you *go*, girl.' But he – Paul, this hideous parody of himself – was sitting there getting sadder and sadder and gloomier and gloomier, and instead of rounding on her and telling her just precisely how wrong and full of shit she was, which of course was what the real Paul would've done, except of course that the real Paul wouldn't go anywhere near Pettingell with rubber gloves and a ten-foot pole – instead of pointing out to her how utterly stupid her arguments and reasoning were, he was just crouching there and taking it, like some kind of emasculated silver-trailing slug.

Really, it was so revolting it was fascinating, and he tuned in to what she was saying, purely out of morbid curiosity; and she was saying that the problem was that although she could talk to him, she couldn't really *talk* to him, because although he listened to her, sometimes she felt he wasn't *really* listening, because she felt that when he listened, he wasn't really hearing what she was saying, only what he thought she was saying, and also the other way round too, because apparently he also had a tendency to say what he thought she wanted to hear rather than what he actually felt, which meant she couldn't say what *she* really wanted to say, she had to say what she thought he wanted her to say so that he'd think she was saying what she was actually trying to say, and couldn't he see that that was really hopeless and it was impossible for them to really communicate—

Helpless in the prison of his own dream-struck mind, Paul howled at Sophie Pettingell to shut the fuck up, but she couldn't hear him; and he was pretty sure that if he had to listen to one more second of this poisonous drivel his sleeping brain would explode through his ears and spray itself on the bedroom walls like aerosol paint. And then he somehow became aware that he wasn't alone inside his head; that there was an alien presence in there with him, not just a submerged part of his own subconscious mind but a genuine outsider, who was talking to him.

'Well,' said the outsider, and he recognised the voice; it was that of Frank Laertides, of all people. 'So what do you think of your choice now?'

'My what?' Paul replied.

'Your choice,' Mr Laertides repeated. 'Your decision to be someone else.'

Weirder and weirder. 'I don't get you,' Paul said.

'Really? Good Lord.' He could hear a grin in Mr Laertides's voice. 'That's significant in itself, I suppose. So, how'd it be if I were to tell you that what you're watching here—'

'This is down to you, is it?' Paul objected angrily. 'Look,

would you please get this shit out of my head, before it gives me a bloody aneurism?'

'What you're watching here,' Mr Laertides went on, ignoring him, 'is the real you, and only a few hours ago, this was your life; or at least, this is how you'd have hoped your life would turn out, because although it doesn't sound all that hopeful to a casual earwigger, actually you and Sophie have just had a major break-through in the peace process and actually resumed a meaningful dialogue in the search for a road map towards a negotiated settlement—'

('What?' mumbled the leggy redhead from the Credit Lyonnais.

'Huh?'

'You just sat bolt upright and screamed,' she mumbled sleep-ily. 'What the hell is the matter with you?'

'Bad dream,' Paul replied. 'Go back to sleep.')

Back in the crummy little sandwich bar, Paul and Sophie both looked round, to see what the loud crashing noise had been; then Sophie resumed her monologue where she'd left off, and Mr Laertides started chuckling annoyingly.

'You're back, then,' he was saying. 'And I guess that sort of answers my question for me. No regrets, in other words.'

'You're saying,' Paul muttered in a hollow, broken voice, 'that there's some kind of ghastly alternate universe where that dis-gusting, snot-nosed, cowering *thing* over there is actually *me*?'

Mr Laertides snickered. 'That,' he said, 'would be telling.'

'No way,' Paul objected. 'Absolutely no frigging way. I'd rather be dead. Seriously.'

'Funny you should say that,' Mr Laertides replied. 'So what you're telling me is, all in all and taking the rough with the smooth, on balance you wouldn't be tempted to change places with that Paul Carpenter sitting over there. Yes? All right,' Mr Laertides added, 'I get the message, please don't scream like that, the acoustics in here – Thanks. So, you're perfectly happy and satisfied with your life, is that it?'

Paul hesitated. It was his own dream, so there wasn't much point in lying. 'Well, no,' he said. 'I wouldn't actually go that far.'

'But I thought—'

'Compared to *that*,' Paul said quickly, 'yes, my life's an absolute bed of bloody roses. But perfectly happy and satisfied would nevertheless be overstating it.'

'I see.' Mr Laertides's voice raised a virtual eyebrow. 'And what would you say is wrong with your life, right now?'

'That bloody woman,' Paul answered without a hint of hesitation. 'Just when I finally get what I truly deserve, what I've slogged my bum off for, the partnership, what do you and that git Tanner and the rest of you go and do? You make her a partner too. I mean, where's the sense in that? It's *stupid*.'

'That's it?' Mr Laertides said. 'That's all, really? The only thing wrong with your life is Sophie Pettingell?'

Paul thought about that for a full third of a second. 'Yes,' he said decisively.

'Fine. And what would you say is your problem with her?'

That took a little bit more thought, a whole half-second. 'I hate her,' Paul said.

'Ah.' Mr Laertides sounded satisfied, as though he'd just reached a conclusion. 'In that case,' he said, 'you can wake up now.'

So Paul woke up.

But he wasn't snuggled in a nice warm bed under expensive Laura Ashley sheets next to a leggy flame-haired banker's moll. It wasn't even morning. He was at home, in his flat, but it was late afternoon and outside the kitchen window rain was drizzling like a selfish child's tears.

'Oh,' he said.

'I just thought,' Mr Laertides said, 'that before you committed yourself to your new life, I'd better check and make sure you actually liked it. I mean, in a sense it's supposed to be your reward, for repairing the space-time continuum and so forth.'

'Reward,' Paul repeated.

'Yes, up to a point,' Mr Laertides replied. 'Or it's an attempt, in my usual flat-footed, cack-handed style, to set things right. Like, maybe that's how you would have turned out if I hadn't interfered and you'd been left to your own devices.'

'I see.'

'Well, quite. So I said to myself,' Mr Laertides went on, 'it'd probably be wise if I did just check, to make absolutely sure. To make absolutely sure,' he repeated slowly, 'that that's how you'd like to be, irrevocably, for the rest of your life.'

Paul didn't say anything. He owed it to himself to make a considered decision for once in his life, rather than just going with instinct and gut reaction. From his mind he plucked the image, only slightly wilted, of himself waking up in bed: himself but not himself, this other person, this stranger—

'Yes, please,' he said.

Possibly it wasn't the reaction Mr Laertides had been expecting. 'Are you sure?'

'Am I sure?' Paul exploded. 'For crying out loud. Weren't you bloody well watching? He's like rich and cool and successful and he gets on with people and he was in bed with this girl with no clothes on . . .' Paul paused a moment to catch his breath. 'Yes,' he said. 'If that could be me, I'm all for it. Absolutely no question whatsoever.'

Mr Laertides frowned. 'But Sophie,' he said. 'What about Sophie?'

'Well—' Paul hesitated. 'If I've got this the right way round, the deal is that if I choose, reality will be like it was in that dream, OK? I'll be normal and successful and I'll have a career and girlfriends and everything; and so will she. I mean, she'll have all the stuff she had in the dream; she'll be a partner too, and—'

'But you'll hate her. And she'll hate you too, probably.'

Paul grinned weakly. 'Omelettes and eggs?' he said.

For a moment Mr Laertides flickered, as if someone was playing about with his vertical hold. 'That's what you really want, is it?'

'Yes. Oh yes.'

'Oh. Right,' Mr Laertides said, sounding somewhat bewildered. 'Fine. You do realise that unless you say otherwise really soon, like in the next five seconds, you'll be stuck like it for ever, for the rest of your life.'

'Smashing,' Paul said. 'All right, have I got to do anything, or does it just happen?'

★

'I had this really weird dream,' Paul said.

His friend wasn't listening. Four pints of Flammenwerfer tends to have that effect. Nevertheless, Paul felt he wanted to tell someone about his dream, and his friend hadn't actually begged him to shut up.

'I had this really weird dream,' he repeated, 'where I was this obnoxious snivelling little git, and God or somebody came to me in a vision and asked me if I wanted to be me, or if I wanted to turn back into the git and get off with Sophie Pettingell.'

At the words *get off with*, his friend's hearing came back on line. 'With who?'

'Sophie Pettingell. You know, that awful bitch at our place, the one who just got made a partner.'

His friend frowned, as though peering through a cloud of amber-coloured fumes. 'I wouldn't if I were you,' he said.

'Wouldn't what?'

'Whatsername, that bird you just said. Anyway, I thought you were after that redhead from the Credit Lyonnais.'

'Snores,' Paul replied succinctly. 'And anyhow, I didn't say I wanted to, I said that in this dream I had, God said I could be this wimp loser and get off with her, if I wanted to.'

His friend seemed to have a problem with that concept. 'God, you say?'

'I think it was God,' Paul replied. 'One of those blokes, anyhow.'

His friend shrugged. 'If I were you,' he said, 'I'd think seriously about my whole religious position. Also, if next time you see Him, He starts on about how there's all these English people buying up farmhouses in the Dordogne and wouldn't it be a good idea to raise an army and drive them into the sea, I think you'd probably be wise to change the subject.'

Paul nodded absently. 'The thing was,' he said, 'it was such a vivid dream. If I close my eyes, I can still see bits of it. And he said, if I chose it'd be for ever, for the rest of my life. Which is really weird, don't you think?'

His friend didn't seem unduly impressed. 'I had this dream once,' he said. 'I dreamt I was a twelve-foot-high bass saxophone, and I was being chased through the corridors of

Broadcasting House by a pack of aubergines. And you know what? Since then, I've never touched the stuff again, and it seems to have done the trick.'

'Maybe you're right,' Paul said vaguely. 'In any case, I think I'll go home now.'

'Oh,' said his friend. 'You're not stopping for the other half.'

'I had the other half two hours ago.' Paul swilled the last drop round in the bottom of his glass and swallowed it. 'Got to be up early,' he said. 'Pre-breakfast meeting with Dennis Tanner. Catch you later, Duncan.'

'Neville.'

'Whatever.' Paul pushed his way through the crowd to the door and walked out into the street. It had turned cold, and the beginnings of rain were feathering down. He'd left his umbrella at the office, but it was too late and too far to go back for it.

'Really weird,' he muttered to himself, as he stepped off the pavement.

Later, at the inquest, the taxi driver said the bloke must've been drunk or something, because he hadn't looked, he'd just charged out into the road.

'Celia Johnson,' said the elderly Chinese gentleman. 'Leslie Howard.'

Paul closed his eyes and opened them again, but the Chinese bloke was still there. 'You what?' he said.

'*Brief Encounter*,' the Chinese bloke said. 'I can't remember if either of them actually says, "*We can't go on meeting like this*" in the film, but you get the idea.' He shrugged his blue silk-clad shoulders. 'Anyway,' he went on, 'you're down for the Scrabble tournament at six-thirty, followed by first steps in basket-weaving at seven-fifteen, followed by gardening club at nine. After that,' he added, 'I haven't bothered, since by then time will have no meaning for you.'

'Excuse me,' Paul said, and he couldn't help but notice that, apart from the elderly Chinese gentleman and his rather garish silk dressing-gown thing, there was nothing at all in any direction, 'but I haven't got the faintest bloody idea where I am or who you are or what the hell is going on or what just happened to me.'

The Chinese gentleman's smile was a salad of pity, cruelty, sadness and triumph. 'Like it matters,' he said.

'So it's just as well,' Mr Laertides said, as Paul's eyes snapped open, 'that there's two of you. Otherwise—'

For the first few seconds of consciousness, Paul was sure that he was dead. He could remember it so clearly: Mr Dao's horrible grin, the terrible sensation of gradually drifting away, the sudden realisation that this time there was no escape, the white curtain being drawn slowly across his mind's eye. 'Where?' he mumbled. 'Am I—?'

'Now,' Mr Laertides was saying, 'there's only one of you, and so that's been put right too. I do like to have everything neat and tidy and sorted when I'm wrapping up a job.'

Paul filled his lungs with air, just to see if he still could. 'Did I just die?'

Mr Laertides's face stretched into a long, annoying grin. 'Don't ask me,' he said, 'I've never tried it myself. You, on the other hand, seem to spend more time down there than up here. Not so much a grave, more a pied-à-terre.' He drew his fingertips down the sides of his nose, and yawned. 'That said,' he went on, 'I'd sort of throttle back on the snuffing-it side of things from now on, if I were you. Might not be so easy to get away, the next time.'

'I died,' Paul repeated. '*Really* died. I was fading away, evaporating—' He stopped; he felt sick, and he was shaking. 'Are you listening to what I'm telling you? I didn't manage to get away at the last minute this time. It happened. I—'

'You woke up,' said Mr Laertides. 'You were having a bad dream. People have them every day.'

'Not like this,' Paul objected hysterically. 'It was so real. It was *real*—' He could feel muscles contracting in his stomach. 'All those other times, somehow I knew it wasn't actually the end, because, well, it wouldn't have been right. But this time—'

'I wouldn't worry about it if I were you.'

'The hell with that,' Paul said. 'It was horrible. It was so absolutely horrible.'

Mr Laertides smiled awkwardly. 'I'm not saying it wasn't,' he said. 'I'm just saying that you shouldn't worry about it, because it doesn't do any good. I mean, it's like spending the whole summer holidays feeling miserable because school starts again in September. You can waste your whole life thinking like that.'

'But I thought—' Paul tried to pull himself together; it was a bit like trying to catch whitebait with a cod-fishing net. 'Mr Dao told me himself. He said that over me death has no jurisdiction.'

'*Had*,' said Mr Laertides gently, almost kindly. 'There was an anomaly. It's been ironed out. That's what I do. Congratulations,' he added, with a slightly forced grin. 'You're now a hundred per cent normal again, at least where mortality's concerned.'

'Oh.' Paul curled up in a ball on the floor, hugging his knees to his chest. 'So some day—'

'Some day,' Mr Laertides repeated. 'But not yet. Anyway,' he added briskly, 'that about wraps things up as far as my side of it goes. I can shove off, go back to sleep until some other dangerous bastard starts mucking about with the foundations of the universe. Thanks for all your help.' His voice was different somehow, Paul noticed. 'You know what?' he went on. 'I'll miss you. Sort of got used to being around people these last thirty years, and watching you grow up and everything. It'd be pushing it a bit to say I'm proud of how you turned out, but you could've been a lot worse.'

Paul opened his eyes and looked up at him. 'Uncle Ken,' he said.

'That's right,' said Mr Laertides; then he flickered one last time into a cloud of pixels, which reshaped themselves into his errant godfather. 'Now you see what I meant when I said I've always been here for you. Looking after your moral and spiritual welfare, that was the job description. I did OK, though I say so myself. So long, son.'

'You're going,' Paul said.

'Well, yes.' He smiled, this time with a hint of genuine warmth, though perhaps that was just an illusion resulting from the change of face. 'Couldn't hang around here even if I wanted to. I'm not so much an actual person, see, more what you'd call a phenomenon; and when my gig's over, I move on to the next one. Bit like Dr Sam Beckett, but without the crinkly blue lights.'

'But you're my godfather,' Paul said. 'I mean, you're *real*.'

'For a while,' Uncle Ken replied. 'Same as everybody else, same as you, even. But all good things come to an end.' He walked to the kitchen door and opened it, and Paul suddenly realised he'd never see him again. 'Thanks for the biscuits and stuff, by the way.'

'Biscuits?'

'The ones I helped myself to, last time I was here. I also nicked the magic sword from under the sofa, while you were in the other room, but that wasn't actually stealing, because I knew I'd be giving it back, at Rosie Tanner's do, when you'd be needing it. Just a minor detail I wanted to set straight,' he added. 'Force of habit. Talking of which: when I was your godfather – well, it wasn't one word so much as two separated by a comma. Or even an ampersand. Be seeing you, our Paul.'

He closed the door after him; tricksy things, doors, as Paul had learned to his cost over the last nine months or so. Paul sat still for a while, musing on his godfather's parting words, which appeared on first hearing to be mere gibberish.

Two words separated by a comma. Or even an ampersand – Oh.

Oh well, Paul thought. That'd explain various things, too: like why Mum had always liked Uncle Ken a lot, but Dad had never seemed to care for him much; indeed, why Dad hadn't liked Paul much, either, or bothered to show up at his funeral. And other stuff, to do with the first of the two words; intriguing but on balance rather less important.

Paul stood up and went to the fridge, but when he opened the door the light didn't come on, and there was nothing in it, not even furry cheese or deliquescent tomatoes. Paul sighed; it wasn't every day that you lost not only your immunity from death and your god and your newly discovered long-lost father but your fridge as well.

'Now what do I do?' he said aloud; whereupon the doorbell rang.

It was a goblin. No, it wasn't, but not far off the mark – it was

Dennis Tanner. He came in without being asked, looked around at the furnishings and decor with a vague, mute blend of disgust and contempt, and sat down on the edge of the better chair.

'You didn't come into the office today,' he said.

'Didn't I?' Paul tried to think what day it actually was. 'Sorry,' he said, 'I've sort of lost track of time lately.'

'Well, that's not good enough,' Mr Tanner said. 'You're fired.'

A very brief spurt of instinctive anger, followed by a slow, glorious sunrise of joy. 'Really?'

'Yes,' Mr Tanner said, and he had the grace to sound a bit uncomfortable about it. 'You'll get a week's pay in lieu of notice, and we'll clear your desk for you in the morning. Don't bother coming in, I'll send it on.'

'That's—' Paul tried to find some words, but they were all out to lunch. 'Thanks,' he said.

Mr Tanner sighed. 'Don't thank me,' he said. 'It wasn't exactly an ordinary management decision. More,' he added, muttering, 'an act of God. Anyhow, that's it as far as you and the firm are concerned. If you were hoping for a gold watch or a card signed by all of us, forget it.'

'I—' Paul shrugged. 'That's all right,' he said.

Mr Tanner got up. 'You may also be interested to know,' he said, 'that I've had to sack Ms Pettingell as well. Pity, we had high hopes of her at one stage, but—'

'Another act of God?'

'More acts than bloody Chipperfield's,' Mr Tanner said bitterly. 'But there you go. She's out of it, and so are you. In fact, it's going to play merry hell with my agoraphobia, what with Theo Van Spee and Ricky Wurmtoter suddenly vanishing off the face of the Earth. You wouldn't happen to know anything about that, would you?'

'Me?' Paul said. 'Sorry, no.'

'Ah.' Mr Tanner shrugged. 'So it'll just be me, Cas Suslowicz and Jack Wells holding the fort. Still, we'll manage. Probably take on a few zombie trainees from MIT come the autumn. They're smart and hard-working, have excellent qualifications and they don't want paying. I'll see myself out.'

The door closed behind him, too. It was being a hungry door

today, gobbling people up and not even spitting out the bones or the boots. On the other hand—

On the other hand, Paul was free, and that was going to take quite some time to sink in. He dreaded to think what kind of threats Mr Laertides – even now he couldn't manage to think of him as Uncle Ken; let alone Dad – must've used to force JWW to let him go, after they'd paid a six-figure sum for him and seen hardly any return on their investment. Under other circumstances (fairly bizarre ones, admittedly) he could have felt sorry for them; but the screeching brakes of the sweet chariot swinging low drowned out any such thoughts. He was free; it was the same sort of relief he'd felt on parting company with Mr Dao—

No, he was under strict orders not to worry about that, so he shoved the thought of Mr Dao out of his mind and slid a chairback under his mind's door knob. Instead, he thought: *So they've let Sophie go, as well. I wonder—*

Freshly canned worms; please dispose of can tidily. Sophie, and yet another ghastly dilemma. Mr Tanner could let her go, release her from her contract and let her get on with her life; all very well for him, all he had to do was tear up a piece of paper. But it didn't end there. If Paul had got the right end of the stick, Sophie was in love with him; she had to be, because she had no choice in the matter, she'd been bred that way, like a variety of geranium. If she was ever to be genuinely free and have some sort of a life without nasty bits of magic embedded in it like impossible-to-operate-on shrapnel, he'd have to find some way of letting her go too. Assuming, of course, that he could bring himself to do that—

He'd tried once already; or at least one of him had, and died in the attempt. Not a good precedent. How do you make people stop loving you, Paul wondered; is there a magic spell or a philtre you can buy that'll do the trick? The impression he'd got back in the office was that there wasn't; in which case, what'd be so bad about leaving well alone, letting the happy ending slouch towards Bethlehem to be born? If Sophie loved him and he loved her; wasn't that what Life's supposed to be all about, according to Hollywood and the music industry and received opinion generally?

But it wouldn't be right. It hadn't been right when she'd

offered to drink the philtre for him, and it wasn't right now. Paul flopped onto the sofa and put a cushion over his face, but he knew perfectly well that the world was still out there, even though he couldn't see it. He wondered where she was, what she was doing, what she was thinking; had Mr Tanner told her the good news yet, and if so—

The phone rang. He dragged himself across the room to answer it.

'Paul. Guess what that bastard's gone and done, he's sacked me. I don't believe it, it's so *unfair*. He said it was because I was ten minutes late getting in on Tuesday the week before last, and I'm too slow sorting the Mortensen printouts, but that's just so not true, it was eight minutes not ten, and nobody's ever said to me when the bloody printouts've got to be done by, they just say here they are, do them. I'm definitely going to take them to the industrial tribunal, they can't get away with stuff like that, this isn't the bloody Middle Ages—'

'Sophie,' Paul said. 'Think about it.'

'What?'

'I said, think about it. They've let you go. You're free of them. For ever.'

Pause. He could hear her thinking, down the other end of the telephone line. Then: 'Paul, what are you still doing at home? Why aren't you at work?'

'I've been sacked too,' Paul replied. 'Isn't it wonderful?'

'Stay there,' Sophie said. 'I'll be right over.'

Click, said the phone in his ear, and he put the reciever down. So she was coming over to see him. That was probably good, except—

Except he was living in a world where true love wasn't possible but magic worked just fine, where death wasn't always fatal, where his dad wasn't his dad, but God was; and he had no job and a broken fridge. He slumped in a chair, his face in his hands. He lived in a world where he was doomed always to do the right thing, even when it was palpably wrong. Also, though it was some way down his prioritised list of things to get in a state over, it wasn't all that long ago that he'd stabbed Ricky Wurmtoter to death with a sword. And that had been the right thing to do; and living happily ever after with Sophie would be the wrong thing to do. The whole business was as crazy as a blenderful of blind ferrets.

It took Sophie an hour and a half to get there; during which time Paul could have grown a dozen stalagmites. When he opened the door, she walked straight past him and dropped down in the good chair like a discarded bag of shopping.

'I've been thinking,' she said. 'We need to have a serious talk about all this.'

Oh joy, he muttered to himself, *a serious talk*. 'Yes,' he said, 'I suppose so. Would you like a cup of coffee before we start?'

She looked at him with vague annoyance. 'We need to talk about us, for one thing,' she said.

'I see. Coffee's out of the question, then.'

Sophie had this way of frowning at him that made him wonder if English really was his first language. 'What?'

'Forget it.' Paul sat down in the bad chair and braced himself for a serious talk. 'You start, then.'

'Well,' she began; and then she hesitated. This was unusual. During the short time they'd lived together, they'd had rather a lot of serious talks, and the format had always been the same. She'd start with a speech-cum-lecture-cum-list-of-charges and he'd sit still and be quiet, trying not to let his attention wander; then there'd be an awkward silence, and then she'd start talking again, usually saying the same things but in a slightly different order. The cycle would repeat itself (rarely more than five times), and at the end either she'd burst into tears and stomp out of the room, lose her temper and stomp out of the room or sit on his lap and start nibbling his ear. Starting the procedure off with an awkward silence was an entirely new approach, and Paul wasn't sure that it was an improvement. 'Well,' she said eventually. 'Say *something*, for crying out loud.'

What, me? He thought hard. 'Actually,' he said, and dried up.

The silence that followed was pretty excruciating, almost to the point where Paul wished the ground would open and swallow him up, but not quite. Accordingly, it was almost a welcome interruption when a door appeared in the middle of the opposite wall and started to swing open.

Sophie had her back to the wall in question and couldn't see it. Paul could see it perfectly well, but the shock paralysed him until it was too late to do anything useful. By the time it had worn off, the door was wide open and Theo Van Spee had climbed through.

The professor wasn't armed, or pointing a magic wand; crackly blue flames weren't flickering out from under his fingernails. He didn't even stride purposefully. In fact, the way he shuffled across the room suggested that more than anything else, he was very tired. It was only when he cleared his throat, a soft, muffled noise like an apple falling off a tree onto deep leaf-mould, that Sophie turned round, saw him and screamed.

A cue, if ever there was one: a damsel in distress, and here was Paul, until recently a professional deputy hero with a leading City firm. He jumped to his feet. But then Professor Van Spee looked at him, and he sat down again, not quite knowing why but painfully aware that he had no choice.

'Mr Carpenter,' the professor said. 'And Ms Pettingell. You will forgive the intrusion.'

It wasn't a request; Paul could practically feel forgiveness being yanked out of him. He started to lift a hand, to gesture the professor to a seat, but such an invitation was redundant. A particularly fine leather armchair that Paul had never seen before had appeared in front of him, and the professor was sitting in it.

'You will excuse my rather melodramatic entrance,' the professor went on. 'But I have very little time, and a great deal to do. The clock on the kitchen wall is six minutes fast, and the light bulb in your bedside lamp needs replacing. You are both considering the use of physical violence, but it would be both futile and counter-productive.' He paused, took off his glasses, polished them on a little bit of soft yellow cloth, and replaced them. 'Mr Carpenter, Ms Pettingell,' he went on, 'you are under the impression that you have won. This is not the case. I regret to have to inform you that you both have less than two minutes left to live. In just over one minute, I shall evacuate all the air from this room, and then you will both suffocate and die.' He sighed, more in sorrow than in anger; in fact there was hardly any anger at all, like vermouth in a really dry martini. God probably sighed like that when he looked at the tree and saw that someone had been scrumping apples. 'Before you die, however,' he went on, 'there is something I would like to ask you, if it's convenient.'

Well, Paul thought; *two minutes, it's not like there's time to start anything else, so why not?* 'Sure,' he said. 'Fire away.'

The professor nodded. 'You will recall,' he said, 'our last meeting.'

Paul had to think. 'The duel,' he said. 'The first one. Ricky killed me.'

'Correct. Can you remember what I was doing?'

'You were reading a book,' Paul replied. 'While Ricky and I were fighting it out, you just leaned up against a rock or something. You were looking the other way the whole time.'

'Quite right,' the professor said. 'And you may remember, I marked my place in the book with a bookmark.'

'Did you?' Paul asked. 'Sorry, but I wasn't—'

He remembered now: a dark green leather bookmark, with gilded writing on it, letters he couldn't read. But so what? Pointless thing to remember.

'Would you happen to remember,' the professor went on, 'what became of that bookmark? I fancy I may have dropped it at some stage. It has sentimental value, nothing more, but—'

'Why aren't you dead?' Sophie demanded.

The professor looked up at her, as though he'd forgotten she was there. 'Ms Pettingell,' he said. 'Since you will shortly be dead yourself, I see little point in telling you. The bookmark, however, is of some trifling significance to me, and I shall still be alive. You wouldn't happen to have seen it, by any chance?'

'I have,' Paul said.

The professor looked up at him sharply. 'Excellent,' he said.

'And I'll tell you where it is,' Paul added, 'if you'll answer her question.'

The professor sighed. 'You are playing for time,' he said. 'A pointless exercise. Still, it'll be quicker to tell you what you want to know than to try and reason with you. The bookmark, and then I'll tell you.'

'Other way round,' Paul said firmly. The professor shrugged.

'As you like,' he said. 'The truth is that when you and that tiresome little man' – Mr Laertides, Paul assumed – 'forced your way into what you both thought was my last secure hiding place, you were both mistaken. It was simply another simulation; not my last refuge, only its counterpart in my synthetic universe. I had already taken steps to remove the real thing, and make it secure. So long as I control it, with the real me safely concealed inside, your enthusiastic but rather dull-witted father can kill me to his heart's content, as often as he likes. All he's killing are replicas, duplicates. In fact,' the professor went on, with a weary smile, 'he has done me a substantial favour. He, and the rest of the powers that be, now believe that I am dead and my private dimension is destroyed or lost for ever; accordingly, I shall be able to continue with my work without any fear of further annoyance. There,' he concluded, 'that's my side of the bargain. Now yours.'

Paul nodded. 'Your bookmark,' he said. 'I picked it up.'

'Really.' The professor raised an eyebrow, neatly as any Vulcan. 'May I trouble you to give it to me, please? I can wait a few seconds and take it from your dead body, but—'

'I picked it up,' Paul said, 'and when I got back here afterwards, I found this bookmark in my pocket. It should still be there.'

'Excellent.'

'In my other jacket,' Paul said. 'In the wardrobe, just behind you.' He smiled pleasantly. 'Go on,' he added, 'it won't bite you.'

The professor looked at him for two and a half seconds. 'I am trying to calculate,' he said eventually, 'whether that is a bluff, a double bluff, a triple bluff or a pathetic attempt to prolong your existence by a few seconds in the vain hope that someone – your father, presumably – will come and rescue you. Based on my evaluation of your intelligence and resourcefulness, I believe that you may have some unpleasant surprise in store for me in there – a pocket demon or a Detlinger's Chasm, or some other low-level magical booby trap that you may have acquired by mail order or found in a Christmas cracker. Accordingly, I shall be obliged if you would open the wardrobe and retrieve the bookmark yourself.'

Paul frowned. 'I'd rather not,' he said.

'In that case, I must insist.'

Paul took a step back. 'No,' he said.

The professor clicked his tongue. 'In that case,' he said, 'I shall make Ms Pettingell do it. Would you like me to—?'

'Shit,' Paul said, and walked across the room to the wardrobe. He closed his eyes as he reached for the doorknob.

'Both of you,' the professor said, his voice unusually harsh, and a moment later Sophie had joined him. With his left hand, Paul grabbed her wrist; with his right, he pulled open the door, located his other suit, fumbled with a pocket flap and pulled out a thick, flat rectangle that should have been too big ever to fit in a jacket pocket. It contained, of course, Mr Laertides's flying-carpet samples.

'Hold on,' Paul yelled to Sophie as he flicked the book open with his forefinger and snatched at the first sample he came to. Then there was a nauseating rush and a blur, a moment of sharp pain as they burst through the glass in the kitchen window, and a tendon-jarring bump as the carpet spilled them off onto the pavement of the street outside.

CHAPTER SEVENTEEN

'What the hell,' Sophie demanded as she pulled her head out from under Paul's leg, 'was that?'

'Me being really clever and resourceful,' Paul answered truthfully. 'You all right?'

'I think so.'

'Great,' Paul replied. 'Run.'

'But—'

'Will you stop arguing with every bloody thing I say and just run? Please?'

'All right, I'll run, if that's what you—'

They ran. Even as he turned the corner and felt the first stitch bite into his ribs, Paul knew that running away from Professor Van Spee was a bit like trying to stab an elephant to death with a darning needle. The master of Custardspace, proprietor of the Acme Portable Door, hardly needed to come sprinting after them, because there was nowhere for them to go. Wherever they ran to, wherever they hid, he could find them and get at them. He was just, as the professor had pointed out, playing for time.

Which only left Paul with the other option, and that was something he really didn't want to have to do. Unfortunately—

'Sophie,' he said, stopping dead, hands on knees, panting

rather shamefully for breath, 'have you got any money on you?'

'Money?' she repeated, as if he'd just asked her for dinosaur eggs. 'What the hell use—?'

'Only I'll need at least fifty pee, and I don't think I've got that much.'

Sophie, who was also more than a little bit out of breath, gave him a long, nasty look. 'Go on,' she said, 'here's a whole pound. You can owe me.'

'Thanks.' He took the coin from her and marched into the newsagent's shop outside which he'd halted. There he bought a cigarette lighter.

'Here's your change,' he said.

'Keep it,' Sophie said munificently. 'Paul, what the bloody hell is going on? And what's that?'

Having looked carefully up and down the street, Paul had taken from his inside pocket the bookmark he'd picked up on Bersa Island, the first time. He was relieved beyond words to find that it was still there. 'Van Spee's bookmark,' he said.

'Fine,' Sophie replied, as Paul flicked at the lighter to get it going. 'And what are you planning to do with it?'

Paul looked at her. 'Commit murder, actually,' he said, as he held the lighter flame under the little tassels at the bottom of the bookmark. For three seconds nothing happened. Then it caught light and slowly began to burn.

'All right,' Sophie growled at him, 'don't explain. Be cryptic. I really don't care any more. Because—'

The bookmark screamed.

It took Paul all his strength to hang on; not because the flames were scorching his fingertips, though they were doing that all right, but because he knew perfectly well what he was doing. As usual, the right thing. He hated it.

'You see,' he said, raising his voice a little to cover the screams, which were pretty faint, 'it's bloody obvious why Van Spee wanted this thing, isn't it? He practically told us himself.'

'What – Oh,' Sophie said.

'"Oh" is right,' Paul said. 'Doors and portals that just roll up and tuck away in a pocket; they're what he does best, right? This—' He nodded toward the scrap of burning leather pinched between his fingers. 'This is Theo van Spee's last hiding place. With Theo Van Spee still in it.'

Sophie's eyes widened. 'Paul—'

He nodded. 'Like I said,' he told her, 'murder. Also,' he added, 'the end of Custardspace, probably also the Portable Doors, any hope of rescuing Ricky Wurmtoter from the Land of the Dead, and I've got a nasty feeling it'll probably do something horrible to Colin the goblin, since you're standing here next to me.' He shook his head. 'Tough,' he said. 'But there you go. According to my dad, I was born to make omelettes.'

'Omelettes—?'

'By breaking eggs,' Paul said; and he dropped the last fragment of charred leather on the pavement and ground it under his heel until it was nothing but black dust. A little spurt of wind caught it and whisked it away. 'Job done,' he said, in a voice with no trace of feeling whatsoever. 'So, shall we go and have some lunch somewhere? Or is it dinner time? I've completely lost track. Time has no meaning for me. Private joke,' he added.

'Paul,' Sophie said. 'Did you just kill Professor Van Spee?'

Paul nodded. 'Mphm.'

'Good.'

He looked at her. 'Good?'

'Yes. He was a bastard. Not just,' she added firmly, 'an employer-boss bastard, but a real arsehole. If you really did kill him just now, I'm glad.'

Paul frowned. 'That's a bit—'

'And now,' Sophie said, grabbing his hand (he winced, because his fingers were burned), 'we'll go and have lunch, and you can start explaining. You can take,' she added grimly, 'as long as you like.'

Since they were now both out of a job, lunch was coffee and a cheese roll each at a sandwich place, but it took longer than many Guildhall banquets. Sophie wanted to know everything; she wanted Paul to begin at the beginning, but got very impatient when he started telling her about Audumla the Great Cow of Heaven. Also, she kept interrupting, making him go back and then forward until he'd completely lost his place. There were bits she couldn't grasp, even when he'd been over them four or five times, and he had to pretend her misunderstandings were what had actually happened, just so as to be able to get on to the next bit. There was quite a lot she refused to believe ('For crying out loud,' Paul said, 'why on Earth would I want to make something like this up?') and times when she'd break in on a complicated bit of explaining, where Paul himself was only just managing to hang on to the thread by one fingernail, to say that something rather like that had happened to a friend of hers, or a cousin, or an aunt. Eventually, though, he ground to a halt, and sat looking at her, waiting for a reaction.

'And that's it?'

He nodded, and waited, and sipped some coffee to keep himself occupied while he was waiting. It was foul coffee and tasted of chemicals; probably the stuff they used to clean out the steel pipes of the cappuccino-frothing machine.

'That's it?' Sophie repeated.

'Yes,' he said, with just a hint of annoyance. 'Enough to be going on with, I'd have thought.'

She sighed. 'It just seems – well, bloody odd, to me.'

'Glad to hear it,' Paul replied. 'If you'd said it sounded normal, I'd be really worried about you.'

That remark apparently qualified for one of her beneath-contempt scowls, after which she went on: 'The thing is, I can't see where the whole horrible mess *started*. Did Van Spee invent Custardspace before or after the second Bersa Island duel? And what happened to the first other-you, the one who was really good at swordfighting? And why did Laertides make you go all round the country doing all those silly things, looking at trees and counting pigeons and so forth?'

Paul thought for a moment. 'I think he explained that,' he said. 'As I understand it, which isn't much, it's a bit like a computer mouse; only on the screen, all the icons are hidden, so you just have to move the mouse around and click at random, in the hope that you'll land on the one you want.'

'And you were the mouse, and the stupid things you had to do were the clicking?'

'Suppose so.' Paul yawned. It wasn't surprising that he was

feeling worn out. He couldn't remember when he'd last slept; it was either just before his most recent death, or just after his death before last, and besides, time hadn't had any meaning for him lately. Probably he wasn't just suffering from exhaustion but time-lag as well. 'The other stuff you asked about—' He yawned again. 'Sorry, I've forgotten. What was it?'

'Something about Custardspace.' Sophie was yawning too. 'I can't remember either, so I don't suppose it was very important.' She frowned, as though trying to round up a flock of stray thoughts with a very slow, lazy sheepdog. 'What is important,' she went on, rubbing her eyelids, 'is us. What happens next? Where do we go from here?'

'Um,' Paul replied, and he knew that yes, this was really important, really *really*, but in spite of that he couldn't seem to keep his eyelids apart. Also, his head was very heavy and his neck disappointingly weak. 'Think I'll just,' he mumbled, and rested his head on his forearms. As he closed his eyes, he heard Sophie yawning hugely.

A couple of minutes later, the little bald, round-headed man who ran the sandwich bar came out from behind the counter, checked to make sure all the other tables and chairs were empty, and turned the sign in the window from OPEN to CLOSED, EVEN FOR THE SALE OF PRANCING PORKER CRISPS. Just to be on the safe side, he shot the bolts on the door and drew the blinds. Then, tiptoeing, he left the room and nipped out into the back, locking the door behind him.

On the other side of the door, he grinned, though there was a smidgeon of sadness in his empty black eyes. In a few minutes he'd cease to exist, at least until the next time (and when that happened and he was jerked back into existence he was pretty sure that he'd wake up as someone else, a slightly but crucially different personality, because that was what always happened. He'd never be Frank Laertides again, at any rate; in which case, even if his son was still alive when the next call to duty came, he wouldn't be Paul's father any more. Pity, that. He'd created worlds and bred countless billions of different forms of life to inhabit them, but he'd never actually been a father before. It had been a strain, all that worry and stress, not to mention frustration and disappointment, but on balance he felt it had enriched him. And been fun.)

But – he shrugged – there you go. Meanwhile, the last step, the last procedure was now under way and, barring horrible accidents, was bound to succeed. Just to be sure, he'd slipped half as much again of the world-famous JWW love philtre as was strictly necessary into Paul and Sophie's coffee. According to the helpful leaflet that came packed in with each bottle, exceeding the recommended dose wasn't bad for you physically, it just enhanced the effect; but it could, in certain cases, make life pretty trying for the relatives, friends and neighbours of the happy couple, particularly if they were cursed with weak stomachs. Not every pair of overdosed lovers would inevitably grow into the sort of nauseating couple who think up cutesy new pet names for each other every week and hold hands in the waiting room at the tax office; but the risk was there, and was not to be underestimated.

On the other hand, he decided, the course of true love never did run smooth. But where the two idiots next door were concerned, so far the course of true love had been a dodgem ride organised by Virgin Atlantic. If ever there was a case for adding an extra tablespoonful just to make absolutely sure, this was it. In fact, he'd have bunged in a bit more, only then there wouldn't have been any room left in the cups for any coffee.

Well, he thought. Time he wasn't here.

He closed his eyes, and when he opened them again he couldn't tell the difference, which told him he'd arrived. Time had no meaning here, of course, so strictly speaking he wasn't late for the afternoon whist drive or the eleven o'clock origami class or the early-evening cookery course (vegan dinner party recipes with Julia Sniff). But he couldn't be bothered right now; they'd always be there and so would he. Instead he relaxed, let go, savoured the experience of no longer existing. He found he didn't like it much, but there wasn't an awful lot he could do about that.

Paul opened his eyes. His neck hurt. 'Sophie?' he said.

'Honeybundle?'

What did she just call me? He lifted his head off the table, straightened his back and looked at her. 'Are you feeling okay?' he asked warily. 'Fluffmuffin,' he added.

They looked at each other for a moment; then, like a rogue asteroid, the penny dropped.

And Paul thought – well, he knew what he thought, though it had taken him all this time to admit it to himself, but it did occur to him to wonder what was passing through her mind. *I would give good money,* he said to himself, *Dad, if you're listening, to know that right now. And you owe me a fiver, if you remember.*

But there wasn't any answer, and he realised that his father – Mr Laertides, Uncle Ken – was gone, wouldn't be coming back. And neither would any of them. And he was alone, which was just a downbeat way of saying free.

Except that he wasn't; because he didn't actually need magic, chocolate-coated dragon droppings or the imp-reflecting mirror in the JWW boardroom or any gadgetry of any kind to see what was going on inside Sophie's head right now. He could read it in her face, in clear, for free.

'That's all right then, is it?' he said.

'Suppose so.' She shrugged. 'Depends on you, really.'

'No, it depends on you.'

'No, it—' Suddenly she looked round. 'Bloody hell,' she said. 'They've locked the doors on us, we're trapped in here.'

Abruptly, the doors blew open, the blinds shot up, and the sign in the window swung round. A tall woman in a light blue coat wandered in and asked for a cup of tea and an almond Danish.

Sophie frowned for a moment, as if struggling to remember where she was, then said, 'Sorry, we're shut.'

'It says you're open on the door,' the woman pointed out.

'Go away,' Sophie said.

The woman stiffened, gave Sophie a poisonous look and drifted out into the street. 'We'd better go,' Paul said.

'All right,' Sophie replied. 'Where?'

'No idea,' Paul said; at which point, something on the blank wall opposite caught his eye. At first sight, he'd taken it for a tourism poster: a map, with big, jaunty, friendly lettering at the top. He stood up and went closer. It was a map, all right, but not of any place he recognised. A slice of coastline, by the look of it, or half an island; and skewering it like a kebab stick, an arrow; and at the thick end of the arrow, the words *You Are Here*.

'Here, Sugar-angel,' he said, 'have a look at this.'

(*Sugar-angel*, he thought, *oh my God*.) 'So what?' Sophie said. 'It's just a map.'

'Yes,' Paul said, 'but it's a map of somewhere that doesn't exist.'

'What?'

'It's a map,' Paul repeated, 'but there's no such place.'

'Yes, there is.'

'No there—' A few headache tendrils probed the tender walls of his skull, but he ignored them. He tried to remember – geography lessons with Miss Hook. Of course, he'd been notorious for not paying attention. 'There is?'

'Of course there is,' Sophie said firmly. 'New Zealand.'

'New what?'

'*Zealand*.'

Paul thought for a moment. 'Never heard of it,' he said.

'Really?'

'Yes. Look—' He stopped. Fine, it slipped neatly into place in a now-familiar pattern. There was stuff he'd been prevented from learning when he was at school, for the sake of the Grand Design. Accordingly, there was a *reason* why he'd not been allowed to know about this island place, New whatsit. And what could that reason possibly be? 'Tell me about it,' he said.

She looked at him. 'Tell you about New Zealand? Now?'

'Yes. Please,' he added, because *please* is like the little paper umbrella you find lolling in the corner of fancy drinks, serving no useful purpose but some people get strangely upset if it's not there. 'I need to know why I've never heard of it.'

'Oh.' Paul watched Sophie play that back in her mind, draw a blank and resolve to overlook it for now. 'Well, I don't actually know a lot. It's sort of near Australia, and the people are sort of Australians only not quite so bouncy, and they filmed *Lord Of The Rings* there, and I think that's about it, really.'

'Thanks. So why does that arrow say, "You are here"?'

'I don't know, Dreampumpkin,' Sophie admitted. 'I mean, it's lying, but there's no reason to believe it's anything to do with us. Maybe the man who owns this place comes from there, or his son's over there working on a bloody sheep ranch.' She shook her head sadly. 'It's working at JWW,' she sighed. 'After a while, you automatically assume that anything weird must be about us personally.'

Paul considered that for a moment. 'Nice idea,' he said, 'but I'm not buying it. Bloody hell, there's this whole island I've never heard of before, and suddenly there's a map of it on a wall.' He frowned. 'Is it big, this New Whatsit place?'

'Fairly.'

'Like, say, the Isle of Wight?'

'Bigger.'

'Bloody hell.' For a moment, Paul couldn't find room in his mind for anything beyond anger at a world that had had so much fun at his expense. Kick him around, don't tell him stuff everybody else knows, kill him repeatedly, and when you've finished with him, flush him round the U-bend where he belongs. Even his happy ending was tainted; it came out of a bottle and it was compulsory, a convenient tying-off of loose ends for God: let's get shot of these two redundant instruments of the Great Plan by making them fall in love. 'Screw it,' he said, with sudden and terrible resolution. 'They can't just fire us. We've got rights.'

'Paul?' *No wonder she's looking at me like that*, Paul thought; *the worm is turning so fast you could use it as a masonry drill.* 'But the whole point is, we wanted them to fire us. We only stayed because that bastard Tanner—'

'Doesn't matter,' Paul shouted. 'Doesn't matter a bit. They can't screw up our entire world and then just shoo us away.' He calmed down a bit, but the determination was still there. 'They've got to do something about it,' he said. 'They can work magic and stuff, they must be able to put us right.'

Sophie frowned, puzzled. 'You mean counselling or something?'

Paul shrugged. 'Don't know, not my department. Up to them. And we're going round there right now, and if they refuse to help, well, God help them.'

'Maybe he will, at that,' Sophie said. 'After all, if you're right, He used to be a partner.'

So they took a taxi to St Mary Axe, and walked up the so-very-familiar pavement to the building they knew so well; and they stopped outside and looked at it for two minutes without moving or saying a word.

It was Sophie who eventually broke the silence. 'Fine,' she said.

'What?'

'I said, "Fine." It's not there any more. Or at least, the building's still there, but now it's a bloody Starbucks. If you ask me, I'd say they've won this round.'

Paul realised he hadn't actually breathed for quite some time. 'No, they haven't,' he said, between gritted teeth. 'They're in there somewhere, hiding.'

'Disguised as Danish pastries, you mean?'

'I mean it's that stuff Countess Judy used to do – effective magic. They've put a spell or a glamour or something on the building, so we'll think it's a coffee shop.' He scowled ferociously. 'Won't work. I know how to break through those things. It's easy, actually. You've got to imagine that what you see is really just old manky wallpaper, and then you find a loose corner and you—' He stood for thirty seconds or so, during which time he pulled some very strange faces. 'You try,' he said.

'Don't be bloody stupid, Sugarwombat,' Sophie snapped. 'It's a real coffee shop. Stop doing whatever it is you're doing, before you give yourself a hernia.'

'It can't be,' Paul protested. 'It wasn't there yesterday, or whenever it was. I'm going in.'

'Please yourself,' Sophie replied. 'I'll just have a cup of tea, though.'

They sat down at a table that should by rights have been the reception desk; but Mr Tanner's mum wasn't there, and although a fairly attractive blonde girl came up to take their order, she didn't grin. 'Excuse me,' Paul asked her.

'Yes?'

'Can you tell me,' he said, 'how long has this place been here?'

The waitress thought for a moment. 'Don't really know,' she

said. 'I've only been here, what, eight months, but Ray, he's the manager, I think he's been here since it opened, and I think he said it was three years, something like that.'

'Three years.'

'Something like that,' the waitress repeated. 'Why, have you been here before or something?'

'We used to work here,' Sophie put in. 'When it was just offices.'

'Ah, right.' The waitress went away, and Paul put his face in his hands. Suddenly he felt very tired.

'All right,' he said. 'I still think they're out back somewhere, hiding. But I can't be bothered any more.'

Sophie reached out and took his left hand in hers. 'Forget about it,' she said. 'The main thing is, we don't have to go back. The rest of our lives belong to us.'

Someone coughed, and they both looked round. A very distinguished-looking Chinese gentleman was standing over them, wearing a beautiful dark blue suit. He nodded politely to Sophie, smiled at Paul and handed him an envelope. Paul took it without thinking; then he dropped it as though it was burning his hand.

'Pardon me for interrupting,' said Mr Dao. 'I thought I might find you here.'

Paul stared at him, with a rare and rather unstable blend of fear and hatred in his eyes. 'What the fuck are you doing here?' he muttered. 'You should be—'

Mr Dao nodded. 'Quite,' he said. 'But, as you may have noticed, the world has changed since we last met. In particular, this building. There are loose ends, formalities; a connecting door that is no longer either required nor authorised, and therefore must be sealed off. Perhaps it wasn't entirely necessary for me to come in person to supervise the arrangements, but—' He shrugged charmingly. 'Everybody likes an excuse to get out of the office for a while every now and again. And besides,' he added, 'I wanted to see you.'

Paul felt his bowels loosen a little. 'Me?'

'Quite so. To tell you that this will be our last meeting for a while. To be precise, for sixty-two years, three months, five days, nine hours, fourteen minutes and' – he counted under his breath for a moment or so – 'forty-five seconds from *now*. And as for you, young lady—' He looked at Sophie for a moment, then shook his head. 'Perhaps you would prefer me not to spoil the surprise.'

Sophie stared at him, then looked away as if she'd just brushed against an electric fence. 'Paul,' she said, 'who the hell's this and what's he talking about?'

'Him?' Paul closed his eyes, then opened them again. 'Oh, that's just Mr Dao. From the Bank. I'm sorry,' he went on, 'but I missed that. Could you just repeat—?'

'No,' said Mr Dao, smiling. 'The letter is not from me, or my associates. Mr Tanner asked me to give it to you. Before you ask, I have no forwarding address for him. I'll be seeing him in—' He glanced at his watch; an original Dali and probably quite valuable. 'In four years or so,' he said. 'I could ask him then, if you like.'

'No,' Paul said quickly, 'that's fine. Thank you.'

'A pleasure.' Mr Dao smiled again. 'I've taken the liberty of putting you down for basket-weaving on Thursdays and beginners' Esperanto on Monday evenings. It's sensible to book well in advance, just to be sure. Ms Pettingell, good day.'

He turned, walked to the doorway and went out. Paul leaned back in his chair, trying to keep his hands and feet still. Sophie leaned across and looked at him.

'Are you all right, Candyfluff?' she asked. 'You've gone as white as a sheet.'

Paul took a deep breath, while he still could. 'Fine,' he replied. 'Look, can you remember what he just said? Sixty-one years, five months, three days—'

Sophie shook her head. 'No,' she said, 'it was sixty-five years, two months—'

'No, it was definitely sixty-one.' Paul scratched his head. 'Or was it sixty-three? Oh Christ, I can't remember.'

'Oh. Was it important?'

Was it important? Oh, eleven out of ten for a really good question. 'No,' he said, 'not terribly.'

'And besides,' Sophie went on, 'he's got to be joking, right? I mean, he was seventy if he's a day. He's not going to be around in sixty-four years—'

'Sixty-two,' Paul said. 'Or something like that. Anyhow, like you said, it's really not important.' He felt the envelope under his hand: heavy, good-quality paper, slightly rough to the touch. JWW's best quality stationery. He turned it over, and there was the monogram, JWW, deeply embossed just above the flap.

'Well,' Sophie said, 'aren't you going to open it?'

Paul nodded, slid a finger under the flap and looked inside. His face fell. 'No cheque,' he said.

'Well, you can't expect miracles,' Sophie replied. 'Are you going to read it, or—?'

'All right, Fluffbunny,' he said. 'Give me a moment.' He unfolded the letter. The familiar letterhead; the list of partners' names – but it was shorter than it used to be.

John W. Wells MAA (Oxon) LLB FIPES DipN

C. N. Suslowicz FSEE AIBG

R. Catherwood-Tanner MA BLG Playmate of the Month August 1967, July 1983

D. Tanner BA (Plymouth) BG

'R. Catherwood-Tanner,' Sophie read aloud. 'Who the bloody hell is that?'

'Mr Tanner's mum,' Paul said, after a moment. 'Must be. She married that clerk we rescued, remember? So they made her a partner.' He actually smiled, a bit. 'Well,' he said, 'that suggests she's still alive, though you can't be sure with these people. Anyway.'

He looked back at the letter.

Dear Cousin Paul –

He shuddered.

Hope this finds you well. Sorry to have missed you, but we've had to clear out in a hurry, on account of some careless fuckwit blowing a hole in the pocket reality we were existing in. (You wouldn't happen to know anything about that, would you? Sarcastic laughter.) It was the only decent day's work Tosser Van Spee ever did for us, and some bugger had to spoil it. Oh well.

Couple of things before we go. One: Mum sends her love. Two: don't come looking for us. Ever. If you do, trust me, all that'll be left of you'll be a few shreds of skin and the echo of a

*scream. (That bit's from me, personally.) Three: severance pay.
Which I don't think you're entitled to, not after all the money
you've cost us, but I was outvoted. Please find enclosed title
deeds to land comprising approx 2500 acres or thereabouts near
Timaru, South Island, New Zealand. If you want you can
share it with that miserable cow but you don't have to.*

'I never liked him one little bit,' Sophie said calmly.

'Nor me,' Paul agreed. 'What title deed? There doesn't seem
to be – wait, what's this?'

He pulled out a small folded piece of paper, the size of a bus
ticket. It unfolded into a legal-looking document, a bit smaller
than *The Times*, with several pages and a front cover, on which
was written *Handle With Care*.

'Why does it say – Ouch,' Paul added, as he dropped the
thing on the table. 'Bloody thing bit me.'

'Bit you?'

'Felt like it. Typical,' he added. 'Should've known anything I
got off Tanner'd try and do me an injury.' He poked it aside with
his elbow and went back to the letter, which went on –

*No, it didn't bite you, you ungrateful sod; it's just an extremely
powerful response, coupled with the fact that, let's face it, you're
naturally one of the most gifted minerals scryers I've ever met, a
talent completely wasted on you but that's life. And I'm disappointed but hardly surprised that, even after nine months with
the firm, you still don't recognise—*

Paul dropped the letter, braced himself, and pressed a fingertip to the title deed. The shock was a bit like sticking his fingers
in a light socket, but it was terribly familiar.

'Bauxite,' he said.

Oh, very well done, the letter continued. *For the record, the
biggest bauxite deposit ever found outside Australia, and the
fourth largest, or maybe the third, in the world. In other words,
you and that soppy tart are going to be very, very rich and I
hope it chokes you. Unless, of course, she won't let you sell the*

rights to one of the big mining cartels because of the environ-
mental damage—

'Actually,' Sophie said, 'screw the environment.'

Thought so, the letter read smugly, *your type are all the same.*
It's all Friends of the Earth and save the whales till you get a
whiff of some serious dosh, and then ethics is just a county in
southern East Anglia. Anyway, that's all you're getting so make
the most of it. Please signify that you accept this offer in full and
final settlement of all claims against JWW by signing and burn-
ing the enclosed copy of this letter; and if you don't, tough.
Look out, the waitress is coming over with your tea. Act nor-
mally till she's gone.

The waitress put down the tray. They thanked her. She went
away again.

Assuming you know how, which I personally doubt. Where was
I? Oh yes. Loose ends. Benny Shumway isn't with the firm
any more, he cleared out the day Theo Van Spee died, took the
petty cash with him, the bastard. I know exactly where he's
gone; you see, when you took out Countess Judy, Jack Wells sent
her away to the Isle of Avalon, along with King Arthur and Sir
Francis Drake and JFK and Elvis and Princess Di and Lord
Lucan and Shergar. But Avalon's just another of Van Spee's
exclusive executive developments, and now he's gone – well,
keep an eye on the newspapers over the next couple of weeks,
that's all I'm saying. My guess is, Benny's gone to rescue the
only woman he ever really loved, which is kind of romantic,
even if she is a psychotic megalomaniac killer elf. A propos of
which, you might consider laying in a stock of really strong
coffee, like the red Lavazza Espresso. Sweet dreams are made of
this, as the old song says. Sinister chuckle.

'Oh God,' Paul murmured.

Quite. I expect he's on her trail right now, your old man; like they say, no rest for the righteous. In which case, Judy and Benny won't be on the loose for very long. Pity about Benny, a sad tendency to think with his dick but a damn competent cashier all the same. But it'll all come right in the end – he'll go down for a very long time and we'll get our money back. I guess you could say Benny's yet another casualty of your bloody heavy-handed interference. Honestly, I know you never liked us much, but you've certainly had your pound of flesh out of the partnership. Humph Wells, Countess Judy, Van Spee, Ricky Wurmtoter, and now Benny Shumway. Anybody'd think you had a grudge against us, or something.

Whatever, whatever. Must stop now, I've got a whole office to unpack, so I'll round off with a bit of advice for the both of you. Look, it's true you've both been buggered about with by the firm, and by Frank Laertides as well, of course, sure as God made little green apples (and that was a dirty trick too). Everything that's made the two of you what you are was part of some other bugger's top-secret agenda, you were bred up specially to be deployed against someone else's enemies, and now the war's over and you're left behind, like all those Soviet nukes when the Berlin Wall came down. The important thing, in that case, is to make sure that you don't fall into the wrong hands, otherwise there's no knowing how much damage you might do. Which is why the last thing Frank did before going away was to dose you up with the famous JWW philtre. You were made for each other, after all, like the Bride of Frankenstein. And yes, I know, you feel pretty hacked off about that; but what the hell. Don't let the self-pity get to you. After all, vast numbers of people came into this world for all the wrong reasons; like, for instance, two hormone-crazed teenagers getting careless behind the bike sheds, or an unhappily married couple who should've divorced years ago thinking that a kid'll put everything right betwen them. But it's not how we got where we are that matters; it's what we do now we're here, while we're here. Look, all this mushy stuff is making me want to puke (and sure enough, the ink on the page was gradually turning green) *so I'd better knock it on the head, but I'll just say this. Doesn't matter why you two pains in the bum are in love, just face the fact that you are. And with patience, understanding, mutual respect, a sense of humour and twelve billion US dollars' worth of premier-grade bauxite, you may just be able to make a go of it, if you want to.*

That's it. Be strangers. Don't keep in touch. Drink your tea, before it gets cold.

Cordially,

Squiggle, pp Dennis Tanner.

For a long time, Paul and Sophie sat still and quiet, carefully not looking at each other. Then Sophie reached out a hand, took the letter and slowly, methodically tore it into little pieces.

'Interfering, dirty-minded prurient little troll,' she said firmly.

'Quite,' Paul said, though he wasn't quite sure he knew what 'prurient' meant. 'But maybe he's got a point.'

'Really?'

'Yes,' Paul said. 'I think he was right. I think we ought to try again.' He rested his hand on top of hers, on top of the small mound of shredded letter. 'For the sake of the bauxite.'

Theo Van Spee had never got around to explaining to Paul how he did that apparent mind-reading thing. But it didn't matter in this case, because Paul didn't need telepathy to figure out what was going on inside Sophie's head. One voice, shouting loudly and angrily; another voice, small and quiet, whispering, *Yes, but true love and twelve billion US dollars;* then the first voice snarling, *Screw the twelve billion dollars,* and trying to sound like it meant it; and the second voice saying, *All right, fine, so that just leaves true love –*

And then she turned her head and looked at him, and said, 'All right.'